DAWNBREAKER

"Gritty action-packed drama so hi-res and real you'll believe you got something in your eye."
Matt Forbeck, author of Amortals *and* Dangerous Games

"*Three* feels like the result of tossing Mad Max, Neuromancer and Metal Gear Solid into a blender. If you don't find that combination appealing, then I do not understand you as a human being."
Anthony Burch, writer for Borderlands 2 *and* Hey Ash Whatcha Playin

"*Three* is a great start into a new series. The post-apocalyptic world that Jay Posey created in *Three* is brilliantly constructed, it's just chock-full of the cool stuff, futuristic gadgets (guns and the like), augmented people and not forget the Weir."
The Book Plank

"*Three* is a post-apocalyptic adventure tale in the vein of The Road Warrior, only with fewer vehicles and a higher tech level and body count... Posey knows how to pour on the tension. 4.5 stars. Now I'll twiddle my thumbs until the next Legends of the Duskwalker book comes out.""
Shelf Inflicted

"Posey kept me on my toes throughout the entire story and left me shocked by the end. This is a really good contender for one of my top 10 books for the year."
Working for the Mandroid

"Stark and powerful, Three is a stunning debut. Reinventing the post-apocalyptic western as a journey across interior badlands as dangerous as the cyborg-haunted terrain his hero must cross, Posey has crafted a story that is impossible to put down."
Richard E Dansky, author of Vaporware *and* Snowbird Gothic

ALSO BY JAY POSEY

Three
Morningside Fall

Jay Posey has asked for a percentage of his fees for
this book to be donated to Hope For The Warriors®.

We are honored to bring Hope to the lives of our
nation's heroes and their families.

RESTORING: Self • Family • Hope

The mission of Hope For The Warriors® is to enhance the
quality of life for post-9/11 service members, their families,
and families of the fallewn who have sustained physical and
psychological wounds in the line of duty. Hope For The
Warriors® is dedicated to restoring a sense of self, restoring
the family unit, and restoring hope for our service
members and our military families.

www.HopeForTheWarriors.org

ANGRY ROBOT

DAWNBREAKER

LEGENDS OF THE DUSKWALKER
BOOK 3

JAY POSEY

ANGRY ROBOT
An imprint of Watkins Media Ltd

Lace Market House,
54-56 High Pavement,
Nottingham,
NG1 1HW
UK

angryrobotbooks.com
twitter.com/angryrobotbooks
Keep fighting

An Angry Robot paperback original 2015

Cover by Steven Meyer-Rassow.
Set in Meridien and Bank Gothic by EpubServices.

Distributed in the United States by Random House, Inc., New York.

ISBN 978 0 85766 448 8
Ebook ISBN 978 0 85766 449 5

Printed in the United States of America

9 8 7 6 5 4 3 2

For those who gave all.

ONE

The chaos of combat echoed sharply through the empty alleyways, a cacophonous swirl of horrifying intensity. It was a sonic storm, growing ever louder as Cass and her companions closed the distance to the structure where they'd left Gamble and the others. White noise shrieks of countless Weir blended into a single, unbroken cascade of sound, like rushing water, punctuated occasionally by the pops and cracks of sporadic gunfire. *Sporadic* gunfire. Not nearly the withering volume of fire she would have expected. How many of her friends had her absence already cost her?

Once-looming buildings slumped on either side of the narrow street, dark concrete and steel with darker emptiness yawning where windows had once been. Wick led the way through the twisting streets and alleys with a broken pace; he moved with a cautious urgency, but Cass could tell by his unsteady gait that his wounds were taking their toll. His face was slick with sweat despite the cold night air and his breath came in erratic puffs. Able glided along slightly behind and to Wick's right, weapon held one-handed, up and ready. The fingertips of his left hand rested lightly on Wick's shoulder, maintaining contact with his teammate. It was hard to tell if he was doing so to coordinate their movement or to help keep Wick steady. Both, maybe.

Cass trailed along a few steps further back, struggling to keep herself from rushing ahead. She could easily outpace the others by twice as much or more and get into the fight that much sooner. But as loud as the fighting was, the way sound ricocheted amongst the urban ruins was disorienting and made it almost impossible to pinpoint the precise location of the battle. Wick might not be able to match her speed, but he would most assuredly take them by the most direct route. All the speed in the world wouldn't matter if she got lost. And judging by the noise, they couldn't afford any detours.

And yet, despite the strain she felt to get into the battle, Cass couldn't escape the fact that every step closer to the fighting was another step further from the tunnel. From Wren. Her boy.

It had seemed so clear in the moment; sending her son back to Greenstone with Chapel, getting him out of harm's way, while she stayed behind to hold the line with the last few defenders. In that instant, her decision had surprised her, but not as much as her certainty had. There'd been no doubt in her mind that it was what she had to do. What she was *meant* to do. It had been only minutes ago. Here, now, she felt the first crack in her resolve. What if it was already too late to help Gamble?

She didn't have time to complete the thought. A blur of unexpected movement snapped Cass back to the moment, a pair of Weir bursting from a cross-alley not fifteen feet away, barreling towards the fighting like hounds on a trail. One glanced their direction just as Able fired two quick bursts. The rounds stitched up its side and shoulder, spinning it off balance. It let out a gurgling squawk as it tried to catch itself but it twisted awkwardly and fell, skidding across the concrete. Before it came to rest, Wick's rifle spat rounds into its companion. The second Weir had turned towards them, and Wick's shots caught it in the upper chest and throat, throwing it backwards. It collapsed and was still.

"Gamble, this is Wick," Wick said, calling to his team leader through their secure connection. "We're inbound, two minutes."

The first Weir writhed where it lay and let out an

unearthly wail, a static-laden and distorted scream. As they drew nearer, it whipped its clawed hands out in a spasm. Able pumped two more rounds into the creature without breaking stride, silencing it.

"Say again," Wick said.

Cass wasn't dialed in to the team's channel, so she couldn't hear the response. Assuming there was one. After a long pause, he spoke again.

"Negative, will not comply."

"What'd she say?" Cass asked. Wick didn't answer. To her surprise, he broke into a jog. It wasn't much faster than they'd been moving before, but he'd already looked like he was on the edge of collapse. Cass found it hard to believe he had any more to give.

"Wick, what'd Gamble say?" she called.

He didn't glance back at her.

"Not to come."

The words made Cass hitch a step. They were going to be too late.

The three of them jogged in strained silence another thirty or forty seconds. Cass noticed the clamor of fighting had turned sharper, individual sounds more distinct. She didn't hear any more gunfire.

Wick took two turns in close proximity and then halted in a wide alley. Able smoothly drew up alongside him. The sudden halt took Cass by surprise but she angled herself fluidly and came to a stop right next to Wick, facing him. He was busy looking up at the rooftops on either side of them. Able kept his weapon shouldered and scanned the alleyway. Wick tapped his shoulder to get his attention.

"I need a boost," he said, motioning upwards to the building on their right. It was a multi-story structure, but some of the rusting girders were showing above street-level where the walls had collapsed or been blasted out. Able shook his head.

I'll go first, Able signed. He waved Cass over. She nodded and moved into position next to the building, her back against the wall, in a partial crouch. When she was set, she nodded again and Able stepped up on her thigh, then on her shoulder. His boots dug in, but she gritted her teeth against the pain and pushed up to her full height. After a few seconds, she felt Able sink down and then push off as he launched himself upwards. He scrabbled his way up into the building. Cass looked up to see his feet disappearing into the hole. A few moments later, a dim red glow emanated above her; Able using his low-intensity light to check the building for threats.

After several tense seconds, Able reappeared. His head and shoulders poked out of the hole, and he stretched his arms down towards them. Cass motioned for Wick, and boosted him in the same fashion. She couldn't help but notice how unsteady he was on her shoulders. Able helped drag him up into the structure, and then returned and stretched as far down as he could to grab Cass's hands. She waved him off and though he looked at her with some confusion, he moved back and to one side. Cass took a few steps away from the wall and then ducked her head and charged at it, leapt, planted a foot and leapt again. Her head cleared the opening as her hands grabbed the lip of the second floor. Able helped pull her in the rest of the way, even though it wasn't necessary. Once she was on her feet, Able retrieved his weapon and they crept towards Wick on the other side of the building.

The entire floor had been completely gutted, but it seemed stable enough. Rows of steel girders broke up the sight-lines amidst the otherwise flat and featureless concrete. The sound, though, was almost unbearable; a wild and fierce thing thrashing against its cage. The echoing howls of the Weir were amplified in that bare space, their waves of harsh cries stacking one atop the other. Cass had to consciously force herself not to cover her ears.

Wick was hunched down a few feet back from another large hole in the exterior wall, scanning the street below, making himself small so his silhouette wouldn't draw any attention. Cass dropped to a low crouch as she approached and from that angle she realized Wick wasn't kneeling. At least not in any kind of controlled, tactical sense. It looked more like he'd just collapsed to his knees.

"Wick?" Cass said. When she was close enough, she reached out and laid a hand on his shoulder. He didn't react and Cass felt her heart turn in her chest. Her mind flashed back to when she'd found Swoop after the first battle outside Morningside; still sitting upright, coated in ichor and surrounded by unnumbered foes slain. Even in death they hadn't been able to bring him down.

Not Wick. Please not Wick.

She moved around in front of him. His hands were limp in his lap, his eyes glassed and staring. His weapon dangled from its sling.

"Wick," she said, "Wick, stay with me."

After a moment, his gaze shifted unsteadily to her. He regarded her as if through a haze, then a few seconds later shook his head slowly and looked back out through the hole in the wall. Cass didn't know what to make of the response. Until she too looked out onto the street below.

Just on the other side, she recognized the squat one-story building where Gamble and her team had stopped to make their stand. Where Cass had left them.

And all around the structure, a host of Weir formed a shrieking, unbroken ring. The first, shocking impression was of numbers beyond counting; Cass nearly cried out at the sight. It was no single line of Weir surrounding the building. It was a churning mass, ten or twenty deep in some places.

But they weren't attacking. Not for the moment, at least.

The slain lay sprawled all about the shelter and so numerous were the dead just outside the main entrance they had fallen in a mound. A few feet further out from that mound stood two figures. To Wick and Able's eyes they wouldn't seem like anything unusual, but through Cass's modified vision, they were radiant; robed in lightning, wreathed in flame. Broadcasting their internal signal in some manner that her enhanced eyes translated into the glowing forms she saw now, standing defiant before the Weir.

Lil. And another of her warriors. Cass crept closer to the hole in the wall and saw there was a third person out there with them, slumped at their feet, but she couldn't make out who it was. Lil and her companion stood on either side of their fallen comrade, long blades held outward and ready. Why the Weir didn't collapse on them, Cass didn't know, but she understood that it wouldn't be that much longer before they did.

"Wick," Cass said, turning back to him. "Does Gamble know we're here yet?"

It took a few moments before Wick responded.

"Finn's in there," he said. Finn. Wick's older brother.

"Wick," she said, more firmly this time. "Tell Gamble we're here."

His eyes flicked to her and then cleared, focused.

"Gamble, Wick," he said. "We're on site. What do you need?"

She felt Able move up beside her, and she glanced over to him. His face was grim, but his eyes moved quickly over the scene and she could see already that his mind was at work.

"Southwest of your location," Wick said, still in conversation with Gamble.

Down below, one Weir broke from the circle, followed quickly by two more. A distinctive hum twice sounded above the clamor, and the first two rag-dolled to the ground. Lil's companion stepped forward and cut down the third. Cass recognized that hum. Sky's rifle. He was still down there, doing his work with deadly efficiency.

Something about that moment brought everything into focus for her. Sky was in there, in that little building, patiently, calmly firing as threats presented themselves. Disciplined. The initial shock passed, and Cass found herself strangely detached. Rather than an innumerable horde, the wall of Weir became many individuals. Any one of them alone posed no threat to her. How many had she slain at

Ninestory? More than she'd thought possible at the time. Would this be any different?

"Negative, boss," Wick said. "We're not leaving."

She hadn't realized it before Ninestory, and she hadn't believed it until that first wave of assault on Morningside. Twice may have been coincidence. A third test was what she needed to prove to herself what she was beginning to suspect. Whatever modifications the Weir had made to her body before Wren had brought her back... whether they had done something special to her, or whether her previous life as a quint user had caused some fundamental change to her physiology, she felt almost certain that she was faster, stronger, more deadly than any of those creatures down below. *Almost* certain.

"I'll draw some of them off," Cass said. "Hit the flank, then fall back."

Wick shook his head. "Too many, Miss Cass. They'd shred you."

"Maybe it'll stretch them enough for our people to punch through."

"More likely it'll get you killed for nothing."

"I can do it, Wick. Think about Ninestory."

"I am," he said. "You'd be dead if we hadn't pulled you out. There's no one to pull you out of this one, Cass."

Cass looked back down at the street below. They were running out of time, but Wick was right. They'd told her she'd killed thirty or forty at Ninestory, but that'd been after Swoop's carefully prepared charge had torn through many of them. Throwing herself into the pack down there now might disrupt them for a minute, but it wouldn't take long for them to overwhelm her. And then what? The Weir would be right back on the people trapped in the building. Even if Gamble and the others fled while Cass attacked, they'd most likely just get tracked down and slaughtered on the run.

On the run, like Wren was now. Thoughts of her son threatened to bubble to the surface... but no, she forced them away. The decision was made. Time and again these

people had come to her aid; Gamble, Mouse, Swoop, Lil...
even Elan, a man she'd hardly known. They'd all risked
their lives. Some had given them. She couldn't abandon
them here. Wouldn't. But what options were there? It was
like watching the ocean roll and searching for a way to stop
the coming waves from crashing on the shoreline. All her
strength, and there was nothing she could do with it.

. And then unbidden a thought sprang to mind.

"What if I hit them from *every* flank?" Cass said.

"What?" said Wick.

She turned back to face him. He was up in a crouch now,
weapon in hand. A good sign. "What if I stay on the move,
attack from different locations?"

"What's that gonna do, Cass?" Wick asked.

"Buy you time," she answered.

"For what? To find a different hole to die in?"

A short burst of gunfire ripped through the air, followed
by another of Sky's shots. No more discussion.

"I'm going. Direct me, Wick. Be my eyes. Set points for
me. I'll move faster if I don't have to decide where to run
next."

Wick set his jaw, but after a heartbeat, he nodded.

We'll go together, Able signed.

"No," Cass said, shaking her head. "You stay with Wick,
keep him covered. If they get me, maybe you'll be able to
direct Gamble out of there, and Wick can't run on his own.
You have any more of those flash grenades?"

Wick shook his head, but Able produced two from his
pack and held them out.

"Throw to the far side," Cass said, pointing to places
where the line of Weir was thinnest. "One there, the other
there. After they go off, I'll open up, then move. Bounce to
a new position, fire, move again. If I can stay ahead of them,
maybe it'll be enough."

"If *they* get ahead of *you*, we're not going to be able to do
anything to help."

"Then don't let them get ahead of me."

Wick unlatched his sling and held out his short-barreled rifle to her. "It's set on burst," he said. "Fire two, then move. Two bursts max. Don't wait around for a third."

She nodded and took the weapon, its sleek metal cold to her already cold hands. It'd been years since she'd fired anything bigger than a pistol, and she'd never run anything quite like Wick's weapon before. But she wasn't about to tell him that. It had a single-point sling attached to the stock, which she slipped over her head and shoulder and then cinched. Wick quickly adjusted it for her so it would hang properly. He handed her two extra magazines.

"Thirty rounds each. Don't try to reload on the run. When you're running, just run. You can reload when you get there. Unless you're dry, then just–"

"I got it, Wick," Cass said, cutting him off. "Find me some places to set up." She squeezed his shoulder, and then Able's arm, and then crossed the empty space to the back side of the building where they'd first climbed up. When she reached the gap in the wall, she forced herself to stop and scan the street below for five deep breaths to make sure it was clear. Satisfied that it was, she crouched low and hopped over the edge. The twelve-foot drop barely registered when she hit the pavement. She crouched again in the moonlit alley and ran her eyes and fingers over the controls on Wick's weapon; fortunately all the essentials were in familiar places. Cass dropped the magazine out of the rifle and swapped in a fresh one, then did it again just to make sure she could. She shouldered it, and snapped the muzzle back and forth between a couple of arbitrary pieces of debris down the alley, gauging the weapon's weight and getting a sense of the sight picture. She knew her way around guns, but they'd never really been her thing. Not as smooth as Wick. She could get the job done well enough... she hoped. At least she was about to get a lot more practice.

An internal ping showed up in her vision, a digital landmark only she could see, off to the northeast. Wick's first point of attack. She took another deep breath to steady herself, and headed out, hunched low but with quick, careful steps. Whether she could see residual heat or some wavelength beyond the normal spectrum, she didn't know, but the night's darkness posed no trouble for her Weir-enhanced eyes.

Cass approached the end of the wide alley and slowed as she reached the corner. Wick's first waypoint was only about thirty yards on the other side of the road. She edged forward and leaned out just far enough for one eye to get a view of what lay down the street. It was empty, except for the raging noise that cascaded down the channel created by the buildings on either side. Cass ducked her head and dashed straight across, forcing herself to keep her eyes fixed on her destination. Once she'd crossed, she slipped around behind a four-story structure, passing a gaping hole in the wall that exposed a skeletal staircase coated in concrete dust and debris. She glanced up at it as she went by and saw that whatever those stairs had led to at one time was gone now. The final steps had sheared off and hung out into space.

Just past the building she paused at another corner, and then covered the remaining ground to the waypoint. As she closed in, though, it vanished. Cass glanced around looking for a good vantage point, but as far as she could see there wasn't anywhere that had a sightline to the Weir. A few seconds later, a second waypoint appeared, further east, maybe thirty yards. Again, she made her way to it and again, as she neared, the waypoint vanished. The position seemed even worse here. Still no clear lines of attack, and even the roar from the Weir seemed dulled. What was Wick doing?

It occurred to her now that she had no way to communicate with him directly. She hadn't thought to ask him to patch her in to the team's secure channel, the low-frequency, low-profile method they used to communicate in the Open without attracting the attention of the Weir. She didn't dare risk a pim to him, knowing the signal would surely reveal her. Maybe he'd misunderstood. Or... was he leading her back towards the tunnel? Trying to send her out of harm's way?

A third waypoint appeared for her, northward, though still with an eastward bend. She stood for a moment, uncertain of his intentions. After a moment she resolved to go to the third point and evaluate. If by then she wasn't seeing a place to ambush, she'd make her way back and hope she got there fast enough before Wick and Able did whatever it was they were really planning to do.

Cass upped her pace to a trot. The third point was slightly elevated, and she had to scramble up and over a low wall to reach it. She didn't like that wall, given the need she was going to have of a quick, direct path out. There was a single-story structure there, some kind of old storage facility she guessed. It had a sloping roof that was only about four feet above the ground in the back and angled to maybe twelve feet in the front. Wick's waypoint hovered midway up the roof. Cass hopped up on to it, dropped to a crouch, and made her way up. She had to move a few steps ahead of the waypoint to get a view on the Weir, but once she did, she realized Wick hadn't led her astray. Far from it. Cass couldn't imagine a better position from which to launch a surprise assault.

Two rows of low buildings separated her from the host of Weir, but the gentle rise of the terrain and the way the buildings lined up gave her a clear field of fire. When her first rounds found their mark, the Weir would most likely turn their attention to the buildings closest to them, giving her plenty of time and cover to make it to the next point.

Cass settled in and tucked the rifle stock tight into the pocket of her shoulder. Sighted in, took a deep breath, held, released. On target, she slipped her finger inside the trigger guard and lightly rested it on the trigger. She wondered briefly how much recoil the weapon had.

And then, as if her thoughts had summoned it, the attack began.

Able's first grenade made a pop Cass could barely hear above the clamor, but there was no missing the flash. Lightning-bright, it made her flinch reflexively even from that distance. The Weir closest to the detonation scattered blindly, and Cass took advantage, sighting in again and firing three bursts in succession at the clusters of Weir gathered on either side of the blast. Able's second grenade went off twenty feet from the first, with similar results. Except this time Cass didn't flinch. She ripped off two, three, four more bursts as the line of Weir rippled and broke open near the blast points. Wick had warned her not to fire more than twice from the same location, but her vantage was so good and the chaos so complete, she couldn't miss the chance to take down as many Weir as possible at the height of their confusion. This first strike was critical.

Cass sighted in on a tight cluster and let off a burst, then snapped her weapon to a second group and fired again. Some Weir stumbled, others fell. Whether they could tell where the shots had come from or not, Cass didn't know. By then, she was too busy leaping down from her perch and dashing towards the low wall. She'd pushed her luck as far as she'd dared. As she scrambled up and over, a new waypoint appeared. Cass sprinted for it.

Five, seven, ten seconds. Each one felt like a potential loss of momentum, a possible unraveling of the plan. Forty-four seconds after her initial attack, Cass slid on her knees into the new position Wick had marked for her. This one low, with a narrow line to the courtyard. Not knowing how many rounds she'd expended, she dropped the magazine out of the rifle and slapped in a fresh one. Then without hesitation, she shouldered Wick's rifle and fired two quick bursts into the thin sliver of the teeming crowd she could see. Her fire was accurate, but she didn't confirm whether or not her targets were dead. Kills were a bonus; chaos, the goal. Already the next waypoint was waiting for her, and speed was of the utmost essence.

Cass vaulted up to a full run, north and west, circling behind a row of squat cement structures. She was only fifteen feet away when the first Weir surged out of a darkened entryway into her path. The creature hesitated for a heartbeat. It was enough. She fired a burst directly into its center of mass, and then leapt and brought her knee high. She caught the creature just under the jaw and rode it to the ground, then rolled and let the momentum carry her back to her feet. The Weir managed a ragged, gurgling howl, but Cass didn't bother to look back. The adrenaline was flowing. She was too fast now. Far too fast. The entire world seemed to have slowed around her, for her, *because* of her.

She reached the waypoint, dropped to a crouch, fired, moved on. She had to stay one step ahead. Two, if possible. But Cass was forced to restrain herself; it was several seconds before Wick marked a new position, and she had to loop back to reach it. Speed was critical to keeping up the illusion, but if she outran Wick, she might end up in a place she couldn't get back out of.

The next waypoint was at an intersection of alleys, and Cass slowed her pace just enough to squeeze off three accurate bursts as she crossed. It took her less than two seconds. And even as she resumed her sprint, she found she could see it all so clearly in her mind's eye; the sight picture the weapon presented, the impact of the rounds, the uncomprehending expressions on the faces of the stricken Weir. Like still frames, each instant perfectly preserved. Like when she'd boosted on quint. *Like*, but not the same. This was clearer somehow, cleaner.

Out there, in that courtyard, the clamor of the Weir was changing, shifting. Cries and howls transformed from savage mockery into anger, confusion, pain. And above it all, an eruption of gunfire. Cass couldn't see the building where Gamble and her team were pinned, but she knew they were fighting now. Not defensively, not conserving ammo. Counter-assaulting.

There was another delay before her beacon showed up, longer this time, and when it finally appeared, it was so close Cass almost overran it. She skidded on the concrete-dusted asphalt as she took the hard corner towards the newest destination. This position was in a tight alley, and

Cass was startled by the number of Weir just at the other end. Wick was taking her much closer to the Weir.

No, not closer. The crowd was breaking up, turning outward. Searching. Seeking.

Two Weir were hunched down, sweeping their heads back and forth in measured movements. Hunting. The waypoint blinked away as she brought the rifle up and on target.

She felt it somehow, just before.

A dread presence, like someone standing too close behind her.

Cass whirled–

Too late. The barrel caught, her burst of fire stitched the wall. The world went sideways.

The impact blacked her vision for an instant, something heavy atop her. Even as her mind swam and fought to recover her scattered senses, her body was in motion, reacting. Automatic. Her claws rent her attacker before she could even see it.

As her vision cleared, she swept the dying Weir to the side with one arm. Still on her back, she arched up and brought her weapon above her head, the world momentarily upside-down as she fired into the two Weir that were now charging at her. One twisted and tumbled into the wall, but the other took the hit and kept coming. Cass rolled to her belly and squeezed the trigger again. Her rifle only clicked. Empty.

She scrambled back on her knees, but didn't have time to make it all the way up to her feet. She let the rifle drop free, trusting the sling to carry it out of the way as she reached out her hands. Time stretched in that final second before contact. The Weir was wounded. Two dark blotches in the upper abdomen. Its right hand was sweeping in, claws extended, aimed at her eyes.

Cass intercepted the creature's wrist with the palm of her left hand, lifted it up just enough to pass it over her head. In the same instant, she stepped up and drove forward with her right shoulder, planting the strike right in the Weir's wounded midsection. It folded over her with a shriek and she continued upwards, using the creature's momentum to carry it off its feet and send it flying face first into the hard concrete. It squawked once as it impacted with a wet slap, but Cass spun and stomped down on the back of its neck before it could recover.

Another group of Weir skidded around the corner, further down the alley, back the direction she had come. They were starting to home in on her. Four of them, thirty feet away and closing fast. Cass swapped the spent magazine for her last one. Fifteen feet. Cold, savage fury rose within her and spilled forth as she advanced to meet them. Her burst of fire killed the first two at nearly point-blank range, and she swept the third's attack aside with the rifle, spinning between the last two as she did so. The Weir seemed sluggish, unable to match her speed or predict her movements; she was behind them before they reacted. She slammed the butt of her rifle into the base of the third Weir's skull, sent it headlong into the fourth. Two bursts into the confused tangle. Then she was off again, at a full sprint.

This was the most dangerous time; the Weir were like hornets, frenzied by the attack. The tight mass of them had begun to break, with many individuals scattering in wild search for their tormentors. A single Weir would be nothing to her, and even a handful could be overcome. But if they got a lock on Cass's position, they would surely kill her with their thousand stings. She'd burned through her ammo much faster than she'd expected to.

And where was the next waypoint? Had she missed it? Was it back the other way? Cass scanned all around her as she ran, searching for her next position. She risked a quick glance back over her shoulder; when she looked forward again, another Weir was just flashing out of an alley ahead and to her right. She touched the trigger but the instant before she squeezed, instinct stopped her. There was only one; ammo was low.

The Weir squawked at her once, hands outstretched. She twisted and punched out with the rifle, one-handed, and jabbed the creature in the forehead with the muzzle, checking its momentum. Its head snapped back with the impact, its hands splayed to the sides. Cass jolted in close and followed with a strike to its exposed throat. The creature managed a broken croak and locked its eyes on hers just before she drove the butt of her gun into its temple.

She was moving too fast to stop. The impact sent a sickening crunch vibrating through her hands. And as the blue-light glow of the creature's eyes doused and it collapsed, the look on its feminine face lingered, fixed in her mind, crystal-clear as if time had frozen. Not the emotionless stare of the dead; not the savage snarl of animal rage. An expression. Wild-eyed, frantic. Lost. Afraid. Not an *it*. A *she*.

What had Cass just killed?

A clatter from behind spurred her forward, even as her mind lagged behind. She leapt over the stricken Weir and ducked into the alley, weapon up in case any others had been trailing the one she'd just slain. There was nothing. Cass quickly swiveled and leaned back around the corner, just enough for the rifle barrel to clear the edge. Nothing there either. Calls were still coming from every direction. And Wick still hadn't sent her a new position.

A pair of Weir raced by the opposite end of the alley, but they didn't look her way. In fact, they looked like they were headed back towards the courtyard. Cass drew in close to one side of the alley and slowed to an aggressive walk.

She had to get some distance to regroup, reassess. She tried to get her bearings as best she could. As she analyzed her surroundings, Cass realized she'd been so intent on Wick's points, she hadn't paid full attention to how she got from one to the next. Surely he'd send her another any second now. Maybe he was tracking her somehow, and her sudden flight from her last position had him scrambling to find her another position. Thin hope in that, but she clung to it.

A single Weir called out somewhere off to her left and Cass swiveled at the waist, weapon leveled in the direction of the cry without interrupting her stride. Wherever it was, she couldn't see it now. And as she turned back to face forward, it suddenly dawned on her. She'd heard that call clearly enough to know it was a single Weir. Things were quieting down. And she couldn't hear any more gunfire.

Cass rounded a corner and saw a gutted three-story building across the street that looked familiar. Something she'd passed before. She checked both directions before crossing to it; there were no Weir in sight. The building had a wide entrance, wide enough for two doors though only one was hanging there now. There were no windows on the lower floor, not even cracks for the moonlight to get in. Even though her modified vision enabled her to see in total darkness, the building had a deathly feel that made her hesitant to enter. Still, she needed cover while she waited for Wick's next update, or until she could figure out what else to do. There was no way to know what she might find inside, no way to tell if Weir had gotten in first, or were searching for her in there even now.

Three Weir appeared further down the wide road and made the decision for her. She pushed into the dusty entryway before they spotted her. There was a lot of clutter in that front room; strange shapes, broken outlines. Cass had never tried to clear a room before, but she'd seen Gamble's team do it a handful of times. She did her best.

She pushed in aggressively, sweeping the corners of the room as she moved to the front-right corner and dropped into a crouch there. She held for five seconds, ten, thirty. Nothing stirred. The room was clear. And as she held her position, glad for something solid at her back, the weight of the moment settled on her.

Her great unspoken fear, come to pass. She was on her own. Cut off. Utterly alone.

And with the Weir scouring the streets, Cass knew that her chances of reconnecting with her companions were slim and growing ever slimmer.

TWO

Wren stood silently at the edge of the roof, staring out over the swirl and churn of Greenstone's midmorning streets as the citizens went about their business and the Greenmen kept careful watch. But despite the clamor below, he wasn't fully aware of his surroundings. Instead, he was locked in a struggle of the mind, stretching out with all his will and might. Somewhere out there, somewhere in the east, were the signals that told the fate of his mother and of his friends and guardians. Somewhere across the vast expanse of the Strand, amongst the ruins of his once-great city, were traces and digital footprints that could tell him whether they still lived, or, if not, at least maybe where and how they had died.

And yet no matter how focused he was or how hard he strove, there was nothing. Or rather, there was Something that hid all else from him, like a great static fog or electric darkness. Digital nightfall. Vast and impenetrable, even to Wren's innate talents.

It was as if everything beyond the Strand had ceased to exist; worse, had never existed at all. Every sign, every imprint, every shadow of what once had been had been swallowed up in the roiling fog. And it was no natural phenomenon. Wren could feel it pushing back against him. It was a gloom born of malice and an evil will, a manifestation of Asher's great and still growing power.

At the same time, Wren dared not probe too deeply.

There was a searching quality to that great shadow, as if something roamed about within it, seeking others to devour. Wren feared drawing its attention. And whenever he extended himself to it, touched it, filaments of it seemed to cling to him when he withdrew. To stretch and trail after him, like threads of a web or heavy strands of tar. The effects of his last encounter with his brother still hadn't worn completely away. Every light seemed too bright, every noise too loud. His head felt too heavy, too full. And a dread lingered over his every moment and thought; the possibility that whatever Asher had done to him had been the result of a mere fraction of Asher's capability.

Asher. His laughter echoed in Wren's memory, and Wren came back to himself with tears in his eyes and a hollow cold in his gut. Fear, anger, frustration. But worst of all, uncertainty. Maybe Mama was still out there, maybe she was gone. And the others. Gamble, Sky, Able. Mouse. It'd been what? Three days now? More than enough time for any survivors to make their way through the underground tunnel that ran beneath the Strand. Bonefolder's trainline. The same path Chapel and he had used to escape. Wouldn't they have followed, if they'd survived to do it?

Of only one thing there was no doubt; Asher would come again. But when, and how, Wren didn't know. It would be in his own time, in his own way, some manner carefully calculated to bring the most pain and terror. Wren knew that even the waiting would be a part of Asher's planned torment; each day haunted by the question *will it be today?*, and thus robbed of any peace. Wren had tried before to stop him and failed catastrophically. When Asher finally did come, Wren would be utterly powerless to prevent it. And he *would* come. As long as Wren remained free, Asher would be seeking him. Pursuing. Bringing wrath wherever Wren had trod.

Unless.

Wren leaned forward and placed his hands on the waist-high wall that enclosed the rooftop. Forty feet below, the streets teemed with Greenstone's citizens. The array of colors was almost dazzling, the droning buzz of voices hypnotic. Theirs was a wild expression of life, a walled city's flagrant protest against the rest of the world's colorless decay.

A little further forward, a small hop; would his death disrupt any of those people below? Might it not even be their salvation?

"Come away from there, child," a voice came from behind. "Such thoughts do not suit one so young."

It was Chapel, Wren's sole remaining guardian. The voice was kind but firm, warm in its command. Wren didn't have a grandfather that he knew of, but he imagined Chapel's voice was how one would sound. The boy lingered, the idea of a final surrender not yet entirely dispelled. But after a moment he drew a breath and without any sort of conscious choice felt his heart resign itself to life. Chapel had said it before; many good men and women had given their lives to preserve Wren's. It would be a mockery of their sacrifice to simply give up now.

Wren wiped his eyes and stood up straight.

"I wasn't going to jump," he said.

"I would not have let you fall."

The people streamed about below, oblivious to the doom that hung over them. The doom that haunted Wren and brought ruin wherever he fled. If Morningside, the great shining city of the east, could fall, what hope was there for any of them?

"Don't you ever think it might just might be easier, though? If I were... you know. If I wasn't around anymore."

"No."

"Never?"

"No."

"How come?"

"Because I believe your life has purpose yet unfulfilled."

"Yeah, well..." Wren said, his mind suddenly flooded with images of faces. "Maybe that's not such a great thing to believe. Everyone else who has ever thought that is dead."

"You seem certain."

Wren turned to face Chapel. The old man seemed to be

staring right at him despite the blindfold that covered his eyes. He was closer than he'd been a few minutes before, now nearly within arm's reach, though Wren had never heard the man move. He realized that even if he *had* tried to jump, Chapel would have snatched him back from the edge in an instant. Wren sat down on the dusty roof, his back against the short wall.

"It's most likely."

"What does your heart tell you?"

Wren shook his head and looked down at the ground. Traced a meaningless design in the dust. Probably Mama was dead. Probably they all were, from what he remembered and from what Chapel had been willing to tell him of the night they'd escaped. Asher's incomprehensible power. The overwhelming numbers of Weir. Painter's betrayal.

And Mama choosing to give Wren over to Chapel, so that she could go back and fight. Only once in his life before had she ever entrusted him to someone else; the first time she had done it because she knew she was near death. And the man who had taken charge of him then too was now dead. But no matter how much Wren's mind tried to imagine it, or how strongly he willed himself to believe that she was gone again, his heart couldn't accept it. Not this time. At least, not yet.

"That she's alive," he said. And then shook his head. "But I think it's just what I hope."

"Hope is a powerful gift. It should not lightly be cast away."

Wren shrugged. He'd heard grownups say *hope against hope* before, but he'd never really understood what that was supposed to mean. Maybe he was starting to figure it out. Even when everything else told him all hope was lost, something down deep held on anyway. Something so deep it almost felt like it might not even be part of him, but rather something Other, forced in from the outside. Or maybe he just didn't want to accept how near the end was, and how in real life the good guys didn't always win. In his case, it was starting to seem like they *never* did.

The door leading out on to the roof eased open, drawing Wren's attention. Behind Chapel, a familiar face peeked through – Mol.

"Hey," she said, quiet and careful in her speech, like she was concerned about intruding.

"Hi, Mol," Wren answered.

"Mind if I come out there for a sec?" Her gentle hesitance was highlighted by the fact that it was her roof in the first place.

"No, ma'am, not at all," Wren said.

She slipped out onto the roof carrying her daughter, Grace; six months old, sleeping peacefully in her mama's arms. The nerve-rig that enabled Mol to walk whirred and clicked softly, stirring strong emotions in Wren. It was a beautiful thing to see; Mol with the baby her body should never have been able to produce. Her own little living miracle. But it raised in him a dull panic as well, knowing that his presence put such a precious thing at risk. Indeed, even if he left today, the mere fact that jCharles and Mol had taken him in again might still invite Asher's eye and vengeance.

"There's someone downstairs," she said. "Down with Twitch." She looked concerned, or puzzled. Maybe both. "Twitch wanted to see if you might feel up to coming down to see to him?"

"Me?" Wren asked.

"Mm-hmm," Mol nodded.

"Who is it?"

"I..." Mol said, and then stopped, her brow furrowed. She shook her head. "I don't even know how to explain, sweetheart. I think maybe Twitch should."

Wren glanced over to Chapel, who stood impassively, head raised slightly like someone catching a scent on the wind.

"OK," Wren said, getting up off the ground. "I guess so. Down in the apartment?"

Mol shook her head. "The bar."

Wren dusted his pants off and moved to the door. Chapel fell wordlessly in behind him. They made their way down the stairs past the apartment where jCharles and Mol lived. Where jCharles, Mol, *and Grace* lived, Wren reminded himself. On the floor below was the Samurai McGann, the bar, or saloon, or whatever the business was that jCharles owned and operated.

There was, in fact, much more that jCharles was involved in, as Wren had learned when Three had first brought him here. It wasn't exactly clear what all jCharles did, but Wren had come to understand that most of the citizens of Greenstone either feared or respected him, or both. Wren also guessed that whatever his other business was, it might not be strictly legal. Then again, the definition of "strictly legal" changed a lot from town to town, and Wren had the impression that in Greenstone there were rules and there were laws, and they could be very different things depending on where you were standing at any particular time.

jCharles was waiting for them at the bottom of the narrow staircase, and he dropped down to a knee as Wren approached.

"Hey, buddy," he said, and placed a hand on Wren's shoulder. He smiled slightly, but it didn't soften the hardness in his eyes. He was either shaken or suspicious, and neither was a good sign to Wren. "There's a guy, just showed up a little while ago." He paused and scratched his upper lip with his thumb. "He's out here asking some questions. I think maybe you're gonna wanna talk to him, but that's up to you, OK? My fellas are all in there, and I'll be there, and I'm sure Mr Chapel will be there, so it'll be safe, we'll make sure of that. But you don't have to say anything you don't want to, OK? You don't even have to go in, unless you want to."

"What kind of questions?" Wren asked. Mol's manner had seemed a little strange, but the way jCharles was acting was starting to make Wren genuinely nervous.

"He's uhh..." jCharles's eyes narrowed and he took a moment before he answered. "He's asking about Three, Wren."

Suddenly the grownups' reactions started to make sense. Maybe there was cause for concern after all.

"We haven't told him much of anything," jCharles added. "But he already knows about you."

"Is it someone you know?" said Wren.

jCharles shook his head. "Never seen him before. Just rolled in, and he's not saying a whole lot. I got some of my guys checking around, but so far nothing's showing up."

"Is that a good thing or a bad thing?"

"Right now, it's just a thing that *is*."

Wren nodded, thought it over. He hadn't much felt like talking to anyone about anything lately. And he knew questions about Three might lead him to remember things he'd been trying to let himself forget. Still. There was something of a mystery there that he might be able to help solve.

"You think I should talk to him?"

"You do what *you* want, Wren."

"But I'm asking... you think I should?"

jCharles hesitated, worked his jaw. Then, finally, "I think so, yeah. Normally, someone walks in poking around like this, I'd just blow him back out the door but this guy..." He trailed off, then shook his head. "I don't know. This one, I wanted you to have a say."

Wren rolled the idea around. Whoever it was, jCharles didn't seem to think he was dangerous. Or rather, maybe jCharles thought the man was a kind of dangerous that could be handled. But what did he want to know? And more importantly, why did he want to know it?

In the end, it wasn't courage or any sense of duty that decided it. It was simple curiosity.

"OK then," he said.

jCharles nodded and stood, squeezing Wren's shoulder as he did so. He took hold of the door handle, but paused before he opened it. "Any time you wanna leave, you just say so. Anything you don't wanna say, you don't say it. You're in control here, 'kay?"

"OK."

jCharles glanced up at Chapel, gave a quick nod, and then pulled the door open and ushered Wren through.

The Samurai McGann wasn't particularly crowded this

early in the day, but the dim and hazy atmosphere had a way of making everything feel close no matter how few people were around. A small knot of men was gathered near the middle of the bar, a little closer to the storefront than to the back hall. Five, maybe six, of jCharles's "fellas"; mostly large, bruiser-looking types who were either employees or the most regular patrons anyone could ever hope for. Their collective mass blocked Wren's view of whoever was at the table. Nimble, the bartender, was at his usual place behind the bar, leaning over it slightly and keeping an attentive watch. His eyes flicked over as the three of them entered and then back again at the group.

Wren walked towards the table with jCharles just behind him, at his left shoulder. Chapel lingered by the door near the back hall.

The man was sitting there with his back to the door, but before Wren could make out any features someone came in off the street. The white light of day shone dazzling through the dusky bar and its radiance masked both the man at the table and the newcomer at the door in silhouette.

Whoever it was at the door must have taken a quick survey of the situation, because he hesitated there in the entrance for a few seconds and then promptly backed out and left. In those few moments, though, Wren's heart nearly burst in his chest. Even though he knew it wasn't so, that it would be impossible, the silhouette of the man sitting at the table was so familiar that hope unbidden leapt forth and for a fleeting second told him that this man was not simply *asking* about Three, but was in fact Three himself, come back from death and desolation.

But no. An instant later the illusion faded, and even before the front door had swung fully closed, Wren saw that the man was shorter than Three had been, stockier in build, skin tone darker. Still, the shock lingered with a wisping trace of disappointment and a renewed sense of loss. Cruel that one's own mind could play such a bitter trick.

And yet there remained a hint of familiarity that he

couldn't completely dismiss. Something vague and elusive that seemed to flutter at the edge of his thoughts, like something seen out of the corner of the eye and gone when looked upon.

Wren's vision readjusted to the dim light and he took in the scene. The man was the only one sitting. For his part, he seemed entirely at ease despite being surrounded by a number of tightly-wound, rough-looking men. His deep eyes were bright and piercingly alert, set in a wide, round face. A dark stubble of hair dusted his head, a few days' growth after a clean shave perhaps. His thick-fingered hands were clasped before him and rested atop what at first appeared to be some sort of thin box. As Wren reached the table though he realized it was not a box at all, but was instead a thick book; leather-bound, battered, dusted with the grime of travel and use.

Wren hovered at the edge of the table, hesitant to sit. He was aware of the others in the room, but his eyes were drawn intently to those of the man across from him. The man gazed back unblinking. For a span, no one spoke; hardly anyone moved.

"Hello," the man said. His voice was warm and vibrant, not particularly deep or loud, but full and rounded.

"Hi," Wren answered.

"I seem to have alarmed your friends," the man said. A gentle smile spread across his face at a speed like that of a man holding up his hands to show he was unarmed.

"I don't think that's wise."

"Neither do I. Nor was it my intent."

Without understanding why, Wren felt some of the tension start to melt away. There was something wholesome about the man; he emanated a kind of steady peace, a quiet strength. Even so, Wren had learned not to trust too readily. He slid into the empty chair directly across from the man, reminding himself to guard his words.

"They said you had questions," Wren said.

The man inclined his head forward.

"I'm looking for someone. A man," he said. "Judging from the reaction, I suspect I'm correct in thinking it was a man you may have traveled with some time ago."

"I've traveled a lot," Wren said, trying to sound casual. "With a lot of different people."

"I suspect this particular individual might stick in one's memory."

"What do you want with him?"

"Nothing insidious," the man answered, raising his hands slightly to give a clearer view of his book. "I'm a chronicler. A historian, of sorts. I know something of his past, but I'm a bit behind." He smiled again. "Just trying to fill in the gaps."

"You knew him? Before?"

The man nodded.

"Then I guess you know how he'd feel about people asking questions about him."

For the first time, the man's eyes left Wren's and flicked down to his own hands. His smile shifted, more inwardly focused. He nodded again. "I do, very well." The man looked back up at Wren. "I see you also knew him well. And that you wish to protect him."

Wren held himself still, but in that moment the vague sense of familiarity snapped into focus. It wasn't a single feature or trait about the man that reminded him of Three, but rather the sum of many ethereal qualities taken together; the man's utter stillness, the fluidity of his few movements, the almost surgical gaze.

The man glanced around at the ring of men that had him surrounded and took a deep breath, then nodded seemingly to himself. He looked back to Wren and leaned forward, as if sharing a secret.

"My name is Haiku," he said. "Of House Eight."

He said it as though it should have more meaning to Wren than it did. He must have read Wren's face, though, because after a moment he leaned a little closer and said something that hit Wren with a fresh storm of emotion.

"Three was my brother."

THREE

Cass focused her attention back to her immediate surroundings. The moon carved a channel of soft light through the darkened room, stark as it spilled across the dusty floor and over the scattered piles of debris. It was odd to see such clutter; much of the area surrounding Morningside had been so thoroughly scavenged over the years as to be almost clean. She wondered just how far out from the city she was now. Or if perhaps there was something about this particular building that had marked it off-limits. Cass tried not to think about what that might mean.

The Weir were still near and active, though their calls to one another were trailing off, coming less frequently. They hadn't seemed to be searching in any organized way, but after a minute or two Cass decided to move out of the front room. If she could get higher up in the building, she might be able to get a better sense of what was going on out there.

There was a door in the back wall, flat grey, slightly recessed. As quietly as she was able, she edged her way to it and found it led to a narrow passage that ended in a stairwell. Cass moved in cautiously and after a moment's consideration, pushed the door nearly shut. There was a handle on this side of it, but she didn't feel quite confident enough to close it all the way.

When Cass reached the base of the stairs, she was relieved to find they were concrete. A cheap, rough cast, they were

uneven, chipped, and cracked. But they weren't likely to
creak when she put her weight on them. She ascended.
The second floor appeared to be laid out much like the
one below it. There were slit windows here though, and
the gloom lay less heavy. The slant of the ceiling above the
steps suggested another staircase. A quick glance through
the nearest window revealed little more than the faces of
the surrounding buildings, so Cass climbed the next flight.

The third floor didn't deviate from the established
floorplan, except that there were no stairs leading further
up. A thin metal railing ran around the top of the stairwell;
a rusting mesh clung to it with haphazard welds. With
each passing minute, Cass became more confident that the
building wasn't harboring any Weir, and after a brief search
of the upper rooms, she allowed herself to relax ever so
slightly. For the first time since she'd entered the building,
she lowered her weapon and let it dangle from its sling. She
kept one hand on it.

As on the floor below, slit windows perforated the thick
outer wall at even intervals. Cass moved to one at the front
right corner, close to the stairs, where she could keep her
back to the adjacent wall while she tried to get her bearings.
She didn't have much of a vantage from the narrow
window, and she'd gotten so turned around she wasn't
even exactly sure where she should be looking anyway. It
took her almost a minute of scanning to find the building
where she'd left Wick and Able. When she did locate it,
the distance surprised her. It seemed farther away than it
should have been. But even from this far out, she could see
the flickering moonlight glow dancing within the hole in
the front of the building.

The Weir. They'd taken the building.

Maybe Wick and Able had made it out. Or maybe they,
like so many others before them, had given their lives to
save the rest of the team. Cass tried not to think about the
likelihood that they were *all* dead, and that she was now
truly alone. But whatever had happened, she was on her

own, if not for good, at least for now.

For a time Cass just stood, scanning the broken horizon, waiting for the flood of emotion to hit her. The weight of the loss and the isolation. But it didn't come. Whether she was too juiced up from the fighting or too exhausted by the same, she simply acknowledged the situation and accepted it for the moment. If she survived till dawn, maybe she'd have her break down then. But not now. For now, there was only *what next*. She dropped down into a crouch by the window and took inventory. It didn't take long. There wasn't much.

Cass dropped the magazine from the rifle and combined the ammunition with what was left of her other unspent magazine. That left her about half a mag. Her go-bag still had a few rations, a couple of water canisters, some extra clothes, a light.

What was the best thing to do now? She'd done all she could for the team. Maybe they'd been able to escape, or maybe they were all lying slaughtered somewhere out there. There was still the tunnel. If she could find her way back to it. She could probably catch up with Chapel and Wren, if not before sunrise certainly before they reached the end of that long darkness.

But no. Even as she pictured it in her mind, she knew she couldn't rejoin them. Not now. Maybe not ever. Asher may have spent his wrath on Morningside, but Cass knew with cold certainty he wouldn't stop there. He might let Wren go, now that he'd inflicted whatever cruelty it was that had left Wren unconscious. Might, if perhaps he could reclaim Cass. Tormenting Wren had mostly been Asher's way of controlling *her*, after all. His threats a way of keeping her in line. Exploiting her greatest vulnerability.

And what of it now? If Wren was beyond his reach... no, whatever Asher had become, Cass very much doubted anyone was truly beyond his reach now. But maybe if she were closer at hand...

Before the idea had fully formed in her conscious mind,

her heart had understood and committed. She knew what she had to do. She would make herself both bait and trap. Not much different than what she had just attempted with the Weir. A greater degree, perhaps. Perhaps a far greater degree. She would tease Asher with her presence; taunt him by dangling herself just beyond his grasp. How she would manage it, Cass would have to figure out later. She was too tired, too mind-numb to do any serious planning. She would keep east of the Strand. Haunt the ruins of Morningside, maybe, and its surroundings. Make it up as she went along.

For the moment, though, she needed to make it through the night. The howls of the Weir were still out there, but they were few and far between. The throng had broken up, or wandered off together. She stood and gazed out of the window again. The building where she'd left Able and Wick was dark now, inside and out, black silhouette against a midnight sky. And though she didn't want to admit it, Cass was loathe to leave the relative safety of her current location. It felt good to have elevation, and sturdy walls around her. From here, she could put her back to the corner and have the drop on anything that came up the stairs. And anything that wanted to get her was going to have to come up those stairs.

After a minute, Cass decided she'd take a little time to rest before she headed back out. That'd give the Weir time to scatter further, and might help her head get clearer. She settled down to the floor, back against the wall under the window. After she loaded her weapon with the half-magazine, she drank some water, and forced herself to eat a little, even though she wasn't remotely hungry. Her eyes were dry and felt too big for their sockets. It was quiet. And she was so weary. Twenty minutes she'd give herself. Twenty minutes, and then she'd go back out into the night. Cass lay Wick's rifle across her lap with her hand on the grip, and let her eyes fall closed.

•••

It was a feeling that woke her more than anything else. The sense that something had changed. Cass checked the time and saw she'd slept for over an hour. She clenched her jaw. Nothing she could do about it now. And she felt certain she had a bigger problem to deal with anyway. She strained to hear over the sound of her own heartbeat, and after a moment, she heard it. A faint, gritty rustle; a concrete whisper. A footstep, its weight carefully, painstakingly shifted to avoid making any sound, betrayed only by the grime on the steps. There was something moving on the stairs below.

Cass clutched the rifle, drew it up slowly from her lap. Sighted in on the lowest stair she could see.

"Sssssst," a hiss came from below, soft but shocking to her senses. Cass forced herself to relax her grip on the rifle and held as still as possible. The stairs took on a reddish hue, as if lit by dying coals.

"Sssst," it came again, quiet but insistent, a breath barely exhaled through clenched teeth.

And then, a shadow of a voice.

"Cass. You up there?"

Cass exhaled, not even having realized she'd been holding her breath.

"Cass, it's Sky. You hear me?"

"Yeah," Cass whispered back, hardly able to believe it, hardly able to get her voice to speak the words. "Sky. Sky, I'm here. Up here."

She lowered her weapon and leaned forward towards the rusted mesh around the stairs. The red light spread further up the stairs and a few moments later the top of Sky's head appeared. His rifle was up at the ready, with its mounted low-intensity red-filtered light switched on. From what Gamble's team had told her, Cass knew the red light didn't spoil their night-adjusted vision, nor did it pose as much risk from the Weir as brighter white light did. Sky was still creeping up the stairs, sweeping the rifle slowly back and forth as he came.

"Here, Sky," she whispered again.

His head flicked around in her direction, and she stood so he could see her over the mesh.

"We clear?" he whispered.

"Yeah, we're good," Cass answered.

"You hurt?" Sky asked.

"No, I'm all right. Sky, what happened out there? Where's the team?"

He held up his hand, and angled his head back down the stairs. Listening. After a moment, he climbed the rest of the steps and joined Cass in her corner.

"We broke out," he said. "Thanks to you."

"You all made it out?"

"Most of us," he said. And then his jaw went tight and even in the gloom Cass saw the unmistakable look on his face.

"Sky..." Cass said, but that was all she could manage.

"I don't want to hang around here long," Sky said. He glanced out the window, and then back at her. "You all right to move?"

"Yeah, I'm good to go."

"It's breaking up pretty good out there. If we're careful and don't take it too fast, we should be able to slip out." He pointed to Wick's rifle hanging by her side. "How's your ammo?"

"About half a mag, I'd guess. That going to be a problem?" Cass asked.

He shook his head. "Hope we won't need any." After a moment he shrugged a shoulder and gave half a smile. "If we do need any, we'll probably need a whole lot more than two of us could carry anyhow." He glanced back out the window again, studied it for a few seconds, and then turned back to her.

"Set?"

"Set."

Sky gave a curt nod, shouldered his weapon, and moved back around to the top of the stairs. He paused there until

Cass moved around behind him and then wordlessly the pair flowed down the steps together. They made their way back down to the ground floor and to the front room, where Sky paused once more at the entrance. He took his time scanning the street to make sure it was clear, and then led the way out.

They set out at a controlled, steady pace. Cass had never traveled with Sky before, not just the two of them with him in the lead. He had a smooth, low-key rhythm to his movement. At first its seeming listlessness kept her on edge, his apparent lack of urgency made her feel unsafe. And in the rare moments he stopped to scan for threats, he never stopped for long. There was an almost carelessness to it all. After a few minutes, however, Cass recognized that it wasn't carelessness at all. Instead, the pace Sky kept enabled him to constantly keep watch, evaluating on the move. She saw how effortless was his awareness, how attentive his gaze was to every potential danger, and she understood why it was that out of all of Gamble's team, he was the one that so often did his work separated and alone. She settled into a matching stride, keeping her share of the watch with no more question of his skill.

They traveled this way for three-quarters of an hour or so, and though they occasionally heard distant cries from the Weir, they never saw any of the creatures. At first, Cass was unsure whether this was because so few remained in the area or because Sky was expertly avoiding them. But during one point when they'd stopped, she couldn't resist asking. She leaned in close, close enough that her mouth was nearly touching Sky's ear.

"Where are all the Weir?" she whispered.

He turned his head so they were a hair's breadth from being cheek to cheek.

"Bunch of 'em went looking for you," he answered. "Bunch of 'em ate a lot of rounds."

He drew back and gave her a little friendly nod and smile. Then they resumed their prowl through the cold and empty streets. They kept to street-level, twisting and turning through streets and alleys, though Sky seemed to prefer moving through wider spaces than Cass was comfortable with. She understood it; less chance of coming around a blind corner and into something nasty that way. Still, she was used to doing that kind of work up close. Sky's proficiency was the other direction; for him, the farther out the better.

It struck her how different everyone's sense of security could be. Perspective was a funny thing. Walls could be a fortress or a prison; open spaces, freedom or exposure. Cass had always prized mobility above all else. She was quick to react, and fast on her feet. Pursuit didn't frighten her, as long as she had room to run. Seemed like she'd been doing a lot of that lately. Too much, maybe.

Sky held up a hand in a fist, signaling a halt. He dropped into a crouch, and Cass followed suit, sidling in close behind him and turning ninety-degrees to provide security. By that time, she guessed it'd been almost two hours since Sky had found her. Now, scanning their surroundings, Cass began to feel a vague familiarity with the area. A few moments later, she realized she was seeing buildings they had passed before, but from the rear. They'd doubled back. Or, more correctly, circled around.

Ahead of her, Sky motioned again and led her forward towards a gutted building. It was a mostly concrete affair, long ago stripped of anything useful and much that wasn't. There weren't even any markings left that identified what it might once have been. The structure had three entrances, wide enough for double doors had there been any doors at all. They ascended a flight of cracked but stable stairs and then up a second, much steeper set of metal steps that led to a narrow hatch. Sky eased it open, scanned for trouble. Satisfied, he swung the hatch open the rest of the way and climbed through out onto the flat roof of the building. Once Cass was through, he closed the hatch again and then moved over to the front, where a low wall marked the edge. They crouched together there, a few feet between them,

taking in the surroundings from their new vantage. The
buildings were more spread out here, with wide avenues
running throughout. And now Sky had his two greatest
allies: distance *and* height.

Cass heard him whispering, but after glancing over at him
she saw that he wasn't talking to her. Calling in to his team,
no doubt. Cass settled back and waited. Sky spoke in quiet
bursts for a minute or so, though his whispers mingled too
fully with the wind for her to listen in. After a few moments
of silence, he turned to her and nodded and then, to Cass's
surprise, he turned fully around and sat down, slouching
back against the low wall. He drew his knees up slightly and
propped his rifle atop them. Cass edged over towards him.

"Now what?" Cass whispered.

"I guess we hang out," he said.

"For how long?"

"Till my girl gets here."

"Oh. OK," Cass said. There was some measure of relief in
that, knowing Gamble was still all right. "What do you want
me to do until then?"

"Well," Sky said. "You could get some sleep, if you want.
Or if you really want something to do, you could hope
nothing bad comes up that hatch." He lifted the back end
of his rifle, raising the stock almost to his shoulder and
Cass saw with that simple motion, his weapon was right on
target, pointing back the way they'd come. He was using his
legs like a bipod. If anything came up that hatch that Sky
didn't like, it wasn't going to be happy.

Cass sat down next to him and laid Wick's weapon across
her lap. She leaned her head back against the cold concrete
wall. There didn't seem to be much else for her to do but, as
tired as she was, the idea of sleeping while Sky kept watch
didn't sit well. She'd already gotten an hour or so of sleep,
and she was certain this was the first chance Sky had had
to sit down since... now that she thought about it, the man
must have been on the move for almost twenty-four hours
now. Maybe more.

"You go on and rest, Sky," she said. "I'll keep an eye out."

He glanced over and gave her a kind smile, but shook his head.

"Thanks, Cass, but if Ace found out I'd made you stand watch while I took a snooze, she'd chew me out non-stop for a month. I'd rather gut it out now and save my ears, if it's all the same by you."

Cass smiled at that. "Fine by me."

"You should catch some sleep though, if you can," he said as he returned his gaze back to the hatch. "I'll wake you if I need you."

"I think I'm good for now. I dozed off for a bit before you found me."

"Good," he said.

"Hey," said Cass, and he looked back at her. "Thank you, Sky. Thanks for coming to get me."

Sky shook his head and made a face like he was mildly insulted she'd said it.

"Come on now. If not for you, we'd have all been killed back there. If anybody owes anyone anything, it's us to you, not the other way around."

"Still. It means a lot."

"You're one of us, Cass. And we don't leave ours behind. Not ever."

Cass wanted to say something more, but couldn't come up with anything appropriate, so she just nodded. They sat in silence again for a minute or so.

"How'd you find me anyway?" Cass asked.

Sky pointed to the weapon laying across her lap. "Wick keeps an eye on her at all times. He sent her signal to me, before he went down."

Those last four words made Cass's chest go tight and her heart cold.

"Wick's gone?"

"Dunno yet. He and Able had to go dark, and Wick didn't want you getting lost out here on your own."

"What happened to them?"

"I'm not sure, Cass. Everything happened pretty fast. They were in some trouble, but you know... we all were. Once you started your run, we had to scramble. But we'll find 'em. Finn and Mouse are out looking for 'em right now."

"I'm sorry, Sky."

"We'll find 'em," he repeated.

They lapsed into silence again for a time, Sky lost in his own thoughts and Cass keeping a quiet respectfulness. Somewhere in the distance the cry of a Weir sounded, echoed. An answer followed so faintly that Cass couldn't be sure she hadn't just imagined it.

Some time later, Sky held up a finger and his eyes got that unfocused look; he was getting an internal message. He answered his caller, "Yeah, check, up top. You want us to come down?... All right, check." Then he looked back to Cass, talking to her again. "We'll see."

He got to his feet and walked over to the hatch. There he knelt, eased the hatch open, and waited in a crouch. A few moments later, Cass saw him smile, broad and genuine, and soon after, Gamble emerged into his waiting embrace. They held each other for a long while, long enough that Cass decided to avert her eyes to avoid intruding on their reunion. At the sound of approaching footsteps, she glanced back towards them and got to her feet. Gamble looked angry.

"What are you doing here, Cass?" she said, her voice low but with a hint of a growl.

"Waiting for you, Gamble."

Gamble didn't slow her approach and didn't hesitate. Before Cass knew it, Gamble had her arms around her in a bear hug.

"That was a supremely stupid thing you did," Gamble said in her ear.

"I know." Cass hugged her back.

When they separated, Gamble's eyes were wet. Nothing else about her expression betrayed any great emotion, but those almost-tears told Cass everything she needed to know.

"I'm not going to say I'm sorry," Cass said.

Gamble grunted; maybe in acknowledgment, maybe in disapproval. Both, probably. Sky walked over and joined them.

"Where'd you stash your boy?" Gamble asked.

"I sent him with Chapel. On to Greenstone."

"All right," Gamble said, nodding, and already Cass could see Gamble factoring that into the plan she was undoubtedly forming. "OK. I don't think we can get you back to the tunnel tonight. But once the sun's up, we'll see what we can do."

Cass shook her head, but Gamble was already looking at Sky. Maybe now wasn't the time for that conversation.

"I want to hold here ten or fifteen," Gamble said to Sky. "Make sure I didn't pick up any tag-alongs."

"You hear from Finn yet?" Sky asked.

"Yeah, just," Gamble answered. "Able's back up. They're moving to him now."

"Wick?" said Sky.

"Breathing, for the moment. But..." Gamble shook her head. "Probably be about forty minutes before they can get to him and Mouse can check him out."

"How's Finn?" Cass asked.

"Keeping it together. Which is pretty heroic, all things considered."

There was a pause in the conversation as the weight of the moment settled on them. Then, before anyone had a chance to say anything more, Gamble switched back to go-mode.

"Sky get that hatch buttoned back up, then get eyes front. I came in south-southeast, so if I picked up stragglers they'll probably be that way."

"No sweat, Ace," he said.

"Cass, I need you on that opposite corner, just in case they get sneaky. You see anything moving around, you let me know immediately."

Cass dipped her head in silent acknowledgment.

"We'll give it fifteen and if all's quiet, I'll take you back to our hole-in-the-wall."

The three broke up and took up positions around the roof. Cass set herself to keep careful watch, knowing all too well that out here in the open, fifteen minutes was plenty of time for everything to go wrong.

FOUR

Painter stood on a high, wide balcony of a building outside the city, six stories up, and watched as dawn broke open and spilled its first light over the high wall of Morningside. The once great city, glittering jewel of the east, was now, just as Asher had proclaimed, a horror to gaze upon. No, not as Asher had proclaimed. As he, Painter, had proclaimed on Asher's behalf. Asher's words, delivered by his mouth. This was his work, too. He could not separate himself from it, no matter how much his heart might repulse at the thought. This was his work. Painter forced his eyes to take it in, to see fully and truly the destruction that he had brought upon the city.

The scale of the devastation was beyond anything he had imagined possible. Painter recalled the night Asher had come to him in a dream, when he had touched Painter's mouth and loosened his tongue.

Tell them I'm coming.

Even then, Painter had known Asher's intent, his thirst for vengeance. It was a thirst Painter had shared, at least in part. But he simply could never have fathomed the full depths of Asher's power, or his wrath. Painter had proclaimed Morningside's coming doom with his own mouth. Only now did he see what those words had truly meant.

But he had made his choice. This was his work. In a way,

Morningside had brought its ruin upon itself. The way its
rulers had treated its people, had assigned value and meted
out punishment or reward as they alone saw fit. Even
Wren. Painter tried not to think too much about Wren. He
had been a friend. But he'd been caught up in the games of
power, he'd taken on authority he was too weak to wield,
and through him others had worked their corruption.
Painter would grieve him. Painter *did* grieve him. But some
casualties were inevitable when justice was done, and he
couldn't completely absolve Wren of guilt. He had played
his own part. He had made his own choices, just as Painter
had. And as horrific as the outcome seemed now, Painter
soothed his troubled spirit with the thought that this was
the price of his own liberty, his ascension. And more than
his own, for Asher had kept his promise.

"Snow," he said, turning to his sister. She was behind
him, sitting on the roof, head lowered and hands folded in
her lap. She looked up at him, her Weir-blue eyes glowing
faintly in the weak light of the new dawn. His sister, once
dead, now returned to him. "Come stand with me," he said.
She stood and crossed to him, and he watched as she came
over. She moved with a dancer's ease and grace, beautiful
to behold, and took her place next to him, gazing out over
the city.

Painter just looked at her for a while, his heart stirred
with overwhelming love. His little sister. Once lost, now
found. His truest and impossible hope, realized. The grief
he felt over the fall of Morningside was a faint shadow
compared to the deep joy in his heart at his sister's return.

"Snow," he said, and she turned her head to look at him.
She responded to her name, but he could see in her eyes
there was no true recognition. Her gaze was dull, mechanical,
and when he looked into those eyes, Painter both loved and
hated her. No, not hated her. Hated her condition, trapped
as she was between life and death, between self and slave.
The Weir had done their work. Asher had found her in
their midst and had... well, Painter wasn't sure what he had

done. Released her somehow. But he hadn't Awakened her, not fully. Not the way Wren could. And so, Painter thought as he looked into his sister's eyes, his impossible hope was perhaps not yet fulfilled. Not yet. But he would find a way.

Long ago, after their father had died and left them alone in the world, there had been many dark and fearful nights when Painter had sworn to Snow that she would never have to worry because he was there, would always be there, would always watch over her. It had cost him much to keep that promise. He looked back over what remained of Morningside. It had cost him and many others. But it seemed a small price to him now. They were together. For the moment, that was all that mattered. She was close, he could watch over her. And in time, he would find a way to bring her back to herself.

The morning light grew stronger as they stood there, not yet strong enough to interfere with Painter's vision but enough to make him uneasy. There was an aversion to sunlight deep in his makeup now, beyond just the discomfort and difficulty it caused his Weir-modified eyes. Something the Weir had done to him that made it feel unnatural and disquieting. His Awakening had given him mastery over his instincts to flee the daylight, but the anxiety it produced had never fully subsided. He wondered what Snow was feeling – if she was in fact feeling anything, or if she was simply an automaton somehow attached to him now, like some lesser process of a higher control program. The Weir could be made to move in broad daylight, could be provoked to endure it. But they suffered under it, just as normal humans naturally feared the dark.

"Come on," Painter said. "We'll find a place for you to rest." He leaned over and drew his sister's head to his lips, kissed her forehead. She accepted it without hesitance or warmth. He led her back inside the abandoned building, and she followed obediently. More like a servant than a sister. Too much like. But that was temporary, Painter reminded himself. He'd find a way.

They descended through the darkened building, looking for an inner room without windows or holes where the light could seep in. There were many to choose from, and though Painter knew Snow would accept any one he selected, he kept searching for one that seemed safest and most comfortable. Like most of the buildings this close to Morningside, anything of value had long ago been stripped out, and much of the debris had been cleared away. Still, it was heavy with dust and the damp, stale smell of long disuse.

As he searched, he felt a vibration in his thoughts, a ripple of something Other, an external impulse; the first sign that Asher was reaching out to him. And even though Painter had accepted it, had invited it, it was nevertheless deeply unnerving each time. The door between his thoughts and Asher's was weak and unlocked. Though Asher had, thus far, always done him the courtesy of requesting access, Painter couldn't help but wonder what the outcome would be if he declined or, worse, resisted. And he wondered briefly if he was even capable of resisting. It was as if Asher stood at the door of his mind, having already turned the knob and opened it a crack before knocking. Painter was free to say *come in*, but there was little question what the result could be if he didn't.

He opened the channel and Asher formed in his mind. More than mere thoughts, more than a voice. A presence. Asher couldn't control Painter directly, but he left no doubt as to his will.

"I have need of you," Asher said, from deep within the recesses of Painter's own mind. Painter stopped his search for a room and waited. It was difficult to do much of anything else when Asher was communicating with him. "What are you doing?"

There was another strange aspect of this... whatever this was. Communion with Asher. He was somehow fully part of Painter's mind, and yet completely separate and distinct. He couldn't read Painter's thoughts, couldn't see

through his eyes, or hear through his ears. To respond,
Painter had to make a conscious effort to direct his thoughts
towards Asher. Though he didn't need to speak aloud, the
mechanism felt almost exactly the same.

"I'm with my sister," Painter responded.

"Yes, obviously," Asher said. He might not be able to
make use of Painter's senses, but he always seemed to know
exactly where he was. Painter wondered if Asher knew the
exact location of every single Weir under his power. "But
what are you *doing*?"

"Finding a place for her to rest."

"She doesn't need it," Asher said dismissively. "I have a
new place for you. I'll send you the location."

A moment later, Painter received a locational ping, a
virtual marker set in the physical world. It was miles away.

"Get started. The rest will be along in a little while."

"Shouldn't I wait until the sun goes down?"

"Why?" Asher said. The impatience was apparent, and
Painter decided not to press it.

"What should I do when I get there?"

"Just get moving. I'll tell you what to do when it's time."

"OK."

Painter waited to see if there was anything more, but
Asher wasn't talking. He wasn't leaving either, though.
Painter looked over at Snow, who was standing dutifully
by, staring off at nothing in particular. It would be a strain
on her to travel through the daylight. He knew she could
endure it, but he didn't like forcing it on her.

After thirty seconds or so, Asher still hadn't disconnected.

"We're going right now," Painter said. "Come on, Snow."
She turned to him, and he took her hand in his. She would
follow him without it of course, but it felt more natural that
way. Like when they were kids.

"Painter," Asher said, and the tone of his voice had
changed. Or, rather, the tone of whatever it was Painter was
experiencing inside his own head had changed. It was less
agitated, less abrasive. Not quite consoling, but there was

a note of reassurance in it. "You are my voice. My herald. You're not like the others. I chose you... I ask more of you because I know you have more to give."

"I understand," Painter answered.

"Good," Asher said, and in the next instant he was gone. That sensation was almost as disruptive as when Asher made his approach; there was, for a moment, what felt like a hole in Painter's mind. His own thoughts rushed like water to fill the void, collided together, churned. It always left him a little disoriented, as if he had walked in a room with a floor tilted ever so slightly to one side. The feeling subsided in a minute or two.

Painter led Snow down several flights of stairs to the ground floor. They stopped at a side entrance near the front of the building, where sunlight was filtering in underneath the door. Snow squawked once, softly, her voice and words still attuned to the static language of the Weir. Painter had lost whatever part of him could interpret that densely packed burst of communication, but he was becoming more skilled at discerning the different timbre of that which had formerly been pure noise. It had shape now, somehow, in his mind. She was worried about the sunlight. Or, if not worried, at least drawing his attention to it.

"It's OK," he reassured his sister. "We need to go out there. We have a long walk to go on, and we have to leave now." She stood placidly by, still holding his hand, but continuing to look down at the light seeping in under the door.

"Here," Painter said, and he got his goggles out of his pocket and placed them over her eyes. She reached up and touched them, trying to back away at first, but he held her steady and gently adjusted the straps to secure them in place. Snow kept one hand on them even after he'd fitted them for her. They were too large for her face, and made her look like a little bug. Painter smiled at the image; with the dark lenses he couldn't see her modified eyes. For a moment, he could almost believe she was wholly herself again. He let the thought linger as long as it would, enjoying the lie even as it fled before him. Finally, he took her hand and then pushed the door open.

She shied away from the burst of sunlight, dazzling in contrast to the dusky stairwell. It made Painter's head hurt almost immediately, and he squinted against it, even though he knew it was yet weak compared to what was still to come. He stepped out into it, drawing Snow gently along behind him. Maybe they'd get lucky and some cloud cover would blow in. He glanced up at the sky; it was pale purple tinged with yellow, and as clear as it could be. It looked like it was going to be a beautiful, sunny day.

And it would be a long day, and the journey longer. But he could bear the intense headache the day would bring, knowing his sister wouldn't have to. He sighed and started off towards the distant mark Asher had set for him, with Snow in her too-big goggles in tow.

FIVE

Wren sat on the couch and stared at his hands clasped in his lap. There was a small red spot beside his left thumbnail where he'd picked at a tag of skin and torn it free. It was a bad habit. Mama always told him not to do that. It hurt when he pressed on it, but he was pressing on it anyway.

They'd moved up from the bar to the apartment above, both for comfort and for privacy. Now they were seated in the front room, Haiku in one chair, jCharles in another, with Wren across from them on the worn leather couch. Wren couldn't quite bring himself to raise his eyes to Haiku; the scene was too strange. It'd been well over a year since he'd sat in the same place, and jCharles had sat in the same spot he was in now, and Three had been there, where Haiku was now sitting. Seeing the reality somehow made the memory more real, more immediate; like maybe if Wren didn't look up, that really would be Three sitting there.

"You don't have to do this, Wren," jCharles said.

Wren nodded, but didn't look up. It was foolish, and he knew it was foolish, but *almost* believing Three was there was *almost* enough to give him courage. Three had called him a soldier once. So many memories of the man rushed and swirled through his mind. Some moments were indistinct, more impression than image. Others were so clear, remembering was nearly the same as experiencing. Except for Three's face. Over time Three's face had become

54

indistinct in Wren's mind, and noticing it now frightened him. Was he forgetting Three? How could he ever do so?

"I know much of his past already," Haiku said, gently reassuring. "Most from having lived it alongside him. Some, I've discovered through searching. But not this chapter of his life. If you could help me record it, it would honor both the man and his House."

Wren glanced up at Haiku, sitting across from him. The man was sitting quietly, his big book open on his lap, pen in hand. His expression was warm and kind, expectant without any trace of impatience or annoyance. Waiting. And looked like he would wait, without complaint, for however long it took. Wren couldn't remember if he'd ever seen someone use an actual pen before.

Tell his story. To honor Three and his House. Wren could do that. A deep breath. Then he let his mind go back, back to a time he'd refused to allow himself to remember for a long time. And having given himself permission, the memory came back, acutely vivid. The bar, the people, the smell. Mama's hand, hard and cold and trembling, squeezing his. The fear.

"He was just sitting there," Wren said, at last. "When we first came in. In the front corner of the place, behind the door. Mama didn't notice him, but I did. Because he was there, but it felt like he shouldn't have been. That was when we met him. That was when I met Three."

Now that the door of his mind was open, Wren couldn't stop the flood of images. Three, sitting at that table, staring down at the drink on it, refusing to look up at Mama or down at him. Three, pulling him away from Mama while she lay dying, leaving her behind in order to save him. Three, lying in Mama's arms as the last of his life seeped away.

"And that's when he began to help you?" Haiku said, a gentle prompt.

Wren shook his head, more to clear it than in answer. "No. That was later."

He continued for a few moments, telling as much of that first encounter as he could recall, surprising himself at just how very much that was. Things he hadn't realized he'd noticed came to him, things that hadn't seemed important at the time that gained new significance in looking back upon them. But as clearly and fully as those first images returned to him, something inside revolted against him and Wren suddenly found it difficult to proceed. The rush was too much, the memories overwhelming. Having fought to keep that part of his life distant and locked away, once freed they came like the ocean to a sinking ship, impossible to resist.

His face flushed hot then suddenly cold, and his heart raced as hard as if he'd been running as fast as he could for a mile. jCharles sat forward, like he was going to stand up, but Haiku stayed him with a raised hand.

"So your mother took you out of the bar through a back door," Haiku said a few moments later, picking up where Wren had left off, gently leading. "And then..."

He trailed off, leaving Wren to once more take up the story from there. The words called him back, fixed his mind on that moment. But Wren found his mouth had gone dry and sticky. The images still swirled.

"Through the back, and..." Haiku repeated.

"And then we went to a chemist," Wren managed to answer. "Can I have some water?"

"Sure, buddy," jCharles said, and as he was standing to get it, Wren heard the clicks and whirs of Mol's approach. She passed by and waved jCharles off, moving towards the kitchen for the water herself. She returned moments later and sat down beside Wren, handing him a plastic cup with her left hand while draping her right arm over his shoulders. Wren sipped the cool water, let it sit in his mouth for a few seconds, feeling how it swished and swirled as he moved his tongue through it. He swallowed, took another sip, then a longer pull.

"And what happened at the chemist's?" Haiku asked.

Wren stared down into his cup. "Bad things."

Telling the story was much harder than he'd expected it to be. After that initial burst of information, Wren spoke little, answered directly, without elaboration. It was easier for him that way, to think of each event in isolation, to tell only what seemed necessary. Eventually he decided he'd been too eager. Told too much, too quickly. This way was better. One step. Don't linger too long, don't rush too far ahead.

But over time, Haiku's careful, respectful tone and insightful questions began to work their cure. His voice was quiet and words kind, and gradually he drew forth the answers he sought. Wren's responses lengthened. Without his notice, he began to share more details, to offer information more freely, to expound without prompting. And all the while, Haiku's pen flowed across the pages, capturing every moment, freezing each in ink.

Cautiously, compassionately, Haiku led Wren through the journey, recording it all in his leatherbound book. Occasionally they stopped for breaks, sometimes at jCharles's or Mol's prompting, sometimes because hunger or thirst or weeping demanded it. Wren hated crying. He fought it off as much as he could. But at times the tears were irresistible. The memory of leaving Mama, knowing she was dying. The shock of the guards' attack when they first reached Morningside, when their journey was so nearly done. Mr Carter's death, and Dagon's. The utter helplessness of being pulled from Three's arms by the surging crowd. Asher's cruelties. His mother's return as a Weir. Mol sat with him as he relived those terrible moments, her arm tight around his shoulders, her cheek pressed to the top of his head, her tears falling freely with his.

Whether it took an hour, or two, or four, Wren didn't know. He completely lost track of time in the telling. But it didn't seem to matter. Once the barriers had been brought down, Wren found the courage and the determination to tell it all. And tell it all he did, right down to the final seconds of Three's life, his death, and the giving of his remains to the fire and the setting sun.

Only once did Wren notice Haiku stop writing. It was when Wren told of how he brought Mama back from being a Weir.

"I don't understand," Haiku said, lifting his pen. "What do you mean she 'came back'?"

"She was a Weir, and then she wasn't." Wren took a drink of water, wiped the corners of his mouth with his fingers. "I mean, she's still kind of one. Her eyes and... stuff. But she was herself again," he said with a shrug. "Like she woke up."

"How is that possible?" Haiku asked, and then looked to jCharles. "That can't be possible."

"I assure you it is so," a voice said from near the door. Everyone jumped, and turned to find Chapel there, leaning against the wall. Wren had no idea how long the man had been standing there.

"*Spatz*, old man!" jCharles said, which earned him a reproving look from Mol. "I swear I'm gonna have to tie a bell around your neck. I thought you went out!"

"I did," said Chapel.

"And?" jCharles asked.

"I am returned."

There entered a side conversation which ran for a long while. Wren did his best to explain what he could about awakening the Weir, which wasn't much. Chapel identified himself as formerly of the Weir, and answered Haiku's questions in his typical enigmatic way. Wren noticed Haiku didn't record anything in his book throughout that discussion. After a time, Haiku returned to the final moments of Wren's tale and resumed writing, though he didn't seem quite satisfied with what they'd told him. Nevertheless, his full attention was once again on Wren, and Wren did his best to finish a full and good account of his time with Three.

By the end, Wren was exhausted emotionally and

physically. But as he slouched back on the couch and let his head rest on its cushioned back, he noticed he felt lighter somehow. Not happy, certainly. But healthier. Relieved. Content, maybe. Like some great burden had been taken from his shoulders, or some deep sickness drawn from his body. The flickering flame of memory he'd fought to quench blazed brighter than ever now. Three's face was as clear and bright in his mind as ever before, and while there was still sorrow, it dimmed in comparison to the love and gratitude Wren felt. Three had died for him. More than that. Far more than that. Three had truly given his life for Wren; not just in that final moment and act, but in every day, in every hour of sacrifice leading up to it. From the moment Three had given his word, he too had given his life. And having told all that Three had done for him, that gift became powerfully real to Wren in that instant, and utterly precious. The weight of it rested upon him, not as a burden, but as a blessing that commanded his affection and his awe.

"How did you know to prepare his body that way?" Haiku asked. Wren noticed the man's eyes were shining like he might cry, but his face also almost looked glad.

"From him. We just did it the same way he showed me. After Mr Carter. And Dagon."

"But you say you waited until the sun was setting," Haiku said.

"Oh," Wren said. "Yeah." He shrugged. "I don't know, it just seemed like the right thing to do."

Haiku smiled and nodded. "It was, more than you know. And now you have done him a double honor. You upheld the tradition of his House, whether you knew it or not, and gave his remains the due tribute he likely would have been denied elsewhere. And the record you have kept, which you have relayed to me," here Haiku held up the book from his lap, "will be preserved. His memory will live on, not just in you, but in those who otherwise would have never known him."

Haiku closed his book and set it aside. He stood and came

to kneel in front of Wren, and looked him squarely in the eye.

"Three could not have been more properly and fully honored had he passed on while our House still stood in its former glory," he said, and then bowed his head. "I am deeply grateful."

"I'm glad I did the right thing," Wren answered.

Haiku looked up at him and smiled, and then rose to his feet.

"Thank you all," he said, looking to jCharles and Mol. "For your hospitality, and your forbearance. I know this was not an easy time for any of you."

"It was well worth it, friend," jCharles responded. "I loved Three like he was my blood. You showing up is like having a piece of him back, in a way. Of course, you know, I don't know how you ever tracked him to us, and normally I wouldn't care too much for that."

Haiku smiled his easy smile. "I assure you it was not easy, nor would it be easily repeatable."

"Yeah, well," jCharles said. "You being Three's kin makes it a little easier to swallow. If you'd given me any other explanation, I'd have blown you right back out that front door. But Three used to pull some of that same business. Spooked me then, still spooks me a little now."

"Serendipity, Coincidence, Destiny, Providence," said Haiku, his eyes twinkling. "The convergence of random events leading to seemingly meaningful moments has many names. Sometimes we just get lucky."

"Yeah," jCharles said with a smirk. "I've heard a few folks cheatin' at cards say things about like that." Haiku just smiled in response.

The mood of the room had altered with the ending of the tale. It had been a solemn time, almost sacred. Now there was an almost casual air, as if everyone were glad to return their focus to the mundane tasks of everyday life. Like after a funeral, when one of the bereaved laughs at some quiet joke, and gives everyone else permission to breathe again. For Wren, however, the sanctity of the story lingered dreamlike. The images and emotions had been refreshed and would not quickly fade. The others seemed like they were speaking too loudly, too quickly.

"So you got your story," jCharles continued. "What now?"

"An excellent question," Haiku said. "I've been on this journey for so long, I'd not given much thought to what might come after."

"Well," jCharles said, "you're more than welcome to stick around here until you get it figured out."

"Thank you, but no," answered Haiku, "I've disrupted your lives far too much as it is."

jCharles casually pointed at Haiku and glanced over at Mol. "Now who's that remind you of?"

Mol smiled and nodded. "Brothers for sure."

"So that's settled then," jCharles said. "You're stayin' for dinner."

"Thank you, but it's really all right," Haiku said in mild protest.

"It's not a request, Haiku," Mol said, rising to her feet. She bent and kissed Wren on the head without hesitation, as if he were her own, and he accepted it as readily. "You made demands on our time, now we're returning the favor."

Haiku smiled and bowed his head in acquiescence. Mol turned back to look at Wren, and ran her fingers through his hair. "Wren darling, would you like to help me in the kitchen?"

Wren knew the offer for what it was. She didn't need the help, but had over the past days found ways to involve him in her daily affairs, keeping him occupied and giving him reason to keep close. Normally he would accept the invitation. At that moment, though, his whole body felt completely spent. A great weariness settled on him.

"Actually, I think I'd like to lie down for a while," he answered. "If that's all right with you, Miss Mol." Her smile trembled at that; Three had always called her "Miss Mol", and Wren realized she too must be feeling the weight of sorrow anew.

"Of course, you must be exhausted," she said. "Just be quiet as you can, Gracie's sleeping back there."

Wren nodded and started towards the back room, where jCharles and Mol had made a pallet for him in an alcove off their bedroom.

"Wren," Haiku called. Wren turned back. "Thank you again." Wren nodded, but he had no more words to give. He silently slipped into the back room and crept to his alcove. It was his intent just to lie there, to get away from everyone else, to let his mind swirl and hopefully settle. Instead, sleep came, swift and heavy.

In the dream, and he knew it was a dream while he dreamed, Wren saw Mama, alone, crouched in a strange place. It was Morningside, or rather, was supposed to be Morningside, though the look of it was wrong and was no part of the city he recognized; no part of the city he once ostensibly ruled over. The sky above was dark with clouds. Or smoke, perhaps, oily and thick, swirling with strange currents and lit from within by a sickly pale light. She seemed to be searching for something amongst the tall and twisted buildings. Her movements were hurried; not frantic, but urgent, and always her head turned this way and that, as if she feared discovery as much as she sought to discover.

Wren tried to call her name, but try as he might, he could not force open his mouth, and as he grunted through clenched jaw, he knew that his voice was sounding in the real world and threatened to chase the dream away. He ceased his struggle, willing himself to stay asleep, to continue the dream, to see his mother for a few seconds more. She saw him, then; her face showed it plainly, joy radiant. She left her place and rushed towards him, and in the final moments, as the dream slipped from him and consciousness arose, the sky shifted with sickening speed. A great black hand of ash and shadow writhed into being from above and swept towards her, and Wren's eyes flashed open, his heart pounding so hard he could feel its beat against the floor beneath him. He didn't stir when he awoke. Mama had long ago taught him to wake in stillness as a safety measure, and he had never lost the ability.

He lay with his eyes open in the darkling room, letting the dream slide away into memory. Seeing his Mama in that dreamscape left him hollow in the middle, reminded him afresh of his loss. And the hand descending from the sky. Asher's reach was long; not even in sleep could Wren escape it. He shivered, though not from cold.

It was a warning, perhaps. His subconscious reminding him of the great risk posed if he tried contacting his mother, or she him. Asher was out there, somehow, with thousands of eyes and ears now, always watching, always listening. If Mama was still alive, and Wren could not yet believe otherwise, pinging her through the digital could expose her and ultimately be her doom. As desperate as Wren was for her voice, to know for certain that she was alive, she had trained him well to suppress those impulses when danger was at hand. Surely she would reach out to him as soon as it was safe.

Outside the sun had sunk below the horizon. The last traces of natural light were bleeding from the room to be replaced by the gaudy artificial light of the neighboring buildings. For a time, Wren just laid there, giving his heart time to settle and his nerves time to remember the real world. With some irritation, he realized his hand was asleep. He lifted it and waved it around, feeling the electric prickling as the dead fingers flopped about. Had today been the day that he'd told Haiku his story? It seemed like a different time to him now.

Muffled voices in the other room told him everyone else was still up, though to his ears it sounded like they were trying to keep the noise down. He considered trying to go back to sleep, but the image of the hand still lingered strong in his mind. And he was actually pretty hungry. With a deep breath, he rolled himself up on his pallet, shook his hand out some more, and then went into the main room.

jCharles and Haiku were standing near the dining table, while Mol was in the kitchen. jCharles was in the middle of some story, which he had to tell with frequent pauses since he was holding Grace and she kept trying to grab his teeth as he talked. Haiku was setting silverware out for everyone, and listened intently, offering the occasional quiet comment that Wren couldn't quite make out from across the room. Chapel was sitting in a chair in a darkened corner, fully removed from the proceedings despite his proximity to them. Surely Chapel knew Wren was there, even though he made no sign that revealed it.

jCharles had to stop for a moment to pull Grace's hand out of his mouth again, and in doing so he noticed Wren.

"Hey, buddy," he said, his voice raised to a normal tone. "Did you sleep?"

Wren nodded.

"Did we wake you?"

Wren shook his head. Mol appeared at the open entrance to the kitchen, wiping her hands on a dish towel.

"Do you feel up to eating something?" she asked.

"I could eat," Wren answered.

"Then you're just in time. Come on in here and help me carry the food to the table, would you?"

"Sure."

Wren followed Mol back into the kitchen where dishes sat filled with steaming vegetables, rice, and some kind of meat with an amber-colored glaze. They weren't *real* vegetables, Wren knew. They were the manufactured kind, not like the ones he'd seen growing straight up out of the ground at Chapel's compound so long ago. The compound that lay in ruins, now. The hand from his dream had laid waste to it, as it had Morningside.

"Hey," Mol said, crouching in front of him. "You OK?"

The dream lingered at the edges of his wakefulness, tinted everything like a thin veil of fog. Wren blinked a few times, and then nodded.

"Still waking up?"

Wren shrugged. Mol made a face like she wanted to say something but didn't know what it was.

"I'm OK, Miss Mol," Wren said. "Just had a weird dream is all." He gave her a smile, though he could tell by the way it felt that it probably looked weak and fake. He picked up the bowl of meat and carried it into the other room. He'd seen Mol carry as many as five dishes before, all at once, so he knew she didn't really need the help, but he was glad to do it anyway. He set it in the middle of the table. Mol followed after him and arranged the rest of the bowls and serving spoons. She said grace over the meal as was her way, and then they all sat down to eat.

"Chapel," Mol called. "Care to join us?"

"Thank you," Chapel answered. "But no."

Mol nodded and started serving out portions. It wasn't a surprise that Chapel remained where he was. With each day that had passed, he'd seemed more withdrawn. He'd gone out several times, for increasingly longer stretches of time. Wren wondered what that all might mean, but he was too worn out to think about it just then, and it didn't really seem like a good time to bring it up.

Over the meal conversation was light and carefully balanced; Wren could sense it in the words and the glances. Haiku asked about Greenstone and jCharles's livelihood. In turn, jCharles prompted Haiku for some history of his travels. No one wanted to venture too far into potentially painful topics after the earlier emotional work of the day. And it seemed like maybe neither jCharles nor Haiku wanted to reveal too much about either of their histories. Wren ate quietly, and though Mol kept glancing over at him to check on him, mostly the adults carried on, content to let him participate when and how he chose.

Try as they might, however, the gravitational pull of their strangely connected history was too great to escape for long, and gradually, inevitably, conversation worked its way towards the unavoidable. There was a pause in the talk that grew longer than the usual break, almost to the point of awkward silence. Finally, jCharles wiped his mouth with his hand and dropped his napkin on the table, and leaned back shaking his head and smiling sadly.

"You know it's weird, though," jCharles said. He looked hard at Haiku then. "I knew Three a long time, and I don't recall him ever mentioning he had a brother. And you really don't look all that much alike, either. But I'm jiggered if you don't *feel* like his own twin."

"I should clarify," Haiku said. "He is not... was not... my brother in the traditional sense. We share no parent, at least that we know. We are not related by blood, but rather by a bond much deeper. He *is* my brother nonetheless. We were raised in the same House."

He put a curious emphasis on the word house when he said it, like it was more than a building.

"Three used to mention it sometimes," Mol said, her voice quiet and still tinged with sorrow. "His House. Only ever in passing, though. What was it?"

Haiku's expression changed then, a slight shift. A cloud passing briefly across the sun.

"Once a place of honor," Haiku said. Then he inclined his head towards his book, lying on a side table nearby. "Now, little more than words on a page."

"Sounds pretty," jCharles said. "For a non-answer." Mol gave him a mildly scolding look, which he shrugged off.

Haiku smiled and offered his own shrug. "It's difficult to explain. The world was so different when House mattered. Much was lost in the falling." The smile faded, his expression darkened; a hardness came into his eyes as he looked off somewhere into his own past. "And much given."

After a moment, Mol offered, "It's OK if you don't want to talk about it."

His eyes shifted to her and cleared but didn't soften. The intensity of the look made Wren's breath catch; he'd seen it before in another man. Then, as if he remembered himself, Haiku smiled again and the look was gone.

"I apologize for my rudeness," he said, dipping his head in an apologetic bow. And then he repeated, "It's... difficult to explain."

"You're like Three," Wren said, drawing all eyes to him. It was the first he'd spoken. Then, realizing what he'd said, and what he'd meant by it, he wondered if he was betraying some secret Haiku did not want known. "I mean..."

Haiku gazed at him for a time, and then dipped his head forward, as if he knew what Wren meant and was giving his permission to speak it aloud.

"I mean," Wren continued, "you're not connected either. Like Three."

Haiku inclined his head to one side. "What makes you think that?"

"I can feel it," Wren answered. He looked back down at his plate. There was still a fair amount of food left. He'd felt a lot hungrier than he'd actually been.

"Feel it?" Haiku said.

"Yeah. I, um..." Wren said. He poked a piece of meat with his fork, pushed it back and forth across the plate, painting a meaningless design with its thin trail of amber glaze. "Well..." he said, then looked up at Haiku and smiled. "It's kind of difficult to explain."

At the far end of the table, jCharles suppressed a chuckle.

"You're correct, Wren," Haiku said. "I am not connected."

"Is that what House Eight was?" Wren asked. "What made it special?"

"No," said Haiku. "No, that's not what made it special. Not that alone. But the House was the first to recognize the value of disconnection in the old world. Some others followed after, though none ever embraced it as truly and fully as House Eight."

The room fell quiet for a span, except for Grace smacking her hands on the tray in front of her. Wren got the impression that Haiku might continue if prompted but likely wasn't going to offer much more on his own. Mol and jCharles both seemed to be waiting, maybe uncertain of how far back to draw the veil. Haiku's past was Three's past, and as much as Wren longed to know, he remembered well how closely Three had guarded himself. It almost felt wrong to dig much deeper.

"And what of you, Wren?" Haiku asked, breaking the silence and taking the opportunity to change the subject. "What brought you back to Greenstone from Morningside?"

The question shocked Wren so violently he actually physically flinched. Mol reflexively shot a look at jCharles, and Haiku, though he had no idea what he had just done, immediately tensed up and searched the faces of the others for some clue. It hadn't occurred to Wren that Haiku might not know of Morningside's fate, but then he couldn't understand why he would have assumed otherwise. News didn't much travel across the Strand. Certainly not quickly. And Wren's own story as he'd told it had ended with Three; he'd had neither the energy nor a reason to tell more.

"I apologize," Haiku said. "Please forgive my ignorance, and my rudeness." Even without knowing why he'd provoked such a response, it was apparent he hoped to undo any hurt he'd caused.

"No, it's uh," jCharles said, "it's my fault, I should've... It's just, you know, we got to talking about Three, and uh..."

Wren didn't really hear whatever else it was that jCharles said. Haiku's question had threatened to bring with it a storm of fresh, raw emotions and Wren thought for certain that all the past days' terror and pain and loss would overwhelm him at any second. But instead, he found himself strangely calm; still and centered. The emotions were there, just beyond him, as if he could reach out and activate them, embrace them, if he so chose. Yet, the decision was his, and in his own stillness he found a small measure of courage.

"Morningside's gone," Wren said. He heard himself say the words, understood what they meant, understood all that those two words didn't say and yet knew the full measure of the loss they implied. But the storm didn't reach him. The quiet calm remained his. "Morningside's gone now," he said again, and for the first time he thought maybe he could talk about it without feeling like he was going to throw up. Whether his subconscious had somehow finally accepted this new reality and adapted, or he was simply too emotionally exhausted to feel anything anymore, Wren didn't know. Nor did it seem to matter for the moment. He took a breath and nodded to himself.

"It fell," he said. "To the Weir."

Haiku blinked back at him, with no sign of understanding, as if Wren were speaking some made up language.

"Morningside?" said Haiku.

"Yes," Wren answered.

"To the Weir?"

"Yes."

Haiku looked to jCharles, then to Mol, then back to Wren again. "... Morningside?"

Wren just nodded.

"When was this?" Haiku asked.

"Three days ago."

"To the Weir?" Haiku repeated. "I don't understand. Morningside has stood for decades. It would take hundreds of Weir to overthrow it."

"Thousands," Chapel said from across the room.

Haiku's brow creased slightly, a look of doubt he probably did not intend to express openly. But Chapel nodded.

"Well. It wasn't *just* the Weir," said Wren. "Not exactly." And in saying it, he knew he would have yet another story to tell. He was tired. Weary, deep into his bones. But the story wanted telling.

"After... after all that," he said, "all the things I told you today. The people made me Governor. Because I was Underdown's son, and because of what I'd done to my brother. I guess they thought I could protect them, the way Underdown had."

Wren went quickly, sparsely, through the history. Not like before, when he'd told it all in the utmost detail he could recall. Now, it was just the barest sketch of events.

Fifteen minutes in the telling, twenty maybe. The council, his personal guards, the attempt on his life. Underdown's machine. Haiku listened intently, watched with eyes hard and piercing. He didn't write any of it down.

"My brother. Asher. I thought he had died, but I was wrong."

Wren went on to tell Haiku of his discovery at Ninestory, his return to Morningside, its turmoil, and its ultimate fall. But most of all about Asher, its conqueror. His brother. Mind of the Weir.

"And Chapel brought me here," he finished. He tried not to think about Mama too much. The strange stillness hadn't yet left him, but thoughts of her were too close to the tempest that churned beyond it. He feared any movement towards those raging winds.

Haiku sat motionless for a span. Behind his eyes, Wren could see him processing all he'd just heard. To the man's credit, he didn't seem to be rejecting it outright. Finally, he spoke.

"What you've told me is nearly too much to comprehend," Haiku said. "If all you say is true, our world has changed in dire ways." His gaze dropped to the table, and he was lost in his own thoughts for a few moments more. Then, he looked up at Wren again.

"This brother of yours, Asher," Haiku said. "He... *controls* the Weir?"

Wren nodded. "Not all of them. But some of them. A lot of them."

"And what does he intend to do with them?"

"I don't know," Wren said. "I don't know what he wants or what he's trying to do. I never have. But he'll come for me. Wherever I am. Some day."

"But you have stopped him before–" Haiku began, and Wren knew where he was headed.

"No," Wren interrupted. "He's too strong. He's so strong now." The memory of his struggle within the machine flashed through his mind, with its terrifying strain, the feeling that Asher was pulling him apart, the sudden blackness. "I think maybe he could have killed me, if he'd wanted to. I know he could have. But he wasn't ready for that yet."

Haiku sat back in his chair and though his eyes remained on Wren, Wren could tell the man wasn't really looking at him. He was lost deep in his own thoughts. Searching. Calculating.

Wren's heart started to race again, and the room was too bright, too loud, too hot. He felt sweat on his forehead, though his hands and feet were ice cold. He took a few deep breaths to steady himself, like Mama had taught him, but it was a losing battle. The emotional toll of the day was coming due, and Wren knew he couldn't take any more.

"I don't feel so good," he said, looking to Mol, knowing she would be the first and strongest ally. "I need to go back to bed." He didn't even wait for a response, he just got up from the table. Mol made some reply, but Wren didn't catch it and didn't feel like turning around. There was panic rising; pure, unfiltered panic at the thought of Asher, out there, always out there, always pursuing. Unbound. Unlimited. Unstoppable.

"Wren," came Haiku's voice. But Wren kept heading for the bedroom.

"Wren," Haiku called again, and this time his voice was more powerful; not louder, but full of authority. Wren couldn't help but respond. He stopped and glanced back. Mol was standing and jCharles was still sitting. Both of them looked concerned and like they had no idea what to do. Haiku alone looked calm. He was turned partway around in his chair to face Wren.

"I know a man who might be able to help," he said.

"Me too," Wren said reflexively, the memory of Three still strong. "But he's dead."

Haiku seemed to read his thoughts.

"Not Three," he replied. The barest hint of a smile touched his eyes. "The man who trained him."

SIX

The wayhouse was cramped and stifling, with a dampness to the air that made everything feel too close. They had waited out their time on the roof and a little more with no sign of any trailing Weir, and afterwards, Gamble had led Cass and Sky back to this latest hiding place. Now, Cass sat on the floor, leaning against the front wall closest to the lone entrance. This particular wayhouse had been built to hold four, maybe five comfortably. They'd managed to pack twelve into the space. The smell of sweat and blood and fear floated thick, almost nauseating. Cass was reminded too much of old haunts; the chem-dens where she used to buy quint, where burnouts lay on dirty mattresses or amongst stained blankets, oblivious to the dank reality around them. She let her eyes float around the room, surveying without any particular intent.

From the look of it the place had been a hasty add-on, wedged in the narrow space between two existing structures and just below street level. It was only one large room, or two if you counted the closet-sized washroom as its own. A flimsy, rubberized curtain hung on a rail and served as the divider between the bunks and the rest of the space. For now, it was pulled back. The ceiling was low, maybe six feet high, and there were no windows, no vents. In one corner of the ceiling was the only entrance: a round, rusted steel-rimmed porthole with a spot-welded ladder through it.

Clambering down into the wayhouse had felt to Cass very much like climbing into a grave. She still hadn't completely shaken that sense. The main lights were all off, and a single red emergency light cast the room in a sinister hue.

The others had been here long enough now that the initial wave of energy and emotion had passed. Cass had missed that part, but she could imagine it. The overwhelming relief, the shock of survival, the guilt. But they'd been here a few hours and now, though a few slept, mostly the rest just sat in stunned silence. Gamble had put them on tight noise discipline, so there was hardly any conversation, save the occasional hushed whisper. One man, Cass didn't know who he was, sobbed softly in the corner. No one tried to comfort or quiet him.

They were all wounded, dirty, exhausted. They'd hardly had time to process their losses, and none at all to grieve them. Though she'd never had time to count them, Cass guessed they'd had around thirty people altogether during their flight from Morningside, holed up in that tiny building to make their stand. Gamble and her team. Lil and her warriors. A few Awakened and a handful of citizens who'd somehow gotten joined up. Over half of them were gone, and even now Cass wasn't sure who had been lost.

Lil, at least, was still with them, and that was something of a victory. She had welcomed Cass warmly, though they had exchanged few words. Lil had been busy tending to others, as was her way, checking their wounds, encouraging them. The exhaustion had finally caught up with her though, and at the moment she was curled up on the floor in one corner of the room, dozing lightly.

Kit, too, was alive. Upon Cass's arrival, Kit had greeted her with a bear hug so tight it nearly stole her breath. Now she was sitting cross-legged by the bunks, on the other side of the wayhouse, staring down at her hands in her lap. Cass watched her for a moment, watched as she spread her fingers and curled them into fists slowly, over and over. Kit had always been full of fire, but Cass doubted the young woman had ever faced the kind of ordeal she'd just come through. Though, then again, as an Awakened, there was really no telling what she may have experienced during her time as an enthralled Weir. Cass knew whatever else Kit was dealing with, her thoughts were almost certainly drawn to Wick. The two had become surprisingly close in a very short amount of time. Cass couldn't help but wonder whether that budding relationship had been cut short.

Sky and Gamble had left almost half an hour earlier to link up with the others, though neither had given any indication about Wick's status. She hadn't expected them to be gone so long and naturally her imagination ran to dark places. If she'd reunited with them only to lose them all again...

Cass was so lost in the spiral of her own thoughts that when she heard a noise at the hatch, her body automatically tensed, ready for combat. The hatch shifted above her. Her claws extended. So far had her fears taken her, even when Sky's face appeared at the entrance, it took her a moment to recognize him and for minutes afterwards, her heart continued to race with adrenaline.

"We're back," Sky said. He quickly swung himself around and came down the ladder so fast Cass almost didn't have time to get out of the way. She retracted her claws and clenched her fists, hoping no one else in the wayhouse had seen them. "All right..." Sky said, and then stopped when he saw her. "Hey, you OK?"

Cass nodded. He gave her a look that said he didn't quite believe her, but there was no time to waste.

"You set?" a voice said from above in a harsh whisper. Male; Mouse or Finn, though Cass couldn't tell which. Sky looked at her, and she nodded again.

"Yeah, go ahead," Sky called back up, his voice low. Moments later, Wick's limp form slid into the entryway and dangled in midair. She could hear the grunts and struggles of those doing the work of lowering him. Somehow those above managed to get Wick low enough that Cass could grab him around the knees. Cass held tight as Sky climbed up one rung to try to steady Wick. He backed out moments later with a surprised look.

"Bring him down, bring him down," he said to Cass, and as he did Wick started dropping lower. Cass felt the weight shift, but she clearly wasn't holding all of it. Sky grabbed hold of Wick's waist as it appeared through the portal, and they backed away from the ladder. A few moments later, other feet appeared on the ladder above Wick. Mouse was climbing down, one hand on the ladder, one hand gripping the back of Wick's vest. Cass marveled at the man's strength.

When they got Wick all the way through, Sky reached up and caught him under the shoulders.

"It's all right, Mouse," he said, "we got him. We got him now, Mouse."

Finally, with those words, Wick's full weight descended upon them as Mouse relinquished his burden. As carefully as they were able, Cass and Sky brought Wick down and laid him on a pallet of coats and blankets they'd prepared for him. The moment Mouse's foot touched down, he went to work. He gently but firmly pulled Cass back away from Wick, and knelt down by his stricken friend's side. After the long, silent wait, the flurry of activity was shocking.

Finn was the next one down the ladder, and he too went straight to Wick's side. Able followed after. When his feet touched the floor, he stumbled from the ladder and collapsed to his hands and knees. Sky dropped and grabbed him, but Able waved him off. Gamble was there a moment later, bending down next to Able, her face two inches from his. Cass had been too distracted with the others to notice when exactly Gamble had shown up. They were all there now. Torn up, beaten down, worn out, but all there. The whole crew reunited. All except Swoop.

For the next ten minutes or so, Cass stood by, wanting to help but feeling like, no matter where she stood, she was in the way. Truth was, that many people stuffed into such tight quarters made it impossible not to be in *somebody*'s way. A few folks stood up and crowded back towards the back wall trying to give the latest arrivals as much room as possible. Kit alone moved forward and, along with Cass, hovered at the edge of usefulness. Cass put her arm around Kit's shoulders and together they stood watch.

Once Mouse had done all he could, he stood and motioned to Kit. The ceiling was so low he had to duck his head and hunch over just to fit. They held quiet conference for a minute or so, after which Kit sat down on the floor next to Wick. She smoothed his sweat-soaked hair back from his forehead, then stretched her hand out and took hold of Finn's. Cass touched Mouse's elbow to get his attention. He looked to her with heavy eyes, the utter exhaustion nearly tangible rolling off him. He gave her a weak smile and squeezed her upper arm.

"It's good to see you, Cass," he said. "Real good."

"Is Wick going to make it?" she asked.

Mouse tossed a glance over his shoulder back at Wick, and when he turned back his expression didn't offer a clear answer. "He's lost a lot of blood and he's been running too hot. Body just cut out on him. He's a fighter though. If we can keep him stable, I think he'll pull through all right. But my medkit's real low, and I don't have a lot of what he needs."

"What about Able?" Cass said, looking over at where Able lay motionless by the ladder. His breathing was deep and even.

"Able?" Mouse said, with a chuckle. "Able's a beast. I reckon he carried Wick seven, maybe eight klicks before we tracked 'em down. He'll probably be the sorest he's ever been in his life tomorrow, but otherwise nothing too bad. How about you?"

"I'm fine."

"Yeah?" His keen eyes narrowed, probing hers. Mouse was ever watchful when it came to others' health, and he never trusted a self-diagnosis.

"Yeah, Mouse. I really am."

"Anything touch you out there? Any falls?"

She couldn't lie. "I had a couple of scuffles. They got the worst of it. I'm fine. Really."

From his look, she could tell he was considering checking her over, but after a moment he just nodded. "All right." The fact that he let it go at that told Cass just how exhausted he must be.

"Are you OK?" she asked.

Mouse smiled at that. "Long night." He ran a hand back over his head, and threw one more look back over at Wick. Then he turned back to her. "I'm sorry, Miss Cass, but we might have to save the rest of the debrief for the morning. I'm smoked."

"Yeah, sure, of course," she said. "Get some rest, Mouse."

He nodded and started towards an open spot on the floor that some of the others had arranged for him, but stopped and turned back.

"Hey. You know you shouldn't be here. And I know that. But it's really good to see you, just the same."

"You too, Mouse. I'm glad you're back safe."

He nodded again and then took his place on the floor, apparently asleep almost as soon as he laid his head on his arm. Cass watched him for a few moments, a strange peacefulness settling on her from his presence. She hadn't realized how concerned she'd been for him until that moment. Mouse had a careful watchfulness over those in his charge that few could match; and if someone was within his sight, he considered them under his charge. She'd seen him in combat before and knew his ferocity well, frightening to behold. He brought that same intensity to guarding the well-being of his companions. Somehow having Mouse safely home, wherever home was for the moment, made her feel like there was some measure of hope after all.

Gamble touched Cass's shoulder and drew her attention.

"Hey," Gamble said. "Go on and try to get some sleep."

"I'm pretty wired," said Cass. "I can stay up. Stand watch."

Gamble shook her head. "We're buttoned up pretty good. We all need to get rest whenever we can. No telling when our next chance may be."

"What's the plan?"

"The plan?" Gamble said. She looked over at Wick, and then shook her head again. "Plan is to sleep. After that, we'll see what the sun brings with it."

Gamble gave her a little nod and then moved off to spread the word to the rest of the survivors. She was right. There were still a few hours before sunrise, and now that they were all safely sealed inside there wasn't much more for anyone to do. They were all too spent, and there were too many unknowns for them to make any kind of serious plans. That would come with the morning.

Cass went to Kit and Finn, pressed her hand into Wick's for a moment, and then found an unclaimed corner to curl into. She stayed sitting up, resting her head against the wall, thinking she might doze lightly at best. It was only a few minutes before she had fallen into a deep sleep.

A hand on Cass's shoulder drew her forth from an intense dream that she couldn't recall when she awoke. Mouse was crouching in front of her, and it took a few seconds for her brain to catch up with her surroundings and her circumstances.

"We're going topside to have a chat," Mouse said. "Think you probably better come with."

Cass nodded and swallowed, suddenly aware of a bitter taste in her mouth. Sleeping with her mouth open, probably. She stood and stretched, trying to work the knots out of her back, and shoulders, and neck, and pretty much everywhere else. Though she was certain the couple of hours of sleep had done her some good, at the moment it sure felt like it had wrecked her. Most of the others were still asleep, or at least sitting or laying with their eyes closed. Kit lay next to Wick, her hand on his chest. It was rising and falling more rapidly than Cass thought normal, and she felt a stab of concern as she followed Mouse up the ladder and into the cold morning air.

Outside, the sun was just cresting the horizon, its first rays melting the dawn grey into life and color. The wayhouse had been nestled between two tall buildings, six stories each, that overshadowed a cluster of smaller structures. There was a small courtyard at the center of them all, and the sunlight filtered through it, striping it with light and shadow. There the others stood waiting, a little distance from the wayhouse entrance. Gamble was already up, which wasn't a surprise to anyone. Finn was there with her, as was Lil. Cass hadn't seen Sky or Able down below, and they weren't around now, which, she guessed, meant they were already out scouting.

"Morning," Gamble said as Cass and Mouse approached. "Sleep well?"

"I slept," Cass answered. "Don't know about well."

"You hear Mouse snoring like an earthquake?" Finn said.

"No," said Cass.

"Then you slept well," Finn replied.

"I don't snore," Mouse said.

"OK big fella," Gamble said. Lil smiled and looked elsewhere. "So," said Gamble, looking to Cass and switching immediately to business-mode. "We've got some plans to make and not a lot of time to make them."

"Shouldn't take long anyway," Lil said. "Come back with us. As soon as everyone's well enough to move. We've got plenty of room and supplies."

"We'd be grateful," Gamble answered, "but I'm afraid it's not that simple."

She cued Mouse with a look.

"Wick's in real bad shape," Mouse said. "He's lost a lot of blood, and when I checked him this morning, his body temp was low. Looks like early stages of a blood infection. If we don't do something soon, we're going to lose him."

Cass looked over at Finn, who was stonefaced. Obviously Mouse had already told him the news.

"Can you cure it?" Lil asked.

"If we had the right meds and time to keep him rested, yeah," Mouse said. "But I don't have what we need in my kit."

Lil hadn't picked up on it yet, but Cass could sense that they were building to something. They already had a plan, they just hadn't told everyone else yet.

"But you know where you can find it," Cass said. Mouse nodded.

"And where's that?" Lil asked.

Mouse glanced at Gamble. She answered.

"Morningside."

The word hung in the air like a thousand-pound bomb moments from impact.

"You can't be serious," Lil said.

"There's more," Mouse said. "Swoop's back there."

"That's... no," Lil said, looking back and forth between Mouse and Gamble. "No, you can't." But they both looked back at her impassively; it was obvious the decision had been made. Lil turned to Cass then, hoping for an ally. "Cass. You saw what they did to the city. Tell them they can't go back!"

Cass agreed with Lil. Returning to Morningside seemed like utter insanity. But she knew in her heart she had no right to oppose Gamble. The team leader would risk anything to save her boys.

"I can't *not* go back, ma'am," Mouse said. "I made a promise to him that I wouldn't let him become one of those things."

"We all did," Gamble added. She shook her head again and looked off across the empty cityscape, back towards the rising sun. Back towards Morningside.

"I understand your loyalty," Lil said to Gamble. "I understand your word, and your honor. But I can't in good conscience let you do this, you're talking about suicide—"

Gamble turned to Lil, a spark of fire kindled. "All due respect, ma'am, I don't think your opinion much weighs in."

"Do you really think Swoop would want—"

"Don't," Gamble said, cutting Lil off. There was a warning growl in her tone, but Lil didn't shrink back. The two stared each other down, and Cass saw laid bare between them the strength of their wills. Different as they were, both were strong, capable warriors; both were gifted leaders. For a few seconds, it didn't look like either one of them was going to back down. But Lil was the first to remember herself.

"I'm sorry," she said. "That was out of line." Gamble continued to stare her down, driving home the point and offering no sign of acceptance or apology. "I just hate to see you throw your lives away."

"If you really knew us, you'd understand," Gamble said.

"You have your people," Finn added, taking his turn to ease the tension. "We have ours. If you were in our place, I'm sure you'd do the same."

Lil nodded, though it seemed to come more from a desire to move past it all than from any agreement on her part.

"If you'd be willing to take the survivors back with you," Mouse said, "we'd be deeply grateful."

"Of course," Lil answered. "Any and all are welcome." She looked at Cass then. "And you?"

Cass looked around at the others.

"You're going on to Greenstone," Gamble said before Cass could answer. "Get back to your boy, Cass. You've already done more for us than you should have."

Cass inhaled, steadied herself. Shook her head.

"I'm not going to Greenstone," she said. "I can't."

"What are you talking about?" Gamble said, her eyes hard.

"I have to stay on this side of the Strand. Keep Asher's eyes on me. He doesn't have any reason to think Wren's anywhere other than where I am. Even if he manages to figure it out, I don't believe he'll go after Wren until he gets to me first. And I don't intend to let him do either."

Cass wanted to continue, to tell them all she was going to head out into the open on her own, but the words caught in her throat. Gamble stood before her, jaw working. Cass awaited the blistering response. But once again, Gamble surprised her.

"If you think that's the best way to protect your son," she said, "then we're with you."

That wasn't at all what Cass had expected, nor was it what she'd been planning. And though she started to protest, once again she couldn't bring herself to confess her intent. Maybe her resolve wasn't as firm as she'd thought.

"We'll work it out when we get back," Gamble said. "Once we know what we've got to work with."

They stood in a brief, awkward silence, no one seeming to know quite what came next. Lil was the first to break it.

"Then I suppose this is where our paths diverge once more," she said.

"Looks like," Gamble replied.

Cass felt the lingering emotional rift and hated it. Here, now, of all times, she knew they should all be supporting one another, not tearing each other down. But the previous night had taken a heavy toll, and careless words were never easy to recover even in the best of circumstances.

"In that case, I would have us part as friends," Lil added quietly.

"More than friends," Cass said, and she stepped forward and embraced her. "You've been a sister to me, Lil."

Lil hugged her back, and then drew away. "Whatever may happen, when your business is done, you'll always have a place with us." She squeezed Cass's arm, and then looked over to Finn, and Mouse, and finally Gamble. "All of you."

"Don't go saying your goodbyes just yet," Gamble said, and though the words were direct, her tone had softened and warmed; the closest thing to an apology she'd give. "We've got logistics to work out." Then she looked to Mouse.

"I want to get Swoop taken care of as much as anyone," Gamble said. "It's worth it to me to see if we can pick up a line on him. But despite some people's impressions, I'm not authorizing a suicide run. We'll run a tight timeline, two objectives. Primary is *resupply*." She emphasized the word. "Can't help Swoop if we're not well ourselves."

Mouse glanced at the sun, already larger on the horizon now. "Maybe I should get a jump on it. Rest of you can catch up."

"That's a negative, Mouse. Sky and Able will be back soon enough. I wanna know if we're going to have to find a new place to hole up before we head out. We'll all go together."

"Not all of us," Mouse said. "We can't move Wick. Not far, anyway. And we can't leave him on his own."

"How much watching does he need?"

Mouse shook his head. "I'll check him again before we head out. Not much we can do for him except keep him still and rested. And, you know... he's not going to be able to pull security real well."

Gamble's eyes narrowed as she looked back towards the wayhouse entrance, evaluating, working on whatever plan she was forming in her head. After a moment, she smiled sadly to herself. "Swoop was always good with this sort of thing."

"You know what he'd say," Mouse replied.

Gamble looked up at him and lowered the pitch of her voice, imitating their fallen comrade. "'Mouse and me can handle it. Rest of you, button up and wait for our knock.'"

The right corner of Mouse's mouth curved upward in a shadow of a smile at the impression. "And then you'd say..."

Gamble chuckled and said in her own voice, "Don't be an idiot. Sky and Able stay with Wick; rest of you with me." After a moment, she looked to Finn. "I'd feel better having you along, if your head's in the right place."

"I'm good to go," Finn answered.

"If it's not, I understand, that's your brother in there," Gamble said. "But I need to know. I don't want you out here if you're running anything less than a hundred percent."

"If Mouse says he'll be OK, he'll be OK," Finn said. "And anyway, if I stayed with him, he'd ride me the whole time for acting like Mom."

"I think Sky ought to come along," Mouse said. "Wick won't need that much watching; Cass and Able can cover it."

"Able won't like us leaving him behind," Finn said.

"None of us would. But he needs rest, too. Only way to get him to take it is to give him something important to do here."

"I'm good with that," Gamble said. She turned to Cass. "Assuming you're intent on staying."

Cass remained convinced that her presence posed a threat to Gamble and her team, but her ultimate concern was Wren. Whatever the team did, as long as Cass was around, Asher's attention would be bent towards her, and therefore them. But if they knew the risks and were willing to accept them, why should she resist? And returning to Morningside? If they were determined to make an attempt, they would need all the help they could get.

"I am," she said. "But I'll be more use if I come with you."

Gamble flicked her eyes to Mouse. He raised his eyebrows and shrugged.

"Not sure there's a place more dangerous," Gamble said to Cass.

"That's probably true for me no matter where I am," Cass answered.

"Then I guess you might as well be with us," Gamble said. "I'm sure we can use the extra eyes. All right, let's get everybody up and accounted for. We all need as much daylight as we can get."

"You got it," Finn said. Mouse nodded and together the two of them headed back towards the wayhouse. Gamble pulled Lil off to the side, and Cass stood there alone, between the wayhouse and the two women, unsure for the moment of what she ought to be doing. There was something more to her decision to stay with the team than she wanted to admit. Though Cass tried to convince herself that it wasn't really part of the equation, the fact was that they'd given her a good excuse not to have to go off on her own. As much as she'd been convinced it was best for everyone, the idea of facing the open on her own was overwhelming. Maybe this wasn't the best way, but maybe it was good enough.

Lil and Gamble stood close together, saying whatever it was they needed to say to one another. Cass couldn't hear any of the words, but she got the impression that the two women would leave as friends. After a minute or two, they embraced. As they parted, Sky and Able reappeared in one of the narrow entrances to the courtyard and approached. Gamble and Lil rejoined Cass, and the three women stood together in silence until the two men joined them.

"Hey, Ace," Sky said, glancing around at everyone's look. "You uh... get it all sorted out?"

"Yep," Gamble said.

"Well all right," he said. "When do we leave?"

"I'd say about now," Gamble said. "We need to have a quick chat, then we'll roll out."

Gamble led them all back to the wayhouse to work out the final details. Cass followed in an almost dreamlike state, dizzy with the unknowns and the possibilities that lay ahead. Nothing was going the way she'd thought it would. In fact, it all seemed to be going exactly the opposite. She'd been expecting her next days, however many or few they were, to be fraught with danger. But she had never for a moment imagined that in just a few minutes, she and her companions would be walking towards the one place they ought to be running the farthest from.

SEVEN

"Come with me," Haiku said.

He watched the boy sitting on the couch across the room; a small and fragile thing. Whatever strength Wren possessed was well-hidden beneath that tiny frame. It would be easy to mistake him, to overlook or dismiss him, if not for the gravity of his gaze, the sharpness in his eyes. Those sea-green eyes had witnessed more than most people beheld in their full lifetimes; far more than any child should have. And more than witnessed. Wren knew the exhilarating horror of battle, and many times over the unspeakable sorrow of sudden loss. His were the eyes of one who knew intimately how thin the membrane between life and death was.

The way the child held himself had already given away his answer; he was shrunken in on himself, shoulders slumped, head bowed, breathing shallow. Haiku waited patiently nonetheless for Wren to give it voice. It had been a long shot, a strange request.

"It's your decision, Wren," jCharles said. "Totally up to you."

Wren nodded. He was seated at one end of the couch, as he had been for most of the day before when he'd related his tale, and Three's. And like the day before, he was now staring at his hands in his lap, picking at a small sore next to the thumbnail on his right hand. The woman, Mol, sat beside him, while jCharles hovered by the window. The old man, Chapel, was leaning against the wall near the door.

"Wren, honey, leave it alone," Mol said. "You'll end up making it a habit."

Wren curled his hands into fists, making his small hands seem even smaller.

"I'm sorry," Wren said finally, and he looked up at Haiku. "I can't go. My Mama will look for me here. I have to wait for her."

It was as Haiku had expected. After Wren had gone to bed the night before, he'd discussed it at length with jCharles and Mol. But he'd waited until morning to extend the invitation, waited until Wren was another day rested, in hopes that he would be more willing to consider the offer. There were ways to manipulate him, of course, and Haiku had discerned them; emotions to stir, memories to evoke. If the Weir had truly been united under a single mind, even just a fraction of their total number, the potential for that one mind to wage war on the fractured world was staggering. It was the very scenario that House Eight had long worked to prevent. And here, now, was a boy with intimate knowledge of that mind. If anything could be done to turn back the tide, this boy would surely play a part in it.

But for Wren to undertake all that Haiku had hoped of him, the boy would have to count the cost on his own and choose for himself. No amount of coercion would be strong enough to sustain his resolve under the pressures he would face. Even so, Haiku had to do everything he could to help Wren understand the magnitude of this moment.

"I understand, Wren," Haiku said. "It would be a big step for you."

"Maybe you could wait," Wren said. "For a while. To see."

"I'm sorry," Haiku said. "I cannot." There were days of travel ahead, and Haiku knew the longer Wren stayed, the less likely he would be to ever leave.

The boy didn't respond. Didn't raise his eyes to meet Haiku's.

"I understand there's no way for you to fully grasp what

I'm offering you. And all I'm truly offering is a hard journey to a harder place. Beyond that, I can make no guarantees to you save one: the opportunity you have before you now won't come again. And it's one that I do not present lightly. It's well-considered, and I believe it's well-deserved. And I'm not the only one who sees that."

Wren had gone back to picking at his thumb, but he stopped at those words and glanced up at Haiku. Haiku read the reaction.

"Three was an excellent judge of people, Wren. I understand why he responded to you as he did. But there is more to you, I believe, than even he recognized. He couldn't possibly have known what the Weir would become, or what role you could play in standing against them. Undoubtedly if he were here now, we would agree. Come with me. Maybe the one I take you to will turn us both away. If so, I'll bring you safely back here again. But if not, Wren, if not, he may well help you find something within yourself that even you do not yet perceive."

It was dangerous to mention Three, dangerously close to using a sense guilt to sway the boy, and for a moment there was a flicker of something in Wren's eye. A spark of intrigue, of courage, maybe even of hope. But as quickly as it sprang to life, so too did it cool and fade, crushed beneath the burden of loss too deep and too recently felt. Haiku tried to salvage the moment before it completely slipped away.

"I don't believe in fate or destiny. I never have. But meeting you, here and now... it's an opportunity that I believe we could turn to *purpose,* if we will take it."

"I'm sorry. I am. But I have to wait for my Mama. She'll look for me here," Wren repeated.

"There are ways for her to find you, Wren, you know," jCharles said, "if that's what you're worried about. You can tell us where you're going, and we'll pass the message along when she gets here."

"I'm afraid that I cannot do," Haiku said gently, and he bowed slightly to take the edge off. "I apologize, but great pains have been taken to keep certain secrets. And even for such a case as this, I cannot reveal them."

jCharles obviously didn't like that, but he didn't let it deter him too much. "A pim then. I'm sure she'll contact you just as soon as she can, and you two can figure it out from there."

"She won't pim," Wren said. "It's too dangerous. Asher might see it. He'll use it to track us both."

"You think they'll come after you here?" jCharles asked, and there was a subtle note of concern in his voice. Not fear exactly. Not yet. But Haiku heard it in his words; the thought that Wren's presence in the city might represent a threat to it was only now beginning to occur to jCharles.

"They'll come," Wren said. "One night. Maybe soon. Maybe a year from now. But they'll come."

"And what if you're not here?" Haiku asked. "What if you're hidden away somewhere else?"

Wren shook his head. "I don't think it'll matter. He destroyed Chapel's village, just because they helped me."

"You don't know that," Mol said.

"I believe it," Wren replied with a shrug. "Just like I believe he'll come here."

"Greenstone is too strong for him," Chapel said. "For now."

Wren shook his head. "You know how quickly Morningside fell, Chapel. And it was way bigger than Greenstone."

"Morningside fell under its own weight," Chapel said. "Its core was rotten. If not for the foolishness at the gate and for your companion's betrayal, the city might still stand, even against such numbers."

"You think we're safe here?" jCharles asked, looking to Chapel.

"For a time," Chapel answered. "But not forever. Preparations should be made."

"Well, I look forward to hearing your suggestions," jCharles said offhandedly.

"I fear you'll have to see your own way through," said Chapel, and there was a note in his words that hinted at the plans he'd made for himself.

"Wait," Wren said, picking up on the tone almost as quickly as Haiku. "You are staying, aren't you?"

"No," Chapel said, simply.

The blow was obviously heavy to the boy, and Haiku suppressed his disappointment that the old blind man had chosen that moment to reveal his intentions. The loss of a protector, the unexpected abandonment. These things would push Wren to cling to known comforts, farther from Haiku's outstretched hand.

"But," Wren said, "you promised. You promised my mom you'd watch over me."

"I promised to see you safely to these people," Chapel answered. "Those promises I give, I keep. But I give few, and those with limits." Chapel strode to Wren then, and knelt in front of him. "I have played my part, child," he said. "And I have other work yet to do."

Wren dropped his head again but Haiku could see the boy was trying to hold back tears.

"I'm sorry to cause you pain," Chapel said. "But I cannot long ignore the iniquity this city harbors. I must leave it, or set myself to rectify it. For your sake, and the sake of these good people, it is better I should go."

"Will you ever come back?" Wren asked. And in his voice, Haiku could hear his chance slip away. Wren wouldn't leave with him now, no matter how long he waited. He was too fixed on what had been, on recovering things lost.

"I have my own path to follow," Chapel said. "As you have yours. For now they part. Who can say where they may meet again?"

Chapel got to his feet and placed his hand on Wren's head, a priest granting a silent blessing.

"There is greatness in you, Wren," he said, after a moment. "If you will embrace it."

Then he turned to the others.

"Judgment will come to this city," he said. "I cannot oppose it. But it is my sincere hope that you will tip the balance in your own favor."

Everyone sat in stunned silence for a time, unsure of what to make of the old man's proclamations. All except for Haiku, who was taking the measure of the room in hopes of finding a moment or thought on which to hang a final appeal.

"Well," jCharles finally said. "When you reckon you'll head out?"

"Soon," Chapel said.

"Figured that," said jCharles.

"I assumed Haiku would be departing shortly," Chapel said, bowing his head towards Haiku. "I thought it best to say all the farewells at one time."

Haiku nodded at that and got to his feet. Chapel moved back to the front door.

"A thoughtful gesture," Haiku said. "And I *should* be on my way." The shift in atmosphere seemed abrupt, a conversation unexpectedly truncated, but Haiku knew lingering wouldn't help his cause. Better to give Wren a clean break.

"I'll be leaving through the Dive," Haiku said, indicating a section of Greenstone on the west side of the city. "In case you change your mind." He said it to Wren, with a smile, but Wren didn't smile back.

Haiku's few belongings were already gathered by the front door to the small apartment. He'd given it his best attempt. There wasn't much more he could do. It was still his sincere belief that having Wren along could have brought a greater good, but it apparently was not to be. There was no use in considering the courses that might have been. All that mattered was what truly was. One journey had ended, and the next had presented itself with its conclusion. Haiku made himself busy with his small pack, giving the others emotional space to say their final goodbyes to Chapel.

"Thanks for all you've done, Chapel," jCharles said. "We

appreciate you getting Wren to us."

Chapel bowed to jCharles and then to Mol. "Thank you for your patience and your hospitality. I am an unusual guest."

"And you're welcome just the same," Mol said.

"Wren," said Chapel. "Be well."

"You too, Chapel. I hope to see you again some day."

The old man bowed his head to the boy and then without further fanfare, he simply turned and left. Everyone was silent for a few moments after. And then jCharles chuckled.

"That's a strange cat right there," he said. "And I do mean cat. Prowling around at odd hours, gone one minute, right behind you the next. I was serious about putting a bell on him, you know."

"Twitch, enough," Mol said, but she was suppressing a smile. "You know you'll miss him." She hugged Wren a little closer. "We all will."

"Yeah, I reckon so," jCharles replied. And then a moment later, he added, "But maybe we can get him to come back around if I leave a little saucer of milk out for him—"

"Oh, you stop," Mol said, and she laughed in spite of herself. And that beautiful sound cleared some of the heaviness out of the room.

Haiku cinched his pack down and stood, slinging the straps over his shoulders as he did.

"Well," he said. "Thank you all again, for your graciousness. Wren, to you especially. You've done great honor to both Three and to our House."

"Thanks, Haiku," the boy answered. "I'm glad we had a chance to meet."

"Me too. jCharles. Mol. My blessings on your household."

Mol nodded and waved. "You take care of yourself out there. It was a real treat having you here. Like having a little piece of old times back for a little while. Stop back any time."

Haiku bowed to her and touched his heart in gratitude. For as much of the land as he'd traveled, he couldn't remember having met anyone with the genuine warmth and sincere openness that Mol had shown him.

"Goodbye," said Haiku.

"Bye, Haiku," Wren said.

Haiku lingered there by the door for a span, just long enough to see if Wren had any final words for him. But the boy had already lowered his eyes back to his own hands again.

"I'll walk you down," jCharles said. He opened the door for Haiku, and Haiku gave a final nod to Mol before moving into the narrow stairwell that led down to the bar below. jCharles followed behind, though he didn't speak again until they'd made it all the way to the front door of the building.

"There anything else you need?" jCharles asked. "You good on food and water?"

"I have all I need," Haiku answered. "Thank you, jCharles. You're a good man."

"Yeah, I don't know about all that."

"I do. Three's friends were few, and he chose them well."

jCharles's eyes narrowed at that. "Just what all do you have in that book of yours anyway?"

Haiku just smiled.

"Yeah. Figures," jCharles said. And then he chuckled and shook his head. "So what'll you do now?"

"The same I would have done had Wren accompanied me. I'll go see the man myself. There may still be something he can do."

jCharles nodded, though he clearly didn't understand. There was no way he could have.

"Well good luck to you, Haiku. Like my lady said, any time you want to stop by, you're more than welcome. Town tends to run a little short on good guys."

"Thank you, jCharles," Haiku said. He would've liked to have added that he'd see the man again some day, but Haiku didn't make promises he wasn't certain he could keep.

•••

After the men had departed, Wren stood by jCharles's bookshelf by the window. He scanned the books there, reading the occasional title, but mostly just taking in the sense and character of each as his eyes passed over. The shelf wasn't very tall, no higher than his chest, being just three levels high. It stretched wide, though, maybe ten feet or more. The shelves were completely filled, end to end, with all sorts of volumes. Books of all sizes, all colors. Some were in better shape than others, but all were to one degree or another worn and battered. Mol had called them jCharles's life work; finding them, buying them, trading for them. Greenstone may very well have been the last place in the world to have a library, and no one who saw the inside of the Samurai McGann would ever guess anything remotely scholarly might reside in the same building. The first time Wren had seen them, he hadn't understood why anyone would spend any effort at all on them, when any of them could instantly access any information at any time through the digital. But as he became more familiar with them, he saw the value of having the books arrayed before him. Who knew what worlds they contained, what stories they might tell? Things he'd never imagined, nor would have, had those books not drawn his eye and awakened him to the possibilities.

They'd given him one for his own, one he'd lost now, with Morningside gone. It had seemed a treasure to him before, a true relic. And it had reminded him of Mol. Having glimpsed Haiku's chronicle, though, these books had become almost magical to him. He ran his fingers across the spine of a titleless blue book, felt the texture of the covering.

"How are you feeling, Wren?" Mol said from behind him. He shrugged. She walked over and sat down on the couch. He noticed she left between herself and the arm, leaving the place open where he'd lately taken to sitting next to her.

"I'm sorry about Chapel," she continued. "I know it's hard to say goodbye. Especially when you aren't sure you'll get a chance to see someone again."

Wren moved his fingers from the spine of the book up to the top where the time-browned pages were pressed together. There was a story hidden in there. The important moments of someone's life, whether they were real or imaginary, were recorded in there for whoever might happen upon those pages. How strange it was that someone's life could leave such footprints that carried so far into the future. The thought made him wonder about his own footprints.

"Did I make the right decision, Miss Mol?"

"If you believe it was the right decision, it was the right decision," she said.

Wren wondered at that. He'd made the decision he *thought* was right, but did he *believe* it? A small voice in his head, his own voice, asked if he'd be standing there wondering about it, if he really and truly believed it. "What if I'm not sure?"

"Then you're human," she answered. There was a smile with the reply; he could hear it in her words. But it didn't settle his uncertainty. A few seconds of silence went by, then Mol continued. "Old as I am, Wren, there are still plenty of times when I don't know if I've made a good decision or a bad one. And you're still a boy yet."

Wren moved his hands over the tops of the books next to the blue one. So many stories. So many lives. What decisions had these people had to make? What part had they played in their own destinies?

"This feels like a big one, though."

"Could be," Mol said. "Sometimes decisions seem big at the time and then turn out not to be what we thought. A lot of times, it's the little decisions that make the biggest difference."

Wren let his hand fall from the books and turned around to look at her.

"But how are you supposed to know?" he asked. "How can you ever tell what you're supposed to do?"

She motioned for him to join her on the couch. Wren

took a seat next to her, and Mol dropped her arm over his shoulders.

"If you figure that one out, you'll be the wisest man in the world, Wren. And then I hope you'll tell me. I'm not sure we can ever know what we're *supposed* to do, because that would mean it's already been decided. That there's some kind of perfect plan out there, already laid out for us. But sometimes, when I don't know which way to go, I try to think of someone I want to be like, and I ask myself what they'd do. Do you have anyone like that?"

As soon as the words left her mouth, Wren's mind was flooded with memories of people. Mama, Gamble, Able, Mouse. Mr Carter, and Chapel, and Lil. And, of course, Three.

"I have a lot of people like that."

"Then you're blessed indeed. Some people don't even have one."

"But all of them are strong and really brave. I'm not like them. I'm not like any of them."

"That's OK, sweetheart. I'm not very brave either. But the question is, what would you do if you were?"

That stirred something within him. It made some sense to wait here in Greenstone. Mama had sent him here because she thought that was best. But Mama couldn't have known what would happen when he got here. None of them could have. And was he really waiting here for Mama? Was he just waiting for the next person to come along and tell him where he should go, what he should do? Was he just hiding?

He'd made a decision once. One time, he'd embraced the fear and done what he thought was best. He'd left Mama behind before, when he returned to Morningside. And the city had paid dearly for it. He'd failed, utterly, completely. Catastrophically.

But that wasn't why he had told Haiku no, and he knew it. He'd said no because he couldn't imagine what might happen next. Here, if he stayed, the possibilities were easy to picture. Maybe Mama would come find him here, and they'd figure out what to do. Or jCharles and Mol would look after him. Or Asher and his Weir would come for one final assault, and it would all be over. But going with Haiku, that was a world completely hidden from him. His mind couldn't comprehend what might wait for him out there, what changes it might require of him. It was the fear that had made his decision, fear of the unknown, fear of another failure. Fear, nothing else.

"If I were brave, I think I would have gone with him," he said.

"Well, honey," Mol said quietly. "It's not too late."

"You think I should go?"

"I don't *want* you to go, Wren. I'd like to keep you here and pretend I could keep you safe. But illusions are dangerous things to base your life on. A lot more dangerous than anything the real world has for us."

"You think I should go."

"I think we're all going to meet our end one day, Wren," Mol said. "One way or another. And when it comes, I hope each of us can say that we gave life our best. That we gave it everything we could. Only you can know whether you're giving it."

Wren sat on the couch, feeling Mol's warmth pressed up against him, her arm over his shoulder protecting him. He knew she would do everything she could to defend him, even though he had no claim on her for it. There was no reason in the world for her to put herself in harm's way for him, to risk her life and the life of her own baby for him, and yet she was willing to do it. So many others had come before her. And he knew that no, this wasn't his best. He hadn't given his all. Not yet. Not by a long shot.

"I need to get my stuff," Wren said.

EIGHT

Cass glanced up at the sky, checking the position of the sun as it rode low in its winter arc. Her veil was down, shielding her modified eyes from the rays that, unfiltered, overwhelmed and confused her vision. It was getting on towards midmorning, and they were only about halfway to Morningside. With Wick out of action, Sky had taken over pathfinding duties. He was plenty good at it, but he didn't have quite the same effortless sense of navigation that Wick possessed. And though none of them had spoken of it, their pace was undoubtedly slowed by the dread that opposed them like a headwind.

It had taken the whole team to convince Able to stay behind. And they'd completely failed to convince Kit to go with Lil and the rest of the survivors. They'd all said their final goodbyes to Lil and her remaining warriors, and sent them off with as many supplies as they could spare, and probably more. Even in his weakened state, Wick had insisted on running a route for them, and ended up plotting three different courses from the wayhouse back to where the rest of Lil's people were waiting.

Now, the team was traveling single file with Cass right in the middle, just in front of Gamble. And though they still tended to arrange themselves to protect her, they had in nearly every way taken her as one of their own. They'd even dialed her in to their secure communication channel, which previously had been off-limits to her except in the worst of emergencies. Sky led the way, with Finn coming behind, then Cass, then Gamble. Mouse trailed behind as rear guard, filling in the position that had long belonged to Swoop. Somehow without Able and Wick along, Cass felt Swoop's absence even more acutely; she could have almost convinced herself that he was back there with his brothers-in-arms. Almost. Knowing he wasn't left a gaping hole in her heart.

The team walked in near silence, communicating little except by way of hand signals. And the nearer they drew to Morningside, the more cautious they all became. Cass had returned Wick's weapon to him and was now armed only with Gamble's sidearm: a jittergun which, while brutally efficient at close range, wasn't intended for much more than last-ditch personal defense. They were all running light on ammo. Gamble had been clear from the first; contact with any Weir and the mission was compromised. They'd break contact and return with all speed to the wayhouse. She hadn't mentioned it, but everyone remembered all too well what had happened at Ninestory. That wasn't the sort of situation you got out of twice. Or usually even once, for that matter.

The approach to the city was agonizing with tension, ever increasing the closer they got. When they were within a half-mile, Sky slowed further, took longer with each decision. No one seemed to mind. There was a disquieting energy over the whole area. It was almost impossible to believe that just the day before, these buildings and streets could have been considered some of the safest in the world. Now they seemed full of danger. Any one of them might house untold numbers of Weir, lightly slumbering in the shadows, just waiting to be provoked by mistake or by chance.

Once the wall came into view, Sky shifted their path to a wide arc more or less following the perimeter of the city from a distance. Communication had dropped to almost zero, and the team had tightened up to no more than eight feet between each member. Weapons were up, breathing shallow.

From the outside, there was hardly any sign of damage. The high wall was intact and obscured any view of the interior. But that didn't make approaching the city any easier. On the contrary, there was something deeply disturbing about such a large settlement being so completely still and silent. They circled the city from maybe two to three hundred yards out, their pace painstakingly cautious. And it was the gates that filled Cass with the most dread. The third gate was just now coming into view and it too, like the others before it, was wide open. Looking through those vast entryways hinted at the horrors within. Even from this distance, Cass could see the destruction spilled out into the streets. This was one of the western gates, and if Cass was reading the city correctly, just one gate over from where they had made their first stand against Asher's hordes. One gate over from where Swoop had fallen.

Up ahead, Sky held up a fist, calling for a halt, and the team smoothly fell into a ring to provide security. He crouched and slowly scanned the city ahead with his optic. After a minute or so, he glanced up and motioned to Gamble. She moved to him and crouched beside him, their faces so close together their noses nearly touched. Cass could see their lips moving but they were whispering so quietly she couldn't hear them even from six feet away. Sky must have given a report, because he did most of the talking. Gamble nodded a few times as Sky motioned with his hands. Finally, Gamble stood and motioned for the others to gather around her.

They drew in as tightly as they could, close enough that Cass could smell the sweat and blood and grime and even the breath of her comrades.

"Four hours," Gamble said, her voice just barely audible. She held up four fingers for clarity. "We go in here, cut across to the gate, start searching there. Work our way

towards the governor's compound unless we find a reason
to go somewhere else." Gamble glanced around, making
eye contact with each of them in turn. No one else seemed
to have any problems with that, but Cass felt cold dread
at the mention of the compound. They'd all seen it the
night before; the Weir had come up through the governor's
compound, that had been their first point of attack inside
the walls.

But she understood. Their team rooms were in the
compound, up on their own floor. The governor's Personal
Guard had access to more weapons, ammunition, and
countless other supplies than nearly the entire City Guard,
most of it locked away in the team rooms, in what they
called "the cage". Anything and everything they might need
for an emergency was there, whether they needed to lock
themselves in against a siege or they needed to evacuate the
city with little advance warning. They could run for a long
time out in the open if they could get to the cage. Assuming
the Weir hadn't gotten to it first.

Gamble paused again, searching the faces of her
teammates for any sign of question or confusion. There was
none. Gamble gave a nod.

"Finn, move to point, Mouse back him up. Sky, you're
rear guard. Cass, on me," she said. "Let's move."

That was all it took. In the next moment, the team shifted
into its new configuration and started off towards the city
that waited for them with the grim silence of a tomb.

Finn led the way, weapon shouldered and scanning for
targets, his every step placed with care, *heel-toe, heel-toe, heel-
toe*. Cass lacked the level of training that her companions
clearly enjoyed, but she was a quick study and emulated
everything she could. She knew enough of the basics to
understand intent of most everything they did: weapons
never swept across anything one didn't want killed; eyes
stayed focused on the assigned sector; movement was
forward or backward, never crisscrossing a teammate's field
of fire.

And then, when they were thirty yards out as they moved in on the city, something clicked and the fear Cass felt started to balance itself with the support she received from the team. Not just *the team*; her teammates. It divided the tension, distributed it evenly; all she had to worry about was her sector. Her teammates had her back, and her flanks. Cass just had to do her part.

She'd always thought of RushRuin as a team, but now she knew there was no comparison. RushRuin had been a crew. A group of individuals with their particular talents and specialties, each playing their part in turn as each job required. This was something different, something higher. She was attuned to the others in a way she'd never experienced before, and even in the face of such danger, it was exhilarating. Maybe *because* of the danger.

The gate loomed large before them, and Finn gave the signal to stop just ten yards from it. He glanced back at the rest of them, one final check before they committed. Gamble gave the OK, and together, they crossed the threshold into the site of recent and utter destruction.

Already Cass could see hints of it. But once they passed through the gateway, her view opened out and revealed a spectacle appalling in appearance, grotesque in scale. Whatever horrible images Cass thought she had prepared herself for were obliterated in that instant, replaced by a reality worse by an order of magnitude. Finn stopped without giving a signal and let out a quiet curse. No one could blame him. The weight of the moment struck them all like a physical force, and for a time there was nothing they could do but stand and stare helplessly at what their once-great city had become.

This portion of Morningside was completely unrecognizable, which made it all the more alien and uncanny. Cass looked back at the gate, and through it, back to landmarks outside the city that still remained untouched. But even with those signposts to help her get her bearings, when she turned back she felt lost and disoriented. She had known these streets once, had known the buildings, and those who owned them. No, not these streets; not *these* streets. These streets were from another world, some alternate reality that had forced itself into her own.

It was as if some great river had washed over the city, had smashed through it, and swept it, and churned it. The streets were filled with such a confusion of debris that it was difficult for Cass's mind to accept. Clothes, wiring, roofing, food, insulation, pipes, store signs, children's toys. A pot, caved in on one side, sat on top of the remains of a window frame, like it'd been arranged for some bizarre art piece. The contents of a thousand lives, torn up and strewn throughout the open. Even the skyline had changed where entire structures had collapsed and spilled themselves out across the streets. The air seemed heavier, thicker, full of dust. Cass had never thought much about how the city had smelled before, but even the scent had become a jumbled mass; metallic, sweet, rancid, dank.

"Finn," Gamble's voice hissed in Cass's head. It was a forceful whisper, thin and processed as it was delivered through the secure channel. "Keep moving."

Her voice brought him back to himself, and he re-centered his weapon and moved forward. The team pressed further in with painstaking caution, now even more vigilant about their footing as they waded through the chaos. They followed the channel of the narrow street that ran alongside the gentle curve of the wall. And as they pressed on, Cass simply could not come to terms with how thoroughly the Weir had ravaged the city. Even witnessing it with her own eyes was not enough for her mind to accept it. It was the kind of scene one might expect from a human invading force, those who might ransack a settlement to carry off its wealth for their own. But the Weir had no need for these things.

The strangeness of it lingered and mixed with the other oddities that surrounded them. Cass had expected the loss of life and the signs of panicked flight. But she hadn't expected the level of wanton, meaningless destruction. The Weir had never seemed interested in anything other than the humans they sought to claim, and yet here they had obviously spent great effort on tearing down not just the citizens, but on all that had had value to those people as well.

But then of course, this wasn't the work of the Weir, Cass reminded herself. This was Asher's doing. And that thought clarified everything in an instant, crystallizing it in a single concept. This hadn't been an attack. It had been a tantrum. Asher's wrath and vengeance poured out upon the city. His rage unleashed and unchecked. Cass's eyes opened to the new perspective and the contrast struck her; how vast the destruction, how childish the execution.

It was about twenty minutes before they reached the western gate where the first wave of the battle had kicked off the night before. This area looked much the same as all they had already passed through. The gate was wide open, and a cursory inspection showed it was intact. The gate hadn't been breached. It had been opened from the inside. A sickening reminder of the betrayal, the fall from within.

Beyond the gate was the site of their first clash with the Weir. The story of that battle was chronicled in the red-black ink of war that stained and splotched the ground.

Here the team would begin their search for their fallen teammate, though even at the first it was without much hope. For all the material that had been scattered, one thing Cass had not yet seen was a single human body. On one hand, that wasn't especially surprising. The Weir nearly always carried off the slain, human and Weir alike. But on the other hand, the sheer number of people that would have had to have been moved was staggering to consider. Where would the Weir have taken them all?

Cass approached the wall just to one side of the gate where she and many others had moved the bodies of their dead after the initial assault had been repelled. She remembered the exact place where Mouse and Able had lain Swoop's body, and she walked to it. Mouse drew up next to her and they both stood in silence, staring at the place they'd seen him last. Mouse made a sound somewhere between choking and clearing his throat, and when Cass looked at him, the tears were already running down his cheeks and dripping from his jaw.

"I'm sorry, brother," he said softly. "I'm gonna make it right, soon as I can."

Cass, unsure of what else to do, laid a hand on his arm and squeezed it.

"I should've lit him," Mouse said. "Soon as we heard 'em coming. I should've lit him."

"You couldn't have known, Mouse," Cass said.

"You don't understand, Cass," he answered without looking at her. There was no reproach in his tone, yet the words were heavy with meaning.

She waited to see if he would continue, but he went quiet and Cass could see from the look in his eye that he was wrestling to get himself back under control. She just stood by his side with her hand still on his arm, not sure how to extract herself from the moment, or even if she should. After a long moment, Mouse exhaled sharply, wiped his face with his hand and then glanced at her. He winked and patted her hand.

"Better get to it," he said. Cass nodded and turned around to find the other three standing nearby, watching them. No, not watching them. Paying their respects, each in their own way.

The team spread out then, though they all stayed close enough together so everyone could still see everyone else. They took their time searching for any sign or trail that might point to where the Weir had gone, but between the debris and the number of people who had moved through the area, all was confusion. Sky was the most skilled tracker among them, and even he looked lost. They spent no more than fifteen minutes there at the gate.

"Come on," Gamble said. "Let's check the compound."

"Gimme five more," Mouse responded.

"He's gone, Mouse. We're not gonna sift all this just for hope. We won't find it here anyway."

Mouse started to say something else, but stopped himself. The two stared at each other for a span, and though Cass couldn't read either one of them, she got the impression there was an entire conversation going on in those looks. Finally, Gamble just said, "Finn." And with a reluctant glance at Mouse, Finn moved out.

The team fell back into their previous formation and started working their way towards the governor's compound. Cass felt the tension rising again. As bad as the initial walk-through had been, at least they'd kept to the perimeter of the city, with the wall on one side. Now they were headed into the centermost part, the heart of Morningside. Even though they hadn't seen a single sign of life or motion, Cass couldn't help but feel like they were being slowly surrounded.

Finn led them with a steady but cautious pace and as they went, Cass noticed that the level of devastation seemed to be gradually lessening. The city was more familiar here, more recognizable. There was still damage everywhere she looked, but more of the buildings were intact, fewer of the streets were choked with wreckage. Nothing had fully escaped the ravages of the Weir, but it was like a fire had spent its fury too soon, leaving a greater portion scorched, coated in ash, but otherwise standing.

Cass estimated they were two hundred yards or so from the compound when she first noticed the change. There was something subtly different, a feeling as she moved along the street, though at first she couldn't quite place what it was. It was several seconds before she realized there was a new component to the unusual scent that clung in the air. It was faint, but sharper, coppery. Once she had identified it, she couldn't help but notice it seemed to be getting gradually stronger. And then she noticed a strange noise accompanying their footfalls; a slight tearing or sucking sound with each step, like peeling something up from

a damp carpet. Like the smell in the air, the sound grew
more distinct the closer they approached to the governor's
compound. Cass had been keeping her eyes up, searching
for threats, but now she glanced down at the ground. The
concrete was darker here than she remembered it, coated in
a gummy grit. That was what had started making the sound;
the ground was sticky.

When she looked back up, the team was just moving into
view of the governor's compound, but though normally
they would have been able to see the main courtyard from
their position, it was obscured by a huge mound of rubble
and debris. The midmorning sun was bright behind it, and
its jagged silhouette made it hard to tell what comprised it,
but it seemed that the Weir had dragged all the wreckage
from the surrounding area and piled it up in front of the
compound. It was hard to judge the scale of it at distance
because it was out in the open area with not much around
it to compare it to. As they continued their approach to the
compound, it became increasingly clear that the pile was
truly enormous; almost a small hill.

Cass's mind started racing. Apart from her experience
at Ninestory, she had no knowledge or memory of where
the Weir typically lived. Did they nest? At Ninestory, they'd
hidden inside the buildings during the day, a fact Wick and
Finn had discovered at frightening cost. But the mountain
of ruin that was before them now looked like a giant anthill,
its material gathered together from whatever could be torn
from the surroundings. That would explain the destruction
they'd seen on the way in, why certain structures had been
targeted while others went untouched. Cass's heart revolted
at the idea that the pile might in fact be a hive full of Weir.
It was strange though. As she'd already noticed, many of
the buildings here were still generally intact. Why had the
Weir dragged so much material back from the outer parts
of the city?

Gamble clicked on through the channel.

"Eyes open. First sign of trouble, we head right back out

the way we came. Finn, take it reeeeal slow."

"Check," Finn responded.

Finn dropped the pace down again as they continued their approach. Within a hundred yards of the debris pile, the tackiness of the ground had increased to the point that Cass could actually feel it pulling at the bottom of her shoes. She glanced down again to see what was causing it. It was almost like a thin layer of tar.

"Dear God," Sky said aloud. Not through the channel, but actually out loud. Cass looked to him and then followed his gaze to what had caused the reaction. A thin cloud had moved across the sun, cutting the glare so that it no longer blinded them to the nature of the heap. Not debris.

Bodies.

Hundreds and hundreds and hundreds of corpses. Death on an unfathomable scale.

Cass looked down at the ground again and knew with sudden, horrible clarity what had so stained the ground. Asher's pronouncement of doom over the city echoed in her mind anew. That he would slake the thirst of Death with their blood, and glut the mouth of hell with their flesh. And here before them now was Asher's great monument, his utter desecration.

When Cass looked upon it again, something inside her broke. She knew she should be feeling horror and revulsion at the abomination outside the governor's gate. Instead, she felt nothing. It was as if her mind, unable to comprehend the reality, had flipped a safety switch and completely detached her emotions. Her eyes roved over the pile, taking in details: faces, hands, shoes. Even those details weren't enough for her mind to grasp hold of, to understand that the hill was not a single entity unto itself, but was instead comprised of countless individuals. Had that mass of dead flesh ever been actual living, breathing people? And yet it was impossible to tear her eyes away, for to look away was to accept what she was seeing as reality or to dismiss it as illusion, and she could do neither.

"Why would they do that?" Finn said, using the secure comm channel, and the question brought Cass back to herself. How long they'd all stood there in silence, Cass didn't know; she realized she'd ceased to notice even time passing. From his voice, she could tell how shaken Finn was.

"They didn't," Cass answered. "It was Asher. That's Asher's doing. His signature, so everyone would know this wasn't just the work of the Weir."

"What are we doin', Ace?" Sky asked. Cass looked over at the team lead; Gamble was staring hard at the pile, her mouth drawn in a tight, thin line. She didn't respond immediately. Several seconds passed.

"Ace?"

"I heard you," she answered, her tone clipped. After a few more seconds, she said. "Circle around, we'll hit the gate on the other side."

"You still wanna go in there?" Finn asked. It wasn't a challenge, but Cass could hear the uncertainty in the words. Uncharacteristic of Finn. Completely understandable.

"If we don't get the gear out of there, we're not gonna be long for this world."

"You think it's clear?" asked Sky.

"We'll find out."

"We have to do something about those bodies," Mouse said.

"Do what, Mouse?" Gamble said.

"We can't just leave 'em like that," Mouse replied. "Out in the open, to rot."

"Brother," Gamble said, turning to him, and her voice was warmer and kinder than Cass could remember ever having heard. "I know. That's my whole life, too. And I can't tell if I'm so angry it's making me sick, or if I'm so sick it's making me angry. But if we had a month with nothing else to do, that right there would still be too much for us."

He was silent while the truth of the matter sank in. Cass's mind hadn't even tried to imagine what Mouse was talking about. What would they do? Bury them? Burn them? The magnitude of either of those tasks was beyond Cass's ability to comprehend in any meaningful way. How could you bury an entire city?

"You think Swoop's in there?" Mouse said.

No one responded at first. And then.

"I could check," Finn answered. He turned to look back over his shoulder at Gamble. "What do you think, G?"

"Tell me about risk level," Gamble said.

Finn gave a little half-shrug. "Maybe none. Might be just the thing to tell the thousand Weir hiding in that compound that we're at the door."

Gamble weighed the options. After a moment, she said, "Hold off for now. I'm gonna go in, see if I can get to the cage. If I don't wake anything up, we'll load what we can. Then you can check for Swoop on our way out."

"Let me," Cass said. "Let me go in."

Gamble glanced over and shook her head.

"Gamble, I'm faster, I'm stronger. I can go where you can't. I can *see* what you can't." Cass removed her veil, revealed her Weir-eyes to emphasize her point. "And if there *are* any Weir in there, they might not even react to me."

"You don't know that," Gamble said.

"No, I don't. But I *do* know how they'd react to you," Cass answered. "Let me go in and scout it out at least."

"I can't allow that, Cass," Gamble said. Cass opened her mouth to argue, but Gamble held up her hand. "I appreciate it, I do. But if something went wrong, you wouldn't be able to coordinate a response. You're right, on your own you're way better suited for this than I am. But this is a team job, and you don't know how to run a team. So it's gotta be me."

"You oughta both go," Mouse said. Gamble looked over at him with a hint of frustration, but Mouse continued with a shrug of one shoulder. "You're both right. So put Miss Cass on point, and you back her up."

Gamble looked around at each of them in turn and when

she reached Cass, she shook her head. She didn't like it, but she couldn't argue.

"You guys are going to be the death of me," she said. And then she held up her pointer finger and made three small circles in the air which, judging from the reaction of the three men, meant something like *let's get to it*.

Finn resumed the point position and led them around to one of the other gates. It too was open, and he paused just outside. Gamble motioned for Sky. He glanced around at the buildings outside the compound and after a few moments, signaled back to her his preferred position. Gamble nodded. Sky winked at her and then headed off across the open ground towards the building he'd indicated, with Finn in tow.

Gamble took over and led Cass and Mouse into the courtyard of the compound. They came in from the side of the main building, moving at a slow walk. Cass scanned the exterior of the building, the place she'd called home for the past year. Inside the compound walls, everything was almost exactly as she remembered it. An island untouched by the storm that had ravaged everything just beyond its borders. Uncanny. The Weir had breached Morningside here, coming up through the emergency tunnel that led from the compound out under the city's wall; the tunnel that had long been a closely-guarded secret. Given the level of destruction outside the compound, Cass had assumed that it would be at its worst here, where the fury of the Weir was first unleashed. Instead, it was as if the compound had been the eye of the storm, the center of calm while the tempest raged all around.

They circled around to the front of the building, where a long concrete staircase led up to the main entrance. The heavy doors at the top were closed. Gamble stopped at the base of the stairs and surveyed the building, searching for signs of what might lay within. Cass and Mouse drew up close on either side of her.

"Hey, Ace," Sky's voice came across the secure channel,

"we're set. I've got eyes on you right now."

"Check," Gamble whispered back. There was a slight echo to it from Cass's perspective; she heard the whisper both from Gamble's mouth and as it transmitted with a slight delay across the comms. Normal pimming was instantaneous, but also sent a burst of signal that the Weir could track. Whatever system Gamble's team had figured out was low-frequency enough to escape the Weir's notice, but the delay was one of the side-effects.

Mouse went up the stairs first and Gamble followed after, but motioned for Cass to hold where she was. At the front entrance they took up positions at the door, off to one side. Gamble was crouched and Mouse stood tight behind her, holding his weapon up and ready with one hand, with the other hand her shoulder. Mouse squeezed Gamble's shoulder and at that signal, she tried the door with painstaking care. Sure enough after a few seconds, Gamble was able to ease the door open just enough to get a glimpse inside. A few moments later she pulled the door silently shut. She and Mouse returned to the bottom of the stairs.

"Door's good," Gamble said. "Front hall's clear."

"You just want to go in that way?" Cass asked.

"Tempting," Gamble answered. "But I think we better take the side passages."

Going through the front would give them the most direct route but they would have to pass through several large open areas with many entryways. There were side entrances they could use that would follow narrower passages, with fewer angles to cover.

"If we have to come out in a hurry, though, it's good to know the front's an option," she added. "Mouse, you're on the door."

"Check," Mouse responded. "Stay in touch."

"Yep."

"You be careful in there," Mouse said, and he said it almost casually, but he was only looking at Cass when he did.

Cass nodded. "See you soon."

Gamble led Cass around to the side of the building, right to the entrance Cass would have chosen if it'd been up to her. There was a stairwell that led down to a door, but before they took it, Gamble stopped and turned to Cass.

"I wish I had time to train you on this before we had to do it live," she said. "But two main rules." She held up one finger. "Constant communication." She held up a second finger. "When in doubt, slow down." Gamble ran her through a few basic hand signals: go, stop, look, I see, I hear, that direction, danger. It didn't take long.

"Also," Gamble said. "Doors. You're going to be doing the opening, so let me show you the routine."

Gamble got very hands-on, moving Cass where she wanted her to stand, positioning her, even putting her hand on top of Cass's when working the door handle to show her just how carefully to open it. Once she got Cass situated, she put her hand on Cass's shoulder.

"You hold just like that until I signal," said Gamble. "And that's like this." A moment later she squeezed Cass's shoulder, slowly and very deliberately.

"Got it," Cass said. Gamble quickly covered other scenarios: doors opening inward, doors opening outward, double doors. But the basics didn't change. Cass understood everything Gamble told her. Even so, Cass had an entirely new appreciation for Gamble and her team. She'd had no idea how complicated it could be to get a couple of people through a door safely.

"Stairs," Gamble said. She paused a moment, and then shook her head. "Never mind. I'll take point on stairs. Going up or coming down, just keep a hand on me so I know where you are."

"OK," Cass said. After the tutorial on doors, it struck Cass that apparently going up or down stairs was too complicated to cover in a short amount of time.

"One more thing," Gamble said. "If the boys start talking to us in there, you can click the channel to acknowledge. If they ask a question, one click for yes, two for no."

"Click the channel?"

"Just open and close the broadcast, without saying anything," Gamble explained. "Like this." And then, over comms, she said, "Boys, I'm going to click the channel, all right?"

"All right, check," Sky answered.

Gamble didn't say anything, but a moment later three clicks sounded on the comm channel.

"Got it?" Gamble asked.

Cass opened and closed the channel; one click for yes. Gamble chuckled once and then nodded.

"Then you're on the door," she said. Cass took her position, just as Gamble had showed her. Or, at least she thought she had, until Gamble gave her elbow a couple of strong pats to remind her to keep it tucked to her side. Cass made the adjustment and felt Gamble's hand drop on her shoulder.

"All right, boys," Gamble said, "we're going in."

NINE

"Haiku!"

The voice was thin and sharp above the noise on the street, but Haiku knew it instantly and smiled to himself. He turned back to find Wren hurrying towards him with jCharles in tow. They caught up quickly, and when Wren reached him, Haiku dipped his head in greeting and waited to hear what the boy had to say.

"I changed my mind," Wren said. "I'd like to come with you. I mean, if that's still OK."

Haiku nodded once and quickly took stock of the boy in front of him. Wren had his pack on, cinched and fitted well on his shoulders; the pack itself was quite compact.

"We'll be walking for a few days," Haiku said. "Are you sure you have everything you'll need?"

Wren nodded. "Yes, sir."

"He's got a good supply of food and water," jCharles added.

"Nights are going to be cold," Haiku said.

Wren nodded again, and Haiku was struck by the change that had come over the boy; he stood taller, his shoulders back, chest out, radiating a sense of confidence. The story Wren had told suggested he was no stranger to travel and hardship, but seeing him now gave Haiku a new perspective. It was one thing to hear the tale, another entirely to see for himself. If Wren was truly prepared for the journey ahead, he'd done a good job of packing only what he'd need. There was a small bulge on one side of the pack, but otherwise it seemed to fit well; not overloaded, not top heavy. It was a small test, and Wren had passed without even having been aware of the testing. Many such tests lay ahead for the boy, but this first, small as it was, lifted Haiku's spirits and gave him hope for the other, larger ones still to come.

"You can take it from here?" jCharles asked.

"Yes, thank you," Haiku said.

"All right... well..." jCharles said. He stood there for a moment, hands at his side. Wren turned back and hugged him around the waist.

"Thanks, jCharles. For taking care of me and everything."

jCharles laid his hands on Wren's back in an awkward embrace, patted the boy's shoulder.

"Sure thing, buddy," he said. "If your mama shows, I'll be sure to get word to you."

"OK."

The two separated, and jCharles looked down at Wren.

"Well. OK," he said. And then he looked up at Haiku, and Haiku could see the emotion there, the tears not yet formed, the uncertainty of what he was feeling or how to express it.

"We should get moving," Haiku said, more to provide jCharles with a way out than because it was true. "Don't worry, jCharles. I'll treat him like he's my own."

"Treat him like he's *my* own," the man said. And then with a final nod and a wave to Wren, he said "See ya, buddy," and quickly turned and headed back down the street. He didn't look back.

"All set?" Haiku asked. Wren nodded. "Then let's go."

Haiku held out a hand before him, and Wren started walking.

"I'm glad I caught up with you," Wren said. "I was afraid I might not be able to find you."

"I'm glad too," Haiku answered. "We're both fortunate." He didn't mention anything about having deliberately slowed his pace on his way out of the city, for just such an occasion.

"Can you tell me where we're going?" Wren asked.

"North for a while," Haiku said. "Then east."

"East?" Wren said. Haiku nodded. "Back towards the Strand?"

"Don't worry about that now, Wren," Haiku said. "We've many miles to go before we reach that point. Who can say what might happen between now and then?"

"I don't think that makes me feel any better."

"Good," Haiku said. "That will help you keep your eyes open and your wits about you, then."

Haiku walked with Wren just at his side, watched the boy's gait for a while, and adjusted his pace and stride to one that he was confident Wren could maintain for the time being. The boy would need all his energy once they got into the open. As they made their way through Greenstone's wild streets, Haiku observed Wren without his notice. In the short walk to the nearest gate, he discerned important facets of Wren's personality. There was hesitancy there, a tendency to rely on the guidance and direction of others, a complacency towards many of the people and activities that went on around him. Disappointing traits, but not unsurprising given the boy's age and recent history. Governor or not, he'd always been led, always been watched over, by his mother or his guardians. It showed in the way he carried himself. And yet, there were flashes here and there, marks of intuition or training unrefined. Occasionally the boy's eyes would linger on a passerby who watched too intently, or would take a second glance at someone changing direction without cause. In none of the cases was any threat presented, and in fact Wren had entirely failed to notice the two men that were actually trailing them. But he was alert and aware, present in the moment more so than most, and that was a start.

Haiku took them towards one of the gates to the west side of the city, avoiding the gate by which he entered the city. Though there was no obvious reason that anyone should have noticed his arrival or cared about his departure, it was nonetheless a valuable habit and one he didn't mind indulging. They were about fifty feet from the gate when Wren spoke.

"Do you think they'll follow us outside the city?" he asked, just loud enough to be heard over the general buzz of the street.

The question caught Haiku off guard, but there was no doubt who Wren had meant.

"I'm not sure," Haiku answered. "Do you recognize them?"

"No."

"When did you first notice them?"

"I'm not sure. I think they were outside the Samurai McGann when we came out. I'm not sure if it's the same people, but I think so."

Haiku nodded but didn't change course. They were too close to the gate now and any sudden deviation could alert their new friends.

"In a few more steps, I want you to stop suddenly," Haiku said. "As if you've forgotten something important. As if you want to go back to get it."

"OK," Wren said. "Say when." Another point in the boy's favor. He didn't question, wasn't confused by the request, just fell into the plan and waited for Haiku's signal.

They continued several more paces towards the gate, and then Haiku dipped his head slightly.

"Now."

Wren stopped immediately and quickly slapped his hand to his pants pocket. Haiku took two more steps and then turned halfway back, looking to Wren. Rather than focusing on the boy, he let his vision go wide and picked out the shapes of the two men he knew to be following them. Wren patted his pants pockets a few times, and then jammed his hand into his jacket, searching with increasing panic through the many pockets.

"I left it!" he said loudly. "I need to go back!"

"We can't," Haiku said, playing the role. "Whatever it is,

you don't need it. Come on."

"No, I can't! I really need it!" Haiku appreciated Wren's commitment. He'd grasped the intent immediately.

Haiku returned to Wren and knelt down in front of him, flicking his eyes first to one side and then to the other, as if in embarrassment at the outburst. In that split second, he'd absorbed all he'd needed. The two men were hanging back and had turned to one side, clumsily attempting to remain inconspicuous. They were trying to look like they were involved in a conversation of their own, but one of them was watching a little too intently out of the corner of his eye. That one had a long brown coat, and from the way he kept his hand in the coat pocket and his arm pressed to his side, Haiku knew he was concealing something long underneath it. A club maybe, or a gun that was something more than a pistol but not quite a long gun.

Haiku bent close to Wren and jabbed a finger in the boy's chest, as though he were quietly chastising him. But while he made an angry face and spoke through his teeth, he said, "They've either got something worked out with the guards at the gate, or they're going to follow us out."

Wren nodded.

"I want you to walk a step behind me, like you're sad, OK? Not too far back, close enough I can reach you if I need to. But let me get a feel for the guards."

Wren nodded. His eyes were clear, focused. He'd definitely done this sort of thing before. As Haiku stood, he noticed Wren had slipped a hand under his jacket and was keeping it there. He was gripping something near his belt.

Haiku turned and resumed his walk towards the gate. Wren trailed behind as instructed, just behind and slightly to his right, doing his best to play the part of the dejected child. Satisfied, Haiku turned his attention to the two Greenmen standing post at the gate. They kept a casual watch, their eyes roving and resting only lightly on any one person. But Haiku could tell from their posture and demeanor that these were seasoned guardsmen, not to be underestimated.

The Greenman on the left was about Haiku's height, solidly built and bearded. His companion was taller, leaner, with a harder look. The bearded man's eyes swept over Haiku once and then came back to meet Haiku's own gaze. Haiku maintained eye contact as he approached, and the guard's posture changed. The man stood up straighter, squared his shoulders, dipped his head forward. But to Haiku's relief, there was no change in the man's eyes, no dilation of the pupils, no sense of recognition. His eyebrows raised slightly as Haiku and Wren drew near, as if he were expecting a question. And most likely, that was all there was to it. The Greenman was reacting to Haiku's body language and was simply expecting to be approached and engaged in conversation.

Haiku smiled and inclined his head in greeting.

"Morning, sir," he said.

"Morning," the Greenman replied. His lean companion glanced over at the exchange, but resumed his languid watch over the crowds.

"I'm sorry to bother you," Haiku said, extending his hand for a handshake, and slowing his pace. In his palm, Haiku had a nanocarb chip, worth twenty Hard. "But there's a man in a brown coat who's been following me this morning. I'm sure it's nothing to be concerned about, but when he comes by, would you be kind enough to ask him what he's got under his coat?" The Greenman, knowing the protocol, shook Haiku's hand and didn't miss a beat in the exchange.

"We're not gonna stop anyone from leaving the city, sir," the Greenman said. Haiku didn't stop moving.

"I understand. But if you could just ask, I'd appreciate it."

The Greenman gave a curt nod as Haiku continued on by, through the gate, and out into the surrounding cityscape. He led Wren to the left out of the gate and once they'd cleared the entrance, he picked up the pace to an easy jog.

"Come quickly, Wren," he said. His eyes scanned their surroundings as they moved, picking up the angles and lines of sight. They only had a few seconds to find what he was looking for, and he found it in a tumbledown building that may once have been a simple storage shed, now little more than a heap of concrete, rebar, and rust.

"Here, in here," Haiku said, directing Wren through a hole in one side. Two walls were still mostly standing, and though the roof had completely caved in, there was a pocket of space large enough for them both. Haiku followed and turned back to watch the gate. The angle was sharper than he would have liked, but the vantage was good enough for his purposes. The two men who'd been following them had already passed through the gate, and at first Haiku was disappointed that his twenty Hard had gone to no use. But moments later, the bearded Greenman appeared, calling after them. The man in the brown coat didn't stop, but his companion glanced back over his shoulder at the guard. The Greenman called to them again, and they stopped. The companion turned fully back to face the guard and did the talking. Browncoat continued to scan the area. He was obviously agitated, searching for any sign or signal that might reveal where their would-be quarry had gone. There was a brief exchange, and the Greenman approached Browncoat with a hand raised in a placating manner. Haiku wondered what story the man was telling.

Browncoat was defensive, but after some back and forth with the Greenman, he finally pulled the coat open and flashed the weapon he'd been conspicuously trying to conceal. Haiku only saw it for an instant, and only in part, but it was enough for his mind to piece together. Not a gun, then. That was enough.

The Greenman nodded and waved the two on, no doubt wishing them a good morning. Browncoat grabbed his companion by the sleeve and dragged him on, headed the direction they'd last seen Haiku and Wren go. For Haiku's part, he'd felt his choice of hiding place had been too obvious, but speed had been of the utmost essence. Fortunately, there were many low buildings crowded together just outside this side of Greenstone's wall, creating many possible routes. The two men split up and dashed from one alley to the next, from one avenue to another, each searching wildly for whichever direction their targets had gone. It apparently hadn't occurred to either man that their potential prey might in fact be hiding instead of fleeing. They had no clue they'd been made.

Haiku considered the options. He had already evaluated the two men, subconsciously, automatically, the long years of training making the process background and nearly instantaneous. But no. He would wait. After two or three minutes, the two men wasted another half minute arguing, and then finally picked a direction and ran off. Haiku gave it another few minutes before he turned to look at Wren. The boy had moved back to the corner of the structure, and was crouched there, perfectly still, perfectly quiet, his eyes fixed intently on Haiku. Again, it was obvious just how used to this sort of situation he seemed to be. Not comfortable exactly, but competent certainly.

"We should be all right," Haiku said.

Wren nodded. Haiku slipped out of the space first and motioned for Wren to follow. The boy dutifully slipped in behind him without a word. They traveled westward, slipping out farther from the city than Haiku had originally planned to before they turned north. The morning was dry and cold, but the sun warmed pleasantly the blue-greys of their surroundings. It was something of a shock to the senses to return to the open after the vibrant chaos of Greenstone. The dead cityscape that stretched for miles in every direction seemed drained and stagnant by comparison. A colorless wash of jagged shapes, the ancient skeleton of a god long dead. But as they walked together in silence, Haiku felt tension seeping from his back and shoulders, and his mind grew quieter, calmer. His focus, sharper. He'd never much cared for crowds. It was good to be back out on the road, on the move.

•••

Wren had a thousand questions running through his mind, but he'd been afraid to ask any of them since they'd hidden from the men near the gate. It seemed safest to keep the silence, even though he wasn't sure if Haiku was wanting it or not. They'd walked a good twenty minutes or so without speaking, with Haiku leading him on a twisting and broken path. The older man changed their pace frequently, sometimes moving casually, other times with urgency and still others stopping altogether. It was an odd, rhythmless way to travel, but Wren had experienced something like it before. Three had had a similar way of moving through the landscape. Though, maybe similar wasn't quite the right idea. Haiku's movements, the way he scanned the environment, the broken rhythm, they were uniquely his own. But when taken all together, there was an underlying foundation that the two men shared. Like two painters who had studied under the same master, each unique expressions of another artist's influence.

Unlike Morningside, where crowds of people had roamed freely outside the wall during the day, Greenstone's populace seemed hesitant to stray too far out. There wasn't really much traffic to or from Greenstone even on the busiest of days, but there were even fewer travelers who would brave the winter months in the open. The byways through which they traveled were empty and undisturbed by any signs of recent travel. Every once in a while Wren heard a distant scuffle or scrape, some unknown source of movement that could have been from their pursuers, or from the wind, or merely from his imagination. Haiku seemed unconcerned by them, or at least no more concerned by them than he was by anything else.

"The men in Greenstone," Haiku said after a time, and Wren jumped at the unexpected sound of his voice. He looked up at the man. "Do you have any guess as to who they might have been?"

Wren shook his head. "Not really, no," he said. "I'd never seen them before." But a moment later, he added,

"Except..." and then trailed off, as something from his subconscious bubbled up. He hadn't thought about it at all before, and hadn't even been consciously thinking about it now. But somewhere inside, his mind had done its own work and suddenly presented him with the idea.

"Oh," he said. "I wonder if they were the Bonefolder's guys."

Haiku nodded once, as if he'd already suspected it. Wren wondered if the man had been looking to him for confirmation, or if he'd already known it himself and was merely testing Wren's observations. It was hard to escape the thought that Haiku had been evaluating everything he did since they first met.

"How far out do you think they'll continue to look for us?"

"I don't know," Wren said. "I don't know what they wanted."

"What do you *think* they wanted?"

Wren was quiet for a few seconds, and then answered, "Me." Haiku dipped his head again in that same ambiguous gesture. "But I don't know what for."

"The Bonefolder has a long memory."

"You know her?"

"Of her," Haiku said. "Though it would be difficult not to."

"Did we lose them?" Wren asked.

"Not exactly," Haiku answered. Wren felt a wave of anxiety rise up, and he glanced back over his shoulder. He'd thought for sure that the men were nowhere around. "Don't worry, they're not following us," Haiku said. "We're following them."

"What?" Wren said. "Why?" He asked the question without really wanting to know the answer.

"How can we be certain to avoid them if we don't know where they are?" Haiku said. Then he looked down at Wren with a slight smile. "I thought they would have given up by now. Let's go see what they want."

Haiku's pace and posture changed immediately, and he strode forward with a boldness that Wren hadn't seen from him before. They moved quickly through the alleys and avenues, and Wren had to walk fast with the occasional jogging step to keep up. He couldn't tell what it was that Haiku was seeing, or how he could possibly know where the other men had gone. But after maybe two minutes Haiku led him out of a narrow lane between two buildings and there, twenty feet away, stood the man in the brown coat and his lanky companion, headed away from them.

"Gentlemen," Haiku said. The two men were startled by the sound of Haiku's voice, and they twisted around, searching for the source. They both looked plenty surprised when they saw who had called them. Browncoat already had his weapon out from under his coat, the first glimpse Wren had of it. He hadn't seen anything quite like it before; it was a narrow cylinder, sleek and very dark blue almost to the point of black, and just a little bit shorter than the man's arm. Browncoat held it towards the end, where it tapered into a grip. A stunstick, maybe, though if so it was bigger than any Wren had seen previously.

"We all seem to be headed the same way," Haiku said, continuing his approach. Wren trailed along behind him, gradually allowing the distance between them to open up. "Perhaps we should walk together."

Browncoat and his friend exchanged a look.

"Well yeah," Browncoat said, and he lowered his weapon to one side, just next to his leg. Not quite hiding it, but maybe trying to make it less conspicuous. "Sure. Where you folks headed?"

"Oh, you know," Haiku said. "Out that way." Wren had fallen back about twelve feet behind Haiku, so he couldn't see his face. But it sounded like he was smiling. He walked right up to the two men, no more than arm's length away, and stopped.

"Well," said Browncoat. "You're welcome to tag along as you like."

"As long as you're not headed back to Greenstone," Haiku said. Browncoat's friend flicked his eyes to Browncoat, but Browncoat kept his eyes on Haiku and just shook his head. The friend settled back a step, just to Haiku's right.

"Naw, friend. We're just leaving there."

Haiku nodded. "Sure. I just thought maybe you might need to get back to the Bonefolder."

Browncoat smiled. Wren reached under his coat and drew his knife.

In the next instant, Browncoat's friend shot forward and wrapped his arm around Haiku's neck in a chokehold, spun him, and then jerked him backwards. Browncoat whipped his weapon up and held it an inch below Haiku's chin. The weapon emitted a menacing hum, like a swarm of hornets. It all happened so fast, so smoothly, that Haiku hadn't even had time to react. He was caught fast between the two of them, his hands by his waist and held out to the sides in surrender. Wren gripped his knife tight in his fist in a reverse grip, the blade along his forearm, and held it down by his side. If they came for him, *when* they came for him, he didn't want them to see the knife before they felt it.

"You seem like a pretty smart fella," Browncoat said to Haiku. "I'm sure you got this all figured out, but just so we're clear, we're just taking the kid. We don't have no problems with you, and we don't have to. You just keep right on walking like you were. No problems."

In the flurry of action, Haiku had gotten turned to the side, so Wren could see the faces of all three men. Haiku seemed perfectly relaxed. Maybe even a little amused. He still had a slight smile on his face.

"I certainly don't want to upset the Bonefolder," Haiku said.

"Like I said," Browncoat answered. "Smart fella."

"So it *is* the Bonefolder then," Haiku said. Browncoat's eyes narrowed and he frowned a little at that. "Unfortunately, we *do* have a problem then. I'm taking this boy to someone else, you see, and I don't want to upset that someone else either."

"Don't think you got much say in the matter, friend."

"What if we split him?" Haiku said. "Then we wouldn't have to argue. I'll even let you have first pick of halves."

"We're taking the kid. Only choice you got is whether you walk away or don't."

"Oh, come now," Haiku said. "I have many more choices than that." And then his smile went away. "Eyes, for example. Knees. Or hands, perhaps."

"What?"

"Tell you what. I'll let *you* choose. Eyes, knees, or hands."

"You uh... you taking the kid to a chop shop?"

"Oh, no no," Haiku said. "We're talking about you. Of those three, which *one* do I allow you to keep?"

"Come on, Rook," Browncoat's friend said. "Just juice him and let's go."

"Shut up, Grigg," Browncoat, or Rook, snarled.

"He can't, Grigg" Haiku said. "Not until you let go. Unless you want to get juiced too."

Just as Grigg seemed to understand the problem, Haiku reached up and casually and locked his grip on Grigg's forearm and wrist.

"So which is it, Rook?" Haiku continued. He hadn't raised his voice at all, or even changed its tone. He was still perfectly calm, perfectly relaxed. "Eyes, knees, or hands. You only get one. What'll you keep?"

Rook just stared back at Haiku, eyes hard, jaw clenched. He was doing his best to look mean and in control, but even from where Wren stood, he could tell all the man's confidence had melted away. Haiku gave it a few beats, and then smiled again.

"Of course, you could just walk away. Tell the Bonefolder you got held up by the Greenmen at the gate, long enough for us to get away. She might be disappointed, but at least you'll have your health."

Rook moved the weapon from under Haiku's chin up to right in front of his face and said "You look here–"

"No," Haiku barked in a loud voice. Rook flinched at the

sound, and Haiku hunched down slightly and Grigg made a sound like he was on fire. Then Haiku stood straight again and Grigg went skidding backwards about eight feet and fell on his backside. Haiku brought his hand up in a half-circle and made a little loop with it, and Wren was still trying to figure out what had happened when he realized that Haiku had the weapon now. He hadn't even moved that fast. But Rook was standing there eyes wide with the business end of his own stick so close to his left eyeball it looked like it might be touching his lashes.

"Eyes, knees, or hands, Rook," Haiku said. Rook didn't make a sound or even blink. Grigg was still sitting on the ground, afraid to make a move. Then Haiku smiled his slow, wide smile. "Or you can walk away."

Rook didn't stir at first, but after a few seconds he held his hands out to the side and took a cautious step backwards. When Haiku didn't react, he took another step back, and then another.

"See," Haiku said. "We're both smart fellas."

Rook glanced over at Wren. "Ah ah," Haiku said sharply. "Best take the long way around."

Rook worked his jaw, but it was obvious any fight he thought he had in him was gone. Haiku stepped to one side and motioned at Grigg to get up. Grigg did so, awkwardly, and limped his way over to Rook.

"No hard feelings, gentlemen," Haiku said. "I'm not a man of grudges."

"We'll be seeing you," Rook said.

"Enjoy it while you can," Haiku answered.

Rook scowled at that last retort, but apparently couldn't come up with one of his own. He backhanded Grigg in the arm and the two of them slunk away. Haiku stood watching them until they were some distance away, and then finally returned to Wren, switching off Rook's weapon as he did so.

As he drew near, he said, "I assume you can contact jCharles?"

Wren nodded. "I can send him a pim."

"You may want to let him know about the Bonefolder."

"OK," Wren said. And he was about to go internal and request the connection when he noticed Haiku's face change to an expression of mild concern, or maybe rebuke.

"Well now, little one," he said. "What were you planning to do with that?"

He nodded towards Wren's side. It took a moment before Wren understood. He looked down at his hand, where he was still gripping his knife.

"I thought we might be in some trouble," Wren said.

"Oh, well, that was nothing for anyone to get hurt over," Haiku answered. "Those poor boys were just doing as they were told. They didn't know any better."

"If you didn't want to fight them, why didn't we just avoid them?"

Haiku looked at him for a moment and a kindness came into his eyes. "We have a long road ahead. I thought you'd sleep easier knowing these fellows weren't going to be a problem."

"I thought we'd already lost them."

"Thinking and knowing aren't the same. You can run away from a thing, Wren, but as long as you're thinking of it, you haven't truly escaped it. And now you know for sure."

He motioned towards the knife. "May I see it?"

Wren nodded and held the knife out grip first for Haiku. The man took it with care and held it, turned it over a couple of times, felt the weight, the balance.

"It's a fine blade," he said. He flipped it around and returned it in the same manner as Wren had presented to him. And then he smiled again, the same, almost sad smile Wren had seen back in the Samurai McGann when they first met. "I recognize the work."

Wren returned the blade to its sheath in his belt under his coat, and Haiku nodded westward. The two fell back into step. Their pace was much smoother now, steadier. Wren pimmed jCharles and briefly explained the encounter with Rook and Grigg. Apparently jCharles knew who the two were and had even seen them nosing around the day before. He apologized several times and said Wren wouldn't have to worry about anything like that happening again. He didn't explain and Wren didn't ask. They said their goodbyes again, and then Wren returned his focus to the journey at hand.

After a few minutes of walking, Haiku stopped Wren with a gesture, and then crossed over to the other side of the street. There was a four-story building there, largely crumbling like its neighbors. Haiku stood a few feet from it and looked up to the higher windows on the upper floors. Wren couldn't tell what he was looking at, or looking for. He couldn't see anything special about it that should draw his attention. Then, in a swift motion, Haiku pitched the weapon he'd plucked from Rook's hand, and it sailed up and through one of the broken-out windows on the third floor. It landed with a ringing clatter, went quiet, and then sounded again with another, more muffled impact, possibly lower down in the building. Haiku returned looking satisfied, and motioned to Wren to carry on.

"Hopefully no one will go looking in there," Haiku said. "But if someone does, I hope it's a good guy who really needs it."

"What was that thing anyway?" Wren asked.

"A sonic baton," Haiku answered. Wren had no idea what that was, and Haiku must have noticed his lack of understanding because a moment later, he continued. "It's a contact weapon that uses sound to do unpleasant things to your insides. Depending on the power, they can be mildly distressing to lethal. That was one of the bad ones." And then after a moment, he said. "I believe the street term for one is a 'juicer', if that tells you anything."

Wren nodded and tried not to think about what that implied.

"You don't think we should have kept it?" he asked.

"I don't typically like to carry weapons," Haiku said.

"Not even a knife?"

"Well, yes, of course, a knife. Everyone should carry a knife. That's just good sense."

"But not other things? A sword or a gun or anything?"

"No."

"And you travel out in the open a lot?"

"I suppose that depends on your definition of 'a lot'."

Wren shrugged. "Everyone I've ever traveled with outside has always carried at least one. Usually a lot more. It just seems like the kind of thing you might need, I guess."

"Well, if I ever really *need* a weapon," Haiku said smiling down at him, "there's usually one around."

After that, they walked on for a time mostly in silence. Haiku didn't seem to mind the occasional question, but Wren did get the impression he preferred the quiet. After an hour or so of mostly westward travel, they took a short break, each sipping water.

"We'll turn north now," Haiku said. "I hope we won't be more than four days, but we'll just have to see what comes our way."

"The man you're taking me to," Wren said. "What's his name?"

Haiku looked at him for a moment and then said, "That, I'm afraid, is not mine to give."

"What do you think he'll do?"

Haiku shook his head. "That too is something we'll just have to see. I have my hopes, but..." He trailed off and looked towards the north. "It is long since he has concerned himself with the troubles of the world. He may very well do nothing."

Wren hadn't yet figured out what he'd been expecting from this journey, but those words certainly weren't anything he'd considered. Was this whole trip going to be wasted? What if Mama came to Greenstone and he wasn't there, and it was all for nothing? He glanced back the way they'd come, thinking about what lay behind.

"As I said before, Wren, there are no guarantees,"

Haiku said. And when Wren looked back, he saw the man was watching him. "But that way," he nodded towards Greenstone, "lies a life paralyzed by fear, marked by inaction. You rejected it before. Do not allow your heart to bend you back with illusions otherwise."

Wren dropped his gaze to the ground, partially out of sadness and partially out of shame that Haiku had read him so completely, and had spoken so truly. They rested a few more minutes in silence and then, at Haiku's signal, they hoisted their packs, turned their faces to the north, and set off together. And though he felt a longing to do so, Wren did not allow himself to look back.

TEN

Painter had delivered his message, just as he'd been instructed. And now he wanted nothing more than to turn away. To hide himself, while the Weir did their work. Asher had led him to the top of a tall building outside the town's wall, commanded him to watch. To bear witness.

The people of this small town had refused his offer. Just as all those other towns before them had done. Just as they always would. Painter knew it was a false choice he presented them, and there was little hope indeed that any would accept his terms. Service to Asher, or annihilation. Who would choose to swear allegiance to a disembodied power?

Briargate, it was called. Named for its single, heavily-fortified main gate, no doubt. It was truly a fearsome thing to behold, covered as it was in sharpened spines as long as a man was tall. They had trusted in their gate, comforted by the knowledge that it had never before been breached. A false hope, the emptiness of which they were only now learning.

There had been a brief battle, as the guards of Briargate had courageously stood their ground against the tide of Asher's thralls. But they had fallen victim to a simple ruse. While Asher had driven countless of the Weir under his control into the barbs of the Briargate, his select few had scaled the wall on the opposite side of the small enclave.

Snow was one of those, her dancer's grace turned to deadly purpose. It hadn't taken them long to cut their way to the gate, and to open it from the inside.

The battle was over, but the massacre continued unabated as Asher poured out his wrath and hatred on those who dared oppose him. It wasn't enough to slay the warriors of the town. The Weir, driven into a frenzy by Asher's malevolence, were tearing the town apart, rending any and all they found. Painter had seen enough. The carnage was overwhelming, the mindless destruction too shocking to behold any longer.

He turned and started back towards the stairwell that would lead him down, away from the madness.

"No!" Asher's voice screamed from the center of his mind. "No, Painter! Return to your place! I have not released you from your duty!" There was a raw anger in his words, but something else. A perverse giddiness, as he tested his control over the numbers of Weir and exacted his vengeance on yet another town full of innocents.

Asher couldn't control him directly, couldn't force Painter to watch. But he still held power over Snow, and that alone was enough to command Painter's obedience. Painter returned to his position, but kept his eyes lowered. Asher might be able to pinpoint his location, but he couldn't see through Painter's eyes. Not yet, anyway.

"You must watch, Painter," Asher said. "You must understand, this is *their* choice. This is the harvest they reap when they refuse my generosity. Behold it! Drink it in! And perhaps next time you will plead with more passion, and I will be able to spare the innocent."

Painter stood on the roof of the building, eyes closed, with the terrible sounds carried on the wind, and Asher lingering in his mind. Asher had said this was their harvest. But Painter could not escape the knowledge that he had planted the seeds.

ELEVEN

There was something deceptive about Haiku's pacing, Wren thought. When they'd started out, he hadn't struggled to keep up at all. It hadn't been *easy* exactly, but he'd been surprised that it hadn't been harder. After Haiku's comment about needing to make good time, Wren had immediately flashed back to his journey across the Strand, when Three had pushed them as hard and as fast as they could possibly go, and even that hadn't been enough. In contrast, Haiku seemed to be holding something back. Even after the first few miles, Wren had felt certain that he could have covered more ground in that time. They finished the first day and though Wren was tired, he was pleased with himself and thought that all the travel he'd done lately must have strengthened him more than he'd realized.

It was early in the second day that he started to feel the first pangs of doubt. By noon, he'd lost his confidence, and by midafternoon he was certain he'd never be able to keep going. It wasn't that Haiku was going too fast. It was that he never slowed. He kept the same, loping gait, hour after hour after hour. And he made no allowance for Wren at all. Breaks were rare, and the few they took were short. Haiku even insisted that they eat on the move. He had some kind of schedule worked out as far as Wren could figure; at times he forced Wren to drink water or to eat, regardless of whether Wren felt hungry or thirsty. Strangely, Haiku's demeanor hadn't changed at all; when he spoke to Wren, his voice was still warm and kind. But his treatment was indifferent, also to the point of callousness. At one point Wren got a small rock in his boot, and Haiku refused to stop even long enough for Wren to remove it. Eventually it got so troublesome that Wren stopped anyway. It only took a few moments to take care of it, but Haiku kept right on walking, and Wren was forced into a light jog to catch back up. That change in rhythm threw his body for a loop, and made the rest of the day's journey even tougher. Within the hour, Wren was already wondering whether or not it would have been better just to keep the rock in his shoe. As they reached into the late afternoon of the second day, he could hardly walk a straight line. His head was light and his legs leaden.

That night they took refuge in a small wayhouse, which offered security but little else; there was no bed, no water filtration system, and only a single, dull light that burned brownish. A concrete cell, eight feet long and six feet wide, with a foul-smelling drain in the center of the room. Wren looked at the floor with its water spots and stains. The thought of having to lie down on that floor made him nauseous, but the idea of trying to stand up the whole night was worse. In the end, he took to sitting in one corner and laying his pack in his lap to prop his head on.

Just before Haiku turned off the light, he came and stood over Wren.

"I know it's hard, Wren," Haiku said. "But we must keep our pace."

"I'm trying, Haiku. I really am. But I just don't think I can."

"You can," Haiku answered. "You may not believe it now, but you will after you've done it. And don't worry. I promise, you won't die walking." He laid a hand on the top of Wren's head. "You'll pass out before that." He smiled, but Wren couldn't tell if he was joking or not.

That night was a torturous one, as Wren's body fought

with itself, desperate for sleep, but unable to shut out the pain from the concrete floor. Somehow it was the longest night Wren could remember having, and yet morning still came too soon.

The third day was a blur of grey landscape and pain. Haiku had steered clear of any known settlements, so there was nothing for Wren's mind to latch onto to separate one mile from the next. For all he knew, Haiku could have been leading him in a circle no more than twenty feet from where they'd started their morning.

Sometime around noon, the hallucinations started. Dreams mixed with reality. More than once, the cityscape became the Strand, Haiku became Three. Wren had been here before. He knew what happened. But where was Mama? Sometimes he would find that he was opening his eyes without any memory of having closed them. How long had they been closed? Had he been sleepwalking? His mind kept returning to the mistake he had made, agreeing to this. Why had he ever thought going with Haiku was what he was supposed to do? He remembered having made the decision, but all the reasons for it had fled. Fragments of thought swept through, flashes of memory, sudden impressions that dissolved before he could capture or recognize them. His mind became a frenzy of disconnected and troubling images like the nightmares brought on by a high fever.

And while Wren was trapped in his own personal hell, Haiku kept walking, and walking, and walking, and somehow Wren's body kept at it too. Mechanically, as if picking a foot up and putting it down again was all he had ever done and all he would ever do.

That night they found an abandoned high-rise and Haiku had him walk up to the sixth floor. The Weir came out as the sun slipped below the horizon, their lonely and mournful cries echoing through the otherwise empty streets and alleyways. Haiku forced Wren to eat some of his rations and once even had to wake him up to finish chewing the bite in his mouth. After that, Wren curled up in one corner with his pack as a pillow and his coat over his head. He slept deeply and unmoving until Haiku woke him at first light.

When he rose that morning, everything hurt. Feet, knees, hips, shoulders, eyes. Every part of him ached with a dull and hollow pain, and Wren felt like he was coated in a clammy film. It was the same feeling he always got right before he threw up, except it didn't go away. He had slept, but his body was far from rested.

It was no easy task getting down the six flights of stairs, with each one threatening to buckle Wren's legs and send him tumbling. He gripped the rusted railing as they descended, knowing full well that if he did fall, he would never be able to stop himself. When they reached the ground floor, his heart dropped to see Haiku resume his long stride again, even, measured, sure-footed, just as if this was the very first day of their journey. Wren hated him then. Not with passion, but with clinical detachment, as if the man was a thing that simply should not be. Always ahead, always threatening to get even farther away.

At some point early on in that fourth day, Wren took to watching the ground just a foot or so in front of him. He'd find a crack or a spot or some swirl in the concrete dust and he'd tell himself to walk that far. And when he reached it, he'd find another. And another. It wasn't quite a game, because there was never any fun or joy in reaching the goal. But it kept him moving and it gave him something to focus his mind on. Letting his mind wander, that had been his mistake from the day before. Today, he would control his attention, fix it on something, anything, to keep it from running wild.

The change was so gradual that Wren didn't notice it at first. Not for a long while, in fact. But as he continued his cheerless "game", it occurred to him that for landmarks he was finding fewer and fewer defects in the pavement, and more and more patterns in the dust. And when his mind awoke to that, he then noticed that his footing was less stable and each step took more effort. Not just from the fatigue.

Wren looked up and found that the landscape had transformed around him. Gone were the recognizable ruins of manmade structures, the ones where most of the original shape and structure could be determined. Here and there were rounded lumps that might once have been buildings. The ground beneath his feet was thick with some combination of concrete dust and ash. Reflexively, Wren stopped and looked around. It was the same in every direction. And it finally struck him, like a surprise punch to the gut.

They'd crossed into the Strand.

And from the looks of it, they'd done so miles ago. A panic surged up in Wren's chest, the associations from his first encounter with the Strand too strong to ignore. This was the place that had given him his first taste of true, soulbreaking loss. This was where Mama had died.

Haiku had told him they'd be going east. Towards the Strand. He hadn't said anything about actually going *into* it. Wren turned back to find Haiku, to call out to him, to ask him what was happening and why they were here. But Haiku, of course, hadn't stopped when Wren had and he'd pulled far enough away that Wren wasn't sure the man would be able to hear him even if he yelled. And he wasn't even sure he *could* yell. Wren started moving again, trying to catch up. The loose powder of the Strand shifted like a fine sand beneath each footstep, making travel more difficult even without the previous three days' worth of exhaustion. It was a mighty struggle, but Wren finally managed to get within what he guessed was earshot.

"Haiku!" he called. The man didn't slow or turn. "Haiku!" he called again.

Haiku looked back over his shoulder but continued his march.

"What are we doing? Where are you taking me?"

"I can't hear you, Wren," Haiku answered. "You'll have to come closer."

"Can't you just wait?" Wren asked, but Haiku had

already turned away. Wren pushed on, gaining ground with bitter slowness. He finally drew up behind Haiku. "What are we doing here?"

"Walking," Haiku said.

"But why? Why the Strand?"

"So we reach our destination."

Wren had run out of patience long ago. The words came out harsh.

"Tell me where we're going! I demand it!"

Haiku looked at him sidelong. "Be careful, little one. You were never governor to *me*."

"Haiku, please," Wren said, exasperated. "I'm too tired."

"Then perhaps you should save your energy for something other than questions," Haiku said, and then he lengthened his stride for a few steps, pulling three feet ahead. Under normal circumstances, that distance would have meant nothing. To Wren, then, at that moment, it was a gulf too wide to cross.

Some time later, Haiku allowed a merciful break. Wren laid down on the concrete silt and fell into a nearly immediate sleep. When Haiku woke him, he was certain that he'd only blinked. But Haiku assured him they had to keep moving. They were in the Strand after all. There would be no wayhouses, no place to hide tonight.

As he'd struggled to his feet and tried to don his pack, Wren lost his balance and went down hard on his hands and knees. For a moment his vision darkened at the edges. It was then he knew his body had reached its absolute physical limit. He'd given all his body had to give, really and truly. Haiku had told him he'd pass out before he died. And here he was, staring over the edge, down into darkness. He'd come as far as his body would allow. Haiku couldn't ask anything more.

"We must go, Wren," Haiku said. "Now."

"I can't, Haiku," Wren said. "My legs. I can't."

Haiku stood over him for a moment. And then he said, "Then you'll have to crawl." He said it without emotion, neither anger nor reproach nor sadness. Simply stated.

And to Wren's utter disbelief, Haiku turned away and started off again. At that ruthless, relentless pace.

Wren stayed there on his hands and knees watching him go. Surely he'd stop. He'd turn back and see that Wren wasn't giving up of his own accord. Surely he'd come back. But Haiku kept getting smaller and smaller and showed no sign of slowing. Wren lowered his head then, rested his forehead on the rough ground, felt the grit grind into his skin. He closed his eyes just for a moment.

And Three was there, crouching next to him.

"Hey, kiddo," Three said.

Wren kept his head on the ground, his eyes squeezed shut. Even in the fog, he knew Three wasn't really there. But Wren needed him to be there, and as long as he kept his eyes closed, he thought maybe Three wouldn't slip away. In his mind's eye, Three was crouched down beside him, sitting back on his heels and resting his forearms on his knees the way he had.

"Bad place for a nap," said Three.

Wren shook his head.

"I can't, Three. I can't keep up."

Three nodded and looked up after Haiku.

"Well," he said. "It'll be a long while yet before he gets out of sight. Don't worry about keeping up." He looked back down at Wren. "How about you just get out of the dirt?"

Wren, in his delirium, opened his eyes to look at Three and in that instant the man was gone. Of course he was gone. He had never been there. But even knowing that, his words hung in Wren's mind. Wren took a deep breath. Just get out of the dirt. Stand up. Even that seemed like too much to ask. But he could at least try. Wren pushed himself back to his knees and then, with all the effort he could muster, he planted one foot and used his hands to lever himself up. It took everything he had. But a few moments later he was standing.

Haiku was by that time a good thirty yards distant. Wren

couldn't keep up. He knew that. But a moment ago, he'd known he couldn't even get to his feet, and yet here he was, standing. Maybe he could take one step.

And he did. And if he had taken that one, could he take just one more?

Yes.

Those first few steps did everything they could to remind him that he had reached the limits of his physical body; they screamed his limitations, his doubts, his failures. But something kindled in his spirit. Through the pain of his body and the anguish of his mind, Wren found his feet taking one more step, and one more, and then another, and another. And the barrier fell.

The torment didn't disappear, not by any means. But it became less important somehow; distant, less meaningful. His body was moving, he was making progress. Wren felt as if he'd been lifted up to some higher place, freed from the confines of his physical world. Maybe not removed, exactly. There was probably a word for it, but Wren couldn't find it at the moment. He was exhausted beyond belief and exhilarated at the same time. He stretched his stride, each step building confidence now instead of robbing it. And to his astonishment, he found himself not just keeping pace with Haiku, but actually gaining ground.

It took him nearly half an hour to catch up. When he did so, Haiku glanced back at him over his shoulder and just smiled. No greeting, no encouragement. But there was something like an I-told-you-so in that look.

From that point on, Wren's entire perspective shifted. The fog burned away and he started noticing more of his surroundings than he ever had, even when they'd first started out. Everything took on a clarity and sharpness that he'd never seen before. Each blown-out foundation and collapsed structure revealed their unique nature as he passed them. The ash and concrete dust under his feet was no longer a single blanket, it was a sea of individual grains beyond counting. All the world seemed to have fallen into a rhythm that matched his own; his breathing, his footsteps, his heartbeat, connected with the world at large.

The Strand lost its dreadful oppressiveness and Wren's eyes opened to the expanse as it truly was rather than as he had first perceived it to be. There was no threat here. The location wasn't evil in its own right. It was a melancholy place, certainly. A monument to the worst that had befallen the old world. But that world was one Wren had never known; he was aware of the weight of history that lay over the Strand, yet it didn't stir any memories of what had been before. And with the fear removed by his inexplicable euphoria, he discovered the peace that the Strand offered as well. Though the air had a powdery scent from the dust he'd kicked up, there was an underlying freshness to it that had previously escaped his notice. The sun was bright, the sky clear. Wren was likely only one of two people for miles around and that thought brought with it a sense of unexpected freedom.

Then again, maybe in his current state he was just imagining it all. Maybe this bizarre sense of well-being that had come upon him was what happened to people right before they died. If so, dying didn't seem quite as bad as he'd imagined. There probably wasn't a better place to do it. At least it was quiet here.

Wren settled into a matched pace with Haiku just a few feet ahead of him. He had a vague notion to say something to the man, but on second thought it seemed unnecessary. Mere words could only detract from the action that had already spoken for itself. And he didn't really care where they were headed anymore.

Over the next hour or so – Wren couldn't be sure because he'd lost all sense of time – the terrain began to change again. The buildings stood a little higher, the ruins clustered a little more tightly. One structure in particular stood out prominently ahead; it was still distant but to Wren's surprise it almost looked like it was intact. It was wider than it was tall and rounded where Wren had expected corners. Some kind of squat plug of a tower, just a couple of stories high. Whatever it was, the building struck such a contrast with its surroundings that Wren knew immediately that it was their destination. It wasn't that far off, and they still had plenty of daylight left, but Haiku maintained the same pace.

They continued on and Wren lost and regained sight of the tower several times as they wound their way through the tumbledown structures that dotted the landscape. Most of the Strand was soft and rolling, covered in that fine, shifting dust and ash that blew and whirled and made walking wearisome. But here the land took on a jagged brokenness; rusting girders jutting at odd angles, like broken finger bones clawing up from their giant's grave below. And once the image fixed in his mind, Wren couldn't escape the feeling that he was walking through a city's skeleton.

It took a lot longer to reach the tower than he'd anticipated, and as they drew nearer, it became clear why. In the absence of familiar landmarks, Wren had judged the building to be three or four stories high at the most. Now he realized he'd horribly misjudged the size. The tower was immense. It was the width that had deceived him; most of the tall buildings he'd seen in his life had been proportioned much differently. This one was half again as wide as it was tall, and now, closer to it, Wren guessed it must have been nearly twelve stories high. There was a thickness to it, too, a massive solidity, like someone had started sculpting it from a single block of steel and lost interest before they'd even gotten halfway done.

The whole thing was a dull, steel grey, somehow duller than the concrete-sand that swirled all around it. There were no windows that Wren could see, though it seemed to have many protrusions and vents all around. As he was studying these things, the world opened up before him into a wide plain. Haiku halted and Wren came to a stop beside him. At first, Wren thought Haiku was scouting out the area ahead. They'd reached a border of some kind, and the next two or three hundred yards were mostly flat and ominously empty. Whether the buildings that once stood there had all been completely destroyed or had never been built in the first place, it was impossible to tell. But there was nothing except open land between them and their destination. Wren scanned the plain, wide and grey. Little eddies of dust swirled up and chased themselves into oblivion. After a moment, something else drew Wren's eye. About a third of the way down from the top of the building, there was a narrow platform or walkway with a thin line of a guardrail.

And there was someone standing at the rail.

It was small and difficult to make out against the mercury-grey backdrop, but once Wren had spotted it, there was no mistaking it for anything else. The figure was just standing there, hands on the rail.

Haiku raised a hand high above his head to signal the figure, or maybe in greeting. The figure made no apparent movement in response.

"Is that the person you're taking me to meet?" Wren asked.

"It is," Haiku said. The figure still hadn't moved.

"Maybe he doesn't see us," Wren said.

"He does," Haiku said as he lowered his hand. "He just doesn't care." He readjusted his pack and resumed walking.

Crossing that final stretch seemed to take three times as long as it should have. Wren's euphoria burned off and anxiety grew as they made their way through the dead space. Some of it came from the natural fear of uncertainty; the journey had so commanded Wren's thoughts that he'd hardly thought about what would happen when they actually reached the end. But walking across that wide open space brought on the uncanny feeling of being watched, not just from the structure but from all around. Wren couldn't stop himself from frequently glancing up at the walkway. And always, the lone figure was there, unmoved.

And then, when they were fifty yards or so away, he looked up and the figure was nowhere to be seen.

From that distance, Wren could see the structure wasn't

like any kind of building he'd seen before. The whole thing seemed to be made entirely of metal. It was smooth with no sign of seams or cracks, which gave the impression that it really had been formed from a single, massive block of steel.

When they finally reached the structure, Haiku led Wren around the base to a single, heavy door. It was the same flat grey color as the rest of the building and heavily riveted. To Wren's surprise, it was also opened inward an inch or two.

Haiku stopped just outside with his hand on the door and looked at Wren.

"If everything goes well, Wren, this is the true beginning of your journey," he said. "All that has come before, all that you've been through to get here will seem small in comparison."

"Do you mean small like, a small price to pay?" Wren asked. "Or small like it was nothing compared to how hard it's about to get?"

Haiku gave him a tired smile. "Both," he said. And then added, "If everything goes well."

He turned back to the door and paused for a long moment, his head dipped. Like he was gathering his thoughts. Or maybe steeling himself.

Finally, Haiku pushed the door inward and motioned Wren inside. It was dark and Wren hesitated at the threshold, testing the air. It was pleasantly warm and though there was an underlying industrial smell, it wasn't stale or moldy or damp. Not at all like he'd expected. The scent was clean and healthy. Maintained. Lived in. This was someone's home.

Haiku closed the door behind them; Wren heard the squeaking crackle of the rubberized seal squeezing into place, followed by a weighty *thunk* of heavy bolts sliding home. Whatever else might happen, there was obviously no reason to worry about the Weir getting in. Or anything else, for that matter. The governor's compound had had its high walls and strong gates, but even that hadn't felt as secure as this place. It was like being *inside* a wall.

Something clicked behind him and a moment later, small

red-orange lights like bright embers flicked on along either side of the floor, illuminating a path down a short corridor.

"This way," Haiku said, and he led Wren through the corridor. There was a set of stairs at the end, leading both up and down. They went up, but Wren looked over the railing into the deep darkness below and wondered just how far down the building went.

Three flights up, they left the stairs and after passing through another short hallway, came out into a wide room, bright with natural sunlight. Wren had to squint at first. Apparently there were windows after all. He saw now that there were indeed large windows set in the exterior wall, made of thick flexiglass. Typically that would have made them nearly indestructible on their own, but Wren saw on the outside there were also slats of half-inch thick steel. They'd been opened like blinds to let the light in, but if closed, they would make a shield of overlapping plates. These were probably what Wren had taken to be vents at first.

The room itself was not at all what he'd expected. There was a pair of comfortable-looking chairs in one corner, sitting atop a colorful and intricately woven rug. On the opposite side was a small kitchenette; counter, sink, small cooking surface. Another doorway was there on the left, though there was no door. It just led to another short hall, as far as Wren could tell. In the center of the room, an oval table sat with six chairs arrayed around it. There was a teapot in the middle of the table and next to it sat four round bowl-like cups, each on its own saucer. Two of them steamed with tea freshly made and recently poured. A plate held what appeared to be a large, round loaf of bread along with a few other items of food Wren didn't immediately recognize. The whole thing was bizarrely out of place, like walking into a refinery and finding someone's living room. The fact that someone had apparently laid out a light meal for them just made it all the more peculiar.

Haiku removed his pack and laid it aside by the door.

"Make yourself comfortable," he said. "He'll be along in his own time. Could be a while." He walked over to the sink and started washing his hands and face.

Wren took off his pack and set it next to Haiku's, but remained by the door. He was lightheaded, coming down from the last bits of his miraculous second wind and on his way, he feared, to a hard crash-landing.

"How many people live here?" he asked.

Haiku dried his face on a towel from the counter.

"Just one," he answered. He walked over and took a seat at the table, tore a hunk off the bread. "You should wash all the road-grime off."

Wren nodded and followed Haiku's example. The water came from the faucet already heated and as it splashed over his hands, the warmth crawled its way up from his palms into his forearms, soothing. He lost himself for a time, letting the water warm him to his core and watching it spill through his fingers as he turned his hands over and back again.

"The tea's better when it's hot," Haiku said from behind him. Wren took the hint, splashed some water on his face, and dried off. He took a seat at the table leaving one chair between Haiku and himself. Haiku pushed the other cup of tea over to him. The cup was white with a simple green line around the top, slightly smaller than the typical tea cup, and it had no handle. It reminded Wren of the ones Mr Sun had had in his teahouse back in Morningside.

He took a sip of the tea, happy to find that it was still hot enough to warm him without being too hot to drink. He hadn't realized how cold he'd been until he'd started washing his hands, and the tea reinforced the point. It was a strong tea with an earthy quality, slightly sweet. He considered the fullness of the flavor; it was stronger, yes, but smoother, rounder somehow, than what he was used to. Briefly he wondered if maybe it was *real* tea instead of synthetic. Wren looked down at the deep ruby-red liquid in the cup, stared into it as he took another, longer sip.

There was something deeply satisfying about the drink, restorative.

When he lowered the cup, there was an old man standing in the doorway. Very, very old, from the looks of him. He was holding a thin vase with a few flowers in it; striking, vibrant red with white accents, simply but dynamically arranged. They gave Wren the impression of sudden movement, like an animal pouncing or the slash of a sword. Haiku stood up, and Wren followed his cue.

"Hello, Haiku," the man said. His voice had a dry quality to it, sharp-edged though he'd spoken softly.

"Father," Haiku answered, bowing as he did so.

The man entered the room without even glancing at Wren, and set the vase on the counter as he passed. He was mostly bald except for the long, thin white wisps that ringed his head; he had a white, patchy beard and eyebrows to match. Taken together, they gave the impression that his face was enshrouded in its own personal fog. He was short, maybe shorter even than Mama, and thin, nearly to the point of frailty. But he moved with effortless grace and confidence, with none of the stiffness or trembling that often accompanied the elderly. The effect was magnified by the simple clothes he wore: baggy pants and a long shirt, both pale blue and made of a light, flowing fabric. At the far end of the table, he drew out a chair and then stood in front of it while he poured himself a cup of tea from the pot. This done, he sat down and took a drink while watching Haiku from over the top of the cup. He set the cup back on its saucer in front of him.

"Please," he said, holding out a hand and inviting them to take their seats again. Haiku sat first and nodded for Wren to do the same. The man still hadn't looked at Wren, or acknowledged him in any way.

"You look tired, son," the man said. Haiku had called him father, and now he'd called Haiku son, but there was a formality to the tone that suggested there was something else to the relationship. Whether it was something more or something less, Wren couldn't tell.

Haiku nodded. "We've been traveling hard for several days."

"And before that?" the man asked.

Haiku smiled to himself, just a little. "Traveling even harder."

"Mm," said the man, something between a grunt and a short hum. He took the teapot again and, to Wren's surprise, refilled Wren's cup. Thus far it'd seemed like he hadn't even noticed Wren sitting there. "And after?"

"After depends on you, Father."

"Mm." The man sipped his own tea again. When he set it down, he tipped his head sideways, towards Wren. "You've brought a friend."

Haiku looked over at Wren, and then back at the old man. "His name is Wren. I met him in Greenstone."

Finally, for the first time, the man looked at Wren. His eyes were dark, keen, and clear, and when they settled on Wren the boy felt very much how he imagined a mouse might feel when first trapped by the gaze of a hawk. He stood and bowed without any conscious thought.

"Hello, sir," Wren said. The old man dipped his head in a bare hint of acknowledgment. And then, because he felt like he should say something more but didn't know what else to say, Wren added, "Thank you for the tea."

"You're welcome, boy," the man said, and then turned his attention back to Haiku. Wren stood there feeling awkward for a few moments, and then quietly eased himself back into his chair. There was a strange tension in the room, like the old man was waiting for Haiku to ask him a question, and Haiku was too afraid to ask. Wren's palms got sweaty. Finally, after a long, uncomfortable span, Haiku spoke.

"Wren was with Three, Father. He traveled with him for a long time."

"Yes," the man said, and Wren couldn't tell from the tone whether that meant he wanted Haiku to continue, or if that was something he'd already known.

"And," Haiku continued, "he carried out the proper rites for Three, according to custom."

Haiku's gentle way of breaking the news of Three's death. The old man simply inclined his head again in a nod.

"Wren very graciously told me all he could about the end of Three's life, in great detail. I've recorded it all."

"Then you are satisfied?" the man asked.

"Yes," Haiku said.

"Mm," said the old man. He took another sip of his tea. When he set his cup down again, he sighed heavily. The formality fell away, as if he'd blown it out of the room. "What do you *want*, Haiku?"

Haiku looked genuinely nervous, and Wren took that as a bad sign.

"I'm not sure where to begin, Father."

"Well it's too late for that anyway," said the old man. "You've completed your history? You want me to applaud you for it? I assume there's something more, else there's no need for this boy here to be drinking my tea."

Haiku nodded. "There is more, Father. Much more." He paused to inhale. "Something has changed."

"As it has ever been. Life is change, Haiku."

"With the Weir, Father."

Haiku explained briefly, without glossing over the important points. He told of Asher, and of Underdown's machine, and of Painter's awful pronouncement, and the fall of Morningside. When he'd finished, the old man poured himself some more tea. He took a sip, wrinkled his nose at it, and replaced the cup on its saucer. Maybe it was starting to get bitter.

"You've been very diligent, Haiku," he said. "But I fail to see how any of this is relevant to me."

"He's using the Weir as a weapon, Father," said Haiku.

"Yes, I understand. And it's an intriguing idea, hijacking them. Highly unlikely, but not completely outside the realm of possibility, given the right tools and skill set."

"But on this scale... think of it. A single mind, directing

them all; he's massing them, driving them. If Morningside has fallen, there are few cities indeed that could withstand such a thing."

"What of it? Are you here looking for refuge?"

"I'm here to ask you to stop him," Haiku said.

"Why?" asked the old man. The question threw Haiku for a loop.

"Why... stop him?" Haiku asked.

"Why ask me? Why would you think I'd *care*, Haiku? I've already given all I had to this world. You know the good it did."

"He's already killed hundreds of people," Wren said. "Maybe thousands."

"Thousands?" said the old man. He leaned towards Wren and looked him straight in the eye. "Boy, how many people's worth of ashes do you think you walked through to get here?"

He said it so casually; hadn't raised his voice, hadn't changed his expression. They could very well have been discussing whether or not it might rain the next day. He sat back and returned his attention to Haiku.

"So why'd you drag the boy along?"

"Because he knows Asher," Haiku said.

"He's my brother," Wren added. "Well, half-brother."

"But it's more than that," Haiku said. "Wren tried to stop it. He fought Asher, through the machine."

"And what was that like," the old man asked Wren. "To fight him, through the machine."

Wren thought back to that terrible struggle, the infinite complexity that had threatened to swallow him, the arctic bolt that had pierced through the center of his mind.

"I... He... he was too... big, I guess," Wren said. "I don't really know how to explain it."

"Mm," the old man made his little noise again.

"I brought him so you could hear of his experience firsthand," Haiku said.

"Perhaps you should've gotten more detail before you

brought him all this way," said the old man.

"And," Haiku continued. "And... to ask you to train him."

A single chuckle escaped the old man's lips, a sharp, rasping exhale that almost sounded like a cough.

"Train him?" he said. "Train him." He tipped his tea cup and looked into it, then set it back. "I don't do that anymore," he said. Then he looked at Wren with a kindly smile. "I'm retired, you see."

"Father, there's something to him," Haiku said. "Something he can do. Tell him, Wren."

"I have... I don't know," Wren said. "I have a gift."

"Oh," the old man said. "A gift, you say?"

Wren felt silly having said it, and he shrugged. "That's what my mom says, anyway."

"Ah yes, and Mama knows, does she?"

"Yes," Wren said. He knew that tone of voice; it was the one grownups used when they weren't really listening. "She knows it very well. Because I brought her back."

"From where, boy?"

"The dead," Wren said. It wasn't strictly true, of course, but he figured saying it that way might get the old man to take him seriously. The old man tilted his head to one side, and his eyes narrowed.

"And what do you mean by that, exactly?" he asked.

"The Weir took her. And I brought her back. I woke her."

"Woke her?" the old man said. And for the first time, Wren felt like the man was actually paying attention to him now. It wasn't a particularly comfortable feeling. "In what way?"

"I mean, she's herself again, like she used to be," Wren said. "Except her body. She still looks like a Weir. But she acts like my Mama. She *is* my Mama. She's awake."

"And not just his mother," Haiku said. "Others, too. Dozens."

"You can do this to anyone?" the old man asked. "Any Weir?"

Wren shook his head. "No, sir. Sometimes I can't. Most

times. It's like... I don't know, like there's no one there. Inside. But sometimes there is. Sometimes there's someone, and they're stuck. And I can help. My friend..." he said, and then trailed off. Maybe it was best not to mention that Painter had been his friend.

The old man pulled at the wispy beard on his chin and seemed to be considering what Wren had said.

"Father, please," Haiku said. "Will you at least evaluate him before you decide?"

Wren didn't know what Haiku meant by *evaluate*, but he didn't like the sound of it.

"How old are you, boy?" asked the old man.

"Almost nine."

"Look at him, Haiku," he said. "Almost nine already. It would take me a year just to teach him to breathe."

"There's more to him than you give him credit for," Haiku said. "I wouldn't have brought him out here if I didn't think he was capable."

"I know, son," the man said. "But for what purpose? I do not know this boy. Neither do you. You say his brother is the one inflicting such havoc on the world, who is to say this one will not do the same?"

"Me," Haiku said. "I will. I'll take the oath, I'll be his pledge."

"No, Haiku," the old man said. "The answer is no. I am an old man now, and I have had the special misery of outliving all but a precious few of my children. I lack the energy to fill another with false hope."

Wren listened to the two men going back and forth, talking about him like he wasn't sitting right there in the room with them. And he thought about Asher, and all Asher had done, and what he was doing, and would continue to do until someone found a way to stop him. Maybe it was anger, maybe it was pride. But Wren hadn't subjected himself to four days of agony just to sit in a room and drink tea while other people discussed his fate like wasn't even there.

"Please, sir," Wren said. "I'll do whatever it takes."

"I beg your pardon?" the old man said.

"If there's a chance, sir, any chance at all, that you can teach me something, or anything really, that could help me stop my brother, I'll do whatever it takes to learn it."

"You do not know what you are asking, boy."

"My name is Wren," Wren said, a little more forcefully than he'd meant to. The old man's eyebrows went up a little at that.

"Determined, are you?" he said.

"Yes," Wren answered.

"Willing to pay any cost?"

"Yes."

"And why, *boy*, do you think I have anything to give that would be worth such a price?"

"Because of Three," Wren said without hesitation. He hadn't even thought it before he said it, it just sort of sprang out of his mouth. But once he'd said it, he knew it was true. "He was the greatest man I ever knew. And if you helped him become who he was, then it's worth anything to me to learn from you too."

The old man pulled on his beard again for a long moment and just stared into Wren's eyes. Wren did his best to return the gaze and hoped it wasn't too obvious just how anxious he felt.

"Well," the old man said. "How about this? I will give you one, simple task. If you complete it to my satisfaction, then I will evaluate you. Only evaluate you, understand. I make no promise beyond that."

"OK," Wren said. "I'll do it."

"You haven't heard the task yet," the old man said.

"It doesn't matter," Wren answered.

"Eager indeed," the old man said to Haiku. "Not the best of the qualities." He turned back to Wren. "Then my task is this. Leave."

The words hit Wren like a block of ice to the gut.

"Leave?" Wren said. "But... where would I go?"

The old man held out a hand towards the windows and slowly swept it across the horizon. "Anywhere you choose," he said. "All that you see out there is open to you."

"Father, please," Haiku said. "I pushed him very hard to get here."

"Then he should have no problem handling one more night."

Wren tried to steady himself. They'd already spent three nights out in the open. It hadn't been *that* bad. Had it?

"It's OK, Haiku. I don't mind, as long as you can find a good place."

"Oh no, Haiku is not going with you," the old man said. "This is your task, and yours alone."

"You can't do that to him," Haiku said.

"Haiku, of all people, I would think you especially should know precisely what I am capable of doing," the man answered. "Besides if you go with him, I would have to assume you did all the work. And I already know what *you* are capable of."

It was too late. Wren had trapped himself. He'd said he was willing to do anything. He couldn't take it back now. No matter how crazy it seemed, or how scary, he had to show this old man that he had the will he'd claimed to have. He glanced out the window. There was still a lot of daylight left. Plenty of time to cross that span of open ground and find a place to hole up.

"I said I would do it," Wren said, and he turned back to the old man. "So I'll do it."

"Very well," the man said, and he stood up. "Haiku can take you down. Come back in the morning, then we shall see if you have anything more than pluck."

"I do," Wren said. "Eagerness." The old man actually smiled at that.

"Yes. Pluck and eagerness." He shook his head. "Not the best of qualities."

With that, the old man turned and left the room. They sat in silence for a few seconds. Haiku was just looking at him like he didn't know what to say. Wren didn't really know what to say either, so he just said, "I take it that means everything didn't go well."

"I'm sorry, Wren. I knew it was a long shot, but I never imagined it would go like this."

"It's not your fault, Haiku," Wren said, and Haiku barked a humorless laugh.

"It is, and it is mine alone. You don't have to do this. I'll talk to him."

Wren shook his head. "I already said I'd do it. I don't think talking him out of it will count."

Haiku opened his mouth to reply, but closed it again without saying anything.

"I guess I should get going," Wren said.

Haiku nodded. They both stood and walked to the door where their packs were laid.

"How are you on supplies?" Haiku asked.

"Fine," Wren said. "Still have some food and water. Enough to get me through the night."

"It's not you starving to death I'm worried about," Haiku said.

Wren just nodded and picked up his pack.

"Head back the way we came," Haiku said. "There were a couple of taller buildings we passed that might be good for you. Look for somewhere high. Somewhere with stairs is OK, but a ladder is better. If you can't find that, try to find a small space, a place you have to crawl to get in."

Haiku led him back down the stairs, feeding him a continuous stream of advice of what to look for and what to avoid. Even after he'd opened the main door and Wren had moved outside, he kept talking for nearly ten more minutes. He pointed out a couple of locations across the open ground that he thought might be good places to start looking for shelter. Eventually Wren's head was so full of things to think about, he was afraid he was going to start forgetting everything. And he was anxious to get on the move.

"OK, Haiku, I've got it. I need to go."

Haiku nodded. "You want me to stand here for a while? So you can see me?"

"No," Wren said. "He said I have to do this on my own. If it's OK with you, I guess I'd rather just go."

"Good luck, Wren," Haiku said. "I know you can do this. I'll see you in the morning."

"OK," Wren said. "You can close the door."

Haiku smiled at him a final time, and then stepped back inside and slowly shut the door. A moment later, the heavy bolts slid into place, and Wren knew he was, possibly for the first time in his life, well and truly alone.

TWELVE

jCharles stood beside the crib, staring down at his sleeping daughter. His little baby girl. Grace. Mol had chosen the name but if there was a more perfect one out there, jCharles didn't know what it was. Grace. Free and unmerited favor. A precious gift, more precious than life itself; that he had neither earned nor deserved. And yet there she was, sound asleep, looking like an angel.

And he couldn't help but think of his other little angel, Jakey, gone many years now. The same tragedy that had robbed Mol of the use of her legs had also stolen the life of his boy. A tragedy that was the fruit born from the life he'd led before, the wages of choices he'd made. He'd buried his child, and with him the hope of ever having another. Yet here he was now, again a father, looking down at a miracle. A second chance. The wonder of it was almost too much to bear.

"Hey," Mol's whisper crept catlike into the room from behind him. jCharles quickly wiped his eyes, turned, smiled at his beautiful wife standing there at the door. "If you wake her, you're the one that has to get her back to sleep."

He nodded, turned back to the crib. Time to let the little lady sleep. He kissed his fingertips, laid them gently on the top of Grace's head. She stirred under the touch, and he held his breath. He loved his daughter more than he'd dreamed possible. But especially when she was sleeping peacefully.

And he knew Mol was serious. It'd taken almost an hour to get Grace asleep the first time around, and if she woke up fussy, it'd take longer the second time. Fortunately, she settled without opening her eyes, and jCharles slowly drew back from the crib and joined Mol in the front room. She was already sitting on the couch, feet curled up underneath her. He stood by the door to the bedroom and just watched her for a time. She was staring up slightly, no doubt scanning some internal application. After a few moments, she turned and looked at him.

"You all right?" she asked.

He smiled. "I sure do love you, Mol."

She chuckled and went back to whatever she'd been working on. "That baby's making you soft, Twitch."

"Don't I know it."

jCharles crossed the room and sat in his chair across from her. There was already a drink waiting for him on the end table. He sure did love his wife. He took a sip, held it in his mouth, laid his head back as the vapors infused his palate. When he swallowed, warmth rolled down his throat, radiated through his chest, where it merged with his sense of gratitude and blossomed into a tranquil contentment. This was his home. It didn't look like much by most standards. There were plenty of folks in Greenstone that had more money, more flash, more stuff. But in that moment, he was dead certain he was the richest man in town. Maybe in the world.

But as he sat there, he felt the disquiet rippling just beneath the surface of his sense of well-being. Something tugging at the corners of his consciousness that he'd been intently trying to ignore. The trouble in the east. Across the Strand. It was an entire world away, a place he'd never been, a place that was more imagined than real to him. And yet out of that distant place, Wren had come to him, broken, defeated, in despair. jCharles had wanted to forget all about what Wren had told him. The story seemed impossible, even though he'd believed every word Wren had told him.

Maybe it hadn't been as bad as Wren had thought, though. He'd been unconscious for the end of it, after all.

But then jCharles thought about Cass out there, somewhere. If she *was* still out there. She'd sent her son back to him. The magnitude of that choice hadn't been lost on him; the desperation of it, the hope in it. Doing whatever she had to, to protect what she most loved. And the fact that she hadn't followed after... She'd sent her son here, trusting that he'd been taken care of.

"You think we did the right thing?" jCharles said.

Mol's eyes refocused, met his. "Which thing, darling?"

"Letting Wren go off with Haiku, instead of keeping him here with us."

She looked at him with a quiet smile, searched his eyes. "We did the right thing," she said, "in recognizing it wasn't our choice to make."

He nodded and sipped his drink. A moment later, she continued.

"He's not Jakey, Twitch. As much as we want him to be."

Hard words spoken in kindness. She'd put her finger right on the heart of his concern, clarified it for him before he'd even recognized it for himself. She'd always had a way of seeing him better than he could see himself. He teared up again at the words, looked down into his drink so she wouldn't see.

"No," jCharles said. "No, he's not. I know that. In my head, I know that." He took another pull of his drink.

"You're not alone in that," Mol said. "And heart's a different matter. It was the hardest thing in the world, him asking me what he should do. Took everything I had not to tell him he ought to stay here with us. Be our boy. But it wouldn't have been fair to ask him to be something for us, instead of what he needs to be for himself."

jCharles wiped a tear out of his eye with his thumb. Looked back up at his wife.

"I don't know when you got so wise," he said with a smile.

"Oh, I've always been this way. It's just that *you're* finally getting wise enough to see it."

"I sure do love you."

"You mentioned."

He drained the rest of his drink, stood and crossed to her, kissed her on the top of her head.

"One of these days," he said, "maybe you'll finally get the kind of man you deserve."

"Maybe," she said. "If you'll ever grow up enough to see he's you."

"Not likely."

"No, but a girl can dream. You headed out?"

jCharles nodded. "Just downstairs."

"Business meeting?"

"Sorta."

"It going to cost us a lot?"

"Not sure yet."

She made a face at him, a playful show of disapproval.

"It'll be worth it, though," he said. "Trying to hire a runner."

The playfulness disappeared from her look. As usual, she understood what he meant before he even had to explain.

"Pay him well."

jCharles nodded and kissed Mol again, and headed to the door.

"Twitch?" she said just before he pulled the door shut. He turned back, poked his head back into the apartment. Mol looked at him gravely. "You're still on duty if Gracie wakes up."

He smiled. "Yes, ma'am."

He closed the door behind him and headed down the narrow staircase to the bar below. Nimble, his long-time bartender and trusted righthand man, was behind the bar, waiting for him. It wasn't as crowded as jCharles would have liked to have seen it for this time of night, but at least it'd be easier to do business. Nimble had kept the rear corner table clear, and all the tables near it. jCharles approached, and Nimble slid him a drink.

"Whatcha got for me, Nim?"

"Nay much," Nimble said. He nodded towards a mismatched couple sitting up front near the door. "'ems two. And I don't care for the fella."

jCharles checked the two runners out from a distance. A man and a woman, about as different as they could be. The man had a clean, professional edge and an air of confident boredom. He was sporting some top-line gear, conspicuous enough to advertise without being an obviously gratuitous display. Clearly a man who knew the value of his own work and wanted to make sure everyone else had a good hint at it too. He was turned sideways in his chair, disgust at his companion thinly veiled.

The woman, on the other hand, was a ragged-looking creature. If she'd bathed, it probably hadn't been this week. She was heavyset but her clothes were oversized, and she looked rumpled and disheveled. She was busy scraping a hunk of bread across the plate in front of her, gathering up every last possible molecule of whatever dish Nimble had served her on the house.

"Good credentials?"

"His come better," Nimble said. "Maybe too much better."

"But you don't like him?"

"Nah."

"Personal prejudice?"

"He don't drink."

jCharles smiled at that. "You want to sit in on this?"

"As you like," Nimble said with a half shrug that suggested he didn't.

"Yeah, I'd like."

Nimble nodded. jCharles picked up his drink and headed for the table in the back. Nimble let out a short, piercing whistle that got the attention of every patron in the room. He motioned to the two runners. Everyone else went back to their own business with new and very obvious signs that they were paying absolutely no attention to anything that didn't concern them. jCharles watched the runners as they came over to his table; sized up what they wore, how they moved, what caught their attention. The man walked with his shoulders back, head high, a pleasant look on his face as he made eye contact with jCharles. The woman hunched in on herself, eyes constantly roving everywhere but where jCharles was sitting.

The two runners sat across from jCharles with a chair between them. Nimble came and leaned against the wall, just behind jCharles.

"Thanks for coming out," jCharles said. The man nodded curtly in acknowledgment. A military bearing. The woman just stared back expectantly, apparently waiting to hear the details of the deal.

"I want to be respectful of your time, so I'll cut right to it. I need someone to make a run to Morningside for me. Out and back, quick as possible."

The man's eyebrows went up in mild surprise. The woman still wore the same expression.

"Trip's easy enough," the man said. "But I'll need very detailed specifications on the cargo. I'll transfer a datasheet for you to fill out–"

"No cargo," jCharles said. "Except information."

"Oh," the man said.

"You've been to Morningside?" jCharles asked.

"Several times," the man answered. "I can transfer a travel log, if you like."

"And you?" jCharles asked the woman. She blinked languidly. Dipped her head. "So what's your base rate?" he asked, turning back to the man.

"A day out, a day back, plus whatever time I have to spend on location," the man said. "Fifteen hundred, plus in-city expenditures. If I'll be making contact with any of your associates, it'll be an extra two to five hundred, based on several metrics I'll need to evaluate. I can transfer a detailed breakdown of the costs, if you like."

"So call it two thousand?" jCharles said, more for the

benefit of the woman who looked like she wasn't really paying attention.

"Depending on associates," the man corrected.

jCharles looked to the woman, pointed at her to make sure she knew he was talking to her now. "How about you? Base rate for a run?"

She made a show of thinking it over, scratched under her jaw with the back of her hand. "Short day make bad runnin'," she said. "Call it t'ree t'ousand out, two when I back." Her accent was heavy, her *th*s rounded.

Nimble let out a low whistle. Usually the runner who offered the second bid tried to at least match the quote of the first.

"*Five* thousand?" jCharles said, and the man across from him chuckled. "You do know that's over twice what your friend here just quoted me?"

She dipped her head again, apparently unconcerned or unimpressed by the proceedings thus far.

"I'll transfer you a cost breakdown," the man said graciously. "I can leave as early as the morning, if you can get me all the information I need and a thirty-percent good-faith payment up front." He stood up, extended his hand to shake and close the deal. jCharles just watched the woman for a span, letting the man's hand hover over the table.

"Your friend here is ready to do business at two thousand," jCharles said. "Should I take it?"

"Sure," she said. "If you don' care abou' Morn'side."

The man looked at her with sharp indignation.

"Excuse me, *ma'am*," he said, as if it physically hurt him to call her ma'am. "I've made that trip several times. I have detailed travel logs. I've been running for twelve years, and I haven't failed a single client."

"May be he run," the woman said, but she wasn't looking at the man. She was talking to jCharles alone, as if the man wasn't even there. "But you believe he cross dat Strand, you deserve you lose your money." She nodded. "Sure I know."

jCharles smiled in spite of himself. The woman's words confirmed his hunch. The man looked the part, certainly. But he had the feel of someone who'd gone well out of his way to do just that, to *look* the part. And here this woman sitting across from him looked closer to a homeless drifter than someone who was a handshake away from a fat wad of money. She was direct, had no patience for expected manners or business etiquette; here for a job, for the price stated, take it or leave it. In other words, a pro.

"Thanks for your time," jCharles said, extending his hand to the man.

"I'll transfer the documents," the man said, smiling while he shook hands.

"That won't be necessary," jCharles replied. The man's fake smile melted away. He just stood there blinking for a moment. "Thanks for your time," jCharles repeated, taking his hand back. The man looked at him, then to the woman. Then up at Nimble.

"Get faffed," Nimble said.

The man made a disgusted noise and then shook his head. "You're a bunch of empty-headed–"

"Faff off, ye!" Nimble barked, and the man flinched. The bar quieted, and a couple of jCharles's regulars started to get out of their seats, just in case things were about to get rowdy. But jCharles stilled them with a mild wave of the hand, and they slowly sank back to sitting. The man turned and tromped away to the front door, muttering to himself. Once he'd exited, jCharles turned his attention back to the woman.

"What's your name, ma'am?"

"Edda," she answered.

"You a good watcher, Edda?"

"Sure."

"Well, Miss Edda, tell you what. I'll pay you your three thousand now, to go out to Morningside and to take a look around. And I'll pay you an additional *five*," he held up five fingers for emphasis, "when you get back. If, and this is the important part, *if* what you tell me matches up with what I already know."

"If it don't?"

"Just tell the truth and it will," jCharles said. "But I'll guarantee you six thousand at a minimum."

Her eyes narrowed. "Dat some high talk."

"It's important."

"Don't sound like usual bidness, neither."

"It isn't. But it *is* important."

"To *you*," she said.

"To everyone."

Edda wiped her nose with the back of her hand. "Out to Morn'side and back, for eight t'ousand."

jCharles nodded.

"Just for what I see."

"Just for what you see."

She waggled her head from side to side, weighing her options. "Eight t'ousand and anot'er plate o' dat mess when I back." She pointed back over her shoulder with her thumb, vaguely towards the empty plate she'd left on the front table. "And I do."

jCharles smiled, but he turned and looked over his shoulder at Nimble. "I don't know, what do you think, Nim? Making you cook for her again going to put us over the top?"

"I'll make it work," Nimble said.

jCharles turned back around. "Sounds like we can do it."

The woman slapped a hand flat on the table with a nod.

"So three thousand up front. Pointcard OK?" jCharles asked. A lot of runners only dealt in Hard, but he really didn't want to try to scrape together that much physical currency if he didn't have to.

"No card," Edda said, rising to her feet. "I send you straight." A straight transfer; that meant she had a third-party holding her wealth in security, which usually required a significant sum. She flashed a smile for the first time, revealing a missing front tooth. "You get how you pay. Dat make me rich, sure. But I get you what you ask."

jCharles stood and shook her hand.

"Be careful out there, Edda," jCharles said. "It might be a lot more dangerous than the last time you were out."

"Dangerous all dere is," she replied. "Sure I know." She glanced over at Nimble, gave him a once over, flashed that smile again. Then back at jCharles. "T'ree day."

"See you then," jCharles said. She gave her lazy nod, turned and made her way through the bar towards the front door. jCharles stood there, watching her go. "Good call, Nimble. You always could pick 'em," he said. "She's something else, huh?"

"A proper woman," Nimble said. jCharles turned and looked at his bartender. Nimble was watching her too, all the way out the front door. He glanced over at jCharles.

jCharles chuckled and slapped Nimble on the shoulder. "Well, Nimble, you sly son. If I didn't know better, I might be tempted to think you were a bit smitten by my new employee."

Nimble shrugged. "Sure, I know." He smiled after he said it, and went back to the bar, taking jCharles's untouched drink with him.

jCharles watched his old friend return to his usual station, and then swept his eyes over his little business, his patrons both new and regular, his livelihood. Whatever news Edda brought him from the east, this was his world. If only he could figure out how to protect it.

THIRTEEN

The side hall was dark and though that didn't affect Cass at all, Gamble was insistent on taking everything nice and slow. Cass had known they'd need to be careful but they were moving with such painstaking slowness that it would have seemed comical, if not for how deadly the whole place felt. It created a strange tension in her body, forcing it to move forward with such deliberation when everything suggested she should be running flat out the other way. And as much as she tried to focus her mind on the task at hand, Cass couldn't completely block out the vivid memory of the abomination that lay just outside. That image feasted on the oppressive atmosphere here inside, grew in her mind, whispered of other horrors yet undiscovered.

It was a short walk from the side entrance they'd used to the first stairwell, but they'd bypassed it in order to get a better idea of the situation before they committed too fully. If they got into trouble, it was a straight shot back to the side entrance, which simplified the retreat. As long as they didn't run past it. There weren't any exterior windows in the hall and even the emergency lights were off. From the temperature in the building, Cass guessed that the power had been cut entirely; no climate control, no backup generators, nothing. Gamble, walking about eight feet behind her, had switched on the red light attached to her weapon at the lowest setting, which meant Cass was likely just at the edge of her companion's visibility. She hoped Gamble would be able to see the hand signals they'd discussed.

As Cass scouted it out, though, she was beginning to feel more confident. From what they'd seen so far, there wasn't much damage to this portion of the building. It didn't really even look like there'd been much traffic through that particular corridor. Under normal circumstances, that hadn't been unusual, at least while Wren had been governor. There wasn't much on that lower floor that had been used in day-to-day activities. The fact that it still seemed to be the case was at least mildly encouraging.

Even so, it was hard to believe this was the same building that Cass had spent over a year living in with Gamble and her team, and with Wren. Even though this particular section looked pretty much exactly the same, it *felt* completely different. Alien. Other. Like returning home for the first time after some horrible crime had been committed there. The air was heavy, thick, as if it was being compressed by the darkness and the silence.

Part of Cass felt it was silly to go at such a slow pace, especially since she could see to the far end of the corridor and knew it was clear. But she dismissed the thought almost as soon as it had arisen. There was no reason to rush, no reason to take any chances, other than her own impatience.

When they reached the target stairwell, the two women repeated their door-opening procedure. On the stairs, they switched roles, with Gamble leading the way, and Cass following behind holding on to a loop on Gamble's pack. It was completely dark here too, and Gamble's dim red light played over the steps and walls like an evil eye searching the night. From watching the way Gamble worked the light, Cass understood why she hadn't bothered to try to explain the tactics. There was simply too much to keep in mind. Though she would occasionally flash the stairs to make sure they were clear, most of the time Gamble kept her weapon and light up, smoothly scanning above them. She walked with a constantly shifting step, sometimes forward, sometimes sideways, sometimes backwards, depending on what angle she was trying to get as they moved up. She wasn't taking any chances. Which turned out to be a good thing indeed.

As they neared the top, Cass became aware of a faint rustling sound, like fingertips running lightly over a rough surface, or whispers from a distant crowd. The stairs led out to a wide landing that in turn opened out to one of the central halls. And all was as they'd feared. The hall was packed with Weir.

To Gamble's credit, she slowed smoothly to a stop rather than doing so suddenly where Cass might bump into her. She cupped a hand over her light, not even wanting to risk the click it made when switching it off. The hall was central to the building without any exterior windows so the darkness was complete. Or would have been, if not for the hundreds of softly radiant eyes that cast a moonlight glow throughout the hall.

The two women stood there together, stunned. Cass thought for certain that the next heartbeat was when she would hear the first shriek from the Weir that would bring the inevitable wave crashing down upon them. But with each heartbeat that went by, that cry seemed less and less likely to sound. Their eyes were open, certainly. She could see them clearly. When she'd recovered from the shock, though, it seemed to her that the electric light in their eyes was a little softer, a little dimmer than usual. She recalled Ninestory, when Finn and Wick had gone into a building and almost hadn't made it back out. How Finn had described the crowd of Weir inside, like they'd been switched off and he and Wick had woken them up.

The Weir were massed in the hall, drawn in tightly with one another as if the center of the room was the last train to safety and they were all trying to get aboard. In fact, it would have looked exactly like a panicked mob except they were all completely still. Or rather, practically so. Cass could see a few of the Weir shifting on their feet or moving their hands.

Idle motions, like those made by people who are bored or dozing lightly. That was the source of the noise. Hundreds of asynchronous, insignificant movements, creating a constant stream of ambient sounds amplified by the vast open space that contained them.

Of course Cass's first instinct was to flee and it took a great deal of effort to maintain her position. Gamble slowly swiveled around. The fear was plainly evident on her face. She raised her hand to signal, though Cass already knew what she was going to indicate. *Go back.*

To Cass's surprise, that wasn't what Gamble motioned at all. She cupped her hand like a question mark, and then motioned forward and up. Not an order to go back; a question of continuing forward. Gamble was asking if Cass was willing to keep going. The stairs leading up to the third floor were just twenty feet away. A straight shot. The floor between them was stone tile, smooth. The path was clear.

The fact that Gamble was even considering it spoke volumes of her courage, and of her concern for the people outside who were counting on them. They'd come this far. If Gamble was willing to try, Cass wasn't going to be the reason she didn't.

Cass moved her hand very slowly and formed a very exaggerated OK. Gamble dipped her head in a giant single nod and turned back around. She kept her weapon pointed downward at about a forty-five degree angle, and shifted off to the right, away from the Weir. If Cass had thought their movement downstairs had been slow, she didn't even have a word to describe their movement now. Glacial, maybe.

They crossed to the next staircase, each step placed with the utmost care. It was almost like trying to walk on a tightrope. Cass seemed to feel every muscle in her body, every fiber being used to keep her balance, to keep her silence. Maybe they were being overly cautious. After all, none of the shifting noises the Weir were making seemed to bother any of them. But if there were ever a time to test the hearing of a Weir, now was most certainly not it.

Gamble reached the stairwell and started up it. The lower portion of the staircase was exposed to the hall below, but only the first third or so. Once they'd passed that point, the tension lessened by a fraction. Cass knew they were still taking a grave risk, but having something solid between them and those unseeing eyes felt a great deal safer than standing right out in the open.

They reached the third floor, which was really considered the second from the main entrance. To their great relief, there were no surprises waiting for them at the top. Gamble did a quick scan of the landing, but their destination was up one more flight, so they didn't hang around. They continued their gradual ascent with Gamble in the lead and finally reached their target floor.

Gamble motioned for Cass to get set on the door, and she moved into position. This one opened outward from the stairs, which was less than ideal. Motion from the door might attract attention before Gamble even had a chance to see what the situation was. Given what they'd just walked past, Cass didn't want to think about what might be waiting for them on the other side. Her mind kept filling in the possibilities for her anyway.

There was the squeeze on her shoulder. Cass applied gentle pressure, easing the door open a half-inch at a time as Gamble leaned and twisted to get a view. When the door was open just enough for Gamble to squeeze through, she did so, and the motion she made was startling in its swiftness after the painfully slow movements they'd been making over the past half-hour.

Gamble stuck a hand back where Cass could see it and motioned for her to follow. The side passage had led them out a bit farther into the building than they needed to be to reach the cage, but the corridor was clear. The hall hadn't fared as well as the first one they'd encountered. There were obvious signs of struggle in both directions. Gamble motioned for Cass to resume the lead, and Cass edged around her, headed towards the team rooms.

She made her way down the hall, careful to step over and around the broken and scattered debris that cluttered the floor. Here and there were dark splotches of dried fluid; in one place it was clear something, or someone, had been dragged away, made apparent by the wide streak that trailed away the opposite direction, thick at one end and dissipating as it went, like a painter's brush gone dry before the end of the stroke.

Some of the doors along the corridor were open, many of them by force. They didn't stop to clear the rooms, but Cass and Gamble each glanced in as they passed, alert for any signs of dormant Weir. Just inside one of the doorways, a dislocator lay abandoned; a non-lethal weapon the city guards used to bring down unruly citizens.

Fortunately, it appeared that the Weir had all congregated below, leaving the upper floors empty. *Appeared*, Cass reminded herself. It was easy to make assumptions without realizing it, and acting on an incorrect assumption was a good way to get everyone killed.

Gamble's team had several rooms on this floor, but it was the main team room they were concerned about. It had two entrances on the left side of the corridor, and when she reached the first, Cass paused and waited for Gamble to catch up. When Gamble was just a few steps away, Cass pointed at the damage to the exterior of the door and around the handle. The team room doors were all reinforced and secured with biometric locks, but someone had done their best to bypass both. It was difficult to judge whether the damage was from humans or the Weir. Possible it was both.

Gamble played her light along the seams of the door from the floor up to the top, and then following the top from right to left. The frame showed some separation in a couple of places, but it looked like it had held fast otherwise. Gamble wasn't one to take any chances. She signaled for Cass to continue further down to the other entrance. That door was in much the same shape; damaged but not breached. Gamble stood at the door with her brow furrowed. Cass had assumed this would be a typical entry, but clearly she was missing something. The biometric locks ran on their own hundred-year batteries, and both she and Gamble had clearance. It should just be a matter of popping the lock and walking in. After twenty seconds or so without any sign from Gamble, Cass signaled for clarification.

Going in?

Gamble held up her left hand, pointer finger up. *Wait.*

A few moments later, Gamble waved Cass closer, and whispered in her ear.

"If survivors, could be trouble," she said.

Of course. Cass hadn't thought about the possibility that someone might have been able to reach the team room and barricade themselves inside. She realized then that she'd assumed the entire populace had been wiped out. Assumptions again.

"Wait here," Gamble whispered, her words barely an interrupted exhale. "On three clicks, open, do not enter."

She leaned back and looked Cass in the eyes to make sure she'd understood. Cass nodded and took a position at the door. Gamble swiveled smoothly and flowed back down the hallway the way they'd come, back to the first entry. A few moments later, Cass heard in the channel, slow and measured like a countdown:

Click.

Click.

Click.

On the third click, Cass pressed her thumb to the biometric pad on the handle and applied gentle pressure. The lock made a cheery beep and snicked. Normally it was an unobtrusive sound, but in those dark and empty hallways, it made Cass wince. She opened the door anyway, at the same speed she would have if Gamble had been standing right with her. As she pushed it wider, though, she edged back, keeping out of sight of anyone who might be waiting inside. Five seconds later, red light flared across the entryway and then swept away again. Cass hadn't heard the lock sound off on Gamble's side, but Gamble was already in there checking things out. In this particular case, each silent second that ticked by was actually a good thing.

The red light reappeared at her door and flashed three times; a signal Cass interpreted as all clear. She leaned around the doorframe and found Gamble standing in the center of the room, with a hint of a smile on her face. It was one of the largest rooms on the floor, but a quick scan told Cass that no one, human or Weir, had made it inside. The blackout shades were still drawn, masking the room in a dull grey murk, but everything seemed to be in good order. Most importantly, the cage was intact; a cornucopia brimming with life and death. She felt a wave of relief, followed quickly by a flood of guilt. Her good fortune had come at a terrible price paid by others.

Cass moved inside and was gently closing the door behind her when she heard a shadow of a sound in the hallway; a short, sharp scrape. She glanced over her shoulder at Gamble, who met her gaze. No longer smiling. Gamble moved quickly, switching off her light and motioning for Cass to get back from the door while she herself closed in. Cass backed against the wall to give as much room as she could. Gamble went to a knee at the door, with one hand on the handle and the other keeping her short rifle at the ready. She kept the door cracked and leaned as close to the wall as she could to get a view down the corridor. They waited a full two minutes in those positions, ears straining for any further sound or sign of what may have caused the first. But nothing came. After those long minutes, Gamble eased the door fully closed. Thankfully, the lock remained silent when it rengaged.

Gamble rose to her feet and motioned for Cass to follow her to the far side of the room, away from the doors. She motioned to the cage.

"Extra rucks are on the left side of the door," she said, indicating the large packs her team used to haul their gear. "I'll handle ammo and medical. You're on food and whatever else seems useful. One ruck for each."

Gamble led the way back over to the cage, which was positioned along the wall between the two entryways. It was aptly named. The cage was ten feet wide, six feet deep, and stretched from floor to ceiling. It was constructed from a robust metal mesh that formed a grid pattern, with holes too small to fit a hand through. Gamble unlocked and opened the single central door and went inside. She motioned to the right side of the cage while she herself went left. Cass grabbed a pair of rucks from a hook by the door and then headed towards the right. As she moved through, she noted how meticulously organized everything was.

The walls of the cage had shelves or hooks for storage, and additional shelves had been hung from the ceiling to create a few aisles. Equipment was grouped by function for easy access and inventory. Though Cass had been aware that Gamble's team was well-supplied, this was her first look at what that actually meant. And now she understood why Gamble had been willing to take such a risk to reach it. Rope, lights, thermal blankets, batteries, ammo, emergency shelters, tools; everything they could possibly need was here. If they were smart, they could run for weeks on their supplies.

Cass tried not to get distracted but she couldn't help but think of what Wren would have said if he could have have seen it all. She could picture him standing there at the entrance, eyes wide, mouth open, and she smiled even as the thought cut her heart.

Stacks of rugged boxes sat in the right front corner, RATIONS hand-stenciled on the exterior. Cass opened one of the empty rucks, broke the seal on the first box, and started transferring the rubberized packages. If she'd had more time, she would have figured out the best way to maximize the space. As it was, she tried to find a balance between organizing well and just dumping everything in. She came down a lot closer to the dumping-everything-in side.

After her first attempt at closing the ruck, she had to pull five packets out in order to get the top flap to tie down. When it was secured, she hoisted both straps over one shoulder and walked it just outside the cage entrance. It was so heavy she almost lost her balance when she went to set it down. She tried not to think about what the walk back out was going to be like. And she still had another entire ruck to fill up.

When she returned to the cage for "whatever else might be useful" Cass felt completely lost. For a moment she stood paralyzed by indecision. Gamble passed by her on the way to the door and stopped.

"Anything's going to be better than what we have right now. Just grab what you can," she whispered. She didn't wait around for a response.

It wasn't much help, but it was permission enough; Cass went to work collecting a few items from each stack, pile, or drawer. Batteries and blankets were obvious choices. Beyond that, she gathered whatever else caught her eye. By the end of it, she had the ruck about three-quarters full of gear. She added a few more packets of food on top and two portable purification devices for water. Once it was all secure, Cass was happy to note the ruck wasn't quite as heavy as the first.

Gamble had already loaded up two rucksacks of her own, and both looked even bulkier than the ones Cass had packed. For a moment the two women stood by the entrance of the cage.

"She's been real good to us," Gamble whispered. She gave the cage a gentle pat, which would have seemed odd if Cass hadn't known it was Gamble's way of saying goodbye not just to the cage but to her entire former way of life. Cass put her hand on Gamble's shoulder. Gamble sniffed once and wiped an eye with the heel of her hand, then looked at Cass. "Ready?"

"Let's do it," Cass said. She didn't know how they were going to pull this off, but she was well past doubting

Gamble's ability to find a way.

"We're not going to risk lugging all this through that hall again," Gamble said. She pointed to one of the rucks, which had a couple of coils of rope and some carabiners attached to it. "I'm thinking we go forward to the balcony, lower the rucks, try to pick 'em up through the front door."

"We climbing down too?"

"If we can do it safely. If not, we'll circle back through the hall, and have Mouse get the rucks." Gamble said it with confidence, but she hesitated afterwards. "What do you think?"

"I think if anyone can pull this off, it's us."

"Roger that," Gamble said with a smile. She bent down and grabbed a ruck in each hand. "Move 'em to the door. I want to take another peek before we commit."

Cass nodded and picked her two bags up. Heavy as they were, at least carrying one in each hand balanced her out. They set the four bags side by side in a row by the door, and then each got into position, Cass with her hand on the handle, Gamble with hers on Cass's shoulder. Cass waited for the signal. Three seconds. Five seconds. Ten seconds. She was just about to turn her head to look at Gamble when the squeeze came. Gently she applied pressure until she felt the door unlatch and then slowly she pulled the door open. A half-second later, Gamble's hand shot up off her shoulder to the door and halted its motion. A moment later, Cass heard it too. A pattering sound, cut off abruptly, followed by a faint hiss, like a dry exhale through a hollow pipe.

There was something walking in the hall.

Cass and Gamble stood frozen in place, listening. The door stood open no more than two inches in maybe the worst possible position from Cass's standpoint. They'd given up the security of the sealed door but hadn't gained any visibility. For all they knew, the Weir – and Cass couldn't believe it was anything other than a Weir – could be standing right outside the room. Cass held still, waiting for some cue or direction from Gamble. Undoubtedly they were both feeling the same tension. The motion from closing the door might attract attention that the small gap hadn't. But if the gap had been noticed, then surely re-securing the room was their only hope.

Long minutes pounded out, the bloodflow throbbing in her head. Then, finally, the patter started again. Moving away from the door, headed the opposite direction from their planned path. When it was quiet again, Gamble gave it another minute or so before she made any movement at all. She gently pushed on the door. Cass closed it again but didn't let it latch. Gamble leaned close.

"Think it's gone for good?" she whispered.

Cass wanted to say yes. But she didn't believe it. "No," she answered.

"Yeah," Gamble said. They returned to silence, Cass waiting for Gamble to puzzle their way out. Gamble quietly cursed instead. And the idea that even Gamble might not be able to solve this one scared Cass more than the noise in the hall.

If the thing was watching the hall, it was over. And even if it wasn't watching, if they bumped into it on the way out, the chances that they'd be able to react fast enough while lugging all that gear were slim to the point of nonexistence. But Cass couldn't let herself believe they'd come this far just to fail now. Gamble would figure it out. She always did.

"What you said before," Gamble whispered. "About them not reacting to you. Tell me how you know that. Not why you *believe* it, Cass. How you *know* it."

"I can't," Cass admitted. "I don't." She *didn't* know. But every other time she'd faced off against the Weir, she'd been on a war footing. Armed, attacking. She'd never tried walking passively amongst them. And Painter... Painter had mentioned something about it, long ago. *Not* so long ago, and yet a lifetime in the past. Hadn't he told them he'd gone out in the night? "But I'm up for trying anyway."

She could see the consternation on Gamble's face; she didn't want to put Cass at risk, but there clearly wasn't any other choice.

"All right," Gamble said. "Scout it out. But don't go far. We'll do it in stages. From here to the stairwell first, no farther."

"Check," Cass said.

Gamble nudged one of the rucksacks with the toe of her boot.

"Still. Maybe a little overzealous. I'm gonna strip it down to one each." Cass started to argue but Gamble cut her off with a look. "Don't push it, Cass. We're not moving this all at once, and we're not making two trips. Be back in five minutes. You get into any trouble, give me three clicks."

Cass nodded.

"When you get back, click twice, take two breaths, click twice again. I'll open from the inside."

"All right."

"I can't believe I'm letting you do this."

"Maybe you'll think of something better by the time I get back."

"Get out of here."

"See you in a few."

They reversed position at the door. Cass felt strange being the one to give the signal to open; she was so used to following Gamble's lead, it almost seemed silly. Gamble looked at her.

"Be careful," she said.

"Yep," Cass answered. She took three breaths to settle herself, and then squeezed Gamble's shoulder. Gamble opened the door smoothly, slowly, giving Cass time to edge around and take in as much as she could before she committed. It was maybe thirty seconds before she convinced herself she'd seen all that she could. A final breath, and she slipped through the partially opened door, back out into the hallway.

Cass dropped into a crouch near the wall and scanned both directions. Thankfully, the corridor was clear from end to end. Even as she looked, though, she was doing most of her work with her ears. First and foremost, she needed to find out where the Weir had gone and do her best to get a sense of whether or not it was likely to return.

She crept back down the hallway, passing the team room. Both doors were shut, of course, even though she hadn't heard Gamble close the one she'd come out of. That, at least, was a good sign. If she hadn't heard it from that distance, then certainly they hadn't alerted the lone Weir. There were doors on either side of the corridor and she gave each a cursory check as she passed by, but none of them appeared to have been disturbed since her initial entrance. She paused every few feet to listen, straining to pick out any warning in the heavy silence. But there was nothing.

At the farthest end of the hall, a set of double doors led to a common area that Gamble and her team had converted into a combination of recreation room and gym, where they'd spent many an odd hour blowing off steam in their particular brand of rough play. One of the doors was ajar. Had it been that way the whole time? Cass tried to picture it from when they'd first come into the corridor, but she couldn't bring it to mind. She just hadn't noticed. She wanted to dismiss it as nothing. But for no obvious reason, her heart quailed at the thought of approaching that room. And thus Cass knew it was where she had to go.

Carefully, quietly, she made her way there. When she reached it, she pressed close to the wall on the left side and held still for a count to ten, listening. All quiet.

She transferred her weight and slowly leaned around the partially opened door. The room revealed itself to her in a shifting slice, like the world glimpsed through a window of a slowly rolling train. And though nothing seemed amiss, her apprehension built with each heartbeat, a rising tide of dread that threatened to swallow her in its inevitability.

The shock was nearly physical when it came into view, as her mind struggled to process its imagined fear made real.

There was a figure standing in the room, with its back to the door. The hollow blue radiance of its eyes cast a muted glow on the wall, like the moon was trapped within. Cass had expected a Weir; she had *known* it would be a Weir. But she couldn't have possibly imagined that she would recognize that silhouette.

It was Swoop.

She remained at the door, paralyzed by the revelation, unable to move, to think, to breathe.

And that was when he turned around.

FOURTEEN

The bartender noticed her first, as usual. He wasn't officially on watch. Never officially. But he usually saw everything before the official watchers did anyway. Still, he hadn't actually seen her come in, which was rare. She was just standing there as if it was where she'd always been, or like she'd just formed out of the haze that clung to the low ceiling in the establishment. The light wasn't great to begin with, but the woman had picked a spot near the entrance where the one good bulb was just behind her, casting her in silhouette. Almost dramatic. Even though clusters of people were on either side of her, no one seemed to be paying her any mind. She stood there like a hole in the crowd, and the usual noise and chaos of the bar seemed to die at her feet; like rain parting for the one person in the crowd who'd thought to bring an umbrella. The bartender looked down and checked the glass in his hands, the one he was about to wash; it wasn't *that* dirty. He set it aside.

When he looked back up, the woman had advanced a few paces further in, into the next pool of light. Her skin was golden-brown, the kind that could have been from almost anywhere. Dark hair, dark eyes, wide cheekbones. And down her left cheek from just under her eyelid nearly to her jawline, a thick, dark line ran as if a tear had fallen and left a scorched trail in her skin. Some kind of intricate tattoo. She wore a faint smile as she surveyed the scenery and pulled off her coat.

Her shirt was missing its sleeves, and the definition of the musculature in her arms drew the bartender's attention; lean, sculpted, hard. Not the contorted look that the grafters and juicers had. She was a natural, as near as he could figure. A specimen. There was something off about her, though, that the bartender couldn't place. Something sharper. Something *other*. He'd gotten pretty good over the years about reading people's intentions, but this one was a complete mystery to him. That rarely meant anything good.

She made her way over to the bar and picked an empty spot towards one end, nearest the door. The bartender figured that was no accident. The fellow next to her swung his head her direction with groggy imprecision and mumbled something the bartender couldn't make out. The guy was a semi-regular, tolerated by the crew that ran the area, but the bartender couldn't remember his name, so he always just called him "chief". The lady didn't say anything in reply; just turned and looked at him full on, her face less than a foot from his. Chief sat there for a second, and then all of a sudden he jerked back, got up from his stool, and weaved his way to the front door. He didn't even finish his drink. The woman looked back over at the bartender and motioned for him.

He took a couple of steps closer. But not too close. "Drink?" he said.

"Something from the top shelf, if you don't mind," she said. Her voice was husky with a touch of a smirk.

"Sure. What'll it be?"

She shrugged one shoulder. "Surprise me."

He nodded and scanned his wares. The weird vibe continued coming off the woman, and he got the distinct impression that his decision was going to be closely evaluated. Lots of clears up there to choose from, and he started to reach for one, but stopped himself. She seemed more like the amber kind to him. The bartender stretched up on his tiptoes to reach one of the dusty flexiglass bottles towards the back. Not the finest in the house, but close enough. Quality, without being conspicuously expensive. He glanced at the glass on the counter he'd been about to wash, but decided to give her one of the actually clean ones from the bottom shelf.

The bartender poured a couple of fingers worth into the glass and then splashed a little extra on top. When he walked back over and set it in front of her, the woman looked down at it and then up at him with a little smile. And the look made his heart stop cold with fear for a couple of beats.

Her eyes were startling; they were red. Not bloodshot. The whites of her eyes were as clear as they could be. But the irises were a bright, vibrant red, flecked with gold. As unusual as her eyes were though, it was the mark on her face that had caused his reaction. From this distance he could see now what he'd missed before: the line running from cheekbone to jaw wasn't a single thick-lined design. It was a string of neo-kanji characters. And from top to bottom, it read "Property of Kyth".

Kyth. It was the name that struck fear in the bartender's heart.

"Fine choice," she said.

"Yeah, uh, well..." he said, trying to recover himself, hoping she wouldn't notice the hitch. "Been doing this a long while, ma'am."

She tapped something lightly on the bar and slid it towards him. When she withdrew her hand, she left a nanocarb chip behind. Fifty Hard.

"No ma'am, drink's on the house," the bartender said.

"It's not for the drink."

The bartender glanced around, but no one else was really paying attention to this newcomer. Not yet, anyway.

"Doesn't matter what it's for, I won't take it," the bartender said. He risked leaning in closer to her, but not so close there was any risk of accidentally touching her in any way. "I don't mind you having a drink, ma'am, but this isn't the kind of place you want to be hanging around for long.

Best if you drink up and scoot on out."

"You think so?" she replied, and she smiled. She did have a very nice smile.

"I'd hate to see anything happen to you."

"Oh, now, what would life be if not for things happening to us," she said, a sparkle in her eye. "It'd be awfully *boring* otherwise, wouldn't you say?"

"Around these parts, boring ain't so bad, ma'am."

There was a loud bark of laughter from one of the corner tables, the particular table that concerned the bartender the most. Corrin was over there, holding court with a few of the local crew, and more than a few who wanted to be part of it. He was just a low-level lieutenant, but this was his little pond and he guarded it jealously. The bartender tolerated it because it was best for business. Safest, anyway.

The woman took a sip of her drink, savored it, nodded in appreciation.

"So that's on the house," the bartender said. "And I don't want any trouble, OK?"

Her eyes smiled at him over the top of her glass as she drained it; or, if it was even possible, her eyes glinted more with a smirk, like he'd said something funny or had just embarrassed himself and didn't realize it. When she finished, she slammed the glass down on the bar top with a sharp crack, loud enough to draw the attention of everyone seated at the bar. The bartender held still, his hands on the bar, hoping that maybe it'd all escape the notice of Corrin's gang.

The laughter and chatter tapered off as she sat there on her barstool, all calm and innocence. Even when silence had fully descended, she didn't stir. Finally a deep voice called to her from a corner.

"Hey, girly. We're closed." Corrin. The bartender hung his head. The woman leaned her head forward towards his, enough to make him draw back out of the way. When he looked up at her, she winked.

"Hey," Corrin said, louder, which wasn't necessary

because everyone else had gone silent. "I said we're closed."

The bartender turned and went back to his usual place behind the bar, did his best to look disinterested. Corrin was an idiot, and, if the rumors were true, Kyth was a true psychopath. If the little lady didn't leave soon, nothing good was going to come out of it.

The red-eyed woman swiveled her head theatrically, sweeping the entire bar with an exaggerated slowness.

"Funny," she answered. "All the folks in here, kinda gives the impression of being open."

"Nah, closed, like, you ain't invited to be here."

"Ah, I see," she said, nodding. She looked back at the bartender, tilted her glass for another. Why was she doing this to him? He took down the bottle again, balanced atop the eggshells between him and her, hoping desperately that if he kept acting like all of this was just business as usual, no one would blow up his bar. He poured another generous dose and retreated back to his corner. Replaced the bottle. Tried to disappear. The woman smiled broadly. The bartender didn't dare look at Corrin.

"You ain't invited, like... Get out," Corrin said.

"In a minute," she replied, glancing over at the big man in the corner. The smile melted to the barest hint of amusement at the corners of her mouth. The bartender thought it might be a good time to loosen the sawed-off he had in a holster under the bar, but when he moved his hands, the woman's eyes flicked to his and he knew it wasn't a good time for that at all. He took a step back and crossed his arms. Once he was motionless, her eyes left his. Still felt like she could see everything he was doing, though.

Corrin flicked a hand at a couple of his juicehead friends; big meaty boys with necks bigger around than most people's thighs. They got up from the table, lumbered over to the bar. Everyone else scooted out of the way right quick, but the woman just looked at them and cocked her head to one side, like she couldn't quite tell if they were serious. One of them drew up short, put his hand on the other to stop his approach. The smarter of the two, apparently. Well out of range.

"I'm sorry," the woman said. "Did you have something to say to me?"

"Just uhhh," said the smart meathead. "You should probably go."

"Yes I heard that the first time," she replied. Then she slid off her barstool and took a couple of steps towards them. They both backed off.

She advanced a little further and other people started getting restless. Several patrons got to their feet, and a few jeered at her from behind the safety of those standing. But Corrin could see his boys were spooked, and he couldn't have that, so he took charge and came to meet her. He pushed them both aside.

"Look, girly, I dunno where you come in from, but you better blow right on back out afore you get blowed." He held his hand out in the shape of a gun and pointed it right in the woman's eye, a hair's breadth from touching her.

"Corrin," the bartender said.

"Shut it," Corrin barked. He didn't look at the bartender when he said it, just kept his eyes on the woman. She held out her fist and opened it slowly, palm up. A flat grey circle rested there; a nanocarb chip worth about twenty Hard. Not a large sum.

Corrin looked down at it.

"What's that supposed to be?"

"My gift," the woman said. "To you."

"Yeah?"

The woman dipped her head, a slow, single nod.

"Don't look like much."

The woman raised one shoulder. "And yet it's all you're worth."

"Come again?"

"Your worth," she said slowly, over enunciating. "As in, how much someone would pay."

"You're sayin' my life is worth twenty Hard?"

"Oh, sorry, no," the woman said. "Not just yours." Then she swept her gaze around the room, resting lightly, briefly on each of those who belonged to Corrin's crew. She knew each and every one of them. The bartender didn't like that one bit.

"Yeah?" Corrin said. The woman dipped her head again. "Yeah, well. Price seems wrong to me."

"Take this. Leave."

"This is my bar, girly."

"I'm not talking about the bar. I mean the town."

"Oh yeah?" Corrin laughed. "Twenty Hard to leave town? Or what?"

"Or that's the best offer you'll get."

"You got some spunk, huh? I like that."

"Corrin," the bartender said, louder, warning.

"Are you talkin' again?" Corrin snapped, looking at him this time. The bartender knew Corrin would take it out of his hide for what he was about to say next, in front of all these people, but he had to stop things before the escalated any further.

"He can't read, lady," the bartender said. "He doesn't know—"

"I told you to shut it!" Corrin shouted, and one of Corrin's cronies threw a bottle at the bartender, who skillfully ducked it.

"Well," she said, "perhaps someone should take this opportunity to educate him."

The smart juicehead leaned over and started to whisper something to Corrin, but Corrin's heat was up too much now. He shoved the man away roughly.

"How about I educate *you*, girly?" And then he slapped the woman's still outstretched hand, sending the nanocarb chip sailing. It tumbled in the air and landed on the rubberized floor with a dull thunk. "You walk in my place with that kinda chat, and *that's* the best *you'll* get. And it all goes worse from there, I promise you that."

The woman blinked at him. "By any chance, are you familiar with the concept of Schelling's dilemma?" she asked, voice perfectly steady, perfectly cool.

"The what?"

"A Hobbesian trap, maybe?"

"Oh, well, yeah, sure," Corrin said. "Ain't that the one where a little thing walks into a place she don't belong and bad things happen to her?"

"Say two fellows are pointing guns at one another. Neither of them has ever killed anyone before, neither wants to start now. But each is terrified that if he lowers his own weapon, the other will do him violence."

"Nah," the big guy said, scratching his throat with the back of his fingers. "Pretty sure it's the one I said."

"The best strategy," the woman continued smoothly, "is for one fellow to lower his weapon. Gain trust. De-escalate the situation." After a moment she added, "But that's not usually the strategy either fellow takes. Usually, it goes to the *second* best strategy."

"Yeah? And what's that one?"

Her smile returned; broad, genuine. The bartender went for his gun.

The woman shot her hand out and Corrin said something that sounded like *hurk!* and then came flying towards the bar, crashed into it, scattered glasses and bottles and a couple of patrons. The bartender brought the sawed-off up, but there were too many paying customers running around for him to do anything with it. Not that he knew what he'd do with it anyway; hitting the woman would have been a death sentence. And now that the unpleasantness had started, he found himself strangely compelled to see how it'd all turn out. Surely he already knew; there was no way that little lady could handle all the folks that had closed in on her. But he was no fan of Corrin, and he kind of wanted to root for her anyway.

In the span of time it'd taken him to complete those thoughts, the woman had felled three more patrons; the two juicehead friends, and one heavyset woman that the bartender had once seen beat a man to death with an unbroken bottle. A guy in a red jacket grabbed her from behind, but the woman melted to the floor down between his legs and somehow came up behind him. She snatched him by his belt with one hand and under his chin with the other and jerked the man's head back and down on to her shoulder. She swung him to one side and then back the other, warding off the others, wielding him like a gibbering shield.

The crowd was confused, and one young man took the opportunity to lunge for her. She met him halfway, thrusting her human shield out and knocking the young man to the floor before drawing back, her captive once again secure before her.

"Twenty Hard was too high an offer for the lot of you," she said. "This man here," she waggled the man in the red jacket back and forth as she spoke, "is already dead. If you love your own life more than you love his, leave now."

Everyone else seemed frozen in place.

"Can't *any* of you idiots read?" the bartender yelled, and he showed the business end of the sawed-off around to whoever was looking his way. "Get outta here!"

For a moment it was silent. Then someone cursed about the same time someone else said *Kyth* and that broke the spell. People started clearing out every which way they could, as long as it didn't take them anywhere near the red-eyed woman. The guy in the red jacket had taken to crying through his teeth, undoubtedly wishing he'd made wiser choices about his life.

The woman held her captive locked in place until the bar was empty of everyone else, save for the four bodies on the floor and the bartender. She looked over at the bartender then, down at the sawed-off he was pointing vaguely her way, then back up at him again. She arched an eyebrow. He put the gun down.

She adjusted her grip on the guy in the red jacket, just enough so he could open his mouth. Immediately a torrent of apologies erupted.

"I didn't know, I swear I didn't know," he said. "I didn't see 'cause I was behind you and I thought you were just some cat, please I swear, I swear!"

"I wish I could say acting out of ignorance was its own punishment," the woman said. "But I can't go around making exceptions. You laid hands on Kyth's property. From your reaction, I judge you're aware of the penalty."

"Please," the guy said, "please, I swear I didn't know." He was almost whispering now. The bartender couldn't watch. He picked up the almost clean glass again and started wiping it out with a towel.

"I can do it now," the woman continued. "And it'll be quick. I let you go, Kyth's still going to have his due. Can't promise you when or how. Might be tomorrow. Might be ten years from now. Only thing I can tell you is it'll be much, much worse."

"Please, please don't kill me."

"Suit yourself," the woman said. Then the bartender heard a thump, a grunt, and the sound of the guy in the red jacket hitting the floor. After that, she returned to her barstool, took a sip of her drink. Plunked something down on the bar.

The bartender didn't want to look at her. "Still on the house."

"Still not for the drink."

He sighed, put the glass down again. Turned to look at her from his safe distance.

"Lady, I'm just trying to make a living here. It's easy for folks like you to roll in off the streets and throw your weight around because it's little people like me that always pay the price for it. I told you before I didn't want any trouble, and you brought me a heap of it." He slung his towel on the bartop and started wiping it just to give himself something to do. "Not that you care about any of that."

"On the contrary, I do care. Quite a bit. That's what this is for," she said, tapping the stack of Hard she'd left on the bar. "So you don't have to pay the price."

"That's not what I meant."

"You won't have to pay *that* price, either," she continued. "The kid in red will wake up in a bit, and live the rest of his days in abject fear, I suppose. Maybe he'll use his time to do some good. And a couple of folks will be around shortly to take care of the others. Things are going to be changing around here."

"Yeah? And why's that?"

"Corrin and his ilk annoyed Kyth."

"Seems like a bad idea."

The woman finished her drink in a strong gulp, placed the glass gently on the top of the bar, and then stood.

"There are two possible outcomes to annoying Kyth," she said while she put on her coat. "One is that he takes away one of your favorite toys."

She stopped there, left him hanging, headed for the door. The curiosity was too strong.

"What's the other?" he called after her. She'd already opened the door partway, but stopped and looked back at him.

"He takes away one of your favorite toys, and then he takes an interest in you," she said, and she flashed that heartmelting smile at him. "What's your name, bartender?"

"Name's Weston," he answered.

"Well, Weston. Thank you for the drinks."

"You're welcome..." he trailed off, leaving room for her to offer her own name. She declined. And he knew it was silly to ask, but he couldn't stop himself from trying. "I don't suppose you got a name?"

"My name's my own," she said flatly. Then that smirk crept back up. "But most people just call me Trouble."

FIFTEEN

When Wren first surveyed the twisted ruins across the open plain, he found himself completely overwhelmed by all the possibilities. At first, he had stood at the door looking back the way they'd come just like Haiku had told him to. But nothing he saw jumped out as an obvious refuge.

Everywhere he looked seemed equally sparse; all bad options and none better than any other. Having all choices was almost as bad as no choices. Maybe worse, because at least having *no* choice gave some direction. Wren adjusted his pack, more for something to do than because it was necessary. He did need to get moving, but the fear of heading the wrong way kept him frozen in place. And more than that, though he tried not to admit it to himself, there was a feeling of security there at the foot of that fortress. Even outside the tower, the strength of the place radiated outward and cut the sense of exposure. To leave it was to invite the malevolent eye of the wide open.

"Any action's better than just standing around," Wren heard Three say. Not quite audibly, but the thought formed so clearly in his mind he almost looked for him. "Get moving. You'll find it."

The weariness of his mind and body blended dreams with the real. But though Wren knew Three was dead and forever gone, his heart still responded to the confidence in the man's voice, imagined or remembered.

You'll find it.

Wren picked a direction more or less in line with the way he'd first come in and forced himself to leave the meager security at the foundation of the steel fortress. That security was an illusion anyway. The first few steps were always the hardest, he told himself. He'd feel better once he was on the move.

But as he walked across the barren plain and the distance between him and the building grew, fear swept in to fill the emptiness behind him. Whatever change of perspective he'd gained about the Strand on his way in had evaporated. Memories haunted his every step, images he'd suppressed awoke with vengeance and torment. Come nightfall, his mind told him, this empty stretch of dead land would be alive with the Weir. This was their land, their home. Wherever he hid, they would find him. He turned back towards the tower.

You'll find it.

The phantom voice echoed amidst his thoughts, a stillness in the heart of the storm. Wren drew his knife and gripped it so hard it hurt. The blade was too small to save him, he was too weak to wield it well, but there was courage in the steel. And Haiku's words as they left Greenstone too came back to him; back there was a life paralyzed by fear, nothing more.

He had already chosen. Now his job was to execute that choice. The fear was the way. And though he didn't feel any safer or any braver, he turned his face away from the tower and into the fear, and with trembling steps, he advanced.

Once Wren had resolved himself, he made much better progress and his mind quieted. In ten minutes, he'd crossed the border of the dead space and reached where the first broken buildings rose. At first, he wasn't sure what to look for. Haiku had told him somewhere high, or somewhere small. That seemed too vague to be of any real help now. He wandered amongst the ruins, searching for a place that looked right. Was the second floor of a building high enough? Was something he could crawl through on his hands and

knees small enough, or did Haiku mean something he had
to get on his belly to enter? He spent maybe half an hour
trying to think of all the things anyone had ever told him
about being out in the open after dark, and using them to
evaluate each option as it presented itself. Nothing seemed
promising.

And then Wren realized he was going about it all wrong.
He'd spent three nights traveling with Haiku, two of those
outside the safety of a wayhouse. Maybe he didn't have to
think about it, maybe it was something he couldn't figure
out just by looking. Maybe he had to find something that
felt right. And the only way to do that was to get inside
some of the places he'd been passing by. It was obvious that
nothing in the immediate area would do; there was hardly
anything with two standing walls here. But armed with a
new perspective, he doubled back.

Wren wandered without any specific direction, turning
whichever way he felt like going. The first place he came to
was a low one-story structure that had caved in on one side.
The only entrance he could find was choked with debris,
but there was a narrow gap that looked just big enough for
him to squeeze through. He stood outside for a good two
or three minutes trying to build up the courage to poke his
head into that space. Ultimately, he couldn't bring himself
to do it, and moved on.

Wren wandered on as the sun slipped lower and the
shadows grew longer, and his barely-suppressed anxiety
threatened to bloom. About ten minutes later, a narrow
three-story building caught his eye. Most of the front of the
building was sheared off, but somehow the rooms inside
were still in place, like some grotesque dollhouse. Both
sides and the rear of the structure were still standing. The
roof had collapsed and dumped a good portion of itself in
the front; where it remained, it was deeply bowed. It was
almost as if some giant hand had descended from the sky
and stuck a finger right down the face of the structure.
On the right side he saw an exterior staircase, rusting and

skeletal, leading up to the second floor. He walked around that side to take a closer look.

The stairs were twisted and sagging, and a section of it had pulled away from the exterior wall, but Wren thought he might be light enough to make it up. He'd always been a pretty good climber. The staircase led to a metal-mesh landing, where a dark and doorless entryway awaited. The fact that it was dark inside probably meant there weren't too many holes in the walls and ceiling. Wren didn't like the look of it all that much, but he knew he was running out of time, and he decided to check it out.

He went to the bottom of the stairs and took hold of the metal railing. It wobbled a little when he took it, but it didn't feel like it was going to break off. Not immediately, anyway. He started up cautiously, testing each step before he committed to it. The first few stairs groaned and creaked under foot, but they held. He took that as a good sign. Maybe not good, exactly, but at least it wasn't a *bad* sign. The section that had pulled away from the building was about six feet above the ground, and it drooped and leaned inward towards the wall. Wren stood at the last stair before that part, looking carefully at how far he had to go before the staircase fully reconnected to the building. He figured it was five stairs. It was too far to jump and now that he was close to it, it didn't seem like the steps in between could bear even his meager weight. He stood there considering for a few moments. The outer frame of the staircase on the high side was wide and still looked like it was in pretty good shape. He thought that if he could keep his balance and walk along the frame, he might be able to get up quickly enough that it wouldn't collapse under him. And if the steps did collapse, well... at least it wasn't *that* far to the ground.

Wren took a deep breath and tested his footing, first with his right foot then, when that felt weird, his left. That actually seemed worse, so he tried leading with his right again. The angle of the railing made it more difficult than he'd expected, but after a couple of false starts, he held on to the rail and took quick, short steps along the outer frame. The metal whined and shifted beneath him. On his fourth step, the whole staircase shuddered and then popped, and Wren felt everything sliding to the right, away from the building. Further up the stairs, he saw another bolt pull free.

His balance had already been off-center and even though he did everything he could to adjust, his next step came down right in the middle of the unsupported section. The staircase shrieked beneath him. He didn't break through immediately, but he could feel the metal flexing and giving way with a sickening, almost mushy sensation. Without thinking, Wren threw himself forward with his arms outstretched.

He didn't get the push-off he had hoped for, and the impact was hard; his chin slammed down on one of the steps. A flash of pain, spots in his eyes. Not a graceful landing at all. But he hadn't fallen through. Wren lay still for a long moment, sprawled flat on the stairs, feeling them vibrate under him. When he felt confident enough that the whole staircase wasn't going to collapse with him on it, he risked lifting himself up and looking back down the steps. His feet were still dangling out over the bent and broken segment, but from the waist up he was laying on the more stable upper portion, where the staircase remained firmly secured to the building.

Wren drew his legs up behind him, and crawled up the few remaining steps to the top. There, he turned and sat on the landing with his feet on the stair below. His chin burned. He touched it lightly, winced, and his fingers came away wet and bright red. He ran his thumb through the fresh blood and then wiped his hand on his pants. From his vantage he could tell the stairs were definitely in worse shape than they had been just before his ascent, and he wondered if he'd have to find an alternate way down. A moment later it occurred to him that, with as much trouble as he'd had coming up, that ruin of a staircase might be almost as good as another wall. A Weir probably wouldn't

try to come up that way without good reason, and even if
it did at least it wouldn't make it to the top without making
a whole lot of noise. It was kind of like having a built-in
early-warning system.

Wren decided to check out the inside of the building. He
touched his chin again, and then had to wipe his hand on
his pants again. The blood was still bright and he noticed
it'd dripped onto the stair at his feet. He was going to have
to do something about that. For the time being, he tugged
the cuff of his shirtsleeve out from his coat and used it to
wipe the blood off the stair. Then he dabbed it gently on
his chin. Wren got to his feet and stepped into the building,
pausing at the entrance for a minute to let his eyes adjust
to the gloom. The air was musty and when he shifted he
could feel the grit on the floor under his feet. The sun was
getting low and the door was facing the north anyway, so
the light didn't penetrate very far, but once his eyes started
to get used to it he saw he had been partially right about the
room. The walls didn't have any holes at all that he could
see. It was the ceiling he'd been wrong about.

The ceiling had collapsed in the middle. Or maybe it
was more accurate to say it was the floor above that had
fallen in. In any case, from where he stood on the second
floor, he looked up through a yawning hole above and into
utter blackness. Whatever else was up there, at least the
roof hadn't caved in over this portion. There was no visible
daylight that he could see. He set his pack down on the
ground there by the doorway and rummaged around for his
chemlight. It took him a while to find it; it had fallen down
into the very bottom, of course. When he finally felt it and
wrapped his fingers around it, his hand brushed against the
cold metal of the bundle he'd carefully packed on one side.
The cloth he'd wrapped it in must have come undone.

Wren crouched by the door. He pulled the chemlight out
and laid it next to the pack on the floor, and then drew out
the bundle and rested it on his lap. The cloth had fallen
away in one part, exposing a portion of the grip and some

of the surrounding steel. He'd intended just to wrap it back up and put it away, but now that he had it out, laid across his legs, he couldn't resist peeling back the rest of the cloth and taking a peek. He drew the cloth away and looked at the heavy prize in his lap.

Three's pistol.

He ran his fingers over it lightly, tracing the cylinder, the grip, the trigger guard. It was unloaded, but even so, he wouldn't touch the trigger. He still remembered the deafening thunderclap that had filled the room and made his insides tremble, the one time he'd seen Three fire it. The pistol was massive but well-balanced. The scuffs and scrapes showed years of hard use; the finely-tuned components told of the great care that had been taken over it. Rugged and resilient. A precise instrument whose design left no doubt as to its purpose. Wren opened the cylinder to see the three empty chambers, then snapped it closed again. After a moment, he repeated the process. There was something almost soothing about the way the mechanisms all worked together. Even so, the pistol felt menacing in his hand. It thrilled him, but also felt wild and uncontrollable, as if at any moment it might turn itself on him.

Mama had kept the pistol for a long time. Right until the end, when she'd passed the weapon on to Chapel, who had in turn presented it to Wren on their second day in Greenstone. Chapel hadn't said much, just that Wren's mother had wished him to have it, and he'd laid it on the table in front of him, with its three remaining rounds of ammunition on the side. It was as if some ancient king had handed down his sword from of old. Wren didn't know the story of the weapon, but he could tell there was one. Three had handled it with both familiarity and reverence. For a long while, Wren had just looked at the gun on the table, too overwhelmed, too afraid to touch it, but too awed to turn away.

It was Mol, of course, who had come to the rescue. She'd brought an aged but fine cloth and helped Wren wrap the weapon securely. The ammunition they kept separate, in a small pouch on the side of Wren's pack. It was too rare to leave behind, and far too dangerous to leave in the gun.

A dark, wet splotch appeared on the grip; it took Wren a moment to recognize his bleeding chin had just dripped. He hurriedly scrubbed the spot on the gun clean with his shirtsleeve and then dabbed his chin again. There was a cheap adhesive bandage or two in his pack. He wrapped the gun back in its covering and returned it to its place in his backpack, and then rummaged around for the bandages. Mama would be upset about him using his sleeve like that. The thought made his chest go tight, but he kept himself under control while he pressed the bandage onto his chin.

With that completed, Wren finally got to the task at hand. He picked up his chemlight and twisted the endcap to ignite it. It glowed yellow-green and illuminated the small room with its soft light. Not that there was much to see. The room was filled with debris, almost as if the room above had been full of concrete and had dumped it all in a pile here below. In fact, that might very well have been what had happened. There was more to the pile than just concrete, of course, but it really did look like someone had poured out a huge bucket of construction material. That didn't leave much room for anything else in there. There were no windows and if there were any connecting rooms, their doors had been completely choked with the rubble.

Wren's spirits dropped. He wasn't sure what exactly he'd been hoping to find, but this certainly wasn't it. The thought of having to find another way down was too discouraging to face. He was standing there with the chemlight down by his side trying to work up the resolve to head back out again, when a glimmer caught his eye. He held the chemlight up above his head, but couldn't see what had caused it. After a moment, he slowly lowered the chemlight. There. He saw it again.

He bent over and held the light out at arm's length, and though he lost sight of whatever had caused the glimmer, he saw now that one of the floorbeams had collapsed at an angle and had helped form a sort of shelf. What had looked like a solid mountain of wreckage actually had at least one cave. Wren walked closer and got down on his hands and knees. Sure enough, there was a small pocket in the debris. It wasn't very deep and the smell of dust was so thick it made him cough. He got up and went back over to the door, and then looked towards the pocket. He could see it now, the variation in depth of the pile, but it wasn't at all obvious that there was a hole in it. If something did come in the room, it'd have to look pretty hard to notice.

Wren returned to the opening and got down on the floor again. He really didn't like the idea of crawling in there. How long, he wondered, had all of that stuff been piled up like that? The thought of him accidentally knocking something loose and being buried alive almost turned him right around, broken stairs or no. But he stuck his chemlight in there and took a look at the top. There was a solid chunk of concrete or marble, still in one piece, that was laid across the angled floorbeam. He pushed on the broken floorbeam a couple of times, but nothing shifted other than a little dust. It seemed stable enough. And even though he was hesitant, he couldn't deny it felt like the right kind of place.

He slid his pack in first, and then crawled after it. There wasn't even enough space for him to sit up all the way, but it was deep enough that he could get all the way inside if he tucked his knees up. It wouldn't be comfortable, that was certain. But it did feel safe.

Wren scooted out backwards and pulled his pack after him. He'd decided. That would be his place for the night. But he wasn't going to spend any more time in it than he absolutely had to. He returned to the doorway and sat down on the floor with his back against the wall so he could look out. The sun had disappeared behind the buildings off to the west. In another hour at most, the Weir would be out. There wasn't much else for him to do before then.

He dug around in his pack and pulled out one of the

ration bars jCharles had given him. Mol had packed some better food, but he'd had to eat that first so it didn't go bad. The bar wasn't terrible, but it wasn't really something anyone could enjoy. It was spongy and bland, with a kind of buttery aftertaste. Wren knew it had a good balance of nutrients. He wouldn't be hungry in the night. But it wasn't very satisfying either. He drank some water and got out his thermal blanket, which he wrapped around his shoulders. He pulled up the hood of his coat. Somewhere behind those buildings, the sun started to set. The sky faded to pale purple and the shadows reached out across the landscape as it was embalmed in twilight. Wren waited as long as he dared. Almost too long.

The first cry was so distant that he initially mistook it for the wind caught and transformed by the ruins. Realization came moments later as an icy shock that woke him to action. Had he dozed off? He got to his feet and hugged his pack to his chest. The room was far too dark now to find his hiding place. A foolish mistake. Now he'd have to risk the light, when he could have, *should* have, already been tucked safely away. A good lesson, if he lived to remember it.

Wren ignited the chemlight and held it close, shielding it with his body and his pack. Where it had seemed weak and mellow in the afternoon light, now it blazed like a beacon in the darkness. He scrambled to the pile and dropped on his hands and knees to find his entry point. Fear was rising now that the reality of his situation had materialized. Night was falling, the Weir were abroad, and Wren was alone. He wasn't panicking yet, but each second he couldn't find the opening threatened to push him over the edge. Was he too far right? Or had he passed it? Everything looked so different in the dark, with only a narrow beam of light showing slivers.

He couldn't help it; he had to take the risk. He held the chemlight up, extended. Maybe it was coincidence that another Weir cried out just then.

There. To his left. He hadn't gone as far back into the

room as he'd thought. He crawled to the opening, shoved his pack through first and scurried in behind it. In his haste, he caught the top of his head on the corner of the floor beam, hard enough that it stopped his forward momentum. He managed not to cry out though the pain of it brought tears to his eyes. He ducked lower and crawled as far into his hiding place as he could and pulled his legs up behind. Wren's heart was pounding and he closed his eyes and tried to focus on his breathing. Deep breaths. Slow it down. It took twenty, maybe thirty seconds before he felt like he had things under control again. And when he opened his eyes, he realized he'd left his chemlight on.

It was still in his hand, glowing happily. With a quick twist of the end cap, he switched it off. The darkness swallowed him in an instant. Wren lay there listening for any sounds that might warn he'd given himself away, but the blood pounding in his ears made it hard to trust anything. For ten, fifteen, twenty minutes, he did nothing other than fight to still himself. He was twisted at an awkward angle, and the concrete under him worked through his hip bone with a dull, aching restlessness. He pressed his head into his pack and set his mind to enduring it.

Just a little longer. Just a little longer.

It was probably a full hour before he gave in and repositioned. When he did finally move, the muscles in his back spasmed to life and even when he'd settled into a new posture it felt like he was lying on a bed of hot needles. And he'd gotten his thermal blanket tangled and caught so that the larger portion was caught beneath him. He couldn't quite keep it pulled over his shoulder and his legs were completely exposed. His hood was still up, but it too was twisted off-center so that his left ear was uncovered. He wasn't too cold yet, but he could feel the temperature dropping as the night air filtered in through the entrance to his hiding place.

It was going to be a very long night.

The good news was he hadn't heard any more cries of

the Weir. Whether that was because they were nowhere
nearby, or because he was too insulated in his hiding
place, he wasn't sure. He wanted to believe the former. His
imagination assured him it was the latter. It was a detail
he hadn't considered, hadn't even *known* to consider. He'd
thought he'd been clever to use the broken staircase as an
alarm. But what good would it do him if he was too buried
under debris to hear the warning?

As the night progressed, that thought grew in his mind
and wreaked havoc with his thoughts. What had begun as a
mere possibility transformed into certainty. It was no longer
a question. There *was* a Weir outside, on the stairs, in the
room. Wren knew at any second the blackness of his hiding
place would vanish, replaced by glow from the light of those
probing eyes. He trembled uncontrollably, and though the
pain of laying in place was great, the fear that paralyzed him
was greater still.

He knew it would come. Any second now. Any second
now.

But it didn't. And just when Wren thought he would
break from the terror, a thought came unbidden. If he
could imagine the worst, could he not also bend his mind
to imagine the best? And his mind argued against itself.
The *best* seemed too much, too distant, too impossible. But
surely he could find something *better*. Even that seemed
foolish. What good was it to pretend there was safety when
danger was crouching at your door?

That thought brought back in a flash the memory of
the night in Morningside when everything had first gone
wrong. The night the girl had come to his room. The night
Snow had come to kill him. He had been frightened then.
Truly and wholly terrified. But he hadn't just stayed there
in his bed, waiting to die. The fear had motivated him, had
given him focus. As it had when he'd gone to his mama
outside the gate, walking out into the sea of Weir to bring
her back.

Wren tried to put himself back in that mindset. To

embrace the fear, rather than resisting it. To draw power
from it instead of letting it drain him. What if there *was*
a Weir out there in his room? What could he do about it
now? How would he respond?

His knife was still in his belt. He was laying on it, though
he thought if he shifted a bit he could draw it. In fact, if he
tucked his elbow into his side and bent his wrist down as
far as he could, his fingertips brushed the grip. He wouldn't
take it out now, but knowing he'd be able to if he needed
it reassured him a little. Not that he was confident it would
do much good. He'd used his knife to defend himself twice
in his life, and both times he'd surprised his attackers. The
second time it had been against Asher and it had ignited his
wrath rather than extinguishing it. Wren figured trying to
fight a Weir would be more like that.

He could of course try to Awaken any Weir that he came
into contact with, but he knew the possibilities were slim.
More often than not, they were too far gone. Or, if the
people that had once been in control were still in there, they
were too distant for him to reach. Maybe one day he'd learn
what he needed to know to help more of them. Maybe the
old man would even be able to help with that. But for now,
the odds figured he'd have even less chance at Awakening a
Weir than he would trying to fight it off.

Broadcasting was an option; the way Lil had taught him.
The way he'd turned back the tide of Weir that almost took
Mama. If a Weir came too close to the entrance, maybe he
could turn it away. But that too carried risk. What sent one
Weir running temporarily might very well alert every other
Weir in the area to his presence. They might coordinate and
return in numbers. Or worse. If Asher were hooked in...

That was too much to consider for now, and Wren
spent the next shivering, aching hours mentally rehearsing
different solutions to his most immediate problem.
Considering options, evaluating the chances of success,
the risks they bore, the likelihood that he could actually
execute them.

Noises drifted in from outside; scrapes, shuffles, moans that might have been wind or a cry from a Weir distorted by his hiding place. Rusted metal sighing. A thump. Had he heard it, or just imagined it? He held his breath, listening. Was this it?

But no, nothing appeared. Not yet. Wren allowed himself to shift positions. He was slipping towards fear again, and to combat it he refocused his mind on tactics. He had to stay on guard. On watch. He had to stay ready. Over time, his plans took on bizarre qualities or he lost his train of thought and had trouble remembering what he'd been trying to figure out.

He didn't even notice when he drifted off to sleep.

SIXTEEN

For a moment, Cass was frozen in place as she locked eyes with Swoop. Or, rather, with the creature that had once been Swoop. There was of course no recognition in his eyes; only a cold electric blue light emanated. She should have killed him, should have done it the instant she saw him, before he'd turned. Her hesitation had doomed her, and probably Gamble and her boys. All that remained was the white-noise scream she knew would come, followed by the torrent of Weir that would surge up from below and sweep her away. Even now, though, while her mind shrieked for her to *kill it, kill it now*, her body refused to obey. This was Swoop. Not *it*. *Him*.

The Weir opened its mouth. The cry that would bring destruction.

Instead, a quiet burst, like a strong exhale blended with a rattle in the throat. If Cass had had any reason to believe it possible, she might have thought the noise almost had the tone of a question. The sound from the Weir dispelled her paralysis and heightened her awareness of the hair's breadth between her and oblivion. It hadn't attacked, hadn't alerted. Yet. Before she'd even thought, Cass did something completely at odds with instinct.

She backed away. One slow step, then another. Out of view. The Swoop-Weir made the same noise again, as Cass backpedaled back down the hall. And then she heard it move.

It was coming. And she knew whatever confusion the creature was experiencing wouldn't last long. It'd taken her for one its own, for the moment. But if she didn't answer back, there was no question what its next move would be.

She had to kill it. She would kill it, or it would kill her. There was no option. When it came to the door, she would kill it.

But no, she wouldn't. She couldn't. Swoop was in there, somewhere.

Her mind scrambled for possibilities, replayed the images from scouting the hall, searched for something, anything, that could change this deadly outcome. Open doors. A place to hide.

And then.

A weapon, abandoned. The dislocator. Nonlethal against human targets. Where was it?

She looked left, then right. She remembered, it was by a door, just inside. But all the doors looked the same now. Behind her?

There, she saw it just as Swoop's shadow fell across the entryway at the end of the hall. Reflex took over. She dove, slid across the ground, wrapped a hand around the grip and brought it on target right as the Swoop-Weir came out of the door. It was just bringing its eyes to hers when she fired.

The dislocator thumped twice, and the Weir made a half-strangled, half-gagging sound as it flopped backwards in a seizure. It shuddered momentarily, and then was still. Cass lay on her back, weapon still pointed at the creature, heart hammering. Three seconds. Five seconds. Silence.

And then, somewhere from far below, an echoing cry.

She'd woken the Weir.

Cass scrambled to her feet and raced to the end of the hall where the Swoop-Weir lay in a heap with its legs bent awkwardly beneath it. When she reached it, an involuntary gasp escaped. The last time she'd seen Swoop, he'd been covered in blood and ichor, and torn with innumerable wounds. But here, before her, the creature was clean and seemingly mended. With its eyes closed, it *was* Swoop. She shook herself, stepped over the body, and then bent down and hooked it under its arms. It was completely limp in her grasp and unwieldy, but she wrestled the dead weight into position and started dragging it down the hall, back towards the team rooms. There wasn't much time. The Weir were growing louder.

She bypassed the first door and as she was approaching the second, she violated Gamble's directive.

"Gamble, open up," she said through the secure channel. "Open up!"

Just as Cass reached the team room door, it flew open and Gamble appeared, weapon at her shoulder and fury on her face. The range of emotions her expressions traveled through in the next two seconds was incredible to behold. Cass didn't stop, just pushed past her into the team room.

Gamble rolled in behind her and shut the door, and then turned on Cass, wild-eyed.

"Swoop," Cass said. "It's Swoop."

"What? Where–" Gamble began.

"They got him, he's a Weir. I hit him with a dislocator. I think it woke 'em all up."

Gamble's mouth dropped open and she blinked.

Cass waited for some kind of response, some outburst or fountain of curses. Instead, Gamble licked her lips and then said, "Mouse, get away from the door." And then a moment later, "Negative, loop back to Sky's position, wait there."

Cass was too busy struggling with Swoop's body to catch what Mouse had said, but it didn't matter. A few seconds later, Gamble was there beside her, hoisting their unconscious once-friend.

"Here, over here," Gamble said, her voice low. She shepherded Cass over to the wall the farthest from the doors. They laid the Weir on the floor under the window, and both crouched down beside it.

"You heard it?" Cass said. "Out there?"

Gamble was looking at Swoop, but she nodded.

"I'm sorry, Gamble. I didn't know what to do. But I couldn't just kill him."

Gamble put her hand on the top of Swoop's head. It was impossible now to think of him as anything other than the man he'd been only the day before.

"You should have, Cass," she said. Her tone was even, controlled, but Cass could hear the storm of emotion behind it. "That's exactly what you should've done."

A tear dropped from Gamble's cheek and spattered on the floor. She reached back behind her and drew the long, curved-bladed knife from the sheath she kept at the small of her back. To Cass's surprise, Gamble bent down and kissed Swoop's forehead. And then she placed the tip of the knife low on his neck, right where it met the shoulder. Cass sucked in her breath, held it, afraid to let Gamble finish the motion, but more afraid of what might happen if she tried to stop it.

The two women stayed frozen in that position for torturously long seconds, Cass's heartbeat in her ears the only sound.

"But," Gamble said, finally, "I understand why you didn't." She didn't take the knife from Swoop's neck, but her shoulders slumped slightly, and with that, the will to carry out the act seemed to melt off her.

"What do you think the chances are that your boy could get him back?" Gamble said.

"I don't know, Gamble," Cass said. "Good, I think. Wren always said it was easier with people who fought it. I don't think I know anyone in the world who'd be better at that than Swoop."

"Yeah," Gamble said. She pulled the knife back off Swoop's neck and laid it flat across her knee. "Too bad none of us are gonna make it out of here."

Cass looked back at the door across the room. She couldn't hear any sound of the Weir out there, but the team rooms had reinforced doors and walls; they weren't quite soundproofed, but they were much closer to it than any other place in the compound.

"You think they're coming?" Cass asked.

"No idea," Gamble said. "But I think we better plan for it." Gamble slapped the blade of her knife on her knee a couple of times and then returned it to its sheath. She then made some adjustment to her rifle. When she brought her hand back up, Cass saw she'd taken the red light off her weapon. Gamble swept the room slowly with the light, scanning for options.

"Try to barricade?" Cass offered.

"Not sure I want to spend my last minutes moving furniture," Gamble answered. "Plus, two doors, not a lot of stuff to go around." She shook her head. "If they can breach the locks on those doors, there's not much else that's going to slow them down. Where you think that vent goes?" She shone her light on one of the adjacent walls. There was a small vent at the bottom, towards one corner. It looked just big enough to get stuck in. "Next door?"

"Maybe," Cass said. "Or straight down. Not sure we could get much through there anyway. Definitely not Swoop."

Gamble looked back down at him, lying there like he was sleeping. "This guy. Always had a knack for showing up places he wasn't supposed to be."

Cass looked at Swoop again then too, and her emotions swam. She'd only been presented bad options; had she picked the worst? "I'm sorry, Gamble. I just... When I saw who it was–"

"Can't undo it by talking about it, Cass. And if you'd killed him, it might've had the same effect anyway. At least this way we have a shot at getting him back." Gamble glanced up at the window, still sealed off with a heavy-duty blackout shade. The windows were oddly set, raised about chest-height off the ground and running nearly all the way up to the ten-foot-high ceiling.

"Hey," Gamble said. "You up for something crazy?"

"What," Cass replied. "Like coming back to Morningside, or sneaking into an infested compound to steal some supplies?"

"I said crazy, not stupid."

"Let's do it."

"Grab the bags and bring 'em over here. They're still by the door. Try to keep it quiet."

"All right," Cass said. She rose and crept over to the rucksacks. Gamble had unloaded a huge quantity of supplies in the short time Cass had been gone. From the looks of it, she must've more or less dumped everything on the ground. It was a wonder that she'd been able to pack any of it back up, though at least it was obvious which two rucks had been repacked. The others were nowhere to be seen, presumably having been buried under the pile of gear they were leaving behind.

Cass grabbed the two rucksacks, one in each hand, and made her way back to the far side of the room. They were still heavy, but not nearly as heavy as they'd been the last time she'd picked them up. Gamble was busy in the cage; her red light swept arcs, making shadows dance on the walls and ceiling like she'd set a fire. While she worked, she came in over the channel.

"Mouse, you make it to Sky's position yet?"

"Negative, not yet," Mouse responded. "Almost there."

"Well scratch that. Change of plans. I need you back at the compound."

"Uh, all right. Where?"

"West side of the building, outside, below the main team room."

"Uh, say again," Mouse said. "You said below it?"

"Yep."

"But outside?"

Gamble was returning from the cage, cradling a bundle in her arms. "Most definitely outside."

"All right, check. Be there in two."

"What's going on in there, Ace?" Sky said.

"Good news and bad," Gamble answered. She crouched by Cass and laid the pile of gear next to Swoop. "Too much to explain, and we're in a hurry."

"You in trouble?" Sky asked.

"Yep," Gamble said. "You got a line on the main room from where you are?"

"Not a good one," Sky said.

"Go ahead and reposition," Gamble said, as she started separating out the pile into its components. Some of it, Cass didn't recognize. Most of it. But one thing was obvious; there was a lot of rope. "Three hundred meters out, minimum. Let me know when you're set."

"Check," answered Sky. "Moving."

"Mouse," Gamble said, "how much longer?"

"Thirty seconds," he replied.

"I need you for some heavy lifting," Gamble said.

"How heavy?"

"Swoop heavy," she said. There was a beat of silence over the channel. Then.

"Say again?"

"We found Swoop," Gamble answered. "But they got him first. We're bringing him out."

Another heavy pause; Cass could almost hear the swirl of emotion and confusion hovering there in the nothingness. Then, Mouse clicked in again.

"Dead?"

"Negative," Gamble responded. "They got him, Mouse. Made him one of theirs. But we're gonna get him back." Cass marveled at how controlled Gamble was now. Her tone was even, all trace of emotion erased.

Mouse said, "How you figure on– "

"Right now I need you outside, Mouse," Gamble said, cutting him off. She didn't raise her voice at all, but her delivery made it clear she wasn't interested in further discussion. "Help me get this on him," she said to Cass. She was holding up what looked like a tangle of straps. Then Gamble spread it, and Cass understood. A harness.

"Understood," Mouse said a moment later.

Cass had never used a harness like it before, didn't know how to even begin fitting it on Swoop's unconscious form. But Gamble was an effective, if impatient, instructor.

"Sit him up," Gamble said, and Cass did. "Buckle these. Waist. Then shoulders." She pointed at the three fasteners in succession as she said it. "Loop in, around, back through here." It took Cass a moment to figure out how to properly thread the straps through, but once she got the first, the others were no problem.

She was just hooking in the third strap when there was a dull thud in the hall. Both women froze. Cass looked up at Gamble, but Gamble kept her focus on what she was doing, paused in mid-motion. After a few seconds of silence, Gamble wordlessly resumed fastening straps around Swoop's thighs. Cass followed suit.

Once the harness was secured, Cass lowered Swoop back to the ground while Gamble clipped on some kind of device to the front. Cass didn't recognize it at first, but as Gamble finished rigging it to Swoop, Cass remembered having seen something like it before. The night they'd had to flee Morningside the first time, after Connor's open betrayal, she'd seen the team use something similar to ascend and descend the city wall. She wasn't quite sure how it was supposed to work now, though, with Swoop incapable of operating it himself.

"How much you weigh?" Gamble asked.

"I'm not sure," Cass said. "Hundred-thirty, hundred-thirty-five pounds maybe?"

"That's what..." Gamble said. "Call it sixty kilos." She picked up one of the ropes and started unwinding it from the hangman's noose-like arrangement it'd been stored in.

"We're going out the window?"

"We're going out the window."

Getting out that way was going to be a trick. The windows were reinforced, and they didn't open.

Another thud sounded in the hall, louder. Closer. No way to know what was going on out there, but anything was probably bad.

"Gamble, Mouse," Mouse said over the channel. "I'm here."

"Check, stand by," she answered. Then, to Cass, "You think you can handle both those rucks?"

"Absolutely," Cass said. She actually wasn't sure, but if that's what Gamble needed from her, she was going to do it.

"All right, Swoop goes out first. Then you with the gear. I'll follow."

"You should go out before me," Cass said. "Just in case."

Gamble stopped in her preparations and held up another device that Cass didn't recognize.

"You know how to run one of these?" she asked.

"No."

"That's why you go," Gamble said. She set it down and went back to playing out the rope in a coil on the floor. She glanced over her shoulder at the doors. "We're gonna have to risk it," she said, mostly to herself. And then to Cass, "Get that shade open."

Cass nodded and started to reach for the switch, then stopped. Power was still out. She was about to ask Gamble what to do but realized the time for that had passed. She was a big girl. She could solve her own problems. Cass extended the claws of her right hand, reached as high as she could, and jabbed them easily through the thick material of the blackout shade. A quick slash to the right and the lower portion of the shade peeled away. Cass caught it with her other hand and lowered it to the ground as the room flooded with daylight, dazzling. She had to shut her eyes against the onslaught that confused her senses. She tugged her veil back down over her face, tucked it into the neck of her coat. When she opened her eyes, she saw even Gamble was squinting against the light streaming in.

The window flexiglass reinforced with a thin nanocarbon mesh; rumor was it could withstand a direct hit from an armor-penetrating shaped charge, though Cass couldn't imagine anyone ever having the opportunity to test such a scenario. Whatever the case, they clearly weren't going to be able to bash their way out with a piece of furniture or the butts of their weapons.

"Gamble, Sky," Sky said in Cass's head. "Finn and I are in position."

"Check," Gamble said. Then to Cass, "I need a boost."

Cass nodded and went down on one knee, keeping her other foot flat on the floor so Gamble could use her thigh as a step. Gamble clambered up and started running what looked like a thin grey cord from one side of the window to the other. It clung to the flexiglass like putty.

A low murmuration filtered in from the hall, the rustle of sand blown across rough concrete. Things were moving out there. A lot of things.

"Sky, how good's your angle?" Gamble asked while she continued laying the cord in a rectangle. She was working fast, but with precision.

"Looking right at you, babe," Sky said. He was doing a good job of keeping the concern out of his voice, but Cass could hear the intensity of his emotion. He was keyed up. They all were. Gamble finished attaching the cord. When she was done, it lay in a rectangle from the bottom of the window, up two and a half feet, and the full width of the flexiglass. She'd left a small gap at the bottom, maybe a half-inch wide. Gamble stepped off Cass's leg.

"This is gonna be a real pain," she said. She was just crouching down next to Swoop again when one of the door handles rattled violently. Both women went still. One heartbeat. Two. Three. The handle fell silent.

Seconds later, the handle at the other door shuddered. Cass held her breath. Time stretched. The blood pounded in her ears.

A scrabbling sound came from the second door, the scrape of claws against the heavy steel. Gamble went back to work.

"Back," she said waving Cass away. When Cass had scooted a few feet away from the window, Gamble twitched something in her hand and the grey cord around the window smoked and glowed red, then orange, then white. The flexiglass hissed and deformed, and the rectangle section drooped slightly inward. It was still smoking when Gamble went to it and jammed her knife blade in one of the new seams on the side. She pried and the window sagged inward as the tiny remaining tab of softened flexiglass bent and gave way.

"Help me," Gamble said, as she caught the panel. Cass grabbed the other side and together they pulled the cut portion free. They laid it on the ground out of the way.

The whispering rustle of the hall grew louder, or rather Cass became aware that it had become so. The same scraping started up at the other door, the sound of many hands clawing. Gamble snatched up one of the devices and began affixing it to the top of the wall where the window had just been. She wasn't even trying to be quiet anymore. The piece of gear clamped on with a mechanical whine. There was a little wheel near the top, covered by a round metal housing.

One of the doors to the room quaked in its frame. There was no doubt now. The Weir weren't just testing; they were intent on getting in. Cass hoped that they'd tried it before and be unable to get through, but she knew better than to trust in optimism. Gamble glanced over at the door while she threaded one end of the rope through the housing on the device.

"In the cage, far left," Gamble said, her voice even but her words clipped. "Bottom shelf, near the front. There's a stack, looks like little green wheels."

"OK," Cass said.

"Get four."

Cass nodded and bounded across the room to the cage. Both doors were rattling now. She forced herself to focus on the task. Far left, near the front, bottom shelf. She scanned over the gear. There. Green, round, five inches across, they looked like canisters that had been compressed. One, two, three, four, she gathered them up and rushed back to Gamble.

"Mouse, almost ready," Gamble said. When Cass reached

her, she'd just finished tying an elaborate knot to a carabiner. She scooped the gear out of Cass's hands, and then thrust the carabiner at her.

"Check," Mouse answered.

"Hook Swoop up," Gamble said, "Then get him up on the window ledge."

Cass bent down and looked for where exactly she was supposed to hook the carabiner on. Gamble went down on her knees near one of the doors, and started working with whatever it was Cass had just handed her. Cass searched the harness, the device on the front, everywhere, but it wasn't obvious where she was supposed to hook in.

"I don't see it," she said to Gamble.

"What?"

"The hook, where do I attach it?"

"On the front, the runner."

Cass looked again, but she didn't see any place that looked like it would hold.

"Where?" she asked.

Gamble let out an exasperated breath and practically leapt across the room. She snatched the carabiner from Cass's hand and shouldered her aside. It was subtle, but there was a hitch in her movement when she went to hook Swoop in. She cursed wordlessly and grabbed the device on the harness. A twist of some hidden mechanism, and a metal ring flipped out.

"There," Gamble said, hooking the rope to it. "Right there. Get him up."

She left Cass's side and rushed back to whatever she was doing by the door. Cass rolled Swoop over onto his stomach and wrestled him up into position so she could drape him across her shoulders. She'd seen Mouse do this maneuver a few times. It'd always looked effortless when he did it. The dead weight was almost more than she could manage, but she got him there. Once he was situated, she stood and struggled to get him on the ledge.

Gamble reappeared and helped get Swoop placed with his

legs dangling out into space. His back was bent awkwardly, but there wasn't much they could do about that now.

"Mouse, we're sending him down," Gamble said.

"Check, ready," he replied.

"Hold him," Gamble said to Cass. "When I say go, lower him out."

"All right," Cass answered.

Gamble grabbed another piece of gear and hooked it onto her own harness. Cass didn't know when the woman had even had time to put it on. Gamble gathered the coil of rope and pulled it taut through the device on the window ledge.

"Go," she said. And Cass gently rolled Swoop out through the window, towards the edge. Even knowing he was securely fastened, her heart dropped as gravity took over and dragged his body over the side.

Gamble sat back against the weight on the rope, anchoring as she fed the line through as quickly as she dared.

"Harness is on the floor by the bags," she said. "Get it on." And then without waiting for a reply from Cass, she switched over to the channel. "Mouse, you see him?" she said.

Cass scooped the harness up from next to the bags and started buckling in.

"Yeah, I see him," he said. "Keep him comin', keep him comin'. Five meters."

Without warning or explanation, the clamor of the Weir at the door ceased. The room fell strangely quiet apart from the gentle whir of the rope running smoothly through its channel.

"Three meters," Mouse said. Then a moment later, "All right, slow it down, slow it down."

Cass looked at the doors then at Gamble. Maybe they'd given up after all.

"OK, G, I got him," said Mouse. "I got him, he's unhooked. Line's clear."

Rolling thunder filled the room as a heavy impact quivered the door with a dull report, as if someone had hammered the reinforced steel plating with a cinder block.

"Go, Mouse," Gamble said as she wound the line back in. "Go now."

"Talk to me, Ace," Sky said.

"No time, babe," Gamble answered, and that's when Cass realized just how scared Gamble actually was, and just how much trouble they were in. Gamble never called Sky *babe* when they were on mission.

The end of the line flipped up over the edge of the window frame just as Cass was cinching the last buckle around her thigh. The door shivered from another powerful blow.

"Bags, get the bags," Gamble said.

"Gamble—"

"Move, Cass!"

Cass snatched the rucks up off the floor, threw the straps over her shoulders so they hung across her body. There had to have been over a hundred pounds of gear in them. She was just fitting the second strap on when Gamble threaded the rope through the straps on her harness and clipped it.

"That's gotta do, go, go, go!" Gamble said.

A third blow trembled the door and Cass heard the shriek of wrenching metal behind her as she flung herself up onto the ledge. The rucksacks dragged at her, pulled her off balance, threatened to take her the wrong way. She scissored her legs, scrambled for purchase. Gamble shoved her hard, and the world tumbled.

A second later, the line snapped tight, jarred Cass to a sudden, agonizing halt as the weight and momentum of the gear threatened to splinter her spine. Disoriented, she spun on the rope and smashed her shoulder into the wall of the compound. Then she was falling again.

No, not falling. Descending on the line, at a rate that felt barely controlled. Cass bumped and scraped the wall and scrabbled to get her feet around to keep herself off it. Above her, through the window, came the terrible banshee wail of flexing steel, followed by an inhuman roar. Unmistakably the cry of a Weir, but amplified, broader of sound, immense.

"Ace!" Sky called through the channel.

"I know, babe, I know!" Gamble said, and there was a note of panic in her voice that Cass had never heard before. "Cass, put your feet down, put your feet down!"

Cass fought to position herself, but the rucksacks had both swung to one side and she couldn't get her balance.

"Sky," Gamble spoke once more over the channel, eerily calm. "Love you, babe."

Cass was still fifteen feet up when the line went slack.

Free fall.

"Ace!" Sky cried out, "No! Ace! Ace!"

For that frozen moment, it seemed to Cass as though she were floating, suspended, in the path of a wrecking ball the size of the world. She wasn't moving; the planet was speeding towards her, intent on smashing her into oblivion. She snaked around, managed to twist in the air into a partial crouch, so that the balls of her feet would hit first. Her hands stretched out to intercept the collision.

Futile.

The shock of the impact was too sudden, too great to absorb. She catapulted to the concrete with a metallic crunch; a lightning strike of pain stole her breath and vision.

When she came to, Sky was screaming over the channel, but she couldn't make sense of the words. If they were words at all. They sounded more like animal cries; rage, despair.

"Cass," came Mouse's voice; strong, insistent, punching through. "Cass, can you hear me?"

"Yeah," she struggled to answer, her voice was a ghost. It was a strain to get the air to move through her lungs. From far above her, a continuous stream of popping, like glass cracking in blistering heat.

"Finn, get Sky off channel! Cass, do you read?"

She'd forgotten to open the channel. Sky's howls squelched, and she tried again. "Yeah, Mouse, I'm here."

"You need to move," he said. "Can you?"

Cass levered herself up and found she couldn't push

off with her left arm. When she looked at it, she saw her forearm was indented and bent outward at a shallow angle, as if she had another joint between wrist and elbow. She'd landed halfway on the rucksacks, which had absorbed some of the force of impact but not nearly enough for her to escape unharmed.

"Finn," Mouse said, "I'm droppin' Swoop, I gotta go back for Cass."

"No," Cass said, her senses coming back online. "No, Mouse, I'm OK. Don't come back."

"I've got a marker set," Finn said. "Can you see it?"

Cass hauled herself to her feet, cradling her left arm close to her body. Finn's beacon showed up superimposed on reality, a small blue circle, faintly pulsing.

"Got it," she answered. "Gamble's not down yet. Gotta wait for her."

A pause.

"No, Cass," Mouse said. "You need to move now. Right now. On your own."

The popping sound from above dwindled away, replaced by clearer calls from the Weir. Their normal, white-noise screams. Not the thundering bellow she'd heard just before she fell. Cass bent and scooped the straps of the rucksacks up, reshouldered them with her good arm. There was no time to get them balanced. As she was standing, she realized she was still hooked in to the rope. How was Gamble getting down? She glanced back up at the window high above, but her friend wasn't there. She couldn't even see the line leading back up.

It was there, on the ground, in a loose pile. And that's when Cass understood that Gamble hadn't fed the rope out at all. She'd cut it free.

She was still in the room. Gamble was still in the room.

"Cass!" Mouse called.

Cass walked to the base of the compound and gathered up the rope. The end was fuzzed where it'd been cleanly severed. She looked back up at the window above. Listened to the mass of cries. They were filling the room. The room where Gamble was.

"Cass!" Mouse barked. "Move! Now!"

His commanding voice burned away the last of her daze and the magnitude of their danger crystallized.

"Moving," Cass said. She didn't bother trying to unhook with one hand, just stuffed the remaining rope into the crook of her left arm, against her body. "Moving to you!"

She took off, running as fast as she could, the rucks bouncing and threatening to overthrow her with every step, while a storm of Weir swirled and raged above and behind her. And as the gap widened and their cries faded, no matter how much she wanted to wake from this new nightmare, Cass knew there was nothing she could do to save her friend and sister now or ever.

SEVENTEEN

jCharles stared out the window of his apartment, watching the sun slide into the horizon, taking his spirits down with it. He hadn't slept much in the past thirty-six hours, and time was dragging, either slowing him down or maybe making the world move faster. Either way, he felt like he was having trouble keeping up.

Edda had said the trip would take her three days. It was now the fourth day since she'd set out for Morningside, and it was drawing to an end with no sign of her. jCharles had spent the day before anxiously expecting her arrival until nightfall, and then spent the night anxiously speculating about what her failure to show might mean. None of the possibilities were good. Maybe she'd just made off with the money. When he considered the idea of Edda being a talented con who'd just taken him for a big chunk of his limited funds, he actually felt a little relief. And when jCharles realized he was considering that the *best* case scenario, it made all the other options seem that much worse.

He was going to have to talk with Hollander. Hollander was one of the top dogs in the Greenmen; the semi-official police force that kept Greenstone's citizens in check and its many conflicts behind the scenes. Not quite a friend, maybe, but a professional with whom jCharles mostly had common cause. Mostly. If jCharles had any hope of defending

Greenstone, Hollander was going to have to be part of the plan. But how could jCharles even begin to explain?

A familiar knock at the apartment door interrupted his thoughts; Nimble. jCharles crossed to it.

"Yeah, Nim," he called through the door, before he reached it. And then, opening it, "What's up?"

"Edda's back," Nimble said. jCharles had gone so far down the rabbit hole of expecting never to see her again that it took a moment for him to understand what Nimble had just said.

"Oh," jCharles said. "Oh, great."

Nimble twitched his head to the side, like maybe it wasn't so great.

"Think maybe you oughta bring her up," he said, "'stead a you goin' down."

That wasn't a good sign. Nimble knew jCharles didn't like doing business anywhere but down in the bar. But jCharles never doubted his man's instincts.

"All right," he said. Nimble headed back downstairs. jCharles left the door cracked, went to his private collection and poured two tumblers of the good stuff. As he was putting the bottle away, Nimble knocked again.

"Yeah, come on," jCharles said. The door pushed open slowly and Nimble ushered Edda in. jCharles could see in an instant she was a changed woman. The lazy self-assuredness was gone, replaced by a barely-restrained wildness about the eyes. He didn't need to hear her story to know what Wren had told him was all true. He handed her the drink as she came in, and she downed it in one long pull. "Edda. I'm... relieved."

She nodded, wiped her mouth with the back of her hand.

"You need another?" he asked, pointing to the empty tumbler. She nodded again. "Come in, have a seat," jCharles said as he took the glass and went to pour her a second, fuller glass. Nimble hovered by the entrance, eyebrows raised while he waited for some direction from jCharles. jCharles gestured that he'd take it from here. Nimble nodded and pulled the door quietly closed behind him as he left.

When jCharles turned around, Edda was still standing near the door, looking awkward.

"Please," he said, holding out a hand towards one of the chairs. She hesitated, then looked down at the clothes. They were grimy, travel-stained. She was worried about getting dirt in his home. The concern was unexpected, and touching. "Don't worry, I track mud in here all the time."

She didn't look convinced.

"Anything gets on the furniture, I won't make Mol clean it up, I promise."

She shrugged a little to herself, then nodded and took the offered seat, and the drink. He was glad to see her sip this one. They sat in silence for a few moments, while she gathered herself.

"Took a day one more," she said. "Sorry 'bout dat."

"It's no problem, Edda."

"I did how you say," she continued. "Morn'side, just for what I see." She stopped, took another sip, stared at her hands. Disappeared into herself.

"And what'd you see?" jCharles prompted. Edda came back to herself, but kept watching her hands.

"Death," she said. "Blood. Rubble." Then she looked up at him. "Dat city, it gone."

jCharles sat back in his chair, sipped his own drink.

"But dat already you know," Edda said, holding up a finger.

"Feared," jCharles said. "Didn't know."

Edda nodded. "And de rest?"

"The rest?"

Edda nodded again, but this to herself, confirming something she'd been uncertain about. "I run up nort', down sout', some bit east. Dat why I'm gone four day." She paused, licked her lips. "Same t'ing all 'round."

"The same... How?"

She shook her head at the remembrance.

"Like hell come eat 'em up and spit de bones."

jCharles had thought he'd been expecting the worst; the reality was somehow worse still.

"How many places did you go?" he asked.

"Yours and t'ree beside." Edda sat back, took another sip of her drink, then set it on the side table between them.

"Anything bigger than Morningside?" jCharles asked. Based on what he'd heard, there weren't many places left as big as Morningside, maybe in the whole world. But he'd never been to see for himself, and he didn't know much about the other cities across the Strand.

"Not much out dat way big as Morn'side. Not much here, eit'er." Edda shook her head. "Dat don't seem to help it, not one bit."

All that jCharles had feared and more. Morningside was truly gone, wiped away by the Weir. No, not by the Weir... by Wren's brother. By Asher. But it hadn't stopped there. With Edda's revelation, he felt a tiny hope die in his heart, not having known until that moment he'd even harbored it. The hope that Morningside's destruction had been an act of vengeance against that city alone, one that would end there. Instead, that had only been its beginning.

Edda was watching him closely, studying his face.

"You t'ink dat comin' west," she said. "Comin' here."

jCharles nodded.

"Well I take dat meal," she said. "But you keep de rest your money. I t'ink maybe you need it more I do." She nodded at him. "Sure I know."

"Deal's a deal, Edda. That money's yours now. All eight thousand." She shook her head and got to her feet. jCharles rose with her. "I appreciate the thought Edda, but I hate to be in debt to anyone."

"What happen out dere, dat I not believe if not I see for my own self," Edda said as she walked over to the door and opened it part way. "What it might be is you just save my life. So I take dat meal. Keep your money, save your own."

jCharles stood next to his chair, blinked back at her, uncertain of what else to say. She gave him another nod and headed down the stairs to collect the only payment she'd accept. A few moments later, Mol came out of the back room holding Grace. It was obvious she'd listened in to the whole conversation.

jCharles walked over, put his arms around both his girls, and held them tight.

Later that night, jCharles found himself seated in Hollander's tiny office, listening to a more detailed accounting of Edda's story. He'd caught up with her down in the bar before she left and convinced her to come along with him to meet with the Greenman. Now, Hollander was leaned back in his chair, chin low, brow furrowed, trying to absorb everything he was hearing. He was a big, dark-skinned man with heavy features; square jaw, strong brow, a cartoon of a law enforcer brought to life.

"And you got all this corroborated," Hollander said, looking at jCharles when Edda was done.

"Yeah," jCharles answered. "Or, well, Edda was my corroboration. The first time I heard about it was from a boy who'd escaped it."

Hollander grunted. "And I can talk to him?"

"No," jCharles said. "He left a few days ago."

"But I took vid while I out dere," Edda said. "If you wanna see for true."

"That's not necessary," Hollander said, holding up a hand. "But uh..." He stopped, sniffed. Shrugged. "I guess I'm just not sure what you're asking for, here, jCharles."

"I'm not asking for anything, Holl," he said. "Not yet, anyway. Seems like the kind of thing you oughta know about though, wouldn't you say?"

"Maybe. I mean, yeah, it's bad news, obviously. But there's not much we can do for anybody over that side."

"That's not what I'm worried about," jCharles said. "I'm worried about when it hits this side."

"I don't see why you think it will," Hollander replied. "Seems like an eastern problem to me."

"It'll spill over the Strand at some point. It's coming, Holl. And we're right out there on the tip of it. When it comes, it's gonna hit us first."

"You sound awfully sure."

"I *am* sure."

"Well," Hollander said. And he shrugged again. "I got about two hundred men and women between active and reserves. Every one of 'em willing to die on that wall if it comes to it. So, again, beyond that, I don't know what to tell you."

"Maybe recruit more? Issue a warning? Something besides sitting around waiting to get smashed?"

"And tell people what, jCharles? That bad things *might* be coming from the east one day? Get everyone all riled up, so they start hoarding everything? Looting? Last thing I want to do is stir up anything that looks like fear. I'm not sure you appreciate just how fine a line we all walk between getting along and tearing ourselves to pieces out here."

"Oh, I do," jCharles said. "Probably more than anyone but you."

"Yeah, well," Hollander said. He laced his fingers together and rested his hands on top of his head. "You have the privilege of walking in the grey there, don't you? I'm the one that's gotta be the white hat."

"You know I do everything I can to help you and your people, Holl."

"You do, and I appreciate it. We all do. Mostly. I just mean people expect different things from me. You can nose around, call in favors, do whatever you need to do, and everybody just assumes you've got some business you're handling that no one else needs to know about. As soon as *I* start that up, people get antsy. Uptown, Downtown, the Dive, doesn't matter... every triggerman out there would assume I'm about to roll on them. Half the time I'm fighting off *baseless* rumors. I can only imagine what might happen if I *actually* started gearing up for something. Particularly something that might not ever happen."

jCharles looked down at Hollander's desk, frustrated. He should've been able to make a better case than he was, but he didn't know how to get through to the man.

"Look at it like this. If it was the Bonefolder sitting here, telling me this instead of you," Hollander continued, "I'd give it about twelve hours until you were knocking on my door, asking about what she had to say. And less than half that if, after she left, I started calling up the reserves. I fully expect I'm gonna hear from her by lunchtime tomorrow already, just on account of this meeting."

"This is bigger than all of that, Holl. Bigger than any of us."

"I'm not arguin' that."

"So you do believe me."

Hollander's top lip disappeared behind his bottom teeth. It reappeared a moment later with a quiet smack. "I believe that you believe."

"All right," jCharles said, and he got to his feet. He knew that was the best he was going to get from Hollander. "Thanks for your time, Holl."

"Door's always open," Hollander said. "Long as you call first."

"Yeah," jCharles answered.

"How's that baby?" Hollander asked.

"Perfect in every way."

Hollander smiled. "Make sure you enjoy every day with her. Even the ones where you feel like a walking dead man."

jCharles nodded, flashed a smile he didn't feel, motioned for Edda to exit ahead of him. She squeezed by and out into the hall. Before jCharles left, Hollander spoke.

"Hey," he said. jCharles looked back; Hollander was leaning forward in his chair now, serious. "Anything comes over that wall, I'll be the first one to meet it. Count on that."

"Yeah, Holl. I know," jCharles said. And then after a moment, added. "I'll be right there with you."

Hollander nodded. "Give my best to Mol."

"Sure thing."

jCharles followed Edda out, down the narrow corridor to the narrow stairs. Everything about Hollander's office seemed about one-third too narrow. They exited on the ground floor, stepped out onto the sidewalk out front. There weren't many people out on the streets at this time of night, the in-between time, after the respectable citizens had closed up and hunkered down and before the less respectable ones were up and about. And it wasn't usually that busy at any time of night over by where the Greenmen had set up shop anyway.

"I run on my way, I reck'n," Edda said.

"You have a place to stay for the night?"

"Sure."

"And you're not going to let me pay you what I owe you?"

"Son, you can send it straight if it make you feel better, but I send it right back."

jCharles chuckled, held out his hand for a shake. Edda took it in both hands, but didn't shake it. Just pressed firmly.

"What'll you do now, Edda?"

"Same as you," she said. "Run west."

jCharles smiled, couldn't quite bring himself to tell her he wouldn't be leaving Greenstone.

"Take care of yourself," he said.

"Sure. And you."

He took back his hand, and they separated. But as he turned to head home, Edda's simple words sunk deep; thoughts of his wife and daughter invaded, shook his resolve. He'd thought he was resolute, ready to guard the city with his life, to protect it at all costs. But what if his wife and child were safe somewhere else? What if he could pack them up, send them away with Edda, with Nimble maybe? Was he willing to stay behind? He turned back.

"Edda," he called. She was crossing the street, but stopped and looked at him. "If you find a place that seems safe enough, you think you could let me know where you end up? In case I might uh... in case I want to follow along?"

"Not dere's much left safe, sure I know," she said. "But you call any time."

She held his gaze for a moment, a look that suggested she understood more than what he'd said, then nodded and turned away into the night.

The walk home was ten minutes by the direct route. jCharles took almost an hour.

As he finally came in sight of the Samurai McGann, he stopped and watched it for a few minutes. The giant cartoon samurai in garish colors painted on the side made him smile despite his heavy thoughts. The warrior was disheveled, shirtless, a piece of straw in his mouth, a sword held over his head, a bottle of whisky in his belt. An old inside joke, referencing a life even older. The hand-painted sign that said Samurai McGann on it was lying to the side of the door, propped against the wall. It'd been down for probably over two years now, and jCharles still hadn't taken the time to put it back up.

He looked at that roughneck samurai, and at what it represented. The more accurate term for the character was *ronin*, a samurai without a master. A wanderer. Just like jCharles had been when he first arrived in Greenstone. How very much had changed. He'd found his place here, allowed roots to grow, to reach down deep. Now that he was looking at his little place again, the thought of tearing those roots up seemed too painful to face. Yet, now that he'd let in the thought of fleeing, he couldn't ignore the possibility. Staying would be utterly foolish. The kind of foolish that usually got renamed to *brave* after the inevitable occurred, by whoever was left behind to do the renaming.

It always seemed to make sense in other people's stories. Facing impossible odds. Dying noble deaths. But jCharles had seen more than a few people die in his day, and he couldn't remember a single one ever seeming noble at the time. The choice wasn't as clear cut, standing right there in the middle of it.

He stared up at the bloodshot eyes of the samurai; eyes

either red with rage or with too much drink. The ronin had his sword out, held aloft. Homeless, masterless, purposeless. Disgraced. Still fighting, even though he'd already lost everything he'd ever fought for.

Then again, maybe not everything. With all else stripped away, his spirit remained yet unconquered.

Easy for him. He was a cartoon. And yet, if Asher and his Weir should come, he would face them, shirtless, bottle in his belt, sword held high. Where would jCharles be?

jCharles chuckled in spite of himself. *At* himself. The lack of sleep was making him ridiculous. He crossed to his place, pushed the door open, made his way through the saloon with a quick nod to Nimble. Nimble made a familiar gesture, asking if he should make jCharles a usual drink, but jCharles waved him off. Up the narrow back stairs. Through the front door.

Mol was curled up on the couch, asleep with the lights on. jCharles closed the door softly behind himself, locked it, crept to his wife. He sat down on the couch by her feet. She stirred at the movement, opened her eyes and looked at him, puzzled. Blinked a few times. When recognition finally came, she took a deep breath and rubbed an eye with the heel of her hand.

"Oh," she said. "Not as late as I thought. Guess I must've been out hard."

"Babies will do that to you."

"Everything go OK with Holl?" she asked as she shifted around on the couch. She sat up straighter in the corner, and stretched her legs out over his lap.

jCharles shrugged. "Said to give you his best."

"But he's not going to do anything?"

jCharles shook his head. "Nothing substantial."

"That's disappointing," she said.

"Well, yeah," he replied. "But I understand where he's coming from. Sort of. I don't think he's convinced there's a real threat. Or that it's as big as I'm claiming. I'm not sure I blame him."

"So what's next?"

He reached over and swept a loose strand of hair out of her eyes. "I've been thinking," he said.

"Uh oh," Mol said.

"There are places further west. Towns small enough to escape notice. Cities big enough to get lost in."

"Mmm-hmm," she said. "Places we left behind for good reason."

"A long time ago, Mol."

"Maybe." She shrugged. "Probably depends on who you ask." She placed a hand on top of his, squeezed it. "Sure. Of course I've thought about it. Of all the people in this crazy town, we're probably some of the best able to make a run for it."

Her tone hinted at which direction her thinking had taken her.

"But..." jCharles prompted.

"*But*... all the things that make it easier to run are the same things that make it easier to stay. The money, the connections. Twitch, we've been blessed in ways most people haven't. Ninety percent of the folks out there don't have anywhere else to go. And even if they did, most of them don't have the means to get there. We can't leave them behind, hoping someone else will stop this thing before it catches up to us."

"It's not like this is something I can do on my own, Mol," jCharles said.

"You've got plenty of friends," she countered. "And plenty more associates you can reach out to. You're a man of influence. If you put your mind to it, I'm sure we could find you a right proper army."

jCharles chuckled and shook his head. He was a businessman, not a general.

Mol squeezed his hand. "Greenstone offered us a new start, Twitch."

"Not entirely new–"

"A second chance," Mol continued over the top of him.

"If there's a place worth fighting for, where is it if not here?" She let him think about that for a second, and then took her hand away. "And quit saying *I*, like I don't know what you're implying. I'm not going anywhere either."

"Mol..." he said, but she wouldn't let him finish.

"Nope, don't even start," she said, holding her hand up to stop him.

"If you and Grace can get away safely, then you should. There's no point in you staying here–"

"No point? *The point* is that a life without you is no life at all, Twitch," she said, getting heated and raising her voice. She glanced at the bedroom door, paused, listened for any sound of Grace waking. Took a deep breath, settled herself, kept her voice down. "Look. I know what you mean by it, I know it's coming from the right place. But it's a little insulting. More than a little."

jCharles had expected resistance, but not quite like what he was hearing at the moment.

"What would you say," she continued, "if I walked in here and told you I wanted you to take our baby and run, while I stayed behind?"

"I would laugh."

"And what if you thought I was serious?"

"I reckon I'd be a little insulted."

"More than a little," she said.

"Well," he said. "What if I tell you you don't have a choice?"

"I'll laugh at you right in your face," she said. "Real loud like. And then you'll have to get Grace back to sleep."

He smiled in spite of himself, shook his head. "Someone once told me I was a man of influence, you know."

"You still are, in the right circles," said Mol. "So use it to do the right thing."

"Why is it that you always seem to know what the right thing is?"

"Obviously so I can tell you what to do."

"Obviously," he said. He sat there for a moment, looking

at his firebrand of a wife. "I just don't think we've got enough muscle here, Mol. Not in Greenstone."

"So we import it."

"Import it? I..." He stopped, corrected himself. "*We* don't have the money to hire the kind of talent we'd need."

"I didn't say hire."

And now he saw where she was going.

"That's dangerous territory, Mol."

"People still owe you from way back. And you've still got friends out there. What about 4jack and Zimm? Or Mr 850?"

Names jCharles hadn't spoken in a decade at least. Maybe closer to two. Had it been that long?

"Or Kyth," Mol said.

"Kyth?" jCharles said, and he chuckled at the thought. "You know, I'd like there to be something left of the city *after* we save it."

"Have to save it first."

jCharles looked back at her, shook his head. The fact that Mol was pushing him to bring Kyth in showed just how serious she was. There'd been some bad blood between the two of them when they parted ways, and as far as he knew they'd never reconciled. But she was right. Of course. If they were going to make a stand here, there was no sense in leaving any option unexplored.

"Call them," Mol said. "Worst thing that happens is they say no."

"I doubt that's the *worst*."

"Call Kyth."

"You sure?"

"Absolutely. You should do it right now. No time like the present."

jCharles shrugged, but he could see his wife was serious. He shook his head again and accessed contact details he hadn't looked at in years. Issued the request. The credentials were synced to the individual, but folks in Kyth's line of work had ways of spoofing identities.

"I don't know if this will even still connect," he said while he was waiting for a response. Even if the creds were good, that was no guarantee Kyth would accept. Mol just watched him expectantly.

A few seconds later, the connection was granted and immediately afterwards a voice came through.

"Twitch?"

"Kyth," jCharles answered. Mol gave a tempered smile.

"That can't be you," Kyth said.

"It's me," jCharles said. "You wanna buy my book?"

Kyth laughed on the other end at the long-unused, long-running joke, probably more from the shock of hearing from a long lost friend than from the joke itself. "*Spatz*, Twitch! I can't believe it! You know certain people have been trying to tell me you died?"

"You could've called to check."

"I would have if I'd believed any of 'em," Kyth said.

"Yeah, well, not dead yet," jCharles said. "But that's kind of why I'm calling."

EIGHTEEN

Wren woke with the thought that he'd fallen out of bed. And when he opened his eyes, he thought for a terrible moment that Asher had come and destroyed jCharles and Mol's home and that he was buried alive beneath the rubble. But sleep fell away with an adrenaline burn and Wren almost laughed with relief as he remembered where he was. jCharles and Mol were alive. *He* was alive. And he couldn't decide whether it was a good sign that he'd slept, or if Haiku would be horrified by it if he ever found out. Whatever the case, there was light at the entrance of his little cave; the warm, golden light of dawn, calling him out of hiding.

Getting out of his hiding place was agony. Every muscle, bone, and joint cried out with each movement, taking their revenge for the punishment he'd delivered them. There was a cold, damp spot inside his hood where he'd apparently drooled. Worse yet, his entire right arm had gone completely numb from being pinched between his body and the floor all night. There wasn't enough room in the hiding place to shake it out and he couldn't trust it to support any of his weight. He ended up scooting out backwards using his knees and his left hand while he dragged his prickling right arm behind.

A cold morning greeted him, much colder than he'd expected. The temperature hadn't been exactly comfortable in his little cave, but it was notably warmer than the air outside. He hadn't realized the heat from his body could be that much of a factor, and he certainly hadn't had any idea that the space he'd hidden in could retain it that well. That was another lesson he'd try to take with him.

He sat on the floor at the entrance to his hiding place for a few minutes, shaking out his arm and enduring the angry prickling fire of his nerves coming back to life. Everything hurt, and he was lightheaded with fatigue. Wren didn't know how many hours he had slept, but it didn't feel like it could have been that many. Certainly not nearly as many as his body needed. If he slept for a full week, he doubted even that would be enough. And he was ravenously hungry.

When he could move his right hand again, Wren crawled back in and pulled his pack out. He adjusted his hood and drew another ration bar and his water out of the pack. These he took over to the doorway, where he wrapped himself up snugly in his thermal blanket and sat down to breakfast. As he ate, he watched the shadows flee back to their own hiding places as the sun painted the grey landscape with its golden-orange rays. Wren hadn't awoken quite at first light, but it was still early. He wondered if Haiku and the old man were awake yet.

After he finished his breakfast, he stayed there by the door watching the sun come up for a time. It was soothing to his soul in a way he hadn't expected. As terrifying as the night had been, the dawn seemed that much warmer, and sweeter, and even deserved. Maybe it was because for the first time, this was a morning that Wren had earned for himself.

When the sun was fully risen, Wren got to his feet, repacked his blanket and chemlight, and gathered up the trash from his ration bars. It seemed strange to be worried about littering when all around him were ruins, but it felt even more wrong to leave anything behind. Both Three and Mama had always made a big deal about not leaving even footprints if you could help it. It was a hard habit to break, and maybe not a bad one to have anyway.

He took a final look around the debris-filled room that had been his one-night home. It looked pretty much the same as when he'd found it, but it felt completely different. Familiar and safe, rather than cold and threatening. Maybe it was just the daylight, but all his fear from the night before seemed silly to him now. If he ever got thrown out of the tower again, he knew he wouldn't have to worry about finding another place to hide. He nodded to himself, slung his pack, and headed out to the landing.

There was, of course, still the matter of getting back down. The fall from the night before had made the problem seem bigger in his mind than it actually was; it turned out to be a lot easier than he'd been expecting. He just went down the steps to the lowest point that was still secure, climbed over the rail, and lowered himself from the frame. Hanging there, the drop was only five feet or so. He released his grip and dropped to the ground below. The impact hurt his heels a little, but otherwise it wasn't too bad. He looked at the staircase one last time. If he ever had to get back up, *that* was going to be tricky.

From there, he headed back through the ruins towards the steel tower where Haiku and the old man were waiting. Wren had passed his first test, as far as he could tell. He'd earned himself the chance for an evaluation, whatever that was. The uncertainty of it all tried to go to work on his mind again, but whether he was still too pleased with himself for his little victory or just too exhausted to care, the anxiety didn't come. There probably wasn't much he could do about it now anyway.

When he reached the border where the buildings gave way to the dead plain that surrounded the tower, Wren paused for a moment and took a deep breath. As he was looking across the expanse, some movement caught his attention. It was hard to see for sure at that distance, but for just a moment Wren thought he could make out a figure by the base of the tower. Before he could be sure, he lost it. A swirl of ash in the wind, maybe. Or someone whose silhouette blended too well with the surroundings. Haiku.

Whether real or imagined, it occurred to Wren for the first time that Haiku might be outside waiting for him. Looking for him. Of course he would be. Wren hadn't even considered what the man might be going through, having brought him all this way just to see him tossed back out in the night. He wondered if Haiku had slept at all himself.

That thought was enough to spur Wren on. He didn't jog but he headed towards the tower at a good pace. He was pleased to discover his sense of direction hadn't led him too far wrong; now that he knew where to look, he could make out the door they'd used the day before, which meant he was coming back in almost along the same path he'd taken on the way out. Not too bad, considering all the mostly aimless wandering he'd done the previous evening. Even at a hundred yards, though, he couldn't see any sign of Haiku. But then again Haiku wouldn't necessarily know that Wren would be coming in from this direction. Maybe he was walking the perimeter of the tower, keeping an eye out.

As Wren was approaching the door, he realized he wasn't sure how he was supposed to let them know he was back. He was pretty sure knocking wasn't going to be any use. It turned out not to matter. When he was maybe ten yards away, something stirred to his right and almost made him cry out in surprise. Mama had done a pretty good job of training him not to vocalize when he was startled, but he certainly flinched in spite of himself. Haiku was getting up from the ground not far from the door. Apparently he'd seen Wren's approach and had sat down to wait.

Wren didn't feel quite so bad about not having seen him sitting there; he was completely coated in the grey dust of the Strand. He was dressed differently than Wren had seen him before, too. He was wearing a heavy sort of tunic or vest over top of everything else. Pants, shirt, gloves, boots, hat; whether they were themselves actually grey or not,

Wren couldn't tell, but he thought they might be. He'd even wrapped a scarf or something around his face, so only his eyes were exposed. Wren wondered just how long Haiku had been out here looking for him.

"Good morning," Haiku said, except his voice was all wrong, and not because it was muffled by the scarf. Because it wasn't Haiku at all. He pulled the scarf down. The old man. "Did you sleep, boy?"

Wren was so surprised he didn't answer immediately. The old man's eyebrows went up and he leaned forward slightly.

"A little," Wren said. "Yes, sir."

"Good, good. And how do you feel? Cold? Hungry? Tired?"

"Yes, sir."

The old man smiled, and Wren was caught completely off guard by the change in the man's personality. The previous day he'd seemed hard and distant. Now, he seemed almost happy to see Wren.

"How's the chin?"

Wren had forgotten about that. He touched the bandage.

"It doesn't hurt too much."

The old man nodded. "I'll have Haiku take a look at it," he said.

"Where is he?" Wren asked.

"Upstairs," the old man said. "Come inside, we'll get you something hot to drink. And eat." He walked over to the door and raised a hand, but just before he touched it, Wren heard the bolts retract and the seal decompress. The old man pushed the door open and stood back, making way for Wren to enter ahead of him. Wren went in and waited by the door while the old man closed it again, and then followed him wordlessly up the stairs.

They returned to the same room from the day before. Haiku was sitting there at the table, but he rose when he saw Wren.

"Here he is," the old man said, though Wren wasn't sure

if he was talking to him or to Haiku. He busied himself in
the small kitchen for a few moments, setting water on to
boil and preparing a pot of tea.

"Wren, how are you?" Haiku asked.

"I'm fine," Wren said. And reflexively he added, "How
are you?"

"I'm well, thank you."

"Haiku, handle the water, if you would please," the old
man said, "while I show Wren where he can get cleaned
up."

"Certainly, Father," Haiku said. "Good to see you, Wren."

Wren nodded.

"Come along, boy," said the old man, moving to the door
by the kitchen. Wren followed obediently. The old man led
him down a short hall, past three doors on the right and
two on the left. The doors were similar in design to the one
that led outside; oval in shape, flat grey metal, though these
interior doors looked lighter than the exterior ones. They
took a right at an intersecting hall, and then stopped at a
door on the left, which the old man opened.

There was a small bedroom beyond. Possibly the smallest
he'd ever seen. Wren guessed it was maybe six feet by six
feet. A bed was shoved against the right wall, and the foot of
it was only three or four inches from blocking the opening
of the door. Maybe bedroom was the wrong word. It looked
more like a cell.

The old man didn't enter but backed away from the
entrance.

"Washroom is on the left," he said. "Join us in the sitting
room when you're ready."

"Yes, sir," Wren said. "Thank you."

Wren stepped in to the little room and the old man closed
the door behind him. There was indeed a washroom just to
his left, about the size of a small closet. Wren switched on
the light. Sink on the left, toilet on the back wall, shower
to the right, and no counters at all. The door retracted
into the frame. The washroom was bright and clean, and

more economical than even the most well-thought-out wayhouses he'd been in. There was absolutely no wasted space.

He set his pack down by the bed and dug out one of his two changes of clothes. He hadn't realized how much his feet were hurting until he took his boots off and felt all the tension roll out. The floor was a rubberized texture, durable and slightly springy. His socks were damp when he pulled them off, and he stood for a few seconds just squishing his toes into the floor covering.

He got undressed and stepped into the shower. There was only a single control for it, a large white push-button in the center of the wall beneath the shower head. He pushed it in and a green ring lit up around it with a pleasant chirp. A moment later a flow of warm water cascaded over him, like divine rays of healing. He stood under the shower stream with his eyes closed for a long while, letting the water wash away the dirt, and the cold, and the bone-deep weariness. Wren smiled in spite of himself. Even knowing all he'd been through and *not* knowing what yet awaited him, for that moment, just being clean and warm was enough.

The button chirped at him twice and when he opened his eyes the green ring had turned yellow. A warning; he was about to use up the water ration. The bandage on his chin was soggy and growing heavy. He peeled it off, winced as it tugged at the skin around the wound. It was stained through. The water ran down the sides of his face and dripped from his chin, sending fire through his jaw. Wren leaned back out of the water stream and tested the wound gently with his thumb. The gash wasn't wide, just barely wider than the tip of his thumb, but it felt deep. When he drew his thumb away and looked at it, traces of bright red quickly rained away to his palm. If Mouse had been around, he probably would have used some of his weird-smelling gel to seal the wound up. As it was, Wren wasn't sure if there was anything he could do about it.

Three more chirps sounded, and the yellow light

switched to red. Wren managed to finish getting clean just a few seconds before the water shut itself off. The air rushed in cold immediately afterward, and motivated him to get dry and dressed quickly.

When he returned to the sitting room, he felt like a different person. Haiku and the old man were both at the table talking quietly. The old man had also changed and appeared to be wearing the same clothes he'd had on the day before. They stopped speaking when he entered. Wren hovered by the door, uncertain, but the old man poured a cup of tea and placed it at one of the empty chairs around the table.

"Have a seat," he said.

Wren went to the appointed place and sat down. In addition to the tea, Haiku pushed a small bowl over to Wren. It was filled with what looked like some kind of dark soup, with a milky texture. The steam rising from it had a spiced aroma that Wren didn't recognize but that made his mouth water anyway. He looked up at his hosts.

"Please," the old man said with a slight nod.

"Thank you," Wren said. He sipped the tea first, and then tried the soup. The flavor was strong; herbal and slightly sweet, with a peppery aftertaste. It wasn't like anything he'd ever had before, but the more he tasted it, the more he liked it. It was surprisingly filling, too. The others sat in silence until he'd finished. They didn't have to wait long.

"Would you care for more?" the old man asked.

"No, thank you," Wren said. In fact, he would have loved more, but he didn't feel comfortable asking for it. And really, he was fairly full. He just enjoyed the taste so much, he knew he could keep eating even if he shouldn't. There was another matter as well; he was ready to get on with things. "Are we going to start the evaluation now?"

"No," the old man said.

"Oh. I thought..." Wren trailed off, wondering if he'd misunderstood. "I thought you said you'd evaluate me this morning, if I came back."

"Mm," the old man said, making that same little noise. "Is that what I said?"

And now Wren really was confused. He looked over at Haiku, who was sitting silently across from him, but the man merely returned the gaze without any show of emotion. Wren thought back over the day before, replayed the moment in his mind. The old man telling him to come back in the morning. He was certain of that.

"Yes, sir. You said if I came back in the morning, you'd see if I had anything more than pluck."

"Mm."

The old man continued to watch him, and Wren got the distinct impression that he was missing something, that he wasn't answering the question that was actually being asked. But he was sure of it, he remembered it clearly. The old man had said that if Wren completed one task to his satisfaction, then he'd evaluate him. Oh. *To his satisfaction.*

"If I completed the task to your satisfaction," Wren said.

"Ah, yes," the old man said. "That sounds like something I'd say."

"Does that mean..." Wren said, and his heart dropped into his stomach. He was almost afraid to say the rest. "I see." He'd failed. All of that, for nothing. What had the old man been looking for?

"I said I would evaluate you if you performed a task to my satisfaction," said the old man. "What was the task I set you to?"

"To survive the night on my own," Wren answered. The man's eyebrows went up at that; a subtle invitation to reconsider. "Or. Well, you said to leave and come back."

"Too much, boy."

The old man was still watching him intently, and Wren felt the frustration rising. There was some game here, some riddle or puzzle that he didn't see. He tried to remember the exact words the old man had said. One simple task. And then it clicked.

"You said to leave. The task was for me to leave."

The old man dipped his head in a subtle nod, in a manner almost identical to the one Three used to have.

"The evaluation began last night," he said. "You must learn to hear what I say, not what you think I say."

Wren's emotions did a somersault. He hadn't failed after all. Or had he? There was no telling what the old man had been looking for; Wren hadn't had any idea that he was already under scrutiny out there in the open. What evaluation could the old man have possibly done?

"This is the final portion," the old man said. "And it will require your full attention. If you feel that you'll be distracted by thirst or hunger, we can tend to those needs first."

"How about being tired?"

"That part is expected," the old man said with a smile. "Are you ready?"

"I think so," Wren answered.

"Don't tell me what you *think*, boy."

"Yes, sir," Wren said. "I'm ready."

"Very well," the old man said. Haiku got up from the table then and without a word quietly left the room. The old man took a small black cylinder from a pocket and placed it on the table between them. "Sit up straight."

Wren did as he was told, and the seriousness of the moment settled on him.

"Tell me," the old man said. "What is this?"

Wren looked at it, there on the table in front of him. It was short, squat, black and seamless. There were no lights or displays. It could have been a solid chunk of metal or plastic, or it could have been filled with sand or ash. But Wren knew there was more to the question than mere guessing would provide. Or rather, a mere guess might tip things the wrong direction. He stretched out through the digital and tried to find a connection to the device. It was there, almost instantly he could see it, or feel it. He didn't really have a word to describe what it was to connect this way because it was both sight and touch, in a way, and yet not really either. There was something to the device. And it *was* a device of some kind, though Wren couldn't see its purpose.

"A device," Wren said.

The old man's facial expression didn't change. Wren continued his interaction to see what more he could learn. The connection was there but it was difficult to latch on to. Evasive. Slippery. Like spots floating in vision, always fleeing when looked for. It was something like Underdown's machine, though not as aggressive. Whereas the machine had actively resisted his attempts to connect remotely, this device seemed to passively avoid it; smoke curling around a grasping hand. Wren glanced back up at the old man who was still watching him intently.

"May I touch it?" Wren asked.

The old man nodded once.

Wren took the device in his hand, rolled it over in his palm. It was heavy, and cool to the touch. And now that he held it, the signal grew stronger in his mind. The connection became easier to hold in focus, though still it escaped his attempts to interface. An odd sensation accompanied it that he couldn't quite place.

"It's a device of some kind," Wren said. "But I can't connect to it."

"Can't?" the old man said, and his tone suggested Wren reconsider his words.

"Well, it's difficult," Wren said. And then a thought occurred to him. He wasn't certain, but the hunch was there, and it came out of his mouth before he had a chance to talk himself out of saying it. "I might be able to get it if you'd quit moving it around."

The old man's face shifted into the barest trace of a smile.

In that moment, Wren realized the mysterious device itself was no longer important. It might not have even been important to begin with. The real test was in finding the old man's signal, to figure out what he was doing, how he was manipulating the device's connection protocols to prevent

Wren from locking on to it. An invisible battle.

Wren had never tried this before, not really. With almost everything else he had ever done through the digital, he hadn't been actively resisted. And that most likely explained the sensation he hadn't been able to place before. The old man was there too, manipulating the device at the same time. Wren had no training for this sort of thing, no experience to draw from.

Except for the Machine. He had fought Asher there, somehow, more out of reflex than with any understanding. He tried to remember what that had felt like. Wren groped his way through the electromagnetic swirl looking not for a way to connect to the device, but for the hidden hand behind the signal. The old man was in there, somewhere. Wren knew it. But no matter where he looked or what he tried, he just couldn't find any trace of him. Five minutes. Ten minutes.

Wren's mind was already fogged with weariness, and now frustration piled on and threatened to give way to panic. This was his moment, his big test, and he was losing. And if he lost, he would fail. And if he failed, he would never forgive himself. But the more he tried to focus, the harder it all became. After twenty minutes, with no warning, the signal vanished.

"Enough," the old man said.

"Wait," Wren said. "I'm not done."

"Yes you are."

"No, please, I can keep going."

"Perhaps you can, boy," the old man said, "but I have learned what I needed to."

"Sir, please–" Wren began, but the old man held up his hand and cut him off. It wasn't the gesture that stopped the words, it was the hard, piercing stare of the man's dark eyes. But Wren was desperate. This was his best chance, his only chance, and it was slipping away. The old man's signal was there, it had to have been. The device was off. Haiku wasn't connected. The only other signal nearby would have to be the old man's.

Wren stretched out again, rode the wave of fear and frustration as it built inside. Invited it. And there, he found the old man's signal, now unguarded. Without plan or purpose, Wren attached to it.

The old man's eyebrows went up, surprised by Wren's connection or maybe by his audacity.

"And what, boy, do you think you're going to do with that?"

Wren didn't know but he didn't care. He had to show this old man what he was capable of, somehow. Attached to the signal, Wren started crawling his way up the chain, looking for something, anything he could grab hold of, or disrupt, or lash out at. It was like the time when Mama had been unconscious, after Painter had killed Connor, and Wren had been so scared and all he knew was that he needed Mama to wake up. Except Mama's signal had been quiet and flat then, an easy, meandering stream. The old man's was like a lightning bolt.

Before Wren could figure out what he was doing, pressure came against him. The old man resisting him, gradually pulling free. Wren had to do something. And he did the first thing he could think of. He broadcast. The way Lil had taught him or, rather, the way he'd figured out how to do it after Lil had taught him. He turned his signal outward, amplified it as much he could, the way he had against the Weir. And with it, the pressure that had threatened to force him out vanished, as if he had broken through it.

"Mm," the old man said.

Wren was doing it. Whatever *it* was, he had broken through the old man's initial defenses. And then, without warning, everything went terribly, terribly wrong. Pain blossomed in the middle of his brain, white hot. His ears rang. Was the old man attacking him back? Wren resisted, pushed harder, bent all his will and effort to boosting his own signal. But the harder he pushed, the greater the pain grew. The old man sat placidly in front of him, as if

completely unaware of, or unmoved by, Wren's distress.
Wren opened his mouth to scream against the searing of his
senses, but nothing came out. His entire body was seized.

And the next moment, it all ceased. Wren slumped
forward with a choking exhale. But almost immediately
he began to recover, the pain fading quickly to memory,
to something imagined. Whatever had just happened to
him didn't seem to have any lasting physical effect. The
psychological impact was far worse.

"Haiku!" the old man called, his voice sharp. Haiku
reappeared and stood at the entry. The old man motioned
to a seat at the table, which Haiku walked over to and took.

The old man looked at Haiku for a span, and then at
Wren for longer. Wren felt himself wilting under the gaze. It
reminded him of the time he'd snuck out of the compound
at Morningside one night. The night he'd found Painter.
And when he'd come back with his shirt torn and bloodied,
Mama had been so furious that, after she'd held him tight
and checked his wounds, she'd sat him in a chair and
stared at him something like that. Eyes smoldering while
she tried to find her way through the emotion to get to the
words underneath. The difference here was that while the
old man's eyes were just as intense, they were completely
unreadable; no anger, no disappointment, no emotion
whatsoever. And somehow that was even worse.

"Your problem, boy," the old man said, "is that you've
been told you are special." He paused and scratched the tip
of his nose with a finger, smoothed his wispy mustache and
beard. "That you have a *gift*. A *gift* you said. Your words.
And worse, you believe it, don't you?"

Wren couldn't withstand the man's gaze or his hard
words. Tears started to form, and he didn't want the old
man to see it. He looked down at his hands in his lap and
started picking at the red spot next to his thumbnail.

"Look at me, boy."

Wren couldn't do it. Not yet. Get it under control.

"Look at me!" the old man said and his voice was so

sharp and powerful that Wren obeyed even against his will. And when his eyes met the old man's, he found he couldn't look away. Tears dripped onto his cheeks.

"You are here, boy, because you believe it," the old man continued, his voice returning to its normal crackly tone and volume. "Because you believe you are *special*. Because you believe you alone can change the course of events. Perhaps you even believe you've been destined for something great. Chosen."

The old man leaned towards him across the table. "Is that what you believe, boy? That you are a Chosen One?"

No. Wren didn't believe that. Did he? He'd never thought of himself as any of this, and yet the man's words were sinking deep into his soul and making him doubt. Making him wonder. And the fact that Wren couldn't be certain shook him.

The old man leaned back in his chair.

"You are many things. Small, frightened, fragile. Weak. But boy, you are most assuredly *not* special."

Wren didn't know what to say. It was clear he'd not only failed, but that he'd failed in some catastrophic way. He wondered if Haiku was going to face the old man's wrath just for having brought Wren to him.

"I have raised many children. This test," he said, holding up the dark cylinder, "was something my children could solve before their sixth birthday. You did not even reach the part meant to be a challenge."

Wren glanced at Haiku, but Haiku was looking down at the table. Maybe he was feeling some of Wren's shame.

"You're too old. It would take months to correct much of the nonsense you've no doubt been filled with, the habits and patterns of thought that you've developed under careless eyes. And some of them you will never unlearn."

That was all Wren could bear. It was bad enough that he'd wasted so much time and effort already. There was no need for him to accept this berating, no matter who the old man was. Wren wiped the stupid tears off his face.

"You can just say no," Wren said. "There's no reason to be so nasty about it."

The old man didn't reply. Haiku had looked up at Wren, and now his eyes were shifting back and forth between him and the old man. After a moment, Wren stood up.

"I'll get my things," he said. "Sorry to have wasted your time."

"Sit," the old man said. Wren remained standing by his chair, hesitating. But the old man inclined his head towards Wren's chair, and Wren felt compelled by the motion to retake his seat.

"These words are hard for you to hear," the old man said, "because they are new to you. But you must hear them if you are to be my student. I am not a man who tolerates illusions. My House deals in realities only, and they are perplexing enough without the confusion of dreams and wishes."

And now Wren was completely confused. After that raw, unambiguous, and vicious account of all of Wren's faults, had the old man just implied that he might actually be considering taking Wren under his teaching?

"You have sensitivity, but no discipline," continued the old man. "Determination without focus. Instinct and will, perhaps. And I will concede that you appear to have some natural talent, however small. In times of great stress or emotion, maybe you have noticed certain abilities manifest or become enhanced?"

Wren almost didn't catch the question, and wasn't even sure if he was supposed to answer. But the words certainly rang true. He remembered how he'd resisted Asher, or first turned back the Weir the night they killed Mama. The feeling that something was growing in his chest that threatened to make him explode.

"Yes, sir," Wren said, when the old man didn't continue. The old man nodded.

"I've spoken at length with Haiku. And though I believe he's overstated a few things, I would never lightly disregard

the recommendation of one of my children. I cannot make
you all that you might have been, but I can fashion you to a
specific purpose, if you are willing to submit to the training."

It took a moment for Wren to realize what the man was
saying. But when he did, his heart surged.

"You mean... you mean you're willing to teach me?"

Again the old man held up his hand, cutting Wren off.

"Don't think for a moment this had anything to do with
your little outburst. I appreciate determination, not rash
behavior where calculated patience is required. And I have
no tolerance for tricks suitable for a circus. None of this will
be easy for you. You are already far behind, and you will
find that much of what you consider your strength is in
fact a snare for you. The only way forward is through pain,
struggle, and trial. I *will* teach you, boy. But I will teach you
as fire teaches flesh."

"I understand," Wren said. The old man smiled at that.

"Not yet."

Wren held the man's gaze. "Whatever it takes."

"Take the day to consider," the old man said. "Eat, sleep,
gather yourself. This is not a decision for you to make
lightly."

"Sir," Wren said. "I made my decision before I left
Greenstone."

"Wren," Haiku said. "To be clear, this isn't something you
can begin and then walk away from. You must be willing to
give up everything from your previous life."

"I'll do anything to stop Asher."

"It's more than that. Much more," Haiku said. "Father is
inviting you to become part of House Eight."

Wren felt the gravity in Haiku's voice, and knew there
was more to them than he understood. "I don't know what
that means," he said.

"This isn't merely a commitment you would make to
me," said the old man. "You would be making it to Haiku as
well. To Three. To all those who came before you. There is
legacy and lineage here. If you accept entrance, then forever

afterward you will belong to House Eight. Even if you were to run to the other side of the world, that would not absolve you of your responsibility to the House."

The world tilted as Wren's entire perspective transformed. All this time he had been looking at the whole experience through a single focus; how this old man could help him overcome his brother. He'd thought all of this was about solving a problem that they were all facing, one he was uniquely positioned to handle. It had never entered his mind that he would have to make any lasting commitment to these people.

"This is why you must count the cost," the old man continued. "The price is your life. Nothing less." He waited a beat while that thought sank in. And then–

"If your mother showed up today and told you to go with her, would you turn her away?"

The question struck Wren like an icy cascade. The old man had found his greatest weakness and struck it precisely, a knife-blade between the ribs.

"I..." Wren said, and then trailed off. The magnitude of the decision was on him with razor-edged clarity. His mind swirled with contrary thoughts. There was a weight of history here that he hadn't anticipated, a world unimagined unfolding itself before him. It was too much to ask of him. He was only a boy. Was it truly worth giving up everything he had known before to cross into a new life he knew nothing about? How could he possibly know that now? And yet, how could he turn away from what was being offered to him? And while his thoughts raced and collided, and his heart pounded with the enormity of the moment, a hidden part of his spirit revealed itself in stillness.

None of what was going on in his mind or body truly mattered. He knew in his spirit there was no real choice here. Whatever else lay ahead, the man was offering ultimate victory at the end. Now that it had been laid before him, as frightening as it was, Wren could not willingly refuse to take it.

"I would have to, sir," he said. And as the words left his mouth, he knew they were true. Some part of him let go, then. Let go of Mama. "The thing you're promising me is the thing I would already give my life for."

"I promise you nothing," the old man said. "Nothing beyond instruction. When the time comes, I cannot guarantee you will succeed."

Mol's words floated back to Wren, the ones that had convinced him to take this journey. Or rather, the words that had given him the courage to do what he knew he should.

"If I die trying," he said, "then at least when the end comes, I'll know I gave all I could."

"Mm," the old man replied. "We'll see." He looked at Wren for a moment and something had shifted in his dark eyes. Still they pierced, though they seemed to search less. Maybe he was at last seeing the strength of Wren's conviction, a conviction that had been absent until moments ago.

The old man stood and Haiku followed suit. Wren likewise got to his feet.

"I have business with Haiku," the old man said. "You are welcome to any food or drink here in the parlor, and the room you used previously is yours. For now, restrict yourself to this room and that. You are free for the day, boy, but I encourage you to rest. In the morning, if you are still determined, we will begin."

"I won't change my mind," Wren said. "I'm ready to start now."

"No, you aren't," said the old man. "But you'd better be come morning."

The old man gestured towards the door that led back downstairs, directing Haiku to head that way. Haiku smiled at Wren and nodded as he passed by, and his face held a strange mix of emotion; a melancholy joy, pride tempered by concern. It was a look meant to reassure, but Wren saw the disquiet underneath. Whether Haiku's distress was over Wren or himself wasn't clear, and Wren wondered what "business" the old man had with Haiku. The old man followed Haiku out.

The old man. Wren had just pledged his life to him, and he didn't even know the old man's name.

"Sir," Wren called, just as the old man was exiting the room. The old man stopped at the doorway and turned back. "You know my name, but I don't know yours."

"You've not earned the right to my name, boy," the old man said.

"But, if I'm going to be your student, what should I call you?" Wren asked.

"Sir. Teacher. Master," said the old man. "Whatever you deem appropriate." He started to turn back towards the door.

"I'd like to call you what *you* think is appropriate, sir."

The old man stopped again and turned his head to answer over his shoulder, looking at Wren out of the corner of his eye. "In that case," the old man said, "you may call me Foe."

He smiled thinly to himself and then exited the room. After a moment, Wren eased himself back into his chair at the table and, with a newborn sense of dreadful wonder, contemplated what fresh terrors and trials he'd invited upon himself.

NINETEEN

By the time Cass closed in on Finn's waypoint, whatever shock had been keeping her from feeling the pain of her fall had worn off. She knew she'd injured more than her arm, but the pain from it blazed so brightly the other hurts were pale and muted behind it, like the last stars at sunrise. Her legs burned, her knees and ankles ached, and not just from the heavy load she was hauling.

The others were waiting for her at street-level, just down the road, thirty yards away. Finn reacted when he saw her, came out a few yards to meet her. She slowed to a jog for the final distance, and slung the rucksacks to the ground at his feet. His face was grim, but stony.

"You OK?" he asked.

Cass nodded. "All but this," she said, pointing to her unnaturally-angled forearm.

Finn sucked air through his teeth. "That looks bad."

"It hurts, yeah," she answered. "But it can wait. What are we doing?"

Finn glanced over his shoulder at the others behind him. Mouse had laid Swoop down and was busy assembling something from his pack. Sky was off to the side, on his knees with his hands in his lap, staring blankly. His rifle lay on the ground next to him, unheeded.

"We gotta get out," Finn said, turning back. "Obviously. Planning to go straight out the nearest gate, soon as we're set. You see anything following you?"

"No, nothing. They were all..."

Cass looked over at Sky, and then back at Finn, but neither of them had any words for the moment. He nodded.

"Daylight's probably making it hard on them," he said.

He looked down at the rope stuffed in her arm. The cut end was jutting out from the haphazardly coiled mass. Finn took it between his fingers, ran his thumb over the frayed strands.

"She cut you loose," he said.

Cass nodded. Finn just shook his head.

"Well, no point in you lugging all that around." He unhooked the carabiner from Cass's harness and unwound the rope from the straps. She winced as he lifted the rope away. "Mouse," he called. "Need you to come look at this."

"Yeah, one sec," Mouse said. He worked a few more seconds and then stood, and Cass saw he'd been putting his emergency litter together. He came over and instantly saw the problem. After a quick evaluation, Mouse stabilized her forearm with a brace from his kit and followed it with an injection of local anesthetic.

"Sorry," he said. "Best I can do for now."

"It's fine, Mouse," Cass said.

Somewhere in the dead city, a cry echoed. It was hard to pinpoint, but Cass was almost certain it hadn't come from the direction of the compound. Mouse and Finn exchanged a look. Cass snatched up one of the rucks again and cinched it tight.

"Gimme a hand with Swoop," Mouse said to Finn, and the two men withdrew to load their recovered teammate onto the litter.

"What if he wakes up?" Cass asked.

"I dosed him pretty good," Mouse said. "He'll be out for a long while."

"Then what?" she said.

Mouse glanced over at her, and then at Finn, and then back down to the litter where he was strapping Swoop down. "Have to figure that out, won't we?"

Once Swoop was secured, Mouse was back on his feet and slinging his pack on backwards, so it hung in front of him. He came over and took up one of the rucks and threw it on his back.

Finn unhooked his rifle and handed it over to Cass.

"I gotta help carry Swoop. You good to run this?"

Cass swept her eyes over the weapon. It had more heft than Wick's; longer barrel, heavier round. But it was built on the same basic platform, with all the controls in the same place.

"Yeah, I'm good," Cass said. "What about Sky?"

Finn glanced over at their companion, still on his knees, unresponsive.

"He's dry," Finn said, voice lowered and shaking his head. "Emptied on that room. You're our shooter."

Finn handed her one magazine.

"Make it count," he said. Another cry sounded, this one closer and from somewhere ahead of them. Definitely not at the compound. There was more ammo for them all in the rucks, but no time to dig it out.

"We're not going to shoot our way out anyway," Mouse said. "Best bet is not to be here."

"Yeah, check, let's get to it," Finn said. "Sky, we're moving, brother."

For a long moment, Sky just stayed there on his knees, staring without seeing towards the compound, oblivious to all else but his loss. Cass's heart wrenched in her chest to see the warrior so completely broken. A Weir cried from behind them, this time in the direction of the compound. They were spreading out in search. Or they were triangulating.

"Sky," Mouse said.

He didn't move, didn't even blink. Mouse and Finn looked at one another, and Cass knew they were going to have to make another terrible decision. They couldn't carry him out. They didn't want to leave him behind. But the scattered calls from the Weir were rising up from all directions now, and increasing in number.

Cass was just about to call him again when Sky reached up and rubbed his mouth with the back of his hand, in a long slow draw. Then, to her astonishment, he grabbed his rifle, got to his feet and strode to Cass.

"I'm on point," he said. "We'll go out tight, five meter separation from me, quick pace. Cass, you're bodyguard. Stay on Mouse like a lover."

He paused and looked each of them in the eye in turn.

"I'll get us home," he said. "And then I'll go insane. But not till then."

He gestured for Cass to hand over Finn's weapon. She glanced at Mouse. He nodded, and Cass exchanged Finn's rifle for Sky's. Cass cradled Sky's rifle in her injured arm, switched back over to the jittergun.

"Don't drop her," he said, while he checked the chamber on Finn's weapon. Then he looked her dead in the eye. "She's all I've got left."

He turned and started towards the nearest gate. Mouse and Finn took their places at the litter, with Finn in the front, and on a quick three count lifted Swoop. Cass swallowed the lump of emotion in her throat and drew up just behind Mouse, an arm's length away.

Sky set a hard pace, just shy of reckless. For the first few hundred yards, Cass wondered if the grief was too much for him, if maybe he'd gone suicidal and was just leading them to what he hoped would be a large enough number of Weir to pour out all his rage on before they brought him down. But as they moved further through the ruins of the city, it became apparent that he'd been moving with the only caution they could afford. As many of the Weir as had been hiding in the compound, there were still more scattered throughout the city, and they were becoming active. Their calls and cries were coming one on top of the other now as the creatures spread throughout the area, but even as their desiccated voices drew closer, so too did they seem to be coming more and more from behind. Cass felt almost like

they were running on the first broken pieces of earth, with
the landslide on their heels.

By the time they came within sight of the gate, the noose
seemed to be tightening just behind them, though Cass knew
better than to let herself hope they'd made their escape. The
last two hundred yards were the most excruciating. Even
though they had a straight shot out, Sky kept leading them
off the main path, ducking into narrow lanes and alleys,
circling buildings, weaving between structures. He probably
doubled the amount of time they spent within the city walls.

When they were thirty yards from the gate, Sky stopped
and kept them bunched up between two buildings. Mouse
and Finn were doing their best to keep their breathing under
control, but it was obvious lugging Swoop all that way was
already starting to take its toll. That didn't bode well for the
much longer trip they still had ahead of them. Cass moved up
beside Sky and crouched next to him to survey the area for
herself. She checked the main thoroughfare, nearby alleys,
doors, windows. It all looked clear. And though the majority
of the Weir cries were towards the city interior, some were
still too close for Cass to feel they could afford the break.

She glanced over at Sky. He too was scanning their
surroundings, but he must have seen her look out of
the corner of his eye because he raised his left hand and
extended his pointer finger towards the gate and then
rotated it slowly up. Cass looked over at the gate and then
followed the line of the wall up. And there she saw what
she had missed before: a single Weir, crouched low, keeping
watch atop the wall. Any concerns Cass had about Sky's
current mindset were completely dispelled. He was in top
form. She didn't know *how* he was managing it, but she was
grateful he was.

Mouse moved in close, just behind them.

"What's the hold up?" he whispered. Sky looked over
his shoulder.

"Sentry on the wall," he answered. "Might have to take it."

Cass kept her eyes on the Weir up there, watching it as

it dipped down behind the low barrier that ran along the top of the wall only to reappear a few seconds later. There was something odd in its behavior that she couldn't quite identify.

"Tough shot?" Mouse asked.

"No," Sky said. "But if I drop it, they'll know which way we went."

A call from a Weir sounded, and the Weir on top of the wall ducked down again. A few moments later it peeked up further down the wall, glancing this way and that. It even looked back behind it, out into the open.

"Think we're gonna have to risk it," said Mouse. "We gotta keep moving."

And then it struck Cass. She'd seen something like it just the night before after she'd launched her ambush, when she'd killed the Weir that had surprised her coming out of the alley. The one whose expression was frozen, perfectly preserved, in her memory; eyes wild, frantic, a thing lost and terrified.

The Weir on the wall didn't look like it was keeping watch. It looked scared.

"Don't," she said. "Don't kill it."

"You think killing it will bring the others?" Mouse asked.

"No," Cass said. "I don't think it's connected to the others."

Mouse just looked at her.

"Look at it. It's not watching for *us*," she said. "It's hiding from *them*."

Mouse glanced at Sky, and Sky shook his head and shrugged a shoulder.

"Come on, fellas," Finn whispered from behind, tension carrying through even in the low tones.

The feeling that the Weir was no threat to them was overwhelming, but Cass didn't know how to explain it. She didn't know how to communicate it to the others and they didn't have time to discuss it. So Cass lifted her veil and stepped out into the open.

Sky cursed as the Weir reacted instantly to the motion. But its reaction wasn't at all what any of them had expected. Except maybe Cass. Rather than scream a warning to the others, the Weir threw itself down behind the barrier.

"What're you *doing*?" Sky hissed.

"Come on," Cass answered, waving them on quickly. "Come on, we can go."

At that point, the boys didn't have any reason to argue. The Weir had clearly already seen them. If it was going to alert the rest of its brood, there was no way to stop it now. Might as well make a break for the gate while they still could.

Sky pushed out aggressively, keeping his weapon pointed up at the top of the gate and ready in case the creature reappeared. If he got the opportunity to fire, Cass was pretty sure he wasn't going to wait this time. Mouse and Finn followed right behind, ignoring the five-meter rule in the final push out of the city. They closed the distance to the gate, passed through it, and into the open beyond. Cass was gratified that the Weir on top of the wall didn't show itself again. She flipped her veil back down and stuck close to Mouse.

Once the group cleared the gate, Sky led them at the same pace for a good mile or mile and a half, twisting and turning seemingly at random through the dead sprawl outside Morningside's perimeter. Only when the calls of the Weir had faded completely in the distance did he signal for a halt. They ducked into a low single-story concrete structure for cover. Mouse and Finn lowered Swoop carefully to the ground inside and both men stayed down on their knees, breathing hard. Mouse dropped the rucksack off his back.

"Don't get too comfortable," Sky said. "We can't be here long. And *you*," he said, jabbing a finger at Cass. His eyes smoldered. "Don't ever pull a stunt like that again. Not ever, you understand me."

"I knew it wasn't connected," Cass said.

"You *said* it," Sky said, and the words came out hot. "You

didn't *know* it. Are you trying to get us *all* killed? Or was my wife enough?"

If he had punched her square in the face, Sky could not have shocked or hurt her more. Cass was so stunned by the words, so deeply wounded, that for a moment she literally couldn't breathe.

"Hey, easy," Mouse said, rising to his feet. He took a couple of steps towards them both, but he angled his body towards Sky. "Easy now." Sky continued to glower at Cass for a few seconds, then turned away and posted up by the entrance.

"I did... everything..." Cass said, and her words came out broken, heavy with the tortured emotion she'd been trying to suppress. But Mouse looked over at her and held up a hand, shaking his head slightly. Cass couldn't tell if he meant *not now* or *no need*, but neither of them took any of the sting away. She'd been trying to keep it all contained, to keep the loss separated and distant until they were all somewhere safe. But Sky's words had cracked the armor plating, and Cass wasn't sure she could contain the surge.

"I need a couple of minutes to catch my breath," Mouse said. "Might as well see what we're lugging around in these packs. Can you give me a hand?"

Cass doubted Mouse really needed the help or the break, but she welcomed the distraction. Sky was standing just inside the entrance to the building, keeping watch. Cass crept to his side and leaned his rifle against the wall next to him, a silent peace offering. He didn't acknowledge her, but as she withdrew she saw him glance over at the weapon.

She joined Mouse back in the middle of the room and together they worked to empty out the two rucksacks and to organize the pile of supplies. It wasn't a precise system; medical, ammunition, other. Once it was all out, for a few moments, Cass and Mouse just sat there looking at the supplies arrayed before them. Knowing how little time Gamble had had to get it all assembled, Cass marveled at how thorough she'd been. It was a little glimpse into the heart and mind of the woman who'd led her team so well for so many years. It was like she'd known exactly what they'd need. She'd even packed the other two empty rucksacks so they could share out the gear once they got somewhere safe.

Under Mouse's direction, Cass and Finn helped divide the supplies into the four rucksacks as equally as they could, as quickly as they could. Afterward, they topped off a number of magazines for both Finn and Sky's weapons, and then loaded up. Cass hadn't realized just how much sixty odd pounds of gear had dragged on her until she secured half that amount on her back. She felt almost as mobile as usual.

Finn loaded a fresh mag into Sky's weapon and traded it with Sky for his own. He then held out his rifle for her to take.

"You see anything," he said, "call it first. Don't engage unless Sky does, all right?" Cass nodded and was about to accept his weapon, but stopped herself. As much as pride wanted her to believe she could, there was no way she would handle an emergency as well as Finn would with his longtime teammate. Sky would have to tell her everything to do. With Finn running the weapon, it would be automatic.

"You shoot," she said. "I'll carry Swoop."

"Not with that busted arm," Mouse said.

Cass held up her left hand opened wide and then clenched it into a fist a few times. "Grip's just fine."

"I don't want you complicating that fracture–" Mouse said, but Cass cut him off.

"If things go bad, you want your best shooters doing the work," she said. "I'll carry."

To emphasize the point, she walked to the head of the litter, leaving Finn standing there with his weapon.

"I've always been better up close anyway," she added.

Mouse glanced at Finn, who gave a little shrug.

"Fine," Mouse said. "But if anything feels like it's going worse with that arm, tell me."

"Sure," Cass said.

"I mean it, Cass."

"I know," she answered. "Daylight's burning."

Mouse moved over to the litter and shooed her to the end with Swoop's feet, the lighter side. He gave a quick three count and they lifted together. Pain exploded in Cass's forearm and surged like electricity up through her shoulder, radiated out into her chest. She grit her teeth, commanding herself not to make a sound. Mouse glanced over his shoulder at her.

"You all right?" he asked.

"Absolutely," she said, keeping her voice cool and flat. Her pinky and ring finger felt like she was gripping a metal rod just shy of molten.

"Sky," Mouse said. "Take us home."

Sky nodded and moved once more out into the street, with Mouse and Cass coming behind, and Finn keeping rear guard.

The next few hours were a white fog of pain for Cass. Every jolt or jostle, each step misplaced or out of sync with Mouse's stride, sent shockwaves rippling out from her arm into every other part of her body. Even the scant few halts were a mixed blessing. Setting Swoop down didn't relieve the pain, and yet taking him up again seemed to multiply it. The anesthesia had clearly worn off, but Cass refused to mention it. Any time Mouse asked how she was, her answer was the same: a wordless nod.

Sky drove a hard pace, with good reason. They were racing the sun. And Cass wasn't entirely sure they were going to win. She didn't want to slow anyone down or force any change in the current arrangement. It was just a matter of will at that point, and she still had plenty of that in reserve. She kept her eyes focused on Mouse's back, and her mind on the next step.

When they stopped for another break, it took Cass a minute to realize the sun was already touching the horizon. She was about to comment that they should probably keep pushing when Sky turned around and said, "We gotta figure out what to do about him." He nodded at Swoop.

Cass blinked through the dull ache that throbbed through her entire being. She recognized this place. The courtyard. They'd made it back to the wayhouse. She swayed on her feet, the relief almost too much to bear.

"What do you mean?" Finn said.

"He means do we take him inside with us," Mouse answered.

"As opposed to what?" Cass said. Mouse looked at her with his steady gaze. "We didn't carry him all this way just to leave him out here."

"No," Mouse said. "We didn't."

"So we're taking him in," she said.

"Not necessarily," said Sky.

"What are we talking about here?" Finn said.

Mouse and Sky exchanged a look.

"Wait, you're thinking about putting him down?" Finn continued. He ran a hand over his face and then back over his head, let out an exasperated sigh. "We could've done that about ten klicks ago, you know. Saved ourselves a lot of trouble."

"Not properly," Mouse said. "But we're on our own doorstep. We've got time to do it right."

"Guys, no," Cass said. "It's Swoop."

"It's not Swoop," Sky said. "Swoop's dead."

"Not yet, he's not," Cass answered.

"That," Sky said, pointing to the litter, "*that* is just a thing using his body."

"But there's a chance we can get him back. That's why I didn't kill him in the first place. And why Gamble wouldn't either. Wren could still save him."

"Wren's not here," Mouse said.

"But you could go to Greenstone. You could take Swoop to Greenstone and get Wren to bring him back."

"That's a long way off," Sky said, "and we've got to make it through tonight first. Even bringing him this far might be inviting more trouble than we can handle."

"Sky, Gamble could've done it," Cass said. "I was right there. She had her knife out, ready to do it. And she didn't. She chose not to. *She* made that decision."

"Don't talk to me about my wife, Cass," he said, and the coolness in his voice was deadly. "You don't want to talk to me about her right now."

Cass turned to Mouse.

"You can keep him under, can't you?"

"For a while," Mouse answered. "But I don't know what that does for us, Cass, not really. Keeps him from carving us up, sure, but I don't know how they work. How they track each other. We might've just brought them all right to our doorstep. But doorstep is better than inside the house."

Cass couldn't believe they were having this conversation. After all Gamble had done to get Swoop out, after all they had done to get him back to the wayhouse, to give up on him now was beyond her comprehension. But as much as she hated to admit it, she couldn't truly argue the logic. To them, the important thing was to put Swoop out of the Weir's reach forever. They'd already buried him in their hearts; the idea of his potential resurrection was too remote, too implausible compared to the likelihood that his presence was a threat to all of them.

"What about you?" Mouse said to Cass, a curious look in his eye.

"What about me?"

"Could you wake him?"

"Me?" Cass said. The thought had never even occurred to her before, and she couldn't understand why it would have occurred to anyone else, either.

"Could you try it?" he said.

"Try it?" she said. "I'm not... No, I've never done anything like that before. I wouldn't even know where to start."

Mouse nodded. He'd obviously expected the response, but even so, Cass saw the ember of hope die in his eyes.

"Then I'm with Sky," he said. "We already lost one today.

I'm not going to risk everyone else on a wish."

"What about Wick and Able?" Finn said. "Shouldn't they get a say?"

"Sure," said Mouse. "Let's go talk to 'em. You want to let 'em know we're here?"

Finn nodded, and then opened the channel. "Wick, it's me, bud. We're outside."

Wick let out something between a whistle and a sigh of relief. "About time. You guys are cutting it nice and close, huh?" he responded. His voice sounded thin, and not just because of the compression on the channel. "Surprised G let you stay out so late."

"Yeah," Finn said, but he let it go at that. Better to deliver the news face-to-face. "Pop the hatch."

"Able's on it," Wick answered. And sure enough, a few moments later, Able emerged from between the buildings where the entrance to the wayhouse was hidden.

His eyes swept their small party; Mouse, Finn, Cass, Sky, Swoop... back to Sky. And then he lowered himself to the ground, a controlled fall as the weight of understanding bore him down. Mouse motioned to Finn, and they took up the litter before Cass had any say. They all crossed the courtyard together. When they reached Able he recovered himself enough to stand and catch Sky up in an embrace. At first, Sky accepted it without returning it, but as Able continued to hold him, he started to pull away, attempting to shrug it off. Still Able clung to him.

"Get off me, Able," Sky said, and he tried to push free. He got loud. "Able, get off me! Get off ME!"

But Able wouldn't release him. And just when Cass was certain Sky was going to break free and take a swing, all that struggling seemed to take the last of whatever energy he'd been using to keep himself in check. His legs buckled, and he let out an utterly inhuman cry of rage and anguish. No, not inhuman. The rawest, most deeply human wail Cass had ever heard; one that told of a fathomless emotion too powerful, too vast to be bound or captured in words.

Finn and Mouse set Swoop down just outside the entryway, and Mouse wrapped his giant arms around both Able and Sky, lending his strength. Finn put a hand on the top of Sky's head and stood there for a few moments, then headed down into the wayhouse, no doubt to fill his brother in. The three other men there, holding one another, sharing their grief, stepping in to bear some portion of their companion's crushing agony, were a sight terrible to behold; terrible and brutally beautiful. And though on the way to Morningside Cass had felt very much like one of the team, here, now, she knew she was still an outsider, and always would be.

She went and sat down next to Swoop, alone in her sorrow. She wept then, wept with soul-deep tears for the loss of the woman she'd come to think of as a sister. And for her son, and for Morningside, and for all that had gone so completely wrong with the world.

Some time later, a hand came gently to her shoulder, and she turned to find Mouse crouched beside her. How long they'd given to their grief, she didn't know. Long enough for the sun to sink low and stripe the sky in orange and pale purple. The others had gone.

"Hey," he said softly. There was kindness in his touch and in his tear-stung eyes. "We're headed down to talk about Swoop. You want to join us?"

Cass wiped her eyes and nose on her sleeve. Did she want to join them? Yes. Yes she did. She wanted to be a part of that family, to belong to something that stood so strong and wonderful even in its darkest moments. But it was not her place, no matter how desperately she desired it.

"No," she said. "No. Thank you, Mouse, but I've said my part. You go on."

"It's all right, Cass," he said. "You're one of us now. You can come down." And he said it so earnestly, Cass thought that she might be able to let herself believe it. But somehow in her heart, she knew it wasn't right. She placed her hand on top of his and squeezed.

"I'll keep watch," she said. "And keep him company."

Mouse opened his mouth to say something more, but changed his mind and closed it again. He squeezed her shoulder and nodded, and then rose and headed to the wayhouse. Cass watched him go with a quiet sadness in her heart. Mouse was a good man. He deserved better than life had given him.

Once he'd gone, she turned her eyes back to the courtyard, and then upwards to the purpling sky above. As she sat staring, a faint point of light timidly revealed itself to her, a softer scar of paleness against a pale sky; the first evening star. And Cass felt a melancholy descend. She was that star. A lone, faded light drifting amidst a sea of emptiness. No connections, no belonging, no significance to anything else around her. Mother to an angel and a demon, neither of whom she could touch or speak to or even likely see ever again.

She was lost. Entirely lost. And somewhere, something deep within her spoke an insight that seemed beyond her own capability to perceive, some wisdom gifted her by the universe in her moment of utter depletion. Of course she felt lost. She was, at last, alone with herself. All else had been stripped away.

Her entire life, from as far back as she could remember to that very point in time, she had always been something to someone else. Been something *through* someone else. Zenith, Underdown, RushRuin, Asher, Wren. Three. Always defined by her relationship to others. Who was she when everything else was gone? She had no idea. And now, everything else *was* gone.

As she sat there, the sun slipped lower, and the pale sky deepened to dusk. And the insignificant star that had so fearfully shone its meager light first in the heavens grew bold against the darkness. Brighter, yes, but more than that; sharper, defiant. Fierce. And though it remained alone and stood no chance at turning back the night, still it shone unconquerable.

She laughed at herself then. Maybe it was the exhaustion. Maybe the grief. Cass had never been much of a romantic. But that didn't steal away the fact that that little star felt an awful lot like a small kindness from the universe, reminding Cass of her individuality, dignifying her suffering.

She looked down at Swoop. Yes, she'd never done anything like it before. Yes, she didn't even know where to start. But yes, she could at very least *try*.

TWENTY

Wren lay on his narrow bed covered by a thin blanket, staring up at the slender ray of orange light that cleanly divided the gloom that clung to the ceiling. The day before, he'd quickly discovered that regardless of the time, switching off the lights in his room plunged him into an immediate and total darkness. There were no windows, no devices with status lights, not even cracks around the door. It made everything feel too close, reminded him too much of times past that had terrified him, and still maintained the power to do so. He'd settled on leaving the bathroom light on with the door cracked, though it made him feel supremely childish. He knew there were no monsters under the bed. But he knew too there were demons in his mind, and that sliver of light seemed to keep some of them at bay.

He'd slept fitfully, the deep exhaustion of the many days demanding its due yet warring against the stress and anxiety that plagued his every thought. It'd created the same sensation that a high fever would; body demanding sleep, but gaining no rest from it. For now, he was floating in a wired equilibrium. Tired, but not sleepy. Restless, but too weary to move. He checked the time; still an hour and a half before sunrise.

Naturally his thoughts turned towards his mother, as they often did. Despite having heard nothing from her in over a week, he felt more confident now that she was out there somewhere, alive. Mama was a survivor. He'd seen it for himself firsthand. And having witnessed how practiced she'd been in it, he knew she always had been, even before he'd been born. But today, he tried to drive his thoughts elsewhere. That life was behind him now, at least for the duration of his training.

His training. He wondered what lay ahead of him under the old man's instruction. The old man. Foe. Maybe he'd meant it as a joke, but Wren couldn't quite bring himself to believe it. It seemed too true, too likely that it really did capture the old man's intentions. To train Wren not as a patient friend, but rather as a determined enemy.

A sliding sound from the door interrupted his thoughts, the well-oiled mechanicals shifting as someone opened it. The door swung slowly open, cutting the narrow beam of light from the bathroom. It was dark in the hall beyond, so Wren couldn't make out who it was entering his room, but the possibilities were pretty limited. After the door closed, a figure glided silently forward, likewise tripping the orange ray, and Wren saw his features in a rapid series of slivers.

"Hi, Haiku," Wren said. The man stopped moving, apparently surprised by Wren's voice.

"Hello, Wren," Haiku said quietly. "Did you sleep?"

"A little."

"Anxious?"

"Yeah."

"It's understandable. You'll sleep well tonight, though," Haiku said, and Wren could hear the smile in his words. "Assuming you're still intent on going forward."

"I am," Wren said.

"Then Father's waiting for you."

"Oh. Already?"

"Yes. The days are going to be long, Wren. Very early mornings, very late nights. You'll probably feel like you want to die for the first little while. But..." Haiku said, and then trailed off.

"I'll adjust?"

"Well," Haiku said. "I was going to say you won't die."

They were both silent for a moment, and then Wren asked, "Should we go now?"

"Yes," Haiku said. "But do whatever you need to beforehand to get ready."

Wren slipped out of bed, grabbed the clothes he'd worn the day before, and padded barefoot to the washroom. The light blazed when he opened the door and made his eyes water. He went to the bathroom and washed his hands and face, got dressed. Looked at himself in the small metal mirror. The image that stared back looked small and scared.

"You can do it," Wren told himself. "You have to." The reflection didn't look convinced.

He opened the washroom door and found Haiku standing by the entrance to his room with the lights on. Wren went to him and Haiku knelt.

"I want to tell you one thing before your training begins, Wren," he said, and his face was grave. "This is important, and you must believe me. This is going to be hard on you. Harder than you can imagine. At times, Father's lessons might even seem cruel to you. But you must understand, you must trust, that Father will never harm you. Everything he does, every lesson however small, is meant to shape you and mold you, never to destroy you. If you will submit yourself to it, if you will let your spirit rest in that knowledge, then the lessons will be easier to withstand."

Wren blinked at Haiku. He wanted to believe the man, but it was a lot to take in all at once. And it didn't seem to match his initial experience with Foe.

"I guess he wasn't that concerned about me before he agreed to train me?" Wren asked.

"What do you mean?"

"When he made me spend the night outside, by myself. He didn't seem worried about me not getting hurt then."

"Oh," Haiku said. "You *will* hurt, Wren. Pain can be a useful instructor when it is directed with purpose, and Father is a master of its art. But you must believe me that though his lessons may bring hurt, Father will never, ever *harm* you."

"There's a difference?" Wren said.

"Yes," Haiku said, as he rose to his feet. "And you'll learn it for yourself better than I can explain it." He stood there by the door and stared down at Wren. Then added, "And you are mistaken. You didn't spend the night outside by yourself."

"Well... I didn't think the Weir counted."

Haiku chuckled at that. "You were never alone out there, Wren," he said. "Father was watching over you the whole time, from the first moment you left the tower."

At first Wren assumed that meant Foe had been using some kind of tracerun to keep track of his location. But then he remembered seeing the old man that morning, waiting outside and coated in dust. Had he really been out there the entire night?

"Come," Haiku said, opening the door. "He's waiting."

Wren followed silently behind. His chest was tight with a dreadful excitement; a thrilling fear that filled him with emotions for which he had no names. And those nameless feelings pushed against the swirling thoughts about all that Haiku had just told him. There was a frightening quality to Haiku's insistence that Foe's cruelties be taken as kindness, that pain was a necessary component to true learning. It seemed more likely Haiku was too afraid to admit Foe was a ruthless old man who took joy in tormenting others.

Foe was sitting in the parlor, in one of the chairs near the outer wall, by a window. Most of the shutters were still closed, but the one nearest Foe was open. He continued to stare out over the empty plain even when they'd come and stood beside him. Through the window, Wren here and there saw faint flickers in the open and amongst the distant ruins, like the shimmer of remote stars. A handful of Weir, roving.

"Tell me, boy," Foe said. "Have you considered?"

"Yes, sir," Wren answered.

"And?"

"I want to learn from you."

"Very well," Foe said. For some reason, Wren had expected one final argument, one last attempt by the old man to dissuade him. But once again, Foe had surprised him with his simple, almost casual response. "Come, sit here," he said, pointing to the floor at his feet. Wren sat down cross-legged in front of him.

"Before we begin, there are two things you must understand," he continued. "First, I will never ask you to do the impossible. Anything I ask you to do *can* be done."

"OK."

"Second, I will never ask you to do anything that will lead to your destruction. Anything I ask you do is for your improvement, not your degradation."

"OK."

Foe leaned forward in his chair and looked Wren intently in the eye. "It is important you hear these things, important that you believe them and trust in them. There will soon be times when you may be tempted to believe otherwise."

"I believe you," Wren said, because he knew he had to believe it to move forward, and he thought that maybe if he said it, he really would believe it. Foe looked at him hard for a few moments longer, and then leaned back in his chair again.

"These two things, I promise to you," he said. "And in return, you must promise to do whatever I ask of you."

"I will," Wren said, and this time he really did mean it. "I promise."

Foe nodded. He was dressed in a loose shirt, or maybe a light jacket, with sleeves wide and draping at the wrist. His right hand disappeared inside his left sleeve, and when he withdrew it, he was holding a slender-bladed, double-edged knife, about the length of his hand from palm to fingertip.

"Stand up," Foe said. "Hold out your hand, boy." Wren held out his left hand, and couldn't prevent his eyes from straying down to the knife. Foe laid the blade flat against

JAY POSEY   281

Wren's palm with one edge pressed tight into the web between his thumb and forefinger. Before Wren could react, Foe gripped Wren's left hand with his own, as though he were about to shake it in greeting with the blade held fast between. There was no doubt how sharp the knife was; it felt honed to a surgical edge. Though it had not yet bitten into his hand, Wren knew that even a slight motion could easily open the soft flesh.

"Haiku?" said Foe, and Haiku stepped closer.

"Wren, I'm going to recite an oath now. It is the one I have sworn to House, as have many before me. Listen carefully, because it is the one you too will have to swear. When I finish, you will have one final opportunity to decide whether or not you wish to take it. Do you understand?"

"Yes," Wren said, and he tried to turn his focus to Haiku, and away from the blade against his flesh and the iron strength in Foe's grip. Haiku cleared his throat, drew a breath, and began.

"In all ways, at all times, I seek truth. With clarity, I see that which is.

"In all ways, at all times, I master myself. Seen or unseen, I am the same.

"In all ways, at all times, I safeguard life. Lost or taken, I cannot restore it."

At first, Wren struggled against his own divided mind; the conscious desire to absorb the significance of the oath wrestled against a raw, instinctual fear of imminent pain and danger. But as Haiku intoned the words of his oath, Wren found himself becoming entranced by them. Haiku's recitation seemed to fill the room, even to expand it. It was more than an oath. It was a litany.

"In all ways, at all times, I walk uprightly. On my shoulders, I bear the legacy of those who have gone before me.

"In all ways, at all times, I serve resolutely. My every strength and skill, I submit to those who call upon me.

"Truth, my foundation.

"Discipline, my shield.

"Life, my charge.

"Honor, my way.

"Service, my strength.

"Through my life or by my death, I will serve my House," Haiku said. "This is my solemn oath and pledge, sworn and sealed by the shedding of my blood."

As Haiku came to the conclusion of the oath, an electric silence descended, weighty but alive with significance. Here were concepts of the highest quality, ideals of true virtue and a weight of history and lineage that stirred Wren's deepest heart and called to him, challenged him to rise to a standard beyond any he had before imagined. Now that his spirit had been awakened to the possibility, how could he choose to be anything other than the kind of person Haiku was describing? And what cost would be too high to attain it? The moment lingered, and Wren's heart beat harder with anticipation.

"Are you willing to take this oath, boy?" Foe said.

Wren licked dry lips with a dry tongue, swallowed with difficulty. This was it. Point of no return. Nothing he'd done in life compared to this moment, not even when he'd taken on the title of governor. He nodded. "I am."

"Haiku," Foe said. "Lead him."

Haiku repeated the oath in segments, and Wren repeated them, taking his time to give each phrase its full due. The words felt heavy in his mouth, substantial. Powerful.

"Truth, my foundation," he said. "Discipline, my shield. Life, my charge. Honor, my way. Service, my strength." When it came to the final line, he stopped and breathed deeply. Sweat broke out on his forehead.

"This is my solemn oath and pledge," he said. Breathe. Swallow. "Sworn and sealed by the shedding of my blood." He shut his eyes, steeling himself against what he knew must come next. Waited.

"Open your eyes, boy," Foe said. Wren obeyed, met Foe's gaze. "Grip the knife."

Wren saw now that Foe was no longer holding the knife by its handle. He reached out and took hold.

"This is *your* oath," Foe said. "I will not spill your blood."

A drop of sweat rolled heavy past Wren's temple, over his cheekbone. The instinct to avoid harming himself fought against the desire to complete his oath, to begin his training, to become that which had been presented as possible. He squeezed the handle of the knife.

"This is my solemn oath and pledge," he repeated. "Sworn and sealed by the shedding of my blood."

Wren tried to pull the knife in a rapid motion, but Foe had such a grip on his hand and the blade that he instead was forced to draw it slowly free. The pain was muted by the sharpness of the knife, but sensation of the flesh separating made his head swim. When the blade was fully clear, Foe swiftly shifted his grip so that their hands met web-to-web. The pressure was accompanied by the first angry sting of the self-inflicted injury and the welling of blood.

"As you have spoken, so shall it be," Foe said. He continued his grip on Wren's hand. "You are a son of House Eight. From this moment forward, you will conduct yourself in a manner worthy of the legacy of this House." Foe released Wren's hand, and added. "I will show you how."

With the pressure released, blood flowed freely from the wound. Twin trails snaked on either side of Wren's hand and met at a point just below his wrist, where they mingled and dripped. Haiku stepped forward and wordlessly set to addressing the laceration, pressing a gauzy material into it. Wren hissed reflexively as the pain exploded and surged through his hand and up into his forearm. The gauze was wet and cold, apparently soaked in some sort of antiseptic chemical, judging from the fire it lit in his nerves. Wren's lips went numb and he felt chilled and strangely light, like all his blood had turned to arctic air.

"Sit down over here," Haiku said, guiding Wren firmly to another chair. Wren let himself be led and did as he was told. Haiku crouched in front of him with a smile. "It's OK," he said. "I almost passed out too when I did it."

Wren blinked several times, trying to chase away the dimness that seemed to be closing in on his vision from the sides. He sat still for a couple of minutes, allowing Haiku to clean his hand up. As he recovered himself, he noticed Foe was no longer sitting across from him, but was instead up by the table in the parlor, wrapping something around his own hand. It looked almost like a bandage. That was the first moment when Wren realized that Foe had shared the shedding of blood. Of course he had. The blade was double-edged. Though the oath had been Wren's alone to give, Foe had participated in its sealing.

"Recite the oath often," Haiku said. "Each morning when you rise, each evening when you lie down, as often throughout the day as you remember. It is your code, and if you hold to it, it will define your life. Each day will deepen your understanding of those words, and you will find that even a lifetime isn't long enough to work out all their promise."

After Foe had finished dressing his own hand, he approached and stood behind Haiku.

"And now," he said, "we will begin." Wren was still feeling shaky, but he didn't want to say anything about it. Foe didn't seem like he would be concerned anyway.

"As I said to you yesterday," Foe continued, "the life you knew before is over. That's the choice you've made, to turn away from everything that has come before. To that end, while you are here under my training, your world is only as big as I allow it to be."

"I won't try to communicate with anyone," Wren said. "I promise."

"The outside world no longer exists to you. And you, likewise, must not exist to it. To begin, I will hide you from it."

"I'm already doing that," Wren said. Foe's eyebrows raised slightly, and he cocked his head to one side. "I had to," Wren continued. "Because of my brother. I had to make sure he couldn't find me."

Foe smiled and shook his head. "Yes, I've seen what you've done, boy. And it is clever, in its way. But it would be easily defeated by anyone who had more than a passing interest in finding you. When I say I will hide you, I mean that you will, for all intents and purposes, vanish. I tell you this because you will likely find the sensation..." He paused, either searching for the word, or to emphasize it. "Disorienting."

Wren felt a fresh burst of anxiety, from the revelation that his technique for masking his signal wasn't as effective as he'd believed. Did that mean that Asher could have been tracking him all this time? And did that mean that what he'd taught Mama wasn't really working either? Mama. That brought its own wave of emotion. If Foe made him impossible to find, what would happen if Mama came looking for him?

He knew he wasn't supposed to be thinking about that now. He'd sworn an oath. But the reality of what it meant in practice was only now beginning to settle on him.

"Do not panic," Foe said.

And before Wren could respond, a vast emptiness fell upon him, an overwhelming sense of his smallness, as if he had been instantly transported to the top of a skyscraper with the ground ten thousand feet below. He was lost, drifting in a sea of silence, utterly isolated. Conflicting emotions raced through him; it felt as if everything had collapsed in upon him, as if all the world had compressed itself into this one room, and yet he was filled with a loneliness so expansive, it seemed impossible that he alone could contain it all.

The isolation was so heavy it was almost tangible, but it was so foreign, so incomprehensible that Wren couldn't process the source or cause. It was like the sudden loss of a sense, the deafness following an explosion, or numbness of a frost-chilled hand. He wondered with sudden horror if this is what it was to be disconnected.

"Breathe, boy," said Foe, and he chuckled, apparently amused by Wren's reaction.

Out of reflex, Wren tried to access something simple; with the flutter of an eye, he issued a request to the local grid to confirm his location. A routine process, normally so immediate that the interval between request and response was imperceptible. Instead, the request stalled, hung there in the ether, without even an echo to mark its existence. Nothing but the dull silence of a dead signal.

"What's happening to me?" Wren said. "Did you..." The thought of it made him want to throw up. "Am I disconnected?"

"He's insulated your signal," Haiku said. "Nothing more."

"All that you need is here before you," said Foe, holding out his bandaged hand to indicate the room around them. "For you, nothing else exists, nothing else need exist."

Wren wanted to believe that everything was all right, that there was no reason for the fear that dominated his every fiber, but his logical mind had no power over the instinct; he felt like he was being smothered.

"As your training progresses, I will allow your world to expand to suit your capacity," Foe continued. "For now, any and all traffic along your connection goes through me."

Internally, Wren thrashed against the suffocating presence, reached out through the digital and felt it now, Foe's own processes hovering above him.

"Please," Wren said. "I won't do anything you don't want me to. Please."

"It's for your safety, Wren," Haiku said. "And for ours."

Foe walked over and stood in front of Wren, placed his hand on top of Wren's head. He tilted Wren's head back and looked him in the eyes. Foe's dark eyes were cool and steady; there was no malice in them.

"Right now, you think you're strong enough," Foe said. "You believe you have willpower enough to maintain the discipline of silence. And at the moment, I believe you do. But soon enough you'll have exhausted your resolve, and

I would not be a very good teacher if I were to leave you helpless in the face of temptation that I could otherwise remove."

The mention of discipline hearkened Wren back to the words of his oath, and he returned to them, recited them.

In all ways, at all times, I seek truth. With clarity, I see that which is. In all ways, at all times, I master myself. Seen or unseen, I am the same.

It didn't make the suffocating feeling go away, but it gave his mind something to hold on to, something to do other than flail.

Foe removed his hand and returned to the table in the middle of the parlor.

"Steady your breathing," Haiku said, as he put the final touches on Wren's bandage. He lowered his voice, as though he were sharing a secret. "It's harder for you, because of your age. Usually when the training begins, the young ones haven't become as dependent on connectedness yet. But you'll be OK."

"You went through this?" Wren asked. He forced himself to take deep breaths.

Haiku smiled and shook his head. "I was never connected."

"Enough coddling, Haiku," Foe called from across the room. "Come along, boy."

Haiku stood and stepped back. Wren got to his feet, flexed his hand, testing it against the tension of the bandage.

"Thanks, Haiku."

Haiku dipped his head in a scant bow. Wren crossed to Foe, who led him out of the parlor and into the stairwell. Moving seemed to help calm the vertigo. Each footfall found something solid beneath it, reminded Wren of his place in space. He found that running a hand along the wall or the railing of the stairs steadied him, as if the physical world served to anchor him in reality.

"My name is Wren," Wren said.

"Mmm?" Foe replied, though the noise was non-

committal; Wren wasn't sure if the old man hadn't
heard what he'd said, or if he'd heard it and was merely
acknowledging the statement.

"I said my name is Wren," he repeated. "Not 'boy'."

Foe stopped, but didn't turn around.

"You have not yet suffered enough to know your true
name," Foe said. "But you will learn it in time."

The answer was wholly unexpected and completely
confusing. Wren immediately regretted having said
anything. They descended in silence past the ground floor
and continued down three more flights before turning
into another passage. Wren glanced back as they left the
stairwell. The stairs continued down into darkness. He
couldn't help but wonder just how far down it went.

The lighting in the passage was minimal; thin fiberlights
ran along the top and bottom of the walls and cast everything
in a grey gloaming. Foe stopped briefly at a small box affixed
to the wall just outside a door. He swept his thumb over a
panel and the front of the case whirred open. The old man
removed something from the box and dropped it casually
into a pocket on his loose shirt, though Wren couldn't see
what it was. He closed the box and then opened the door
next to it.

Wren followed him in. As they entered, the lights came
up with a hum and washed over the room with a blue-
white intensity. The room was a large square, maybe thirty
feet to a side, but oddly constructed. Wren stood next to Foe
on what seemed to be a ledge or catwalk about four feet
wide. Beyond that, the floor dropped seven feet or so to a
lower level. Where the catwalk was grated metal, the lower
section appeared to be flat, pale blue concrete. Short, round
poles or pillars, narrow and flat on top, stood scattered on
the concrete with no apparent design or pattern Wren could
detect. The catwalk ran all the way around the sunken
portion of the room. A slick touch-panel was inset in the
wall by the door, dark and dormant.

Next to Wren, Foe was busy taking off his shoes.

"You may want to do the same," Foe said. Wren didn't understand why, but he sat down and started taking his boots off anyway. While he was doing that, Foe went to the touch-panel. It lit up under his fingers. As Wren was wondering whether he should remove his socks as well, the walls of the room groaned and clanked. A hissing sound rose from the lower section, and a few seconds later water burbled up from some great number of unseen jets. Wren pulled off his socks.

Foe returned to him as he was standing up and held out his hand. Across his palm lay a small, horn-shaped device in silver and bright blue.

"Have you seen one of these before, boy?" Foe asked.

Wren shook his head. "No, sir."

Foe nodded and gripped the device around the narrow end and pointed the rounded, blunt end at Wren. There was a tiny rectangle at the center. Wren was just about to ask what it was when the device clicked, the rectangle lit with a lightning blue, and a needle-prick pain lanced through Wren's chest. He yelped at the pain, and pressed his fingers against the place between his ribs where he'd felt the jolt. Already the pain was subsiding to a mild burn. There was no hole or mark on Wren's shirt.

"We just call them clickers," Foe said casually as he held the device back out across his palm. "Go on, take it." Wren took the clicker from Foe. Below them, water continued to fill the sunken portion. "Do you see how to operate it?"

Wren turned the device over in his hand, ran a thumb along its smooth back. There was a hint of play in the curve, just behind the broad head of the device. Wren made sure the blunt end was facing Foe and pressed. The device clicked. Foe didn't react.

"Good," he said. He glanced down at the water below, and then turned back to the panel. The hissing ceased. Foe went to edge of the ledge and turned around. "Down."

He bent down and descended, making use of a ladder embedded in the side of the concrete that Wren hadn't noticed. Wren waited until Foe was down and then followed after. The old man waded out from the ladder to the center of the pool, weaving through the poles as he went. Wren estimated the water was about two feet deep. And when his foot touched it, he sucked in his breath at the cold.

"Quickly, boy," Foe called to him. Wren held his breath and forced his foot down into the frigid water. The water came up to the middle of his thighs, and drained all the heat from his body as he trudged his way out to where Foe was waiting. By the time he got there, his teeth were already chattering. Foe seemed disappointed. "You'll want to control that," he said flatly. And then, "Take a look around. Get a good sense of where you are, where I am, and what surrounds us." He paused while Wren glanced around at the poles, the walls, the water. Wren wasn't sure what exactly he was supposed to be looking for. He crossed his arms, hugging himself against his shivering.

"Have you seen enough?" Foe asked.

Wren nodded.

"This is the Waiting Room," Foe said. "You will spend a great deal of time here, and it will teach you many things. But the most important thing you will learn here is *patience*."

The idea of standing in freezing cold water didn't sound at all like a good way to learn patience, Wren thought. How was Foe so calm? The water didn't seem to be bothering him at all.

"For now, we will begin with something simple. You have your clicker?"

Wren unfolded his arms and held up his clicker. Foe drew a second clicker from his pocket.

"A simple game, with simple rules. When I tell you to begin, try to hit me. Don't get hit."

"That's it?" Wren asked. Foe dipped his head in a nod. Wren glanced around again. The poles weren't wide enough for him to hide behind completely, and they were only about three feet tall. Maybe he could use them for a little bit of cover at least.

"Ready?" Foe asked.

"Yes, sir," Wren said. He hunched down, clicker at the ready. When Foe said to begin, Wren would feint to his right, and then dodge left. There was a cluster of poles that direction.

"Very well," Foe said. Wren tensed, waiting for the signal. Instead, the lights went out. Total darkness.

"Begin," said Foe. And in the next instant, a single spark flared and pain bored right through the center of Wren's chest. He cried out at the shock, and Foe's clicker glinted again, stinging Wren in nearly the exact same place.

In the surprise and confusion, Wren forgot all about his previous tactics and lurched to his right. Another click, another ember of pain, this one catching him in the neck just under his jaw. He splashed on, operating purely in reaction, with no plan or purpose. *Click, click.* Two more stings, one on top of the other in his shoulder-blade.

"Remember, boy," Foe called. "You're trying *not* to get hit."

The voice came from behind him, to his left. Wren spun and fired towards it as fast as he could, *click click click click click.* Silence.

Then.

Click.

Lightning struck right between his eyes. Wren cried out again, earning himself another sting. He stepped back, caught his heel on one of the poles, went over backwards. And before he hit the water, Foe stung him again.

Wren splashed down completely submerged, sucked in icy water, came up spluttering. As he tried to recover, over and over he felt Foe's stinging attacks.

"Stop, Foe!" he yelled at the blackness. "Stop it!"

Click. A pang seared his cheek. Nothing he did seemed to matter; every move, every action, invited Foe's deadly aim. And now, he was helpless and choking in the freezing water. The pain, the frustration, the debilitating cold; there was nothing to learn here, nothing except how to be a victim. He hugged the pole he'd tripped against, made himself as small against it as possible. His clicker was gone, lost somewhere beneath the glacial water.

"Please, stop!" Wren screamed. He squeezed his eyes shut against the pain he knew was coming. But only silence followed. Not total silence; he could hear the water sloshing against the walls, the sound of his own troubled breathing. He opened his eyes, though it made no difference in what he could see. The darkness was absolute. "Foe?" he said. And then louder. "Foe?"

The lights came on, blinding. Wren squeezed his eyes shut against the brilliance.

"Recover your clicker, boy," came Foe's voice from behind him and close. Wren turned and cracked an eye. Foe was standing over him, three feet away. When he saw Wren looking at him, the old man pointed away to his right. Wren followed the gesture and saw the shimmering shape of his lost clicker, distorted by the undulating water.

"You didn't tell me you were going to turn off the lights," Wren said.

In response, Foe clicked him. "Recover your clicker."

Wren dragged himself out of the water and sloshed over to where his clicker lay. His entire body trembled with cold. Capturing the device proved more of a challenge than it should have been as his chill-numbed fingers knocked it about in the water. Once he managed to collect the clicker, he stood and hugged himself again, trying to salvage any body heat he might possibly still possess.

The lights switched off.

"Again."

A splinter of fire shot through the middle of Wren's back, and the pain tipped him over the edge. He cried then, cried at the unfairness of it, and at the joy this man he'd pledged himself to seemed to take in his suffering. Not loud sobbing, for he knew that would only give him away. Wren kept his mouth open, let the tears fall unrestrained. He was soaking wet anyway.

Foe's clicker fired again, stinging him at the base of the neck. Wren whirled in a rage, cried out, fired his clicker in a wild arc. For the outburst, he earned a rash of stabbing pain that stitched up his right side.

"Remember your oath, boy," Foe said.

Was this really training? Throwing Wren into the middle of something and tormenting him while he flailed helplessly without guidance or direction? What good did it do to remember his oath, here in the middle of this senseless abuse?

Another sting. He didn't need an oath. He needed something to hide behind. A wall, or a shield. A shield.

Discipline, my shield.

The words came back at the same moment that Foe hit him again from another side. Wren clenched his teeth against it and just managed to stop himself from mindlessly lashing out in response.

In all ways, at all times, I master myself.

Another click, another scorching pain. Still, Wren kept his place, shuddering, tears streaking his face. At least he wasn't splashing around.

I master myself.

Yet again, Foe jolted him. It hurt, yes, but Haiku had said Foe would never actually harm him. No permanent damage. Wren pressed his chilled hands to his face.

Discipline, my shield.

"Good," Foe said from somewhere in the darkness. Good? What did that mean? Surely Wren was failing utterly. He took his hands away from his face. Drew a deep breath as quietly as he was able.

"Of course I know where you are," Foe said, and he fired his clicker again to demonstrate the point. "But that is because I know you have not yet learned to move quietly." Wren wiped his running nose on his drenched sleeve. He turned at the waist in the direction of Foe's voice.

"Are you going to teach me that?" he asked. And he saw the blue flash of Foe's clicker, took the hit, aimed his own at the afterimage still floating in his eyes, and returned fire *click click*.

And then he lowered himself slowly into a crouch, down into the water, until it was over his shoulders. Foe fired again, from somewhere further to the right than he'd been when he'd taken his previous shot. But for the first time, Wren felt no pain. Foe had fired high.

Wren brought his clicker up out of the water to fire back, but too quickly; his hand splashed as it broke the surface and undoubtedly Foe saw the flicker of Wren's device low to the water. As if to draw attention to Wren's mistake, Foe's shot stung Wren right in the knuckle.

Immediately after, the lights came on again. When Wren's eyes adjusted, he saw Foe standing over by the ladder, quite a bit farther away than Wren had expected. He didn't look happy, but he didn't look upset either.

Foe nodded at him. "Good," he said. Wren stood up out of water, hopeful. A small victory. And Foe was standing by the ladder. Maybe that would be enough for the day. Wren couldn't help but notice the old man was barely wet, except for where his legs were actually in the water.

"Does that mean we're done?" Wren asked.

"Done?" Foe chuckled, and the lights went out. "No, boy. We've only just begun."

TWENTY-ONE

Painter reached over and took Snow's hand. It was comforting to him, even though he knew it had no effect on her. They were sitting together in the shadow of a building, resting after their journey. And waiting for word from Asher, of course. Snow was wearing his goggles again, since Asher had once again driven them through the day to yet another enclave. Painter had genuinely lost count of how many towns they'd hit since Morningside fell. Six? Eight?

His stomach churned whenever he thought about it, so mostly he tried not to. Sometimes his mind would wander back to the night when Asher had come to him, and he would find himself wondering what he had been so angry about, what injustice had been so great as to justify what he was now enabling. But he would never allow himself to linger on such thoughts for long. He'd made his choice, he'd chosen his side. These were the consequences. There was nothing to be done about it now. Painter squeezed Snow's hand, drew strength from it. She was his reward.

And yet, even his sister brought him pain now. Asher had given her to him, but he still made use of her for his attacks. She'd proven herself a deadly weapon, and once Asher had seen her effectiveness, he'd refused to let her stay behind. She'd become one of his favorite tools, in fact. For all his power, Asher still didn't seem to have precise control over his armies of Weir. But there were a few that stood above all the rest. The ones Asher called his Hands. Snow was one of those. Painter had witnessed for himself just how effective she could be when they hit Briargate. He wished he could leave her here. Leave her to rest and to keep her out of what lay ahead. It was too late for him, he knew. But one day, he'd find a way to get his sister free.

A ripple across his mind interrupted his thoughts; Asher seeking connection. Painter delayed opening the channel. He was exhausted, and the thought of having Asher in his head seemed for a moment like more than he could bear. The impulse grew stronger with each second. It was the strangest feeling, like a bulge in his thought patterns, something beneath the surface threatening to tear its way through. Painter was tempted to see what would happen if he refused the connection, but the fear that the outcome would be irreversible damage overcame his curiosity. He opened the channel, and Asher's presence exploded into his mind.

"What were you doing?" he snapped. "You answer when I call!"

"Sorry," Painter answered. "I'm... I'm just really tired."

"Whatever, it's time," Asher said, ignoring him. "Get moving. Offer the same."

"They won't accept it," Painter replied before he thought about it. He was so tired, he'd communicated it before he'd considered what he was saying. Asher didn't like to be challenged. Painter had to be more careful.

"Well they *should*," Asher said. "It'd be a lot easier for everybody. Hurry up. I need you to meet up with Roh."

Roh. Even now the name sparked embers of anger in him. Roh was another Awakened from Morningside; fully Awakened, like Painter. And like Painter, he'd pledged himself to Asher's service. Painter had known Roh, or at least known of him, in Morningside. He'd been Awakened a couple of months before Painter and had always had a chip on his shoulder. Though he didn't want to admit it, Painter knew there was some aspect of... well, he wasn't quite sure what it was. Not quite jealousy. But Painter had believed he'd been chosen by Asher above all others, to be his Voice. It had made him significant. Roh's presence reminded him that maybe he wasn't as important as he'd let himself believe.

A location appeared in his mind, a beacon marking the rendezvous point with Roh.

"Come on, Snow," Painter said, getting to his feet. He drew her up, led her towards the beacon. It was several seconds before he realized that Asher was still hanging around.

"Do you think I *want* to eradicate all these places?" Asher asked.

Painter didn't trust himself to answer.

"I don't," Asher continued. "But you see how they force my hand. There have to be consequences. They don't understand how I'm helping them."

Painter couldn't prevent himself from responding. "Helping them?"

"Yes, *helping* them, Painter. You've seen how they live. What about you? What were you before I found you? Before I *chose* you?" he said. "Nothing! And now look!"

"By enslaving them?"

"No!" Asher yelled, his voice sharp in Painter's mind. And then, softened. "No, Painter. Listen. It's not like it will be like this forever. It's just for now. I just need everyone for now. When I'm done, I'm going to let them all go. Like I did with your sister. You know that, right?"

There was a strange note in Asher's words, an almost desperation that Painter had never heard before. Asher hadn't been in the habit of explaining himself. It was this unpredictability that made Asher so fearful a master. But now he seemed conflicted, trapped between a need to be obeyed without question and a desire to be understood.

"What will you do with us?" Painter asked. Asher's words had sparked new hope in him, even though Painter knew better than to let himself trust them fully.

"I don't know. Whatever you want. It's just... I have some things I need to do first. But when I'm done, you'll see. The world will be a better place. Far better. You can't see what I can—"

He cut off suddenly. Not just his words. He vanished from Painter's mind, left a sudden vacuum. Painter stopped and closed his eyes until the sensation passed.

Afterwards, he pressed on to the meeting point, where Roh was already waiting for him, as expected. What Painter had *not* expected were the two giant Weir standing with Roh, one on each side. The Weir weren't exactly natural to begin with, but there was something positively abominable about these two creatures, as if some otherworldly creature had found its way into human frame and corrupted it utterly. Painter had never seen anything like them before. Weir, certainly, or had been as a start. But they'd been heavily modified with grafted musculature, reinforced with some combination of organic and mechanical constructs.

Human war machines.

"About time," Roh said. "I need your skinny sister to get around behind the town."

"What... are those?" Painter asked.

"Something Asher's been working on. Don't worry, they won't bite," he said with a smirk. "Just don't get in front of them when we go knocking."

Painter didn't want to look at the creatures anymore, but he couldn't pull his eyes away. And Roh. How could Roh be so oblivious to the horror? They weren't animals. Those things had been people once. Even if they *had* been animals, Painter would have revolted at what had been done to them.

"Come on, everyone's waiting on us. Go give your little speech so we can get to work."

Painter nodded.

"Unless you want to skip it," Roh said. "You know what the answer's gonna be." He smiled with wicked intent. And for the first time Painter realized that Roh was actually enjoying this.

A lightning flash of pressure exploded in his Painter's mind, so forceful he actually physically staggered. Asher had reformed in his mind, had forced himself into Painter's thoughts, uninvited, unannounced.

"I'm taking a quarter, I need them," he said. There was an almost manic intensity in his voice, or in his projection. "If they don't surrender, burn it to the ground."

And then he vanished again, just as suddenly as he'd appeared.

Not appeared. Intruded.

"Asher's taking some of the Weir," Painter told Roh.

"How many?"

"He said a quarter of them."

Roh made a face. "Why?"

"Didn't say."

"Must've found a hot target," Roh said. "Maybe he found who he's looking for."

Painter tried not to let his face reveal any emotion in response. Asher had never said anything to him about looking for anyone. What had he been telling Roh? There were only two people he could imagine Asher scouring so broad a region for. Cass and Wren. If he was looking for them, that meant they'd escaped and were alive. Or at least one of them was.

Painter felt himself tearing through the middle. The idea that one or both of them were still alive was elating. The thought that Asher was burning the whole world to the ground to find them was horrifying. In that moment, Painter couldn't remember what he'd ever thought Asher was doing, or what he'd ever believed would be worth so much death and destruction.

"Go give 'em your talk," Roh said. "Maybe these ones'll surprise us."

Painter nodded numbly and started towards the enclave. Roh had always talked about how Asher was reordering the world, and how superior he was to regular humans now. How he and Painter were the prototypes for a far better humanity. Painter had allowed himself to entertain similar thoughts. Now he realized just how far from humanity he'd come.

TWENTY-TWO

Cass started by thinking back to the things Wren had told her about; about how to mask her own signal, and how he could find and open electronic locks. His description of Awakening others, and especially his story of Kit: how he said she'd "sprung open", like she'd been fighting for it herself. Connections, signals, the digital swirl that bathed the planet ceaselessly. Cass had never concerned herself much about it beyond the necessary basics. She'd always had others around to take care of the intangible, and her talents had always been geared more towards the real. But she wasn't that woman anymore. She was changed. Transformed.

And her mind went back to that moment, that rebirth, when her son had called her back to herself, and she had answered. Cass looked down at Swoop, lying in front of her. She leaned forward and placed her hand on his chest, felt it rising and falling gently beneath her touch. With his eyes closed, it wasn't hard to imagine that he really was just asleep; the same man he'd been just two days before, now enjoying a well-deserved rest. Why the Weir had taken and converted him when they'd left so many others to rot in the open, she didn't know. There was an ominous implication there that Cass wanted to ignore. That it had been no accident. That Asher had known exactly what he was after when he took Swoop into the fold.

But that didn't matter now. Swoop was in there somewhere, and Cass was going to find him, and she was going to bring him back.

"Swoop," she said. "I'm coming to get you, OK?"

And with that, she closed her eyes and looked for his signal. For five or ten minutes, she searched, with all the concentration she could muster, focused on finding some way to establish a connection with her friend. At times, there were glimmers; flashes of images or stabs of emotion that felt like someone else. But they were too faint, too fragmented for her to latch onto. In her effort, she squeezed her eyes so tightly shut they began to ache. And ultimately, her striving was all in vain.

Cass opened her eyes and blinked away the spots. She took her hand off Swoop's chest and laid it on his forehead. She could almost feel him in there, trapped inside his own mind while his body obeyed another's commands. And as she looked on his face, his eyelids fluttered. Cass gasped and pulled her hand back. She started up to a crouch, thinking that he was about to come to. There was no telling what might happen if he woke up now. But his eyes stilled, and a few moments later, Cass eased herself back down by his side. Surely it had been a coincidence, and nothing that she had done.

But hadn't that been just like Wren's descriptions of his abilities? Something he *felt* rather than *did*? Cass put her hand on Swoop's forehead again, and this time, instead of trying to find him, she focused merely on what her instincts told her. At first, there was no change. But as she controlled her breathing and consciously forced herself to relax, slowly an image began to form in her mind's eye: an image of Swoop, or rather an *impression* of him. A blur of color and emotion. Personality. Determination. A fluttering, like a moth in a web. Swoop. Swoop was there, fighting to break free. Cass felt herself reaching out without striving, without even knowing how she was doing it. And she *was* doing something. But just as the slow invasion of wakefulness disintegrates a dream, her awareness of the connection seemed to dissolve it even as she fought to keep it intact.

"No," she said aloud, "No, Swoop! Swoop, come back!" But it was no use. It all came apart in her hands, water streaming through her fist as she strove to grasp it. She came back to herself without even realizing she hadn't been seeing the world around her. It was darker now, the edge of dusk. Mouse, Finn, and Able were standing in a semi-circle beside her. A rolling wave of pressure coursed from the base of her skull to her temples. She closed her eyes, pinched the bridge of her nose.

"You OK, Cass?" Mouse asked.

The pressure evolved, spread tendrils of frost through her brain.

"I almost had him," she answered. She opened her eyes and looked up at the three men, blinked against the onset of a headache unlike any she'd experienced before; different in kind, not degree. "He was right there, and I lost him."

"What do you mean you lost him?" said Finn.

The pain of the headache was mild, but the discomfort it caused was disproportionate. Fibers aching from overuse, except instead of muscle, it was almost as if she was feeling the neural connections of her brain overheated.

"He's in there, I can see him. Or, feel him," Cass said. She shook her head to clear some of the fog. "He's there. I just can't reach him."

Finn looked over at Mouse.

"Wren could do it," Cass continued. "I know he could."

"If he were here," Mouse added, finishing Cass's unspoken thought. He said it delicately, making the point without salting the wound.

Cass nodded.

"I just can't keep the connection," Cass said. "If I had more time, I might be able to figure it out, but..."

"Yeah," Mouse said. He looked up at the sky for a span, and then back to her. "And that's the thing we're all out of."

He held out a hand to her, helped her to her feet. His

hand lingered, holding hers. She only noticed it because of how quickly he let go when he realized he was still holding on.

"I think you probably want to go on to the wayhouse," he said gently. "We'll be along in a bit."

It was such a waste. Such a tragic, terrible waste of life. But she couldn't quite bring herself to blame them, much as she wanted to. This was their teammate, a man whose life they'd sworn to protect with their own. A man whose body they'd sworn to deny to the Weir, if ever it came to that. She wanted to do something, anything to change their minds. And she could think of nothing.

"Please," Cass said. She could hear the tone in her own voice, knew she sounded desperate. But she didn't know how to make them understand that her belief was based on anything more than wild hope.

Mouse looked at her with a sadness in his eyes so deep it broke her heart. "Go on, Cass."

She saw the torment now, just beneath the surface of his calm. Mouse, the healer, the lifegiver. He'd be the one to carry out the final act. And he'd desperately hoped for another way. He'd given her the chance, even knowing the odds were a million to one against. He'd hoped for a miracle, and she hadn't been able to deliver. Worse than that. Cass hadn't thought of it at the time, but her insistence that Swoop was still in there, that he could still be rescued under the right circumstances, was a crushing blow to his teammates. Better if she had told them he was gone.

"I'm sorry, Mouse," she said. He nodded and dropped his gaze to the ground. "I'm sorry," she said to the others, and she turned and headed for the wayhouse entrance.

"If the connection was stable," Finn said from behind her. "You could do it?"

Cass stopped, looked back. Mouse was watching Finn closely.

"I think so, yeah," she said.

"You *think* so?" Finn asked. He was throwing her a

lifeline, hoping she'd take it.

"Yeah," Cass said, turning back around. "Well, no, I don't *think* so, I'm sure I could. I almost had him."

"Finn," Mouse said. "We all decided."

"We all decided *if* she couldn't bring him back," Finn said. "Maybe I can help her."

Mouse and Finn just stared at each other for a span. Able stood nearby, arms crossed, his eyes shifting between his two teammates. He had to read their lips to follow any spoken conversation, but Cass got the feeling he was reading the silent communication taking place between the other two men just as perfectly.

And then back behind the three men, a motion caught Cass's eye. She caught only a fleeting glimpse, but the streak of blue light was unmistakable. A Weir, ducking behind a building. Mouse read her movement, turned around to see what caused her reaction, then looked back at her.

"Was that what I think it was?" he said.

Cass nodded.

"Did it see us?"

"I don't know how it could've missed us."

"We better go track it down before it brings friends," Finn said. He checked his rifle, readied it. "Which way?"

Cass looked at the spot, replayed the moment in her mind. Strange. Weir didn't hide.

"Maybe it didn't squawk because it saw me and thought I was... one of them," she said. "I'll go after it."

Mouse looked at her, and Cass knew he was about to tell her why she couldn't. Instead, he said, "Not alone, you won't."

"It was only one," Cass said.

"Not a discussion," Mouse said. "Finn, need your rifle."

"I'll go with her," Finn said.

"Negative," Mouse said, holding out his hand. Finn didn't argue. He quickly unslung his weapon and handed it over.

"If we can't find it in five minutes, we'll come back," Mouse said as he rechecked Finn's weapon. And then added, "If we're not back in ten, lock it up."

"Check," Finn said. Then he looked down at Swoop. "What do you want me to do about him?"

Mouse stared down at Swoop for a few seconds, brow furrowed. Then.

"Get him inside."

Cass's heart leapt at the reprieve, and was quickly tempered by the realization that it might have come simply because the threat of discovery was no longer just a threat. It wouldn't matter if Swoop was with them now, if the Weir already knew right where they were.

"Yeah, roger that," Finn said. "Be careful. See you in five."

"Yep," Mouse responded, then to Cass, "All right, lady. Lead on."

She nodded and started off in the direction of the Weir. Hearing Mouse call her *lady* seemed strangely foreign, even though up until a few days ago it'd been a regular part of formal address. Cass couldn't shake the feeling that the person that title had been attached to no longer existed.

Mouse followed closely behind, weapon shouldered and ready. As Cass led the way to where she'd last seen the Weir, she realized her headache had subsided. And she wasn't afraid. There was no obvious reason for it; in fact everything about the situation should have been screaming warnings. Dusk was upon them. The Weir would be out in numbers soon, if they weren't already. One of their kind had quite possibly just identified the team's hiding place, and concealment was the greater portion of the meager protection they had. And yet Cass was more curious than fearful.

They reached the corner around which the Weir had disappeared. She eased up to the edge of the building, leaned slowly around to get a view. It was a wide back alley separating two rows of buildings with their backs to each other. A shallow cement-lined channel ran down the center, dotted regularly with rusted grates. It was cluttered on both sides with scrapped tech, stripped hulks of machinery, steel crates disfigured by partial harvesting or aimless vandalism. A thousand places to hide. No sign of the Weir.

Cass looked back at Mouse and gestured in the direction she'd seen the Weir go. He nodded and motioned for her to get behind him. And inexplicably, Cass found herself shaking her head. She would lead.

Without waiting for a response, she peeled around the corner and continued with careful steps down the alley. She hunched her shoulders, brought her hands up, readying herself for the creature to spring out. But Cass realized she wasn't expecting it to attack her; she was expecting it to try to escape. She couldn't puzzle out why, but her instincts told her there was something about what she'd seen–

It came from her left, just as she'd been looking right. Her blind spot.

Reflexes took over, her left arm flashing up to intercept the attack, right drawing in and back to deliver a counter. But the attack never came. The Weir skittered across the alley in front of her, leapt a pile of debris, and disappeared between two buildings. Mouse raced past, in pursuit. Cass followed a footstep behind.

Mouse slowed for two steps while he cleared the corner, weapon up, looking for a shot, but the Weir had ducked left out of sight just in time. Mouse accelerated, swung around in a wide arc to deny the creature a chance at ambushing him. Cass, instead, cut the corner and got there first, but not by much.

And there, ten feet away crouched the Weir, boxed in by a deceptive U-bend in the building. In the half-heartbeat before Mouse got around the corner, it all snapped into place; Cass saw the Weir, recognized the terror in its eyes. More. Recognized the Weir. It was the same one she'd seen at the gate.

Mouse was there, weapon swinging to target. Without thinking, Cass slapped the barrel up and away. Mouse fired, the round went high and right. The Weir leapt, bodychecked

Cass back into Mouse, sent them both sprawling. And in the scramble, the creature made a dash back the way they'd come. Mouse threw Cass aside with one arm and was up in the next instant, rushing after the Weir. He paused at the corner to scan, and then ran around the building out of view. Cass recovered herself and followed.

When she came around the corner, Mouse had slowed to an aggressive walk. He was hunched over his weapon, sweeping it back and forth as he progressed, covering each likely hiding place or escape path as he came to it. Cass closed the distance between them to ten feet and then maintained the space. They continued down the alley that way for ten, twenty, thirty yards, until it became too apparent to deny. The creature had gotten away.

At that point, Mouse's posture changed. He straightened up, his shoulders came back, the rifle lowered fifteen degrees. But he didn't turn around. Not immediately. When he did, the look on his face was more frightening than anything that had just happened.

"You got something you wanna tell me?"

"I'm sorry, Mouse," Cass said, holding up a hand. "But there's something going on with that Weir."

"Yeah, it's off getting its friends instead of bleeding out in that alley."

"No, it's... You didn't recognize it?"

"Should I have?"

"It's the one from the gate. The one we saw when we left Morningside this afternoon."

Mouse's lower jaw jutted out, then shifted to one side like he was grinding something between his teeth.

"I think it followed us," she added

"That's why it oughta be dead, Cass."

"Mouse, I think it's Awake. I saw something like it before, last night. A different one. And I killed it. I killed it without a thought. But the way it looked at me right before I did... it was scared. It was scared, Mouse, and lost, and I killed it. I killed *her*."

"And I've got what's left of a team I'm trying to hold together out here, Cass. I'm barely hanging on myself. I don't know why any of what you just said matters right now."

"Because you're not a murderer, Mouse. And that Weir might have been an innocent person."

"*Might* have been," he said, smoldering. "You've been getting in the way a lot lately, with your mights and maybes. It needs to stop."

Cass didn't have a response. Whether he'd meant to or not, Mouse's choice of words had gone straight into her heart, struck her right at what she'd feared; she'd been *getting in the way*. Is that what he thought of her?

And as if to emphasize his point, a Weir cried out somewhere in the distance. They were out. Hunting. Mouse shook his head and turned back towards the wayhouse.

Cass followed along behind, feeling like her soul had been stretched to its absolute limits. Maybe beyond. She thought she was right about Swoop, and about the Weir from the gate. She thought she was doing the right thing. But it seemed like all she'd done was make everything worse. Maybe it was better for her to head off on her own. Better for everyone.

She'd taken that evening star as a sign that she wasn't lost or useless. Maybe it *had* been a sign, but not the one she'd taken it for. Maybe it was warning her that the only way to protect those around her was to get as far away from them as possible.

As they made their way back to the wayhouse in strained silence, Cass resolved to set things right. She would give it one more try, take one more shot to do what she could for Swoop. Then, maybe she would just say her goodbyes, the way she should have before, come morning.

Assuming they lived to see it.

TWENTY-THREE

"Again," Haiku said.

Wren struggled to keep his eyes open, even though he was standing in the middle of a training room, within arm's reach of Haiku. This was significant because Haiku was armed with a knife, and that knife was now seeking Wren's heart. Wren twisted and intercepted Haiku's arm, redirected it, stepped behind the attack so he could check any follow up. He felt clumsy; the execution was sloppy and mechanical. When Haiku had done it, it had looked more like he'd been dancing than fighting. Haiku glided; Wren stomped.

"What's that left hand doing?" Haiku said, as he reset his stance. Wren looked at his own left hand, still bandaged, hanging down by his waist. Away from the action. "You have two hands for a reason."

It still stung a little if he opened his hand out wide, but the cut hadn't been deep. Just through the loose fold of skin between thumb and forefinger. Wren wasn't protecting it on purpose. He'd just forgotten what he was supposed to be doing with it. Haiku had shown him a basic defensive drill utilizing both hands, a point he had repeatedly emphasized. It wasn't complicated. It wasn't even completely unfamiliar. Three had taught Wren ways to protect himself, and already he recognized some common elements between what he'd learned from Three and what Haiku was teaching him now.

But proper execution required a level of physical awareness that Wren didn't yet possess. Footwork, hand positions, body angle. Each was simple on its own. When combined, though, he regularly missed one component; focusing on correcting one aspect usually led him to make a mistake with another.

Haiku stepped forward at half speed, executing a telegraphed slashing attack from a different angle. Wren saw it coming, tried to remember the steps. He ended up confusing two movements and collided with the rounded blade instead of avoiding it.

"Relax," Haiku said. "You're overthinking it."

Wren wanted to believe it would all be going more smoothly if he wasn't so exhausted. The best he could tell, he'd gotten just under four hours of sleep after his first day of training. A day that had started early and had been relentless until well into the night. And now here he was again, already well into his second day. The sun wasn't up, and wouldn't be for another hour yet.

"I'm just so tired, Haiku."

Haiku nodded. "One more. An easy one."

He stepped back, and then launched another attack, this one a straight thrust, even slower. He talked Wren through each step as he executed.

"Turn, sweep, step, check," he said. "Good. Perfect." Haiku stepped back and assumed a position that Wren mirrored. Wren bowed in the traditional manner that Haiku had taught him, and Haiku returned it. Even that simple action felt foreign to Wren's body. He waited as Haiku left the training area and set the knife on a small table by the wall. There were a number of other training weapons arrayed on it, and a few devices that Wren couldn't identify. He suspected he'd be familiar with them all at some point.

"It's always good to finish on a success," Haiku said. "It's what your body will remember best for next time. Are you hungry?"

Wren wasn't, but he nodded anyway because the

question sounded like an invitation to take a break. Haiku motioned for him to follow. They exited to the stairwell. Thankfully, that particular training room was only a floor below the main parlor where they took all their meals. Wren clumped up the steps behind Haiku. His entire body was sore. Even his scalp felt wrong, like it'd been sunburned or frostbitten.

"You're doing well," Haiku said over his shoulder. "These first few days are always the hardest." And then as they reached the landing, "How's the hand?"

At first, Wren wasn't sure what Haiku meant. Was something wrong with them? He looked down, saw the bandage around his left hand. Oh.

"It's fine," he answered. And for the most part, it was. It stung when he stretched his thumb away from his other fingers, but otherwise it mostly just felt like he had something stuck in the web of his hand; an itchy, foreign pressure.

They entered the parlor, and Wren was surprised to find a large covered dish waiting on the center of the table, two bowls stacked next to it. Haiku had Wren take a seat while he ladled out the contents of the dish. A few moments later, he pushed the bowl over in front Wren, followed by a spoon.

Wren stared into the bowl of soup that sat steaming before him. It was the same that he'd eaten before, and he knew he liked it. He knew he should be hungry. He knew his body needed the food. But the only thing Wren actually wanted at that moment was to go back to bed. And the bed they'd given him wasn't even that comfortable.

"Eat, Wren," Haiku said. "It will help."

Haiku took a seat next to him and started in on his own portion. Foe was nowhere to be seen, but Wren figured the old man was already off somewhere in the immense building, preparing some new torment for him. Wren picked up his spoon, and even that simple act was a test of will against the aching stiffness that infected his every cell.

He dipped a spoonful of broth out, brought it with effort to his lips. But he was nauseous with weariness, and he let the spoon hover there.

"Your body needs the nutrients," Haiku said. "The sooner you get them in, the sooner you'll start feeling better. Stronger."

Wren took a deep breath, steeled himself, sipped the soup. To his surprise, he managed to keep it down. He took another tentative taste, and found that one was a little easier than the first had been. As he forced himself to eat there was a strange disconnect between his mind and his body, an apparent delay between his intent and its execution. As if he could feel the thoughts forming, or the impulse traveling from brain to muscle. He kept the spoon moving, down, submerge, up, sip. Mechanical. A series of repeated motions. For a time it didn't register that he was actually eating.

His first day of training had been a seemingly random collection of pointless exercises, meaningless torment, and mindnumbing drudgery. Breaks for food had been short. No more than fifteen minutes at a time. After two and a half hours in the Waiting Room, Wren had been subjected to a good hour of vigorous physical exercises that seemed to have been designed specifically to make him throw up. The only highlight of the day had been some light training in hand-to-hand combat for a couple of hours in the evening, when Haiku had first taught him the defensive moves they'd just been reviewing. And even that hadn't been particularly fun or interesting. A few simple defensive moves, endlessly repeated. Over and over and over and over.

If that had been the highlight, undoubtedly the lowest point had been the single hour Foe had spent training him in the digital. And that was the most bewildering detail. It was through the digital that Wren would confront Asher. The only way he *could* face his brother. The only thing that really mattered. And it was there that Foe had revealed his true disdain for Wren. The entire hour had been spent on the most rudimentary elements, things Wren had already been doing for as long as he could remember, and yet, of course, he couldn't do them to Foe's satisfaction. The simplest interaction, initiating a mutual connection request, took half an hour of constant correction; the rest of the hour was spent practicing the same mundane task in precisely the manner that Foe demanded.

"Don't worry," Haiku said. "Whatever you're feeling is normal."

The man's voice brought Wren back to himself. Wren noticed the soup was almost gone. He still felt terrible.

"Normal, like, this is how I'm going to feel from now on?" he asked.

Haiku smiled. "Normal as in, your body is responding as expected to the hardship. You aren't sick, even though you almost certainly feel like it."

Wren lowered his spoon again, but didn't feel like he could bear to lift it another time. He let it rest in the bowl.

"I don't think I can do this, Haiku."

"That is also normal."

"I mean it."

"I know. But that is part of what Father will teach you. You are capable of more than you believe. Far more."

Wren stared down at the spoon sitting in his bowl. When something like picking up a spoon seemed too much to bear, he couldn't imagine how he'd react when Foe took him to his next training exercise.

"I'll share a secret with you," Haiku said. "When I began my training, I struggled more than others. More than most. It took me longer to understand my lessons, more practice to perfect the required techniques. Often I had to stay up after the others had been released to sleep for the night. Sometimes I would even have to work until morning."

Wren was sure Haiku was telling him all of this with the intent of helping him feel better. It wasn't working.

"I was certain I would fail. Certain that Father would eventually realize I wasn't capable of the things he asked of me. Certain that he would give up on me." Haiku paused for a moment. Leaned closer. "And there were many, many times that I hoped he would." He sat back again and then continued. "But he never did."

"One night, I was maybe eight years old at the time, after all the others had gone to sleep, Father was working with me in the Waiting Room. We had been there for perhaps an hour, and I was failing. I knew it, absolutely. And worse, I felt like I had forgotten everything I had learned up to that point. Father turned the lights on, and I could tell he was upset. Worse, he was disappointed. He walked over and just stood there in front of me, looking down, and I remember thinking 'This is it. He's going to get rid of me.' And then he did something most unexpected. Something I had never seen him do before."

Wren's mind filled with vague but terrible visions of punishment. But Haiku smiled to himself. "He picked me up.

"He didn't say anything to me, didn't scold me, or tell me everything was going to be OK. He just picked me up and carried me outside. It was quiet, cold, in the deep night. He took me up on the roof, out under the stars and set me down next to him. And only after we had sat there for a time did he finally speak. I'll never forget his words. 'We must remember, my son, that one man is much the same as another. He is best who is trained in the severest of schools.'" Haiku paused and gazed into his empty bowl on the table for a span, reflecting on the moment. Then his eyes cleared and he looked back to Wren with a mild smile.

"That's it?" Wren asked. And then he realized how that sounded, and clarified what he meant. "I mean, that's all he said?"

"Yes," Haiku said. "After that he sent me to bed. Training carried on as usual. I didn't find out until much later that it was actually a quote from an ancient man of war."

"And what he said... that made it easier?"

"Oh no," Haiku said, laughing. "Never easier. But it

corrected something I had misunderstood about Father. During those many nights, I had come to believe that he was a cruel perfectionist whose standards were impossible to meet. *That* night I learned Father's heart. You see, he does not demand perfection for his own sake, not for some arbitrary whim or for brutal amusement. He does so because he knows he must send his children out into the world, and he knows that once he does, the only protection he can offer them, springs from the way he has shown them to live. Any failing of one of his children he believes is not their fault, but his alone."

Wren didn't quite know how to take what Haiku was telling him. Certainly he'd only just met Foe and didn't know him well at all, but he hadn't seen any side of the old man that he could consider soft or caring. And yet Haiku's words were full of obvious affection for him, even while acknowledging the severity of his training. *One man is much the same as another.* There was something oddly comforting about that sentiment. Foe had said it more bluntly: Wren wasn't special. At the time, Wren had taken it as an insult. But hearing Haiku's story gave him a different perspective. Perhaps the old man was necessarily tearing down a lie that Wren had believed about himself; not that he *was* special, but that he *had to be* special to do anything significant. In some strange way, that thought gave Wren a glimmer of hope. His ability to overcome Asher had less to do with whether or not he was talented enough, and everything to do with whether or not he would allow himself to learn the lessons in this "severest of schools".

And Haiku's story had another effect. Even though Wren had known that Haiku had been Foe's student, somehow it hadn't occurred to Wren that they had any shared experiences. But apparently they had.

"You trained in the Waiting Room?" Wren asked.

"Yes," Haiku said. "Not the same one that you know here, of course. This was in our old home. But yours is a good approximation of the original, with all the important features," he said, adding a knowing smile to his aside. "Dark. Cold. Painful."

"How did you do it, Haiku? How did you get through it?"

"A minute at a time," Haiku answered. And then added, "And I had a little help from another instructor. I could do the same for you, if you'd like."

"I need all the help I can get," Wren said. "Anything."

Haiku nodded. "It's a small thing, but often it is the small things that mean the most." Haiku reached into a pocket, and then placed his closed fist on the table in front of Wren. "A game."

Haiku smiled, and turned his hand over, opened it. There on his palm lay a small metallic sphere, colored a cheery yellow. And painted on it in black, in an uneven hand, were two dots and a wavering line curving slightly upwards. A smiley face. The paint was dull and cracked, even chipped away in some places. It was obviously an old trinket. Wren wondered how long Haiku had had it. ·

"What kind of game?"

"It's very simple," Haiku said. "Each day, I'll hide this little fellow somewhere. And at the end of the day, you tell me where he was."

"That's it?"

"That's it."

Wren wasn't sure how that was supposed to count as a game. It didn't sound particularly fun. But he didn't want to seem rude.

"OK," he said. "I guess."

"I know it doesn't sound like much," Haiku said. "But he's very crafty. You never know where he might show up, or when." Haiku rolled the ball around on the palm of his hand, and then out on to his fingers. It danced lightly across his extended fingers as if it were trying to escape, but each time Wren thought it would drop, Haiku would make some deft move and recapture it without ever letting it come to rest. He had a magician's hands; the fluidity of his movements was mesmerizing. The ball ran across the backs of his fingers, around the edge of his hand only to be scooped back into the cupped palm again. "The only thing is," and here Haiku leaned even closer, "you mustn't mention it to Father. When you see it, try not to draw attention to it."

"If it's somewhere I can see it, he'll notice it for sure," Wren said.

"He'll probably notice it," Haiku said. "But as long as it's not distracting to you, he won't mind. And if it is distracting you, he'll teach you not to let it."

"I don't want to get you in trouble."

"You won't. What do you think? Sounds fun?"

"Sure," Wren lied.

"No it doesn't," Haiku said, smiling. "It sounds stupid. But if you're willing to give it a chance, I think you'll find that it helps you through the day."

"OK, Haiku. I'll do it."

"Excellent," Haiku said, and he closed his fist, made three quick circles with his hand, and thrust it forward towards Wren and opened it. Wren flinched, expecting the little yellow ball to come flying out at him. But no, there was nothing in Haiku's hand now. A simple "magic" trick. Haiku mimed surprise at his own hand. "Look at that. Gone already. There's no telling where he's gotten to."

"It's in your lap," Wren said. "Or your other hand. Whichever place you dropped it when you were doing the circles."

Haiku smiled and then held up his left hand from under the table, and showed the yellow ball. "Kind of a stupid trick, huh? But that one doesn't count. I'll hide him somewhere better for today."

"OK."

"Don't worry, Wren," he said. "It was no mistake, you coming here."

Light footsteps sounded in the hallway; Foe was coming up from the lower levels, or maybe down from the higher ones. Either way, Wren knew his training was about to begin. Haiku tucked the ball away as Foe entered the room.

"Did you get enough to eat, boy?" Foe said.

Wren looked down at his soup. There was still about a quarter of a bowl left, but he just couldn't bring himself to eat anymore.

"Yes, sir."

"Then come with me."

Foe didn't wait for him, just turned and exited the room again, the way he'd come in. Wren dutifully got up from the table, winced at the pain in his legs when he stood, and had to take a few quick steps to catch up. By the time he got out of the room, Foe was already on his way upstairs. Wren hurried up behind the old man, having learned his lesson the day before about responding promptly to Foe's instruction. Foe had made several remarks about Wren's "leisurely" response times; apparently the "rest" that Wren gained from his "dawdling" meant he could continue training even longer.

Foe led him up two flights of stairs to a small, mostly empty room; bare walls, bare floor, industrial blue-white lights. Off to one side stood some odd contraption that looked as if it'd been constructed without any sort of plan or purpose in mind. It was about six feet tall and had what appeared to be a small sack on top, plump, and made from some vaguely shiny textile that Wren couldn't identify. A large spout or pipe jutted out from one side, over a dark circle on the floor, that appeared to be of the same material as the sack. Wren decided it almost looked like some of the showers he'd seen in wayhouses, except put together all wrong. In one corner of the room, a staff leaned against a wall. Wren did a double take. Not a staff. A broom. Beside it was a deflated sack like the one on top of the machine.

"Stand there," Foe said, pointing to the circle on the floor. Wren walked over and stood in the center of it. The material was slightly squishy under his feet. Some kind of padding. He glanced up and noted the wide, bell-shaped mouth of the pipe opening above him. It was affixed to a bulb of pipe that looked like some kind of swivel joint, allowing the pipe to rotate to different angles without interrupting whatever was going to be flowing into or out of it. Wren still couldn't tell what it was for, though the fact that he was standing under it made him imagine something unpleasant would be pouring over him soon.

"Catch only the red ones," Foe said. Wren started to ask what Foe meant by *the red ones* but he suppressed the question. Another lesson he'd learned yesterday. Foe didn't typically respond to questions when the answer was obvious, or would be soon. A moment later the contraption came to life with a clank and a whir. "Do not leave the circle," Foe added.

Above Wren, the opening of the pipe started swiveling in lazy circles, first one way, then the other, and changing angle unpredictably. A few seconds later, a burst of white flakes coughed out and scattered, drifting to the floor in a chaotic current like a snowfall. It took a moment for Wren to recognize what they were; small leaves or possibly flower petals. He reached out for one, but stopped himself. *Only the red ones*, Foe had said. After the initial eruption, the petals continued to disperse all around him in a gentle trickle of three or five a second, falling slightly heavier wherever the funnel of the pipe was pointed.

"Missed one," Foe said casually.

Wren turned and looked behind him, just in time to see a red petal come to rest outside the circle. Out of the corner of his eye, he caught a flash of color to his left. He turned and reached out for it, but too quickly; the motion of his hand interrupted the flow of the petals, chased the red out of his grasp. He stepped forward and managed to capture it just before it escaped, crushing it into his palm in his clenched fist.

"Do *not* leave the circle," Foe said sharply.

Wren looked down and saw the toes of his left foot had crossed the border between the pad and the floor.

"If you cannot tell the difference between the floor and the pad, your senses are worse than I feared," Foe said.

Wren pulled his foot back.

"Missed one," Foe said again. And Wren looked up to see another petal reach the floor.

There weren't too many petals in the air at any one time, but Wren felt himself stretched by all the things he had to keep in mind at once. Watching the petals, he'd forgotten about the circle. Thinking of the circle had distracted him from the petals. But Wren had already learned that Foe had a way of giving instruction without overtly telling him what he should be doing. The comments he made were sometimes hints, though it had taken Wren until the end of the previous day to recognize it.

"And another," Foe said. "You do understand you are supposed to *catch* the red ones, yes?"

Wren ignored the remark. Foe's comments were also sometimes meant merely to distract, and Wren had enough of that going on already. Like the Waiting Room, nothing in this room was an accident; each piece had its purpose. The feel of the circular pad was distinct under Wren's feet, now that it had been called to his attention. He re-centered himself in the circle, rolled his feet around on the mat to get a better feel for it; heels, toes, balls of his feet. His feet would tell him when he was out of position, if he could remember to listen to them. And now, his eyes could focus on the petals alone. Scattered on the floor, the red petals were vibrant and easy to spot amongst the white, so it was surprising just how well they could hide in the fluttering chaos of the drift.

He took to turning a slow, continuous circle, scanning from side to side.

"Missed one," Foe said.

Wren spotted a red petal drifting down from his right, turned and scooped his hand out underneath it, allowing the petal to fall into his hand rather than trying to snatch it from the air. He drew his hand back before any of the trailing white petals could join it.

He turned to Foe, showed him the red petal in his palm.

"What do I do with it now?"

"Missed one," Foe said.

Wren tucked his lone petal into his left hand, kept it gripped there, and went back to work. One more thing to keep track of. He tried to tune out all else, focused on the drifting petals. Eventually, even Foe's admonitions of his misses fell into the background. He found that by crouching slightly and keeping his hands raised just below his shoulders, he was able to react more quickly. Soon full minutes were passing without a miss.

For fifteen, twenty, thirty minutes, Wren continued his watch over the gentle flow, carefully capturing the red petals he could spot, letting others pass when they floated too far. At some point, he fell into a state of consciousness that he'd not experienced before; an effortless awareness, where his mind seemed to disconnect from his body. Though he wasn't consciously trying to keep track of whether he was completely on the pad or not, any time a toe or heel made contact with the hard floor, he immediately corrected his stance before Foe could reprimand him. The petals didn't necessarily seem to fall less quickly or more predictably, and yet Wren felt himself anticipating and adjusting without trying to do so. For a few minutes, it felt like he could continue this bizarre exercise forever, and successfully.

Unfortunately, the feeling was short-lived. The room was warm, and the droning of the machine threatened to lull him into a daze. The lack of sleep from the night before hung heavy on his eyes; his vision was easily confused by the constant fall. Soon it became a battle of will to maintain his focus for however long it was that Foe kept him at it.

"Good," Foe said, at some point long after Wren had lost his sense of time. The machine shut off. A last trickle of petals floated out as Wren stood straighter and let his arms hang at his sides. His shoulders were knotted and stiff, the muscles on fire from keeping his hands aloft for so long. And now that he'd stopped his slow circling, he realized he was slightly dizzy. Foe stood there watching him for a moment, then the old man's eyes flicked to Wren's left. Instinctively Wren followed the gaze and saw one last red petal floating to the floor. He made a grab for it, but too late. Foe smiled but, thankfully, didn't comment. Wren opened his left hand, where his collection of petals clung to each other in a sweaty clump. He estimated he'd managed to capture a good fifty or so. He had no idea how many of them he'd missed.

All around him the pad was ringed softly with white petals, dotted here and there with the occasional red. Foe approached and held out his hand. Wren gave him the squished wad of red petals he'd collected.

"You seem to have finally grasped the basics," Foe said as he dropped the petals into the pocket of his shirt. "We can begin training now."

Wren tried his best not to show the crushing disappointment he felt. He'd hoped that maybe they were done with this ridiculous exercise, though based on his experiences yesterday he knew that he should always expect to continue a thing at least three times as long as seemed necessary.

"Catch only the red ones," Foe said. "And do not leave the circle."

Wren took a deep, settling breath. The machine clanked and whirred. The petals drifted down. Wren resumed his position. There were more petals falling than before. A lot more.

"See wide," Foe said.

"I don't know what that means," Wren said.

"Missed one," Foe replied. He was walking a slow circle around Wren, watching. "Expand your vision. Do not hunt. Observe. Notice."

Wren still had no idea what the old man was talking about. He was too busy searching the fluttering cloud descending all around him to ponder riddles. There were glimpses of red amongst the flurry, and he did his best to collect the proper petals just as he had before. But Foe's warnings came faster this time around, far more frequent, and Wren knew he was failing yet again. There were just too many of them in the air at once. There was no way he could see them all, let alone catch them.

"Missed another," Foe said. "And another."

"There are too many!" Wren said.

"There are not too many, boy. You are too slow."

Wren clenched his teeth, swallowed the response he wanted to give. Talking back to Foe hadn't yet proved helpful. He redoubled his efforts, swept his eyes back and forth through the cascade more quickly. That actually seemed to make things worse. There were too many petals.

"This is impossible!" Wren said, more to himself than to Foe. And in the next instant, the machine shut off.

Foe stood there with a finger raised, staring right at Wren with a stern expression on his face. The remaining petals drifted to the ground, and even though a red one fell between the two of them, Foe didn't say anything about it.

"What was the first promise I made to you?" Foe said.

Wren had to think back for the answer, for the exact words from the conversation he'd had days earlier. No. No, it had just been yesterday. That, too, seemed impossible.

"That you would never ask me to do anything impossible?"

Foe continued to stare at him a moment longer and Wren thought the old man was waiting for him to continue or to provide a different answer. But then the machine started up again and Foe resumed his slow circling walk. Apparently he'd made his point.

Wren tried to reset himself. The pause had cleared the air, and now there were only a few petals falling. If he could just keep up, not get so behind this time, maybe he could manage it. But before the first minute was up, he could tell he was losing ground. The curtain of petals descended to the ground, the false snowfall unrelenting. He was soon again overwhelmed, but there was nothing else for him to do but keep at it, keep trying, until Foe ended the exercise. Talking about it certainly didn't help. He shifted his eyes, started again from the top, giving up any red petals he'd already missed as lost.

There, to his right, a dash of color caught his eye.

And as he reached out for it, Foe took everything a step further. Just as Wren was about to catch the coveted red petal, Foe suddenly shoved his shoulder from behind. Not violently, but enough to cause Wren to lose his balance. He had to step forward and to the side to catch himself; he felt the hard surface of the floor beneath his foot. The petal floated away.

"Do not leave the circle," Foe said, as if he hadn't just pushed Wren out of it. Wren stepped back onto the mat, and almost immediately Foe pushed him again. "Missed one."

Wren steadied himself with a big, deep breath. This was the game. He'd learned it yesterday in the Waiting Room. Foe would do everything he could to test Wren's limits; to distract him, to throw him off, to anger him. It was all part of the test. And, Wren realized now, this was a test of focus.

In all ways, at all times, I master myself.

Wren resumed his partial crouch.

Discipline, my shield.

"See wide," Foe repeated. "Expand your vision."

"I still don't know what you mean," Wren said. He lunged for a nearby red petal, captured it, tucked it quickly into his left fist. A moment later, Foe shot his hand out from Wren's left side, the fingers darting in towards his temple. Wren reflexively ducked his head away from the attack, and then looked at Foe, startled.

Foe didn't say anything; he just looked back with his eyebrows slightly raised, as if he'd asked Wren a question and was waiting for a response. And then a moment later, "Missed one."

It was Foe's way never to explain anything directly, rather preferring to demonstrate his point in some roundabout way and then to leave Wren to figure out what he was supposed to be doing.

"I don't mind if you just tell me what to do," Wren said, as he resumed his search, "instead of making me try to guess all the time."

"Telling is not teaching," Foe said. And he extended his hand to push Wren off balance again. Wren didn't have time to think about it, he just reacted; turn, sweep, step, check. His body executed the technique while his mind was busy elsewhere. Wren stopped, momentarily surprised by himself. Foe smiled.

"Missed one."

Wren recovered himself. *See wide*, Foe had said. *Do not hunt*. The jab at his temple had drawn Wren's attention to his peripheral vision.

Of course.

Now that he made the connection, he couldn't believe he hadn't figured it out sooner. He was trying too hard to focus on each petal as an individual, treating them all as equals when there were in fact only a few he cared about. His vision was too narrow, his effort spent trying to isolate each petal in turn amongst the drift. It wasn't that he needed to focus *more*; he was focusing *too much*. He needed to take advantage of his peripheral vision, to *see wide*, as Foe had said. And as the lesson clicked into place in his mind, Wren felt a little burst of satisfaction at the achievement. One of Foe's riddles solved.

Understanding it intellectually was different than knowing how to do it, though. But he gave it his best attempt. Wren let his eyes relax, lowered them slightly to a more distant point, seeing *through* the cloud that enveloped him rather than looking at it directly. To his amazement, the effect was immediate. Low left by his knee, high and further left above his shoulder. Two blotches of color that naturally drew his eye. He made a grab for the lowest one and managed to snag it, though when he looked back up for the one by his shoulder, he'd again disturbed the current and lost track of it. But that was a minor loss. He understood now.

The next few minutes became an exercise of learning how to transition his vision from a wide, relaxed observation to a targeted focus and back again, as the situation required. Foe continued to disrupt Wren occasionally, sometimes nudging him, sometimes merely reaching out as if to do so without actually making contact. Whenever Foe launched one of his mild attacks, Wren parried it aside the way Haiku had taught him, or at least attempted to do so. It wasn't always effective but it seemed to be what Foe had in mind.

Once again Wren fell back into that effortless awareness that he'd briefly experienced before. This time, however, he realized that his mind had not disconnected from his body at all. The two had become so integrated that the separation between them was impossible to distinguish. His soreness and fatigue remained, but seemed somehow less important. Additional inputs.

"Good," Foe said. It was the highest praise Wren had received from the old man; a mere *good* had come to mean that he'd managed to demonstrate something worthwhile. "You're wasting far too much energy." He raised a hand and Wren reacted, bringing his hands up in defense, even though Foe didn't actually attempt to shove him. Foe looked at him, raised his eyebrows slightly. The subtle look he gave when he'd just provided a lesson, if only Wren would notice it. And Wren was beginning to notice. Wasting too much energy...

"Ten minutes," Foe said, as he walked to the corner of the room where the broom was. "Then the Waiting Room."

A ten minute break. It wasn't much, but Wren had already learned to be grateful for any moment of rest he could find. He went and sat on the floor by the door, leaned back against the wall and closed his eyes. Sleep rushed up from where he'd been fighting to keep it at bay; even though he could hear Foe walking across the room, already dreams were beginning to form.

"You may rest," Foe said, "*after*."

Wren wrestled his eyes open to find the old man standing

over him, holding out the broom, the empty sack at his feet. For a moment Wren just looked at the old man and wondered what the punishment would be if he refused.

"Your every strength, submitted to those who call upon it," Foe said, recalling the words of the oath Wren had sworn. *Service, my strength.* At the time, Wren had imagined that line to mean something more glorious; facing down evil, fighting battles on behalf of the oppressed. Not menial labor. "I'm disappointed I had to ask," Foe added. And there again was a subtle note; a hint at some deeper meaning than Wren understood. He was too tired to care.

Getting up off the floor was a harder task than any the old man had set him to yet. Wren had let himself relax just for a moment, had allowed himself to believe that it was safe to rest, and now he had to force himself into action again. But Wren won the battle over himself. Clambered to his feet. Took the broom.

"Ten minutes," Foe said. "Then the Waiting Room."

And with that, the old man left. Wren looked at the broom in his hand. The severest of schools. And not for the first time, he feared the gulf between his shining oath and the dim reality might be too vast for him to cross.

TWENTY-FOUR

"You ready to uh..." Mouse said to Cass, and he nodded at Swoop, "give this a shot?"

Cass didn't feel ready, but she knew it was time regardless of how she felt. She'd insisted on keeping watch the entire night while the others slept. Her penance for having let the strange Weir escape.

"Sure," she answered.

Mouse and Able had already gone out to scout around. The sun was up and from their report, they hadn't seen any sign that their hiding place had been discovered in the night. Everyone was awake now, except Sky, who was still under the influence of whatever Mouse had dosed him with to help him sleep. Even Wick, pale and weak as he was, seemed much improved after a night hooked up to the meds Mouse had recovered at so dear a price.

"I don't want to do it in here," Mouse said. "Might be fine if it goes well, but if not..." He paused, shook his head. "Well. I reckon it'd be better to move him outside."

"Yeah," Cass said.

Able nodded and he and Mouse went to work unstrapping Swoop from the litter. Once Swoop was free, Finn and Able went up the ladder, and Mouse rolled Swoop over and up into a fireman's carry. It took a couple of minutes, but between the three of them, they got Swoop up top.

Mouse secured Swoop back on the litter in case things

went bad, and then rose and joined the others in a half-circle around their fallen friend. All eyes went to Cass.

"I think it might be a little easier if I don't have an audience," Cass said.

"We're as small as we're gonna get," Mouse said. Cass didn't care for the added anxiety of trying this under scrutiny. Mouse responded to her expression. "Finn's gotta help you," he said. "Able's here for security. And if we have to put Swoop down... well, that falls on me."

Cass still didn't like it, but she couldn't argue with it.

"OK," she said. "I guess we should get started then." She looked over at Finn, who nodded.

"So, the way this is going to work," Finn said. "I don't know exactly what you're looking for, but once you connect, if you can feed me the signal, I'll see what I can do about boosting it. Once we get that going, maybe I'll be able to keep you connected, so you can just worry about doing uh... you know. Whatever you're going to do."

"It might take me a couple of minutes to find it again," Cass said.

"Sure," Finn said. "Take your time. No pressure."

Right. Just a friend's life hanging in the balance. No pressure.

"Ready?" Finn asked. Cass nodded. For a moment she just stood there, looking down at Swoop still asleep at her feet. She didn't know why, but she felt strangely embarrassed having anyone watch her while she made the attempt. But this was for Swoop. Not for her. A deep breath. She knelt beside Swoop and placed her hand on his forehead, like she'd done the night before.

Relax, she told herself. *Breathe.*

Cass directed her thoughts to the experience she'd had the night before. Remembered the sensation, the impressions of personality. Hoped she hadn't just imagined them. The minutes ticked by. And she was painfully aware of the minutes now, far more so than she'd been the first time around. One of the men shifted his stance. Restless, or getting impatient. Losing faith.

After ten minutes, Cass was no closer to finding Swoop again than she'd been when she started. And with each minute that passed, her confidence drained further and further away. Whatever she'd experienced the night before was gone. She'd lost him.

Cass opened her eyes and looked at Swoop. He was gone. And the wave of emotion that rolled over her was the same as if he'd died for the first time. No tears, no cries of anguish. Just a cold numbness. Her mind's initial refusal to accept the reality.

Mouse crouched down on the other side of Swoop, placed his hand on his fallen friend's shoulder.

"It's OK, Cass," he said. He kept his eyes on Swoop. "We all knew it was a long shot."

Memories broke open, spilled over with no coherence: the first time Cass had met Swoop, when she'd been intimidated by his rough look; the startled expression on his face when he'd accidentally walked in on her changing, and how he'd tripped over himself in his hurry to get back out; his grim determination at the gate of Morningside, with poison in his blood.

She slid her hand down to the side of his face. So serious. Even asleep, his brow was slightly furrowed, his jaw clenched, as if he was watching something intently or mildly annoyed. He'd never been much of one for smiling. Even less for laughing. It made the few times she'd seen either all the more precious. An image came back to her of the last time she'd heard him laugh. Something Wick had said at Mouse's expense. She couldn't even remember what it was now, or why it was so funny at the time. But Swoop had laughed, and the unrestrained fullness of it had surprised her. She smiled in spite of herself, in spite of the moment, remembering that uninhibited burst of laughter from so serious a man.

And in that instant, she found him again. The connection rushed upon her almost too forcefully for her to control, and there in the midst of the churning datastream, some part of

Swoop's personality swirled. Reflexively, she reached out to him through the ether. And just as before, as she strove to reach Swoop, the connection began to recede.

"Finn," she said, "Finn, I need you."

Finn came alive, dropped to a knee.

"Yeah, send it," Finn said.

He'd told her to feed him the signal, but in that moment of intensity, Cass wasn't sure exactly what to send. And the connection was thinning rapidly.

"I'm losing it!" she said.

"Gimme something," Finn said. "Anything!"

Cass issued a basic connection request to Finn. The datastream wasn't any less turbulent, but it seemed to be growing smaller in her mind, more distant. Taking Swoop as it went.

And then it came speeding back towards her, solidified.

"Got it," Finn said. "I got it, Cass. I'll keep it stable."

Without the pressure of trying to maintain her connection, Cass felt a release; a sense of calm descended. Patience. A chance to observe. And what she saw in her mind's eye enthralled her. It was as if she'd made an incision in the skin of the world, peeled back a layer of reality, to see its hidden workings; an electromagnetic bloodflow. To her surprise, it wasn't as alien as it should have been. Though she experienced it only in her mind, the essence was familiar. Of a kind with something she'd perceived with the eyes the Weir had given her. Not *seen*, exactly. Cass still didn't have a way to describe the sensation. But whenever a human accessed the digital, she detected it in a way that felt like seeing. And whatever it was that she could "see" with her modified eyes was a mere shadow of what she now beheld, with Finn's help. Raw, pure connection. This was the secret world that Wren knew so well.

The datastream ran wild, a roiling torrent of information, and there, out there in it, like a drowning man fighting to keep his head above water in the raging current, was Swoop. She started to make another grab for him, but an instinct checked her. Once Swoop was out, she didn't know when she'd get another chance to experience so strong and secure a connection. Cass gave herself a moment to investigate whatever else she could find. And under her careful observation, other details started to emerge. Flickers of emotion. Fear. Anger. Lust. Hunger. Others, like Swoop, trapped and enslaved in the datastream. The Weir. All connected. And Swoop among them.

Underneath it all, was some sense of Finn. She couldn't explain it even to herself, but somehow in all of it, and yet separate, floated some essence of the other man. As she bent her mind towards him, a solution unfolded itself to her, an understanding of the digital that had escaped her before. She perceived in her mind how he worked to stabilize the signal, how he supported the connection she had created. At the same time, she saw how faint his... *Finn*-ness was in that realm of existence; shimmering, refracted, indistinct. As if she were submerged in a swiftly moving river, and he stood on its bank.

That was enough for her, almost more than she could handle. Cass turned her focus back to Swoop, concentrated on that impression of him. Stretched herself out to him. Thought his name.

Though there was no representation of their physical bodies, Cass experienced the moment exactly as if Swoop had reached out and grabbed her hand. Sudden contact, a wrenching sensation that threatened to pull her off balance, to drag her forward to him, instead of him out to her. She strained against the force. And then, a release. Swoop came free.

And with him, something else. A wave of force that dissipated on impact and scattered frost across her nerves; like getting hit in the face with a snowball thrown with murderous intent.

The sensation was so tangible she actually fell backwards, physically, and sat down hard on the concrete. And behind that initial force, something immense rose up. The current of the datastream swirled around itself, bubbled up, began to take shape; a digital leviathan rising from the deep. Pale tendrils stretched as it rushed towards her. And then–

–the incision in reality sealed itself, the connection vanished. Finn and Mouse both snapped their attention to her.

"Cass!" Mouse called. "Are you OK?"

Cass blinked at the stars of pain and ice-stung synapses. She knew Mouse had said something to her, but she couldn't make any sense of the words. He came up out of his crouch and started towards her.

"Cass?" he said. She held up a hand, signaled she was fine.

"I'm all right," she mumbled, though the words came out wrong. She looked at Swoop, expecting to see him, with his eyes open and straining against his bindings. Instead, he was laying there perfectly still, just like he'd been when she'd started the process. That didn't make any sense. Shouldn't he be back?

"Did you... did *you* do that?" Finn asked.

Cass nodded. The initial daze seemed to be wearing off. Words made sense again. "Swoop. I got him."

Mouse and Finn looked at Swoop, then at each other.

"Didn't you see it, Finn?" she asked. "Or feel it?"

"Something happened, yeah," he answered. "But, uh... I don't think it was Swoop."

"What are you talking about?" Cass asked.

"I mean, maybe you got Swoop too, I don't know," Finn said. "But there was something else. Something came up the connection." He shook his head. "Bad package. And something after. I had to kill the signal before it hit."

Cass's brain still tingled, and when she turned her head she found she was mildly dizzy. Why did her neck hurt?

"I think maybe it hit anyway," she said. "Something doesn't feel right."

"Could be," Finn said. "There were two things. A quick pulse, came out of nowhere. And then after that something big. Something *real* big. It was moving pretty fast."

"What was the big thing?" Mouse asked.

"No idea," Finn said. "Nothing good. Didn't want to wait around to see."

"Cass?" Mouse looked to her.

"It came up with Swoop," Cass said. She massaged her temples; the external pressure soothed some of the internal freeze. "When I brought him out. Like it was, I don't know, tied to him or something. Or like..."

Her subconscious made the connection and spat it out fully formed.

"A trap."

"A trap?" Mouse echoed. "What kind of trap?" He looked first to Cass, then to Finn, then back to Cass again.

Cass shook her head. It made the ground tilt under her.

"I don't know."

"Something for Wren, I think," Finn said. Cass looked over at him, saw his eyes had the soft, unfocused look of someone running internal accesses.

"What do you mean 'for Wren'?" Cass asked. Even in her fog, she could feel her mind working in the background. "What does it do?"

"Hard to say exactly," he continued, "just got a couple of fragments I grabbed. But it's a custom payload for sure. I don't think you got hit with the whole thing. Even if you did, though, I'm not sure it would've done whatever it was supposed to."

Cass's brain worked on its own, started putting all the pieces together for her. She remembered the apprehension she'd felt the night before, the instinctive warnings she'd ignored. That Asher had selected Swoop for a purpose.

"Back at Morningside," Finn said. "That night, when I was helping Wren keep a connection so he could work with that machine. This thing had the same kinda feel to it. Same signature."

"Same author," Cass said.

"You're all right now?" Mouse asked.

Cass nodded. "Yeah." Her mind seemed to be thawing, even though her equilibrium was off.

If it had indeed been a trap for Wren, maybe that wasn't an entirely bad sign. If nothing else, it meant Asher didn't know where her son was. Her *other* son. And his trap must have been a shot in the dark. A fallback scenario, just in case. There was no way Asher could have known that they'd come back for Swoop. Unless he'd thought that Wren was capable of Awakening Weir without being near them. As far as Cass knew, she was the only one Wren had ever woken without direct, physical contact, and even then they'd been only a few feet from each other.

Maybe that was it. Maybe Asher had converted Swoop as bait, thinking Wren would try to Awaken him from some distant location. And here Cass had taken the hit instead, absorbing whatever damage her older son had intended for her youngest. The important question now was what effect did the payload have on her?

At least part of the answer was obvious. The... thing... that had risen up after the initial impact. Asher himself, or rather, his consciousness. The trap had almost certainly alerted Asher to the fact that she was alive, and maybe had even given up her location. Alive and still close to Morningside. There may have been more to it than that, but it was highly unlikely there was less. She'd still been thinking she'd go off on her own anyway; now she was resolute.

"All right... well," Mouse said. "You've done what you can for Swoop?"

"What?" Cass said, distracted. She looked at Mouse, then down at Swoop, who still looked for all the world like he was sleeping peacefully. She'd been so certain. Surely she hadn't just imagined it all. And yet there he lay, with no apparent change whatsoever.

Wait. That wasn't quite true. She'd missed it before, but she saw it now. He *was* sleeping peacefully, and it was the *peacefully* that made the difference. The intensity was gone from his face, the brow and jawline relaxed.

"Yeah, Mouse, he's good," Cass said.

Mouse nodded.

"Just so we all agree," Mouse said. "You gave it your try. If I wake him up, and he's not himself, I'm gonna put him down for good."

"He's back," Cass said. "I know he is. If you wake him up right now, it'll be Swoop looking back at you."

"I hope so," Mouse said. "But if it's not, don't get in my way."

Cass nodded. She was still feeling woozy from whatever had ambushed her. Even if she'd wanted to get in Mouse's way, she didn't think it would have been particularly effective.

Mouse went to his med pack and spent a couple of minutes gathering up the supplies he needed. He returned to Swoop's side with his med injector in one hand and his sidearm in the other. He knelt down at Swoop's side, and said something to him, too quietly for Cass to make out. And then, he placed the injector against the side of Swoop's neck. The device hissed softly. Everyone went still.

At first, there was no effect. Then after a moment Swoop's head turned slowly one direction, then back the other just as slowly. His mouth opened, but no sound came out. He relaxed, like he'd fallen back asleep.

And then, without warning, his hands shot up from his waist, and the litter hopped from the force. Swoop's eyes popped open, wild and electric blue, and he raged violently against his bindings. Mouse slid back like he was on rails, brought his sidearm up as Swoop's head snapped around from side to side. Swoop was cuffed at the wrists, and the cuffs were secured through the straps on the litter, so there wasn't much he could do. But that didn't stop him from trying.

And then Swoop went still, his eyes on Cass. He blinked and squinted against the early morning light. Looked over at the others.

"Mouse?" he said. And Cass's breath escaped in a rush of relief and joy. Mouse slowly lowered his weapon.

"Swoop?" Mouse said.

"Somethin's wrong with my eyes," he said. Then he looked down at his own body, at the straps around his arms, waist, legs, at his hands bound. Then back up at his companions. "Must've been a bad night."

Everyone stood stunned for a few seconds, and then launched into a flurry of activity, getting Swoop free of his restraints, hugging him, laughing, crying. After Finn got Swoop's feet unbound, he popped up and ran over to the wayhouse hatch.

"She did it!" he called. "She got Swoop! He's back!"

Mouse helped Swoop up to a sitting position, despite Swoop's protests.

"All right, all right now," he said, pushing the others off him goodnaturedly. "I ain't your dog, quit your fussin'."

He looked over at Cass, still sitting by him, and their eyes met. For a moment, she wondered if he understood what had happened to him. How he'd been changed. But in that look, she saw it. He understood. Or at least, he knew he was different. It'd probably be a long while before he really *understood*.

"Lady Cass," he said, dipping his head.

"Swoop."

"I knew you'd be back to get me. After the first time," he said. He looked down at his hands, then back up at her. "Reckon I'm gonna need a few pointers."

Cass crawled up to her knees and wrapped her arms around him. He patted her back with one hand, clearly uncomfortable with the show of affection. Definitely back to himself.

"I don't know what you did," he said quietly, "or how. But thank you."

"Couldn't have done it without your help," she said as she leaned back from him. And when she did, the whole world swam away from her. Swoop's hands closed tightly on her arms, kept her from falling backwards again.

"Whoa now," Swoop said.

A moment later, Mouse was there.

"Easy, Cass," he said. "Easy now." He wrapped his arms around her shoulders, held her steady. Swoop released her and even though Mouse was still holding her, she felt like she was sliding backwards along the shifting ground. She was aware of some commotion going on around her, though it felt muted and distant. At one point, Kit and Wick both appeared, came over to see the miracle of Swoop's return. Mouse was saying something to Cass again, and again she couldn't understand the words. A strange flutter rippled across her mind, like a burst of a multitude of voices speaking gibberish, then suddenly silenced.

"I'm all right, Mouse," she said, and even she didn't believe it.

Mouse had her in his arms now, was laying her back on the concrete with his hand cushioning her head. It seemed harder to breathe than it should have been.

"What's going on, Cass?" Mouse said. "Can you tell me?"

"I just feel..." Cass said. "I feel really tired. Dizzy."

"OK," Mouse said. "Well I need you to stay awake right now, OK? I need you to keep your eyes open."

"OK." And Cass did. She stared up at the sky as it brightened above her. It seemed fitting; day break. A new start. She lay there for a few minutes, while Mouse ran some checks on her, tracked her pulse, shined a light in her eyes. During his evaluation, whatever shadow had come over her seemed to pass again and her head cleared.

"I'm all right now," she said. "Really, this time."

Mouse looked down at her, obviously not taking her at her word.

"No, really," she said. And to prove her point, she sat up under her own power. To her satisfaction, her head didn't swim when she was upright. The others had moved some distance away, across the courtyard, and were gathered in a knot around Swoop. She hadn't noticed when they'd done that.

Mouse ran her through a couple of other tests, and even though she apparently passed them all, he didn't seem as pleased about it as he should have been. Unsatisfied that he hadn't diagnosed the problem. He poked and prodded at her a little longer, asked her a few more questions. She told him about the strange headache she'd gotten after her first attempt at freeing Swoop, guessed maybe it was related. Something about the strain of the connection. Wren had never mentioned it hurting him to wake the Weir, but now Cass wondered. Was this how he felt each time?

After that discussion, Mouse still didn't seem content, but he gave up trying to diagnose her for the moment. Cass shifted her attention back to the team across the courtyard. It was strange, of course, seeing them all there together again. Almost as if time had been rewound, or shifted to some alternate history. Even having been so sure that she'd Awakened Swoop, it seemed impossible to accept that he was really there, that she'd really done it. The certainty and the reality somehow failed to connect. The change was almost too significant, too sudden to embrace. Just the night before, Cass, along with everyone else, had believed waking the Weir was something only Wren was capable of. No. Not *everyone* else.

"How did you know, Mouse?" Cass said.

He followed her gaze over to Swoop. Shook his head. "Oh, I didn't *know*."

"But last night. I wouldn't have even tried if you hadn't asked. Never would have even *thought* to try it. What made you think it was even remotely possible?"

Mouse sat down beside her, shoulder to shoulder, and joined her watching the others across the courtyard. He took a moment to gather his thoughts.

"You know, it's funny, Cass... how much what we believe about ourselves affects what we *perceive* about ourselves."

"I don't understand what you mean."

"I know," he said, and he smiled at her with kindness. "Your boys. They're both pretty gifted, huh?"

It was strange to Cass to hear Asher spoken of that way. Wren, certainly. But Asher... what he'd chosen to become was truly terrible. It was hard to think of his power as any sort of *gift*. But she couldn't deny the talent he had.

"Yes," she said.

"*Both* your sons," he said. He paused. Then added. "Brothers."

Cass nodded, but corrected him. "Half-brothers."

Mouse nodded, a trace of his smile still lingering. Like he knew something...

And then like the sun burning away a cloud, she understood what he was suggesting. *Half*-brothers. *Her* sons. Whatever natural talent her boys shared must have come through their common parent. Her.

She blinked at Mouse, at what he was saying, at what it implied. He read her look, the dawning that overtook her, smiled again with a little shrug.

"You think..." she started, struggling to wrap her mind around a concept at once so foreign and so personal. "You think *I'm* like them?"

"It's something I suspected for a while now," he said. "Nice to be proven right every now and again."

Cass felt a blossoming in her soul at the revelation, even as she rejected it. It couldn't possibly be true. She'd never been done any heavy hacking with RushRuin; physical security was more of her thing. The real world, not the other one. But as she resisted this radical shift in perspective, she began to recall little moments in her past that had previously been unconnected in her mind. Her old boyfriend Zenith's early fascination with her; how she'd always been the one to fill in on small jobs for RushRuin, even over Jez and Ran; how quickly she learned Wren's tricks for masking her signal when they fled RushRuin; how long she'd managed to evade Asher's determined search. She hadn't ever really trained for it, but now that she reflected back it seemed undeniable to her that she'd always had a sensitivity to the digital realm. She'd just always assumed because her son's fathers were gifted, they'd been responsible for the boys' talents. But no, Zenith hadn't really been a man of the same quality. Underdown, Wren's father, had been elegant. But Asher's father, Zenith, had been more of a brute-force kind of guy. A thug. Even as a young boy, Asher had easily outclassed his father.

Was it really possible? Did *she* possess that talent? Looking across the courtyard at the man she'd just brought back from enslavement to the Weir, it seemed more than just possible.

She shook her head. "I don't know, Mouse," she said. "I don't think I could've done it if I hadn't been through it myself. Not if Wren hadn't showed me the way."

"I don't see why any of that matters," Mouse said. "Fact is you did it."

"Once," she said. "I did it once. It helped that I knew Swoop. That I could remember him. It helped me find him, somehow. I don't think I could do it again."

Mouse shrugged. "Only one way to find out."

She glanced over at him, and he looked back at her, smiling. Then his eyes went sad and some deep hurt revealed itself, and he looked away quickly.

"Anyway. Thing is, you did it. When it mattered. When we needed it. So maybe don't sweat the how or why so much, and just celebrate it. For now." He gave her side glance and leaned his shoulder into hers, pushing her gently off-balance. "You sure you're all right?"

Cass nodded. "Just a lot to deal with, I think. Haven't had much sleep lately."

"Yeah. Well you can rest up today. Judging from what Able and I saw when we scouted it out this morning, I think we'll be pretty safe here for a couple of days at least. As long as we stay smart."

The casual way he mentioned it, his assumption that she was staying with them, sent a pang of emotion through Cass's heart. Guilt? Sadness?

"Mouse," she said. "I think something happened when I

brought Swoop back. I think Asher knows. He knows I'm alive. And maybe he knows where I am. I can't stay, not even if everyone wanted me to."

He was looking at her again now, unfiltered concern in his eyes. He shook his head.

"No, you'll stay with us, Cass. We already talked about this. We're not just letting you go off somewhere to try to make it on your own."

"That was when we still had Gamble. Look at your team, Mouse. It's broken right now, and I'm the one that broke it."

"That's not true, Cass–"

"You've all sacrificed so much for me, for my son. I'm not going to bring any more danger down on you."

"I'm not having this same conversation with you again–"

"It's not a conversation, Mouse!" Cass said, a little more sharply than she meant. She tried to soften her next words. "This isn't theoretical anymore. Asher knows. It's best for everyone if I leave."

"For everyone?"

"In your heart, you know it."

Mouse looked away again. "I don't think you know my heart as well as you think you do."

"I know you don't like it. *I* don't like it. And believe me, if there were another way, I'd take it."

"There is. Stay. We'll face it together."

Cass shook her head. "There's no doubt you'll be safer without me," she said. And though she knew it would hurt him to hear her next words, she felt like they had to be spoken, for his own good. "And I'll probably be safer without you."

Mouse just sat there next to her for a few seconds in silence, staring at his feet, jaw working.

"If this is on account of what I said last night–"

"No, Mouse," she said over the top of him but he continued.

"No, look. I said some things I shouldn't have. Some things I didn't mean..."

"It's not about that," she said. "I wish it were. I wish this was a thing that could be fixed with words. But it's not."

His brow furrowed. And then, unexpectedly, he got to his feet. "You know, I thought we'd lost you one time. Thought I'd seen the last of you, when you took your boy on to that tunnel."

Cass looked up at him towering above her. He turned away from her. Stood in silence for a span. Then.

"I don't know if I can say goodbye to you again," he said, and he walked off towards the others.

For a time, Cass continued to sit there on her own, watching the rest of the team. Even Sky had shown up, his happiness at Swoop's return tempered by his own raw grief. But he was taking part. They were all circled up around Swoop. He stood in front of them all, arms crossed, head slightly lowered, a look of vague dissatisfaction on his face. In other words, looking every bit himself. The tone of the chatter had settled and taken a heavier turn. The others filling him in on all he'd missed, most likely.

While she sat alone, thinking about her next steps, Cass felt a tickle in her ear, as if a tiny bug had flown into it and was struggling weakly. It took a moment for her to realize it was a sound, not a feeling. A faint hiss and crackle. And judging from the reaction from the rest of the team, she wasn't the only one hearing it. She got up and walked over towards the others. As she made her way over, she heard it again.

"What is that?" she asked.

Wick shook his head and looked to his brother. "Some kind of interference, maybe?"

Cass's heart dropped. Had Asher found them already? Was he hacking into their secure communications?

"No," Finn answered. "It's internal. Noise in the channel. It's weird though, I haven't had trouble with it before."

The sound rippled again, a white noise whisper. Cass had never heard it before, but it was strangely unsettling; too much like a sound a Weir might make.

"I don't know," Finn said. "It's almost like..." His eyes narrowed. Searching for an answer. Any answer. And then his eyes went wide, and his head snapped up. "No way. No way!" He turned away from them all, took three or five quick steps.

"What?" Wick said. "What, Finn?" Finn didn't respond, he was either too stunned or too terrified. "Finn!"

And then Cass realized Finn was neither stunned nor frightened; he was busy doing something to the channel. The white noise crackled, momentarily louder, then squelched. He was trying to clean up the signal, maybe, or boosting it.

Finn whirled, a bewildering expression on his face; equal parts shock, disbelief, and... joy?

"It's Gamble!"

No one knew what he was saying.

"Gamble! It's Gamble!" he repeated.

"Finn," Mouse said, steady. "What do you mean it's Gamble?"

Finn was smiling, but his eyes were so wild he actually looked more insane than happy.

"I mean it's Gamble! She's alive! She's alive and coming this way!"

"She's... she's *alive*?" Sky asked, and Cass could hear the fear in his voice, knew exactly what he was asking. Was it really Gamble, really alive? Or was it just what remained of his wife, animated by another force?

Finn crossed to Sky, grabbed him by the shoulders.

"Brother, I don't know how," Finn said, eyes shining. "I don't *care* how. Your girl is back."

Sky's legs started to buckle, but he grabbed on to Finn. Finn laughed aloud, wrapped his arms around Sky in a bear hug, lifted him off the ground. The crackle sounded again, but this time buried down deep in the static, Cass thought she could hear the shadow of a voice. Maybe she'd just imagined it, because of what Finn had said, and because she so badly wanted to believe.

Finn set Sky back on his feet again, and then held up a hand, gesturing for them all to wait a second. Something happened to the channel again; another series of jagged pops of static and audio artifacts.

And then.

"... copy, over..." Two words amidst the jumble. Two words. Gamble's voice. Cass found herself in Mouse's arms without knowing how she got there. Laughing, crying, cheering. Everyone was hugging everyone else. And then amidst the cacophony, Finn's voice rose up calling for quiet. When he got it, he looked at Sky, pointed and nodded.

Sky blinked. And then, over the channel. "Ace?"

There was no immediate response. Cass held her breath.

"Ace, do you read?" Sky said again.

Still no answer. Then a crackle.

"Hey, babe," said Gamble. "You still at the same place?" The channel still had static in it, but her words were breaking through more clearly now. Either Finn had boosted the range, or she was getting closer. Maybe both.

Sky sank to the ground, on to his knees, his face a collage of emotion: shock, relief, elation, confusion. His mouth worked, but he didn't respond.

"Yeah, G," Finn said, jumping in. "We're all here. We're all right here. What happened? Where are you?"

"Not a hundred percent sure. In range, I guess."

"Yeah," Finn said. "Well, you're just outside normal... I had to boost you pretty good. So that's probably... I don't know maybe four or five klicks out?"

"You tell me, Finn. I'm just walking here."

"What's your status?" Mouse asked.

"Tired. Sore. Smell terrible."

"Hang tight, we'll come get you," Mouse said.

"Negative, stay put," Gamble said. Her voice had lost some of its snap, but there was no doubt it was her. "Not like you're gonna carry me in, and I'm already walking as fast as I can. Just give me a waypoint so I can quit wandering around."

"Let us meet you halfway at least," Mouse said.

"No, Mouse, just stay there. No need to risk everybody looking for everybody else out here. Wick, you online?"

"Yeah, I'm here," Wick said.

"You feel like pinging me a route?"

"No, G, I don't," Wick answered. "I feel like running out there and carrying you home on my shoulders. But I'll send you a route anyway. Gimme a couple."

"Check," Gamble replied. "You got my position?"

"I do now."

"I'm coming out to meet you, Ace," Sky said. He was back on his feet; he still looked a little bewildered, but his joy was radiant. "I'm on my way to you, babe."

"Check," Gamble said. "I'm all right with that."

"Wick," Sky said, but Wick was already on it.

"Yeah, buddy, go," he said. "I'll set you a rendezvous on the way."

"I'm gone," Sky said, and then through the channel, "Sky, moving to you."

Sky started off at a jog, but Mouse called to him.

"Sky, hold up!" Mouse said, as he ran over to the wayhouse and disappeared down the hatch.

"What, man?" Sky answered. He stood actually bouncing up and down while he waited for a response. "Come on, I gotta go get my girl!"

A few moments later Mouse reappeared with Sky's rifle in hand. He jogged over.

"*Now* go get her," Mouse said, tossing the rifle across to Sky.

Sky caught it and took off.

After Sky left, the small band was positively giddy. Cass couldn't remember ever having seen them so chatty. No one seemed to know quite what to do with themselves. Except for Cass. She quietly slipped away to the wayhouse to gather her belongings and her share of the supplies. When the time came, she would say her goodbyes on her way out. If she was already loaded up, there was less opportunity for the others to try to stop her. She flexed her left hand, made a fist, tested it. Mouse's brace was still fastened securely around her forearm, but already the pain from the break was gone. She knew Mouse wouldn't be happy about her testing things without his supervision, but she unstrapped the brace anyway and tried rotating her wrist. It felt smooth, no hitches, no pain. Good enough for her.

"You look like you're headin' somewhere," came a voice behind her. She started at the sound, and glanced over her shoulder at its source. Swoop. Of course. Cass chuckled.

"Still not sure how you manage to do that all the time," she said, turning back to make her final preparations.

"Do what?"

"Show up places you're not supposed to be."

"Oh, I tend to think I'm where I'm *supposed* to be, Cass. Just maybe not where other people expect, is all."

Cass closed up her pack, tested its weight. Not bad. She turned back to face Swoop. Apart from the moonlight glow of his pupils, he looked exactly the same. Same posture, same mannerisms, same expression.

"Don't reckon anyone's gonna be happy about you tryin' to walk off on your own," he said.

"I have to leave, Swoop," Cass said. She'd been hoping to talk to everyone at the same time; she really didn't want to have to explain herself over and over again.

"I know," he said, taking her by surprise. "I saw it."

"Saw... *what*?" she asked cautiously.

"It," he said. "Him. Asher. Whatever that was, comin' up out of the deep."

"So you understand, then?"

"Yes," he said after a moment. "And no. I understand why you *think* you gotta leave."

"Please, Swoop. I can't keep having this conversation–"

He held up his hand, shook his head. Then said, "Let me come with you."

Cass hadn't expected that. But then, this was Swoop. She should have known he'd find some way to surprise her.

"Be easier to convince the others if you ain't out there on your own," he continued, making his case. "Like we say; two is one, one is none. And I don't pose the same risk they do. I'm more like you than I am like them now."

And though she'd resigned herself to going out on her own, Cass felt relief roll over her at the offer. She hadn't considered it at all, but Swoop was right. He was Awakened now. Less likely to draw the attention of the Weir out there in the open. His risks were the same as hers, and no greater. He'd be an extra set of ears, and of eyes. And his skill set was immense; for as long as she'd known him, she felt like she still didn't know all he was capable of. She wouldn't have to face the dreadful, oppressive loneliness of the dead expanse.

And undoubtedly he would benefit from her company as well, as he came to terms with the changes that had been forced upon him. It only made sense for him to accompany her, to guide her, to guard her. It was the obvious choice, the most logical.

She nodded.

"Thank you, Swoop," she said. "But no."

Most logical, maybe, but not the best choice. Without fully understanding her own reasoning, she knew somewhere in her heart that this was *her* time. With all else stripped away, there was an opportunity before her she'd never before known.

"This is something I have to do on my own," she continued. And then added, "Something I *want* to do on my own."

For the first time in long years, maybe for the first time ever, she saw a moment of decision with utter clarity. Would she continue to allow circumstances and those around her to dictate her choices? Or did she have the courage to stop hiding behind others and to test herself against the world? To accept Swoop's help was to reject her... what? She couldn't bring herself to think of it as destiny. It wasn't. There was no path laid out before her, no unseen hand guiding her to some purpose. *Potential*, maybe. The decision was clearly hers to make. And she decided to face her fear. More. To face herself.

And with that decision, she felt liberated. The same power that enabled her to free Swoop from his bondage had revealed to Cass just how little she actually knew herself. Her *own* potential, her *own* capability. Not as a mother, not as a lover. Not as an object of someone else's affection or lust or worship. As her own being, complete, whole, powerful. The dread she'd been feeling about facing the others melted away, as if their arguments could no longer touch her.

Whether it was her words alone, or if Swoop could sense the change that had come over her, he didn't try to argue. He nodded again. "You'll wait till Gamble shows, though." He made it a statement, though it was actually a question.

Cass nodded. "Of course."

"All right then," he said. He looked at her for a bit longer, then nodded to himself and headed back up the ladder, leaving her alone in the wayhouse.

Cass moved her pack over to the wall by the ladder, and then went and sat down on the bunk where Sky had spent the night. She thought about trying to sleep a little, knowing she'd wake up when she heard the welcome Gamble would surely receive on her return. Lying down was no use, though. The momentum was building; she was anxious to get underway.

It was almost an hour later that she heard the cries and cheers of the team outside. Gamble's return. Cass bolted up, grabbed her pack, and climbed out into the open as fast as she could. By the time she reached the top, Gamble and Sky were in the middle of the courtyard, having already been intercepted by the rest of the team. Swoop caught Cass's eye as she approached; he was hanging back slightly, allowing the others to have their moment. Worried, maybe, about how Gamble would react. He needn't have been. As soon as the crowd parted enough for her to see him, she walked over and wrapped her arms around his neck.

He hugged her back for a few seconds and then let go, but she held on anyway. After about thirty seconds he started squirming.

"All right," he said. "All right now, G." He said it gently, though, not forcing her away; consoling in his own way. When Gamble did finally back off, she wiped her eyes with the back of her hand, sniffed once, and then punched Swoop right in the chest.

"Don't ever do that to me again," she said, and then she laughed and hugged him once more.

"Yes, ma'am," Swoop answered.

Cass was next in line when Gamble separated from Swoop. Cass set her pack down and Gamble gave her a strong embrace. A heavy, sickly-sweet stench hung on her.

"Thank you," Gamble said. "Thank you for getting my boys home."

"Wish I could take credit," Cass said.

"You did your part," Gamble said. "And Swoop... I don't know how. But thank you."

Cass guessed Sky must have filled Gamble in on the way back. Either that, or Gamble was taking everything in her stride surprisingly well. They withdrew from one another.

"Why didn't you tell us you were still in there?" Cass asked. "Let us know you were still alive?"

"I thought I was dead," Gamble said with a shrug. "Didn't want you hanging around and getting caught for nothing. And, by the way, you were right about that vent."

"How's that?" Cass said.

"Straight down," Gamble said, with a chuckle. She gave them all a brief recount of her narrowly death-defying escape; between the sunlight in the room, the anti-personnel mines, and Sky's covering fire, she'd managed to make it to the vent in the corner of the room. "Connected to the floor below, I guess. That's where I fell through the ceiling, anyway. Most of the Weir must've been upstairs. Just made a run for the front door then."

"Wow," Wick said. "You were *not* kidding about smelling terrible. Ugh, what *is* that?"

"Well," Gamble said, looking at him. "I just spent twelve hours buried in a pile of corpses, Wick. Think I'm doing all right, all things considered."

That was all the explanation Cass needed. Gamble had broken contact with the Weir long enough to make it to the front of the compound. She must have hidden herself in that mountain of the dead, spent the night in their midst.

Gamble gave Cass a once over, looked back down at the pack by her feet. "Going somewhere?"

Cass took a deep breath. This was the moment. One final argument to get through, and then she could go.

"I'll bring you up to speed, boss," Swoop said, before Cass began.

Gamble looked at Swoop, and then back at Cass. "Leaving?"

Cass nodded.

"Still think Asher's looking for you?" Gamble asked.

"Certain of it, now."

Gamble stood there looking at her for a few moments and then shook her head. "I'd fight harder to convince you to stay if I weren't so smoked," she said.

Cass smiled. "We'll pretend you tried." She looked around at the others. They were all concerned, maybe sad. But no one was surprised. Cass realized then that Swoop must have already broken the news, paved the way for her. No one seemed to want her to go, but no one offered any more argument. "What about you guys?" Cass asked.

"Well," Gamble said. "I'm going to take a shower. After that, sounds like we got a lot to talk about. Your boy know we're alive yet?"

"*One* of them does," Cass said. "But not the right one. Much as I want to, I think it's too dangerous even to pim Wren."

"Even coming from one of us?" Gamble asked.

Cass nodded.

"I agree," Finn said. "After that thing with Swoop, I think we need to run it as low profile as possible."

Cass was struck by the familiarity of the moment. Standing around with the team, talking about her striking out on her own, and the team going to Greenstone to guard Wren. Hadn't they just done this? And yet, as similar as the circumstances were, the other version felt alien; from a different world, rather than a different day. It was strange to stand in the same place as a completely different person.

"You'll still go to Greenstone, though?" she asked. "To find Wren?"

Gamble nodded. "We'll give it a couple of days. Rest up, heal up, make sure we're not taking the heat along with us. If we're cool, we'll go see about your son."

"Will you explain?"

"We'll do our best, Cass. What about you?"

Cass looked away out of the courtyard. How could she find a thing if she wasn't sure what she was looking for? She shook her head.

"If I get safe, I'll come find you."

"See that you do," Gamble said. "So no goodbye, then. Let's call it a see-you-around."

"I'd like that." Cass held out the jittergun, offering the weapon back to its owner. Gamble glanced down at it, and then shook her head.

"Keep it," she said. "You can give it back to me later."

Cass smiled.

And that was how the moment arrived. No heated debate, no emotional pleas. It just seemed like there was nothing else to say. Cass made the rounds, said a few words to each person in turn; some mix of thank yous, and take cares, and be safes. Finn made her take one of their concussion/pulse grenades, even though she had no idea what she'd do with it.

"Just in case," he said. She clipped it to her belt and gave him a hug.

Mouse embraced her, kissed her on the cheek, but didn't say anything to her. Kit cried, but didn't beg her not to go.

Sky was the one that surprised her the most.

"You remember now," Sky said. "Family doesn't always mean blood."

It took her a second to understand what he meant; when she did, it made her heart strangely warm. She might not ever be a fully integrated part of the team when it came to tactics. But Sky was letting her know that she was part of something even better, with bonds even stronger. Not the team. The family.

With tears in her eyes, Cass hefted her pack, slid her arms through the straps, and cinched it down tight. She guessed she still had a good seven hours or so of daylight, and she fully intended to put as much distance between them as she could. Crossing the courtyard was the hardest part. Once she got out into the open, her steps felt freer, her mind clearer, and sharper. Even though she didn't have a plan completely worked out yet, even that didn't bother her. She was on her own, now. Responsible only for herself, and only to herself. And that fact was liberating in a way she'd never imagined. Maybe had never allowed herself to imagine. Exhilarating.

Cass spent the rest of the day headed north by northwest at a good pace with few breaks.

It wasn't until dusk was coming on and she'd begun to search for a place to lay low for the night that she realized she was being followed.

TWENTY-FIVE

Wren awoke in a panic, startled by the fact that he'd been asleep for so long. He didn't know exactly what time it was, but he could tell he'd slept for long hours; far more than he'd slept all at once over the past week. Possibly more than he'd slept all week, hours combined. Haiku hadn't come to wake him. Was he supposed to have awoken himself at the proper time? Was this a test he'd failed?

He scrambled out of bed and dressed hastily, fearing what displeasure he might face but knowing that any longer delay only made it worse. When Wren reached the parlor, though, Haiku was sitting in a chair by the window, enjoying a leisurely cup of tea. The shutters were open, and the sun was already high in the sky; late morning, drawing close to noon.

"Morning," Haiku said.

"Hi," Wren said. He stood at the door feeling awkward.

"Sleep well?"

"Yes, thanks," Wren answered. After a moment, he added, "Was I supposed to sleep that long?"

"You're supposed to sleep as long as you need to today," Haiku said. He got up from his chair and moved over towards the kitchenette. "Hungry?" Wren nodded. "Have a seat, I'll get something for you." There was already a pot on the cooking surface.

"Thank you," Wren said, and he took a seat at the table.

354

"So I didn't oversleep? I didn't miss any training?"

Haiku chuckled. "Do you think Father would let you miss any training?"

Wren shook his head.

"I'm sorry no one told you," Haiku said, as he carried a bowl over to Wren and set it in front of him. "But this is the schedule you can expect while you're here. Six days of training, one day of rest. Father may have some lessons for you on rest days, but they will be easy."

Six days. Had it been six days already? Had it only been six days? For the most part, time had ceased to have any meaning to Wren. If Haiku had told him it'd been a month or a day, he probably would've believed it. Wren looked down at the bowl in front of him, expecting the usual soup he'd had for breakfast every day since his arrival but found instead a brothy noodle dish. Haiku brought water for Wren to drink and then retrieved his own teacup and sat down next to him.

"So," Haiku said, and he produced his yellow ball with the smiley face on it. He set it on the table. "Yesterday?"

Wren took a taste of the broth; it was light, flavorful and slightly spicy.

"In the Waiting Room, under the catwalk towards the back, left side," he answered after he'd swallowed. "And then when we were eating in the evening, it was behind the vase."

"That was all?" Haiku asked.

Wren thought back through the day. He was pretty sure those were the only two times he'd seen Haiku's little friend. Had he missed one? Or was Haiku just testing him? Haiku waited expectantly.

"That was it," Wren said. "Just two places yesterday."

Haiku smiled. "I think we might have to start making this more of a challenge," he said. "At this rate, you'll be hiding him for me in a few weeks."

Wren took another spoonful, slurped some of the wide, chewy noodles up. One of them slapped his chin as it went by and left a dribble of broth on his shirt. Haiku handed him a napkin, which he gratefully accepted. Haiku's statement sparked a question Wren had been wondering about, but hadn't found the opportunity to ask yet. This seemed like as good an opening as any.

"Haiku, how long do you think I'll be here?" Wren asked.

Haiku shook his head. "That will be up to Father," he said. "And to you. How long do *you* think you'll be here?"

It was an odd question. As if Wren had any control over that.

"Until I learn everything I need to?" he answered.

"Then that would be a long time indeed," Haiku said with a smile. "I left many years ago, and I'm still learning."

"I mean, to deal with Asher," Wren said. "It's already been a week and I haven't done anything yet that's going to help me against him."

"Oh?" Haiku said. "What have you been doing with your time then?"

"All the exercises. The Waiting Room, that thing with the petals. The only things we've done with connections is all stuff I already knew."

"I see," Haiku said, and he smiled again.

"What?" Wren asked.

"So this week has been a waste of time?"

"It seems like it."

Haiku nodded. "*Seems* is a good choice of words."

Wren shrugged. "I'm doing my best to do what Foe tells me. I just don't see why we spend so much time on things that don't matter."

"And which things are those?"

Wren didn't want to seem ungrateful or dismissive, but now that the conversation had started he wanted to be honest. Truth, after all, was supposed to be his foundation.

"Well," he said. "Like the stuff you've been teaching me. Fighting with my hands and stuff. I appreciate it, I really do. But that's not going to help when I face Asher."

"And why is that?"

"Because it doesn't work like that," Wren said. "He doesn't really even have a body."

Haiku took a sip of his tea. "When we first began, how often could you escape my attacks?"

"Never," Wren said. "Unless you let me."

"And now?"

"Sometimes, I guess."

"More than sometimes," Haiku said. "You've improved a great deal, and very quickly. You're learning much faster than I ever did. You're perceiving threats sooner, your reaction times are faster."

"I guess," Wren said. He took a drink of water and shrugged. "But Asher... he just thinks, and he does it that fast. I can't ever be that fast."

Wren set his cup back down and just as he was taking his hand away, Haiku leaned forward and put his elbows on the table, bumped the cup, tipped it. In reflex, Wren's hand shot out and steadied it before it could spill. He looked over at Haiku, who was usually anything but clumsy.

"When you have trained your body," Haiku said. "You can move without thinking."

Not an accident. An object lesson.

"You are learning more than you realize," Haiku continued. "That is very much by design, and the point of Father's methods. It is often better to discover than to be told."

"Telling isn't teaching," Wren said, repeating Foe's words from many lessons ago. And then a thought occurred to him. "But, he told me that, and I learned it."

"You heard it," Haiku said. "But would you have understood what he meant by it, if not for his other lessons? Do you not understand it more today than you did a week ago?"

Wren considered. It was a fair point. Foe's statement hadn't been a lesson in and of itself; it had merely revealed a truth borne out in experience.

"And now you're just being argumentative," Haiku said,

smiling again. "Word games can be fun, as long as everyone agrees you're playing them."

Wren went back to his meal, pondering Haiku's claim. Much of what Wren had learned had been through doing, discoveries he felt he'd made on his own through the forced, repeated practice. Foe had corrected and guided him more by questions and implications than by any direct statement. He'd told Wren what to accomplish, but rarely, if ever, had he told Wren *how* to do so.

"Father has trained hundreds, Wren," Haiku said. "And he is harder on himself than he is on any of his pupils. He has refined his techniques to be as efficient and effective as he can make them. It may seem like you are simply repeating the same things over and over again, but even that is part of the training."

"I guess I just don't see the point of mastering how to catch petals," Wren said.

"Don't confuse the *method* of practice for the *skill* that practice is developing," Haiku replied. "Practice develops habit. Habit forms character."

Wren still didn't quite know what Haiku meant by that, but he got the message well enough. As bizarre and unnecessary as they seemed, Foe's lessons weren't wasted. Maybe Wren hadn't been able to recognize their value yet, but that didn't mean they weren't accomplishing their intent. Still, it was hard for Wren to consciously accept the idea that he was learning when his mind couldn't grab onto what it was he had learned. Maybe that too was its own lesson. To trust. Haiku obviously trusted Foe's methods. He'd been through them himself. Had apparently seen their effect on hundreds of others.

Hundreds of others. The number hadn't really struck Wren when Haiku had said it, but now it stuck out to him. Hundreds. Wren looked down at the web of his left hand, at the thin, pale line of the wound he'd inflicted on himself when he took his oath. The slash was nearly healed already, and though it had not been deep or jagged, it was clearly going to leave a scar. Had been *intended* to leave one. He moved his thumb back towards his hand, watched the injury vanish into the fold of skin. Unless someone were looking for it, it'd be impossible to notice. A reminder of his oath, for him and him alone.

Wren looked up to find Haiku with his own left hand outstretched, opened flat with thumb extended to the side. Showing his own scar. Kinship.

Did hundreds of others bear that same mark? How long had Foe been training his "children"? And what had he trained them for?

"Can I ask you something?" Wren said. "About House Eight?"

"Of course," Haiku said, withdrawing his hand.

"What exactly was it? You know. Before."

Haiku sat back in his chair and crossed his arms. Gathered his thoughts. After a time, he answered.

"We were the balance." A small smile flitted across his face after he said it, though there was sadness in it. "The world was very different before you were born, Wren. Too different for you to even comprehend. It was a world full of people, billions and billions of them. You will find this difficult to believe, but in that world, *small* cities were ten times the size of Morningside. Morningside would have been considered an enclave at best. Maybe large enough to be called a town, but certainly not a city."

It wasn't the first time Wren had heard such a claim, but he still found it impossible to picture in any meaningful way. Cities bigger than Morningside? He could barely imagine a city twice as big, let alone ten times.

"In that world, everyone and everything was connected, geography no longer mattered, and one man clever enough could wage war on a billion. The potential for sudden, catastrophic shifts in power was incredible. Potential of a magnitude that might as well be counted inevitable. House Eight wasn't the first to recognize the need for watchers. But it was one of the first to organize."

"Organize to do what?" Wren asked.

"To observe. And to safeguard. Much of what held society together in that world was vulnerable beyond the comprehension of most. Fragile. Very few understood the dangers. Even fewer took precautions." Haiku took another sip of tea, returned the cup to the table. "Think of the harm your brother was capable of causing when he directed RushRuin. In this world, before he became what he is now, his potential was somewhat contained. Localized to a city, or a region. In the old world, those with such skill and... moral deficiencies had an unlimited reach. Such people were our primary concern."

"You know about RushRuin?" Wren said. He'd mentioned it to Haiku before, but not in detail.

Haiku nodded. "Father has been busy."

"So that's why you're helping me? Why Foe agreed to train me? Because you know what Asher was like before."

"And because of what he's become. That is part of the reason, yes. The threat your brother poses now is of a kind this House was created to resist."

"If that's true, why train me at all then?" Wren asked. "Why doesn't Foe just take care of him? Surely he can do a lot more than I'll ever be able to."

Haiku smiled sadly and shook his head. "In his prime, I have no doubt he would have, perhaps with little trouble. But Father is... not all that he once was, Wren."

"Seems like he's doing pretty well for someone as old as he is."

Haiku chuckled. "He is. He's doing very well. But no, it's not his age." He sipped his tea again. When he set the cup back on the table, he turned it slowly with his fingers, staring at it for a time.

"Is he sick?" Wren asked.

Haiku shook his head.

"Another secret, then."

"It's not a secret, Wren. It just matters very little now," Haiku answered. For a moment it seemed like that was all he was going to say, but then he shook his head slightly, as if arguing with himself. He continued, "When the world changed, House Eight suffered. We did everything we could to prevent the collapse. And when we couldn't prevent it, we gave ourselves to slowing it. It destroyed the House. Father bore the brunt. Few survived. Father would not have, had he been any less. And after... though he doesn't show it, he is in pain almost constantly. He is still capable of a great deal, but he has limited himself by necessity. And more so, by choice."

Haiku's countenance darkened as he said those words, and Wren felt he'd crossed into territory he should have better left undisturbed. "I'm sorry, Haiku. I'm sorry I brought it up."

Haiku shook his head, "No, there's no need to apologize. This is your House too, now. You should know. But..." He paused, searched for the words. "Sometimes when you rake through ashes, you find only more ashes."

They sat in silence for a span, Haiku lost in his thoughts, Wren hesitant to say more, not knowing how to change the subject, or even if he should. Haiku eventually continued.

"House had two tiers of operatives. Those like Father, and like you, who dealt in the connected world. We lost them all. Except for Father, obviously."

"What happened to the others? I mean... the ones who weren't connected. Like you and Three."

"Scattered. Many of us were out on assignment when the final blow fell. Some returned. Most did not."

Haiku's arrival in Greenstone made more sense now; his big book took on a new significance.

"That's why you have your book," Wren said. "Three wasn't the only one you were looking for."

Haiku nodded.

"Did you find them?"

"Some. We are few enough as it is. And notoriously difficult to track."

The comment sparked a new thought in Wren's mind,

or rather drew it to the surface; he thought about Three and the things he'd been able to do. How he'd been able to move in the open at night. How Asher had posed no threat to him. The puzzle began clicking together in Wren's mind, a fuller picture slowly forming from the broken pieces.

"But that was the point, wasn't it?" Wren said. "Your purpose, in the old world. So you could go places and do things without anyone being able to track you. So you were protected from certain kinds of attack."

Haiku nodded.

"But not everyone had people like that?"

"No. Only a few other houses. Eighteen Zulu, the Fell, the Empty Frost. You must understand, at that time, disconnection was considered a punishment worse than death. It was reserved for the most terrible of offenders, whose desire to do harm was so great they could not be trusted with even the most basic contact with others. House was one of the first and few to recognize the value that it offered."

There was more than Haiku was saying; there was a hole in the midst of the words, like water flowing around a stone beneath the surface. Wren could feel it tugging at the corners of his mind as his subconscious continued assembling the pieces. His heart beat faster, though he didn't know why.

"So, you were what, then?" Wren asked.

"Whatever we needed to be. Messengers, couriers, protectors, observers. Gatherers of information."

And though he didn't want to hear the answer, Wren couldn't stop his mouth from forming the word.

"Assassins?"

Haiku looked to him then, for a long moment. "Sometimes."

"Is that what you were? Is that what... is that what Three was?" Wren asked. He didn't want to think of Three that way, didn't want to think of him as a trained killer, but he had to know. He feared he already did.

"Three," Haiku said. He paused, obviously choosing his words with care. "Three was many things, Wren."

"But he killed people? For the House?"

Haiku drew a deep breath, exhaled. Nodded. Wren's heart dropped at the confirmation, his body cold. Everything he knew about Three, everything he believed about the man, obliterated into chaos.

"There is more than you know," Haiku said. "More than you can understand. Three was no murderer. He was a great man. One of the greatest."

"I don't know how you can say that."

"Because I knew him, Wren. I know the burden he bore."

Wren's mind swirled. He'd come here, to train under Foe, specifically because of Three. Only because of Three. Only because he believed that if there was any chance of ever becoming like him, that was his best hope for the world. Had it all been for an illusion? For a lie? He didn't want to be a killer.

"But I don't understand," Wren said. "The oath. What about 'In all ways, at all times, I safeguard life'? What about 'Life, my charge'? How can you say you're protecting life if you're a house full of killers?"

"I should certainly hope my children are not *killers*," Foe said from behind. Wren whirled around at the sound of his voice, startled. The old man was in the doorway, leaning against the frame. How long had he been standing there? "And I'm certain my son would not call his own brothers and sisters such a thing."

"But..." Wren responded, "Haiku just said..."

"Assassins, boy," Foe said, walking into the room. "I would not expect you to understand the difference, nor is it a distinction most people have the clarity of perception to make. But I must insist upon it. An assassin is not merely a killer. A killer cannot rightly be called an *assassin* just because it makes him feel better about his deed."

"It doesn't matter what you call it," Wren said. "It's still taking a life."

Foe searched his eyes for several seconds. Then he pulled out a chair at the table, angled it so that it faced Wren. As he lowered himself into the seat, the corner of his eyes wrinkled ever so slightly as he sat down, as if it hurt him to do so. Though maybe Wren only imagined it because of what Haiku had told him.

"Your brother," Foe said. "Asher. When your time here is done, what is your intent for him?"

It was a question Wren should have had an answer for by now. In truth, he hadn't fully considered it. Or rather, he had refused to let himself think too deeply about the reality. Foe must have read it on his expression.

"My House is not one of illusions, boy. You know the answer, though you do not wish to see it."

"I just want him to stop," Wren answered quietly.

"'Whatever it takes'," Foe said, "I believe those were your words."

It was true, that's what Wren had said. And at the time, he had meant it. Now, with the spotlight shined on the reality of what lay ahead, it once again looked nothing like he had imagined. How had he ever imagined turning Asher back without realizing what that would actually require?

"I don't want to be a killer," he said, and the words seemed weak and full of fear.

"I should certainly hope not," Foe replied. "It takes no special skill or talent or training to be a killer. You want to take a life? Easiest thing in the world. A knife. A rock. Hands." Foe snapped his fingers. "There, you took it. Stole it. It's yours now. What will you do with it?

"Can't sell it. Can't give it back or give it away. It's yours now, you took it. Yours, always and forever."

He leaned forward and looked Wren in the eye.

"How many lives can you live, boy?"

He continued to stare into Wren's eyes for a few seconds, searching them as he so often did. He seemed satisfied with whatever he found there, or perhaps simply felt that his point had been made. He sat back again and stroked his beard once more.

"I should be very disappointed if you thought I was

teaching you all this merely to turn you into a trained *killer*," Foe said. "An assassin, however, is something far greater; one who knows that necessary violence, precisely channeled, can affect change far beyond any one individual's usual reach or impact. Empires have been raised and have fallen at the hand of one skilled assassin. Unfortunately most of history is filled with too many killers and of true assassins, far too few.

"This is a heavier subject than I wanted to cover with you this soon," he said. "But since the discussion has already begun..." He sat back, gathered his beard in his hand, stroked it. "You have lived out in the world. You've seen the trouble people face from day to day, the suffering they endure. What, from your observation, would you say is the basis for such suffering?"

The magnitude of the question was well beyond Wren's ability to answer; he at least had the wisdom to recognize that he was far too young to answer such a complex and deeply philosophical question.

"I have no idea," he said.

"Ah, come now," Foe said. "Surely you are still young enough to see it."

Still *young* enough?

"I don't know, Foe," Wren said.

"What do you *think* then? There's no penalty for being wrong."

Wren thought about all the things he'd experienced in his few years: his time with Mama and RushRuin; their escape and Asher's pursuit; Morningside's rise and fall. Was there a common thread? Something present in all of it?

"Fear?" he guessed.

Foe dipped his head slightly. "A good guess," he said, "and partially true. But deeper than fear. Fear must have a cause."

Wren thought about fear, something he knew very well. And there were so many things to fear: pain, thirst, lack, loss of loved ones, uncertainty. He shook his head, not even willing to venture a guess.

"There are many variations on the theme, many ways that we react, and lash out, and damage one another. Even the most well-meaning of us. But taken on a grand scale, above the individual, above the community, there is a central problem of humanity, and it is one of *justice*. A great deal of our troubles arise because evil flourishes while goodness is ground under its heel. The sense that something is wrong with reality, that the world is broken, flows from the suffering of the innocent."

Wren didn't have to hear any more to know where this was going. He might not have known much about history, but he knew enough to recognize the direction Foe was taking him.

"So you just kill the people you think are evil?"

"No," Foe said sharply. Then he softened, "No, boy, that way lies nothing but wasteland. When you start down that path, you are quickly on your way to genocide. We are no purifiers. This is why truth must be our foundation. We must perceive the world as it truly is, not as we would wish it to be. That includes rightly perceiving ourselves, and knowing our own nature. Regardless of intentions, given enough power, our nature would drive us to become the very thing we were established to war against. We are, therefore, first and foremost, at war with ourselves.

"But the wisdom of your youth has revealed the snare. In developing the capability to defeat evil, we empower ourselves to become that which we were created to restrain. That, in fact, is the natural outcome of such things. Without vigilance, it is the inevitable end. Now, I hope, you begin to see the importance of the oath you have sworn. Why it is necessary."

Wren recalled the high ideals embedded in the words he'd sworn with the shedding of his blood: truth, discipline, life, honor, service.

"It all sounds like exactly the opposite of what you actually do," he replied.

Foe smiled. "As intended by design. Even when taking

one life in order to preserve others, that final act must be ingrained as a *violation* of our nature, rather than as its fulfillment. That is the only way to ensure that the decision is treated with the proper care and gravity.

"Violence is rarely a good solution to a problem, boy. Unfortunately, when it *is* a good solution, it is usually the *only* solution. A sad reality, but one we do not shy away from acknowledging. Sometimes the only counter to an evil, violent man is a good man more skilled in violence."

Wren shook his head, though not necessarily because he disagreed with what Foe had said. It was a lot to process. Too much, maybe.

"Stand up, boy," Foe said. "Here, next to me."

Wren stood up out of his chair, and obediently took his place next to his teacher. Foe reached down and gently took Wren's hand in his, felt each of the small fingers in turn. Then, with a fluid motion, Foe wrapped his hand around Wren's pinky and swiftly bent it. Pain lanced through Wren's hand, down through his wrist and up into his forearm; cold and electric, it stole his breath.

"With the correct pressure, properly applied to even the smallest member, I exert my will upon you," Foe said. "I can make you kneel." He flexed Wren's finger down and back, and in response Wren dropped to a knee. "I can make you rise," Foe said. He twisted Wren's finger a new direction and helplessly Wren followed back up to his feet. Foe released the finger and placed his hand on top of Wren's head. "When the pain commands, the body seeks escape, no matter how small the threat. Animal, man, community, nation. It is no different."

He reached down again to take Wren's hand, but Wren was too quick; he pulled his hand away and took a step back. Foe smiled.

"And already you have learned the second lesson," he said. "When my nature is properly understood, I can exert my will with no pressure at all. You may sit."

Wren returned to his seat and massaged his hand. And

though he understood the supposed wisdom of the method, he wished very much that Foe had other ways to practically demonstrate his lessons that didn't involve pain.

"The reality is that this works for good or for ill. The laws of society operate on this principle. For some, punishment is required to understand the law. For others, the mere threat of punishment is enough. But what happens when those who victimize the innocent become too powerful to be confronted by those who would enforce the law? Or when the law itself is unjust? When the innocent suffer under laws written not to restrain evil, but instead to benefit a favored few?"

He let the questions hang in the air; questions of depth and weight that Wren had never even thought to consider.

"When a malignant cell grows and spreads," Foe continued, "is it better to let it continue until it destroys the entire body? Or is it best to cut it out while it is still small, before its corruption is complete?

"This is one of the purposes for which House Eight was built. To exert the proper pressure on the smallest possible member, to correct course when all other options have been exhausted. Above nation, above race or creed. We stand apart. In the world, but not of it... It is a terrible responsibility to bear, and one we accept with trembling."

Foe's explanations had begun to work on Wren; already he felt his perception shifting. He'd never considered how a law wasn't the same thing as justice before. But hadn't he seen it for himself, firsthand? Wasn't that just what had happened in Morningside, even when he himself sat as governor? Even so, for all of Foe's words, there was one question the old man hadn't answered. And maybe couldn't.

"But how do you know you're right?"

Foe raised his finger and then pointed at Wren, as if to say Wren had just put his finger on the very heart of the matter. "When you are young, you are clear-eyed; you are not confused about what is good and what is evil. It is

only as one ages that one becomes seduced and persuaded
by the illusions that convert one to the other. In the old
way, we dealt primarily in information. Gathering it,
disseminating it, evaluating it. Often we were the liaison
between bitter enemies, without their knowledge. I do not
exaggerate when I say wars were averted because of it. But
when it came time to act rather than advise, we did not
trust ourselves alone. Other Houses operated independently
from ours. Only when consensus was reached did we move
forward. But even then, we can never be *absolutely* certain.
Absolute certainty is the province of madmen alone.

"In reality, the mathematics of death are not complicated.
It is the *uncertainty* that stops most people, the gap in which
they allow themselves the illusion that perhaps with a little
more time, another solution will appear. Countless souls
have been lost to such vain hope, long after it was proven
baseless. But there is a necessary precision to the calculation
that escapes most. When removing a cancer, taking too
much is just as deadly as taking too little.

"It is important that you understand the place that
assassination has in your House. It is only a sliver of the
service we performed, but it is the darkest and most difficult.
You are right to wrestle with the knowledge, but you must
not shy away from the reality of its necessity either. For all
else we provided this world, we each will go to our graves
with blood on our hands. It is the burden we bear, in service
to those who could not bear it themselves."

At long last, Foe seemed to have reached the end of his
philosophical discourse on a topic Wren could have gone
his whole life without discussing. And yet, now that the veil
had been drawn back, he knew it was his responsibility to
consider all that had been said, to weigh it, and to work out
what it meant for him and his life.

"Perhaps now you can understand about Three, Wren,"
Haiku said. "Why there was more to him than you first
imagined."

Wren wanted to believe, but nothing Foe had said had

really changed anything. Whether House Eight considered it justified or not, Three was still ultimately a man trained to kill.

"Think about Father," Haiku continued. "The immense skill and power he possessed. And think of all those he trained, of all those he released into the world, each armed with the knowledge and the skill to destroy it."

Haiku sat forward, lowered his head so his eyes were level with Wren's.

"Sometimes the power was too much. The temptations too great. And those who fell away posed the greatest threat," he said. "You must understand, Three was charged with protecting the world *from his own House*. From his own brothers and sisters."

He left the rest unsaid, just allowed the weight of implication to carry over and settle on Wren. For some reason, that made the revelation more powerful. Three hadn't just been deployed to eliminate strangers at the word of his House. He'd hunted down men and women he'd grown up with, people who'd undergone the same training, who'd sworn the same oath. And with that realization, Wren felt profoundly sorry for Three, for the burden he must have carried, and the loneliness he must have harbored always within him.

The realization had another, unexpected effect as well. Portions of an earlier conversation came suddenly to mind, one between Haiku and Foe, the day Wren first arrived. Foe had asked what guarantee there was that Wren wouldn't cause the same havoc as Asher; Haiku had responded that he would take "the oath", that he would be Wren's "pledge". Wren looked at Haiku then, chilled by the thought.

"That's what you meant when you said you'd be my pledge?" he asked. "If I go bad, you're the one that will come after me?"

Haiku seemed genuinely surprised that Wren had worked that out; it was the first time Wren had even seen that expression on his face before. Haiku shot a glance at Foe, who simply smiled.

"When you leave here, and you return to that world," Foe said, nodding towards the window. "You will walk among those people as a god. Few will be able to prevent you from exerting your will. And so, out there, you will decide whether to live as a son of the dawn or as a servant of the night. The choice is yours. But if you choose to abandon your oath, then rest assured, judgment will follow."

"You're wrong," Wren said, shaking his head. "I won't be their god."

"When the time comes, that choice won't be yours to make. You will act. They will respond. You cannot decide what people worship."

"But I don't want it."

"Good," Foe said. "But that makes it all the more likely."

Wren shook his head again. "... I won't be their god."

Foe inhaled deeply, and when he exhaled he slapped his thighs.

"Well," he said. "Too much talk, too heavy a topic for what was to be so restful a day." He rose swiftly to his feet. "Come with me, boy," he said, the way it seemed he did a thousand times a day.

The abruptness of it all stunned Wren momentarily, but he quickly recovered himself and followed obediently. As usual, Foe didn't comment on where he was taking Wren or what he should expect. Haiku had said that any training would be light, but Wren knew his definition of easy wasn't anything like Foe's. To Wren's surprise, though, Foe led him up past all the usual floors and onto one he hadn't been allowed to visit yet. Rather than opening out to a landing or a corridor, there was simply a door at the top of the stairs. This was, apparently, the top of the tower. Foe stood facing the door, and a moment later it slid open. Wren was immediately inundated by a warm and scented breeze.

Foe stepped into the room. Wren followed after and froze at the entry way. The room was massive, the largest he'd seen yet. Long and wide, sprawling. It was warmer by at least ten degrees than everywhere else he'd been, and the air was sweet and fresh. And everywhere he looked, color. Bright, vibrant oranges, and reds, and yellows, along with muted pinks and purples, amidst lush greens. Electric lights burned with an intensity Wren hadn't seen anywhere else in the tower, almost overpowering.

"What... what is all of this?" he asked.

Foe paused in the middle of the room and turned back. "Flowers, boy."

And so they were. Laid out in elevated beds, arranged in a grid, with narrow aisles separating each from the other.

"Come along," Foe said, and continued down the centermost aisle. Wren hurried to catch up, his eyes roving the entire time across the explosion of life and color that surrounded him. He'd never seen such a thing, had never imagined it. He'd seen flowers before, of course, though they'd mostly been synthetic ones. But never had he seen flowers of any kind in this quantity. It was astounding and dazzling to his senses.

Foe led him to what appeared to be a tall workbench along the back wall. On it were a number of tools, as well as several bundles of various flowers, recently cut. Dozens of vases hung on a rack above it, but one small blue vase sat on the workbench to one side. Three tall stools sat in front of the bench, all pushed into a neat row along its right side.

"That," Foe said, pointing to the vase, "is for you."

Wren looked at the vase. It was deep blue, glass or something like it; a bulb at the base narrowing into a long stem, sort of like the flasks he used to see at the chemist's when his Mama made her buys.

"Thank you," he said automatically. And then, "What do I do with it?"

"You put flowers in it," Foe said with a chuckle. He swept his hand vaguely over the variety of flowers laid out on the workbench. "Take any from here that you like."

The flowers on the workbench had been laid in bundles by kind, fifteen or so by quick estimate. Large blossoms of rich purple, vivid orange, fiery red. And with them, lighter, more delicate varieties; white buds like snowflakes, or threadlike stems tipped with pale pink, so thin Wren feared a too-strong exhale might melt them to nothing. Foe stood by, watching him as he looked over his options. There was a test here, Wren sensed, but he had no idea what it was.

"I like these orange ones," he said. It was true, he did like them, but he mostly only said it to buy himself some time to figure out what he was really supposed to be doing.

"Those only?" Foe said, after a moment of silence.

"And the little white ones," Wren said, though he made no motion towards either. Now that he was aware of Foe's gaze, he was afraid of committing some grievous error. What was he missing? He stood there, hands at his sides, for thirty or forty seconds, weighing his choices, searching for that hidden option he hadn't yet detected.

"Boy," Foe said finally. "Take the flowers you like and place them in your vase in a way that suits you. There is no trap here."

Reluctantly, Wren gathered a few of the orange-blossomed flowers along with the spidery ones with the white buds. He didn't know the names of either of them, nor indeed of any of the others on the table. Roses he knew, and sunflowers, but that was it. He started to put the long-stemmed orange flowers in but stopped himself. Better to put the white ones in first, he thought. He tried it that way and found that the many-branched stems of the white flowers supported the orange ones and filled out the space in a way that was pleasant to him, even though he hadn't necessarily planned it. It seemed nice enough, the orange and white. But it was incomplete. He scanned the workbench again and his eye came to rest on the few yellow flowers that lay together. There were only three of them. The stems were dark, long, and slender to the point of almost fragility, with a yellow bloom explosion on top. When he picked one up, though, he found the stem was woody; flexible but strong. Something about it reminded him of his Mama. Wren tucked the flower in amongst the others, and its blossom stood just above the rest, a yellow sunburst atop a fiery sky.

"Mm," Foe said, his signature noise that Wren still didn't know how to interpret.

"I thought you said there wasn't a trap," Wren said.

"So I did, and so I meant," Foe replied, but he evaluated the flowers as if there was meaning hidden within. "Bright colors, that is encouraging. Good balance, if not symmetry... And who does the yellow flower represent, I wonder?" This last he said with a knowing smile as he looked at Wren out of the corner of his eye. He dragged a stool over beside Wren. "Sit."

Wren climbed up on to the stool while Foe took down a vase from the rack above the workbench. The old man began selecting several flowers from among the variety.

"Tell me, boy," he said. "What is your purpose?"

He asked the question casually, as if he'd asked Wren's opinion on the weather or his meals.

"For... for what?" Wren said.

"For *yourself*," Foe said. He didn't look at Wren; he was focused on his flowers, which he was now placing into his own vase with deliberate care.

As if that clarified anything. Wren didn't have to think about his answer for that long, though; he spent more time trying to find the words to make it sound as noble as he hoped it was.

"To protect the world from the threat that my brother poses to it," he said.

"Mm," Foe hummed. "And if you are successful?"

It seemed like something Wren should have had an answer to, but the question caught him off guard. He'd been focused on the confrontation, on the slender hope he had in overcoming Asher. The idea that something might come after it hadn't yet occurred to him.

"Mm," Foe said again, off Wren's hesitant silence. "If you are successful, what will you do then, boy? What will define your life, when you have your revenge?"

The word struck Wren more harshly than the question.

"It's not revenge," he said.

"Is it not?" Foe said. Still he placed his flowers in the vase before him.

"No," Wren said, but the fact that Foe had asked planted a seed of doubt.

"Not for your city? For the loss of your title and authority?"

"No," Wren said again. It wasn't just revenge, was it?

"For Three?"

Wren felt the hurt as if Foe had struck an unprotected nerve, and the intensity of the emotion surprised him. It was a question he didn't want to answer. A question he didn't want to let himself even consider. What Asher had done to Morningside was horrific beyond Wren's imagining. But somehow the loss of the city was less personal, the pain less acute, than what Asher had taken away when he'd killed Three. Now, confronted with the question, Wren found himself filled with a burning anger. An anger he knew he could draw upon when the time was right. Did that make it revenge?

"Revenge will consume you, boy, and leave you an empty husk of a better man," Foe said, and he turned away from his flowers then and looked Wren in the eye. "It is beneath this House."

After a long moment, he turned away and slid his vase closer to Wren. Now it contained just a few flowers, beautifully arranged. The arrangement was not just of pretty colors, but was masterfully structured in a way that evoked motion, and life. Foe took down another vase, identical to his, and placed it in front of Wren. "Recreate this," he said, motioning to the arrangement.

He sat down on a stool of his own. Wren stood, his mind swirling with thoughts of Asher and Three and revenge and purpose, and already felt defeated. There was no way he could recreate the work of art before him. He stood there, overwhelmed.

"One flower at a time," Foe said.

Wren took a deep breath and looked more closely at the arrangement, not as a whole, but in its individual components. One at a time. He began by counting how many of each flower he would need.

"Purpose and code, boy," Foe said. "Purpose, and code. These are the boundaries that channel a man's intensity to useful ends." He paused for a moment while Wren finished selecting the necessary flowers. Once Wren had the right components, he began replicating the arrangement as best as he could.

Foe continued as Wren worked.

"A code without purpose, and he becomes a slave, obeying without judgment, passion, or understanding. Purpose without code, and he will be a force of chaos, leaving a path of destruction and brokenness in his wake as he undertakes any means to achieve his ends. Without either, he is nothing more than an animal, chasing the moment's desire, living at the mercy of his basest instincts. But a man with both, ah, now there is a power to behold."

Wren placed his flowers as carefully as he was able, but even with only the first few in the vase he could tell something wasn't right. Even so, there was something soothing about the process, something almost hypnotic in the recreation. Foe's words, half attended to, somehow seemed to find their way straight into his heart.

"The oath you have sworn will serve as a code for the rest of your life, if you will embrace it and allow it to guide you," Foe said. "But no one can tell you your purpose. And without it, you will be only a shadow of the man you are intended to be."

Wren finished placing the last flower into the vase. He'd chosen the right flowers, and the correct number, and as far as he could tell he'd put them in the right positions, but something was lacking. His arrangement didn't have the same expression, the same vitality that Foe's did.

"It's not quite right," Wren said, stepping back from the

workbench. "But I don't know what's wrong."

"Mm," Foe said. "A fair attempt. You have the eye for detail. It is in the hand that you lack." He placed a hand on top of Wren's head. "Do not be discouraged. I have practiced for many decades and I too still have much to learn.'

"Purpose," Foe said a moment later. "This you will contemplate tonight, in the open."

"Outside?" Wren asked.

"Yes, boy," Foe replied.

Wren's head still hadn't cleared from all he'd been hit with throughout the day. This last shock hardly had the impact that it might have otherwise. The fear rose up, but it was muted.

"You may leave whenever you are ready," Foe said, and then added, "It is not punishment."

Wren nodded, though he couldn't quite bring himself to believe it.

"You may take your flowers to your room," Foe said. Wren nodded, numbly took the blue vase from the workbench, followed Foe out of the flower room.

The rest of the day was thin with tension; Wren's understanding of having to find a place to hide for the night overpowered by his desire to soak up every last bit of comfort he could find within the tower. He spent most of the afternoon sitting on his bed, looking at his little flower arrangement, thinking of his Mama, and of Three, and of his purpose, and of revenge. But time slipped by and towards the late afternoon, Wren asked Haiku to escort him downstairs to the front of the tower.

And so it was that as the sun sank towards the horizon, he found himself once more locked outside, alone and facing the night.

TWENTY-SIX

jCharles picked three drinks up off the bar and turned back towards his business table, in the back corner of the place. 4jack and Mr 850 were both hanging out there; 4jack, leaning back in his chair with his feet on the table, was blabbing away about something or other while Mr 850 was looking down at the table, not even bothering to pretend he was listening. It'd probably been twelve or fourteen years since they'd seen each other. It'd only taken about three minutes for them to fall right back into old patterns. jCharles weaved his way around the tables, headed towards his friends.

"... which is what I had tried to tell them all in the first place, see?" 4jack was saying. He didn't even pause to take a breath when jCharles set the drinks down on the table and took a seat. "I mean we're talking something like ten kilos of exumite, and they took the whole heap in with 'em, even though I told them it was probably five times more than they needed."

4jack's shirt was completely unbuttoned, and hanging open. He was a little guy, five-foot-five, maybe a hundred and thirty pounds, but he was still as ripped as he'd been in his twenties. Which is probably why his shirt was completely unbuttoned. Plus, he'd always been proud of the tattoos that covered his torso, arms, and legs. They were all quotes from stories or poems, in different languages, and all manner of scripts and fonts. 4jack shared jCharles's love for books, and he spoke something like twenty-seven languages.

"So you can bet I was standing far enough away when the whole thing went up," he continued, "but of course that's the only thing anyone remembers about the incident. Somehow, they say, somehow ol' 4jack's the only one don't get crisped up, which is like, well yeah man, remember how I said exumite burns about a thousand times hotter and faster than anything you're used to? Remember that time I told you how you were using five times more than you should've been?"

"Exumite only burns at 3,206 degrees Celsius," Mr 850 said quietly. Not loudly enough to interrupt, really, but the fact that he'd spoken at all threw 4jack for a loop.

"What?" 4jack said.

"Exumite doesn't burn hotter than 3,206 degrees," repeated Mr 850. "Celsius."

"OK?"

Mr 850 shrugged. He was still looking at the table. "You said a thousand times hotter. Even a methyl ethyl ketone cool flame runs about 265 degrees, so mathematically..."

4jack blinked at his old friend. "... Well... yeah, I was trying to make a point, Fifty, not a scientific assessment."

Mr 850 shrugged again. jCharles took his opportunity.

"Man, I can't tell you how good it is to see you guys again," he said. Mr 850 glanced up at him, smiled his broad, genuine smile. Dark-skinned, dark-eyed, he'd always been a little pudgy and baby-faced. jCharles had never known anyone more sincere than Mr 850. Taken all together, it was hard not to feel like he was just a really big kid. Really big, and really, *really* smart.

4jack leaned forward, took his drink, tipped it forward towards jCharles and then downed half of it.

"I really appreciate you coming," jCharles said.

"Yeah, well, it's not every day a dead man calls you for help," 4jack said. He flashed a quick smile.

"Heard that too, huh?" said jCharles.

"Common knowledge, buddy-o," 4jack said. He drained the rest of his drink. "Easy enough to believe, for anyone who doesn't really know you. You gonna give us the run down?"

"When Kyth gets here."

"Any ETA on that?"

"Should've been the first one in," jCharles said, and he shrugged. "Coming in from Halfway, though, and you know... Kyth runs on Kyth time."

Just then, the front door of the Samurai McGann swung open, and a woman walked in. She stood at the front for a moment, scanning the crowd. Broad shouldered, golden skinned, red-eyed.

"Oh boy," jCharles said. "Here comes trouble."

The others followed his gaze. They all saw each other about the same time. The woman's face lit up, and she made her way through the bar back to where they were seated. The three men all got to their feet to greet her.

"Heya, Ky–" 4jack said as she drew close, and she immediately clapped a rough hand over his mouth.

"Shhhh," she said. "We don't use that name so much anymore."

4jack shrugged and nodded. The woman took her hand away, looked him up and down, and then picked him up in a crushing bear hug.

"Ah, 4jack," she said. "One of these days I'm going to put you in my pocket and keep you for a pet."

She put him back down on his feet, and held her arms out to jCharles. He stepped around the table and leaned in, gave her a one-armed hug.

"Good to see you again, K," he said.

"Not as good as it is to see you," she replied. "How's your lady?"

"Which one?" jCharles said as he pulled away. He smiled at her. "Got a daughter now."

"Breaking my heart," she said. "Whatever happened to there only being one girl for you?"

jCharles didn't take the bait. "What are we calling you these days, my dear?"

"Trouble," she answered.

jCharles laughed. "It suits," he said.

"I thought so."

"So what's with the tattoo?" 4jack asked. "Property of Kyth?"

"Got tired of leaving it implied," said "Trouble". Kyth. JCharles couldn't think of her as anything other than her real name, even though Trouble was so perfectly appropriate. She smiled after she said it. She always did have a killer smile. "And more tired of people not respecting it."

"Kind of high-profile for someone who doesn't want her uh... identity known," 4jack said.

"Not when everyone believes she's someone else," she responded.

"I'm sorry, I'm confused," Mr 850 said. "*You're...*" he made a little motion with his hand, and then he leaned forward and said very quietly. "Him?"

Kyth leaned in even closer, nodded as if bringing him in on a grand conspiracy. Winked at him.

"Oh," Mr 850 said, and he leaned back, clearly not understanding and more than a little uncomfortable with her proximity.

"You must be Mr 850," she said. "It's a pleasure." She stuck her hand out. He shook it timidly. "Twitch speaks very highly of you."

Mr 850 nodded, still in a daze.

"You may have noticed that in certain lines of work," she explained, "sometimes certain kinds of men find it difficult to respond to a woman in as professional a manner as they might to one of their own. This way makes it easier for them."

"Kyth has something of a reputation," 4jack said. Behind him a couple of patrons must have caught his use of the name, because they both looked over, then looked at each other, then tried to move to another table without making it obvious.

"I've heard," Mr 850 said, entranced by her. jCharles got the impression that maybe his friend was rapidly developing a crush. jCharles waved his companions to take a seat at his table.

"Drink?" he asked Kyth.

"Sure, thanks," she replied, and she picked his up from the table and took a long pull while she watched him over the top of the glass, smiling with her eyes. jCharles slid back into his seat.

They spent the next half hour or so catching up. But after the small talk wound down, jCharles took the three of them up to the apartment. He'd told them each enough to get them to agree to come to Greenstone, but he hadn't tried to explain everything. Now, in the quiet of his front room, he laid out everything he knew, and everything he feared. They all sat, listening intently, as he told them about Morningside, the Weir, Asher, and what Edda had found when she'd crossed the Strand. Kyth and 4jack interjected occasional questions, but Mr 850 just sat there and soaked in his words. By the time he reached the end of it, his friends had all fallen quiet, and looked troubled.

"It's a lot to take in, I know," he said as he closed. "And I'm not asking for any of you to stay here to fight. I don't expect that of any of you. But I just can't figure this one out on my own. I need you to help me find a way."

The other three sat in silence for a span, processing.

"Well," Mr 850 said, finally. "I guess we better get to work."

That seemed to kick the others into go mode.

"What's the division of labor?" Kyth asked.

jCharles pointed at 4jack. "Personnel," he said, and then pointed to Mr 850, "groundwork." Finally he looked at Kyth. "Firepower."

"Who's running logistics?" 4jack asked.

"On me I guess," jCharles answered.

"Oh, well," Kyth said, and she smiled at him. "Then obviously we're doomed."

"*You're* doomed," 4jack answered. "I'll come out all right, be sure of that."

"I've got a lot help these days," jCharles said. "The puzzle's just too big for me to see it all."

"Yeah, buddy-o, no sweat," 4jack said. "We'll get it figured out."

"I've got you set up at a couple of places around town," jCharles said. "Figured the least I could do is make sure you had a good bed to sleep on. How long do you think you'll need to get a feel for things?"

"Couple of days, maybe," Kyth said.

And almost simultaneously, Mr 850 said, "Thirty-eight hours."

jCharles smiled to himself.

"All right. You guys should have free run of the town, except for one area. I'll mark it off for you. It's the Bonefolder's prime territory. If her people see you sniffing around there, we might have some friction, and I'd rather not have to deal with that right now. Anything you need, you let me know, and if you can't find me, Nimble can handle it. Any questions?"

jCharles looked around at his friends. The troubled expressions they'd been wearing a few minutes ago had all melted away; already they were in problem-solving mode. They didn't have any questions.

"Try to keep it low-profile, huh?" jCharles said. "I've already got a lot of eyes on me."

"Why are you looking at me?" Kyth said, her hands raised in a show of innocence.

"You have something of a reputation," Mr 850 said. And he smiled sheepishly and looked at his feet, partly embarrassed that he'd said it, and clearly pleased with himself that he had.

"Better watch that one," Kyth said to jCharles. "I might take him home with me."

4jack stood up and buttoned his shirt. Off jCharles's look, he said, "You said low-profile. Hard to blend in with the locals when I'm walking around looking like a god."

jCharles chuckled and shook his head. "I think you're right, Kyth," he said.

"Of course I am," she said. "About what?"

"We're doomed," he answered. The others rose to their feet, said their goodbyes. jCharles directed them to the accommodations he'd had prepared for them, each in a different section of town. After he saw them out, he returned to his front room. He poured himself a drink, sat down in his chair, switched out the light. It felt strange to sit there in the dark; jCharles was a hustler by nature. But he'd done all he knew to do for now, and there wasn't any point in burning himself out with activity for activity's sake. There'd be plenty to do when his friends got everything sorted out. For now, his job was to wait.

And there was nothing jCharles hated quite as much as waiting.

"Can't be done," Mr 850 said, thirty-seven hours and forty-two minutes later.

They'd all reconvened in the apartment.

"That seems... pretty pessimistic," jCharles said.

Mr 850 shrugged. "Sorry, Twitch. I hate to see you lose. You know I do. But if you try to hold the wall, that's the only outcome."

jCharles looked around at the other two. They didn't offer any argument with Mr 850's assessment. That wasn't what he'd expected, and it certainly wasn't encouraging.

"Maybe that's why you were having such a hard time figuring it out on your own," Mr 850 added, an awkward attempt to give jCharles something positive to cling to.

"So that's it?" jCharles said. "Can't be done? We're going to lose the city, no matter what?"

"It's just too spread out," Mr 850 said. "Layout's all wrong. If I'm the bad guy, I'm leading a vanguard force against the front gate. Once you're committed, I bring in my larger body to hit from the other side. Two other sides if I've got the numbers for it. Assuming your estimates are right, you just don't have the people to cover all the angles of attack."

"Even if it's the entire city on the wall?" jCharles asked. Wildly optimistic, he knew.

"They're hard enough folks," 4jack interjected. "Got some real pipe hitters in this town. They'll put up a good fight. It's the organization that's the problem. Loyalties are too small. When the trouble comes, it's going to be every man for himself."

"If what you say about the Weir is true," Mr 850 said, "if they really are being controlled by one mind, then it's inevitable, Twitch. I'm sorry. Even a small disciplined force can decimate a much larger, poorly-coordinated one. And it sounds like they've got the numbers."

"But Greenstone is these people's home," he said, grasping for anything.

"It's not a question of will," 4jack said. "I meant it when I said they'll put up a good fight. But Fifty's right. Any kind of serious, organized attack is going to run right through them."

jCharles sat back in his chair, crushed. Not because any of this came as a surprise; it was because it confirmed what he'd feared was true. In all the greatest epics, all his favorite stories, the good guys always faced impossible odds, and yet they always found a way to overcome. It *felt* like that was how things were supposed to be in real life, too.

"So what if we don't save the city?" Kyth said. jCharles looked over at her.

"I'm not running away," he said.

"That's not what I said," she replied. "You asked us to figure out how to protect the city. The answer is, it can't be done. Let's spend our time figuring out what we *can* do. So, tell me, if we're not worried about saving the city itself, what should we be saving?"

"The people," Mr 850 answered. Kyth winked at him and nodded.

"The people," she repeated. "Look at it that way, and what options open out to us?"

"I'm not sure how it's any different," 4jack said. "Call it what you want, but it's the same thing either way."

"Downtown," Mr 850 said, ignoring 4jack's statement. He let it hang in the air, as if having said it explained all that he meant by it.

"What about Downtown, Fifty?" jCharles prompted.

"You might be able to defend it," he said. "If you could get everyone to hold their ground."

"There's a lot of ground to cover between the wall and Downtown," jCharles said. "I don't see how that helps us."

"We use it," Kyth said, and she looked meaningfully at Mr 850. The two of them were obviously on some page that jCharles hadn't gotten to yet. Mr 850 nodded.

"Thin the numbers along the way," he said.

"Spread them out," she added.

And finally jCharles understood where they were headed.

"You're talking about *letting* them into Greenstone?"

"They're going to get in anyway," Kyth said. "We might as well decide the terms."

"How smart is this Asher guy?" 4jack asked.

"Extremely," jCharles said.

"Arrogant?"

"I imagine so."

"Then we might have a chance," 4jack said. "Just have to make it look good."

jCharles looked at 4jack, then Mr 850, and finally at Kyth. "You're going to destroy my city, aren't you?"

"Not *all* of it," she replied. "And what did you expect? I have something of a reputation."

jCharles chuckled and shook his head. "I'm gonna need a drink."

They spent the next few hours talking through the whole concept from a high, strategic level, offering ideas, rejecting them, refining them. Plans were formed, scrapped, resurrected, reimagined. But the heart of the concept never changed.

They were going to convert Greenstone into an ambush-laden maze. A trap, the size of an entire city.

"There's one major obstacle we have to get past," jCharles said, as evening was coming on.

"Little short there, buddy-o," 4jack said. "I count at least forty."

"Oh I'm not talking about the insane amount of work and supplies and manpower," jCharles said. "All that's easy compared to the big one."

"Which is?"

"The Bonefolder," jCharles answered. "I can get a good chunk of folks on board. And we'll have to keep as much of it under wraps as we can. But Bonefolder's already on edge. We're going to have to deal with her, probably sooner rather than later."

"What about the Greenmen?" Kyth asked.

"They won't go near her," jCharles said.

"No, I mean, are they going to be a problem? Can we count on them?"

"Oh. Yeah, I think I can bring Hollander around," jCharles said. "If I propose it as an emergency plan, maybe. An evacuation route, that sort of thing. Just in case. Maybe we don't tell him too much about all the other parts of it. Not until we need to. But even if they were a hundred percent on board, I don't see how we make it work with the Bonefolder. She's got too many connections, too many favors to call in."

"So let's go talk to her," Kyth said.

"I hadn't been thinking about it being a conversation," jCharles said.

"Maybe you should," she replied. "I know you don't like dealing with her, but think about how much faster everything would go if we had her kids helping out."

"Whoa, wait now," 4jack said. "You want to *team up* with the Bonefolder?"

"Gee, I don't know, 4jack, what'd you have in mind? You want to go pick a fight with her?"

"No, but there's a pretty big gap between fighting and being friends."

"Not as much as you might think," Kyth said. Then she shook her head and laughed. "Boys are so silly. Come on, Twitch. Set it up. I'll go with you."

"I don't think that's a good idea," jCharles said.

"Nonsense. Get over yourself, jCharles." She never called him jCharles, except when she wanted to get under his skin. "Let's go chat with her."

And that was how jCharles found himself standing across the street from the Bonefolder's place the next morning, Kyth at his side. There was a tall, lean man at the door, watching them with a dead expression on his face. jCharles recognized him as Bonefolder's nephew, Sander. Opening the front door was about all she allowed him to do anymore, on account of his handling of the situation with Cass long ago. Nice to see he still had work, at least.

"Just follow my lead," jCharles said. "And keep your hands where everybody can see them."

"OK, slugger," Kyth said, and she slapped him on the backside, and then walked right up to Sander. "Hey, sweetheart," she said, "We're expected." And she leaned in close.

Sander was about to respond when he apparently figured out what Kyth's tattoo said. Then he pressed himself back up against the wall to avoid contact.

"Sander," jCharles said.

"Yeah, go on in," he said, and reached over and fiddled with the handle to let them pass, careful to keep as much distance between himself and Kyth as he could manage in that narrow space.

jCharles followed Kyth in, whispered, "Why do you have to give everyone such a hard time?"

"Aw come on, we're all having fun here."

The place still looked exactly the same as it had the last

time jCharles had seen it, so much so that he felt a wave of deja vu; the main difference was that he was with Kyth instead of Three. The room was a wide open space, containing a number of tables. A far more upscale version of the Samurai McGann. Same idea, but highly refined. Bonefolder would have been horrified if she ever found out that her place and his had occurred together in the same thought. The bartender stood behind the bar on the left; in his sixties, and still looked like he could bite through a steel bar. The bartender dipped his head in greeting. jCharles nodded back. He scanned the balcony, where three men were arrayed around it, keeping watch over the floor below. And there, at her usual table, alone, sat the Bonefolder. Still just as old, just as severe as she'd ever been. The woman was like an ancient tree that just seemed to get stronger even as she got more gnarled. Impeccably dressed, as usual. But her face was even more sour than usual.

"Sit," she said sharply. Didn't even offer them a drink. jCharles led the way, pulled a chair out for Kyth, who flopped into it. She was being even more gregarious than usual. He took a seat next to her.

"How should I address this one?" Bonefolder asked jCharles, waving a dismissive hand Kyth's direction.

"You can call me Trouble," Kyth said before jCharles could answer. "And you can talk to me directly. I don't let other people speak for me."

Bonefolder turned her withering disapproval towards Kyth, but it bounced right off Kyth's gleaming smile.

"Trouble is not a *name*," she said, but whatever else she was going to say caught in her mouth. She closed it with a snap, frowned, and then continued. "Oh. Oh now that *is* unfortunate. Tell me, my dear, why would you let anyone devalue you in that manner?"

"I'm sorry?" Kyth said.

"Another man's property, indeed. I find that repugnant." Which was an odd thing to hear her say, since jCharles knew for a fact that Bonefolder had shuttled slavers around, and made a good chunk of money off it.

"Oh," Kyth said, and she pointed up at her tattoo. "This?"

The Bonefolder dipped her head in her slow, mechanical nod.

"This is just stating the obvious," Kyth said. She glanced over at jCharles for the first time, gave him a look. From anyone else, the look would have been asking for permission; from Kyth, it was just a warning about what she was going to do. He shrugged.

Kyth leaned forward across the table, lowered her voice. "*I'm* Kyth."

For the first time in jCharles's life, he saw Bonefolder look confused. It was a subtle expression; a mild pursing of the lips, a small furrow in her brow. It was magnificent to behold.

"I beg your pardon," she said.

"I'm Kyth," Kyth repeated. "I know you've probably heard otherwise, but that's by design."

She sat back in her chair. "Can I get a drink or something?"

Bonefolder looked at her for a long moment, like an algorithm someone had just fed a bunch of garbage data to. It went on so long that jCharles started to think the whole thing was blown; that the Bonefolder was so offended she was busy calculating the consequences she would have to face if she just had both of them killed on the spot. Even a couple of the guys on the balcony started shifting, like they knew something was up.

Then Bonefolder flicked a finger at the bartender.

"What can I get you, ma'am?" he asked.

She turned and fixed him with her gaze. "Surprise me."

"Please don't," jCharles said.

The bartender ignored the comment and went to work.

"I assure you," Bonefolder said, "this is not a game you want to play with me."

"No game," Kyth said, holding her hands up. "Our business has overlapped once before. I'm sure you recall it. You got a good deal. Taught me a good lesson about keeping tabs on who's on the local security payroll, too, so it was win-win. Even though you won bigger." She smiled when she said it.

The Bonefolder's eyes narrowed. Whatever Kyth was referring to must have given her claim some credibility. The bartender walked over and placed a glass in front of Kyth.

"Thanks, fella," she said. She took a sip, rolled it around in her mouth. Nodded.

"I made the whole Kyth-is-a-guy thing up," Kyth continued. "Pretty early on, I got tired of having to prove myself every time some boy wanted to do business with me. So I just started giving credit to Kyth, as if *he* was my boss, and let *him* take all the credit for my work. Once word got around of how protective *he* was about his property, I had this done." She indicated her tattoo again. "And hey, what do you know, suddenly business was a lot less of an argument. I'm sure you know how boys can be."

And now jCharles was doubly blessed, nearly miraculously so. Bonefolder's expression shifted from confusion to one that he didn't believe was even possible. She smiled. Not in her usual condescending manner that actually communicated disdain. A real life, honest to goodness, smile. At least, her mouth drew into a thin line that was vaguely curved upward at the corners. jCharles imagined that maybe those muscles hadn't been used in something like a hundred years.

"How remarkable," Bonefolder said. "Remarkable indeed."

She relaxed visibly, as much as anyone with her perfect posture could be said to relax. "It's so refreshing to see a young lady having such success. And so clever. I'm delighted."

Kyth shrugged. "It's kind of taking the easy way out, I know. But I don't have the patience that you must."

"Indeed," Bonefolder said. "Few do."

And for all her ridiculousness, jCharles realized that Kyth had just accomplished something no one else had ever done. She'd established a rapport with the Bonefolder.

"Tell me, Ms Kyth," Bonefolder said, "what is the purpose of your visit today?"

More than established a rapport. Apparently she'd just usurped jCharles's position at the table.

"Bad news," Kyth said. "I'm sure you're aware that something's going on across the Strand."

Bonefolder made no indication one way or the other.

"Well, whatever you think is happening over there, it's much, much worse." From there, Kyth launched into a brief recap of everything jCharles had told her. Listening to her, he couldn't help but be impressed. She didn't tell it the way jCharles would have at all, and yet as she did, he couldn't remember why he'd thought his way had been a good idea at all. Kyth seemed to know exactly which points to emphasize, which to ignore, and how to set up the request. Strangely, though, when it came time to lay out what they needed, instead of asking for anything she and jCharles had discussed, Kyth just ended and took a sip of her drink. Bonefolder was silent for a few moments.

"A bit farfetched," she said finally. "Even if only half true."

"If I were lying," Kyth said, "trust me, I would have told you something that was a whole lot easier to believe."

Bonefolder twitched her little smile again.

"Materials," she said. "Personnel. Additional funding, I imagine. These are what you will require."

Kyth smiled.

"You will be overseeing this initiative?" the Bonefolder asked, eyes still on Kyth.

"Not my show," Kyth said. "This is Twitch's bag."

The corners of Bonefolder's mouth turned down as if she'd just bitten into something intensely bitter. She blinked slowly, and then, with effort, turned to face him.

"We have often been at crosspurposes," she said to jCharles. "I expect we will continue to be so in the future. But as this seems to involve more than either of us could prepare for individually, I acquiesce."

She turned back to Kyth. "For you, Ms Kyth, I will see what can be arranged."

"I'd appreciate that very much," Kyth said brightly. "Thanks for your time. And for this," she said, tipping her glass forward. "A high-class establishment in every respect."

"Allow me to return the compliment," Bonefolder replied. "It is rare that I have the opportunity to enjoy the company of a person of substance. I had almost forgotten it was possible. A pleasant change."

She didn't look at jCharles of course, but he knew the comment was pointed his direction.

"I will deal with you directly," she continued. "Keep me apprised."

"Yes, ma'am," Kyth said. jCharles couldn't remember ever having heard Kyth call anyone ma'am before.

"You may go," the Bonefolder said, and that was the end of the conversation. jCharles followed Kyth out in a mild daze.

"What exactly did I just witness?" he said as they crossed the street and started back towards the Samurai McGann. Kyth laughed.

"It's called shared experience," she said. "I could try to explain it, but I don't think you'd get it."

jCharles shook his head and chuckled. "Well I hope whatever magic you did lasts long enough to get this all done."

Kyth wrapped her arm inside of jCharles's, laid her head on his shoulder. "You really need to let yourself have a little more fun with life, Twitch. You try too hard." He peeled her hand off his bicep, shrugged her off his shoulder.

"I'm having all the fun I can stand, Trouble," he said. "I gotta check in with Nimble, see if anything blew up while you were having your tea party." Kyth smiled at him.

jCharles pimmed Nimble to let him know they were out of the Bonefolder's place and on their way back.

"Good to hear," Nimble said. "Hollander come lookin' for ye."

"Uh oh," jCharles said. Hollander typically didn't like to initiate contact because it made other elements in Greenstone jumpy. "What's the problem?"

"Crew came in haulin' hardware ta make your eyes pop out. Greens stopped 'em at the gate, Hollander's got 'em now. Guess they're askin' for ye."

"A crew?"

"Aye, two ladies, six rough lookin' fellas," Nimble said.

"You get a name?"

"Just one, the girl's," Nimble said. "Call herself Gamble."

TWENTY-SEVEN

It was the sound that first caught Cass's attention. A shadow of her footfalls, haunting her trail. Initially she wrote it off as an echo of her own movements, enhanced by the ghost of her weary imagination; she hadn't slept in nearly two days, after all, and she'd covered a lot of ground in that time. But as the day grew older, the noise grew more distinct, less synchronized with her own steps. Someone *was* following her, and either becoming less cautious or too tired to continue timing their movement with hers. The recognition triggered an all-too familiar fight-or-flight reaction. And Cass had never been much of one for flight.

She fell back onto paths well worn by habit. Her years of running with RushRuin had given her plenty of experience at detecting and shaking off anyone who tried to tail her. And all of her practice with increasingly risky chem deals had made her adept at drawing would-be followers into an ambush of her own design. Cass maintained her pace, scanned her surroundings with new purpose. Large blocks of crumbled, collapsed, and rounded architecture formed narrow corridors; cheaply-constructed five- and six-story buildings wasted and blown out, fortresses of concrete snow beneath the unblinking sun.

It seemed unlikely that anyone who'd started trailing her out here had anything good in mind for her, but that didn't necessarily mean they'd continue to stick with her if she proved herself to be something other than easy prey. Unfortunately she didn't know exactly how long her pursuer had been following her, so she didn't have a good gauge of how determined the person was. Time to put it to the test. She passed a lane on her right and began counting the seconds until she reached the next. When she reached it, she turned the corner, continuing to count, and took her next available right. Her route didn't take her around in a perfect loop, but it was close enough. When she came out in a place near her original starting point, she turned right again and took off at a full sprint. Best estimate, she needed four seconds in the clear to make it to the next turn.

She cut the corner at three and a half and held there, crouched, pressed up against the dry and dusted exterior wall of a building, and counted down. Six... five... four... She slipped the edge to get a glimpse, exposing as little of herself as possible. Her count was off by about nine seconds, but sure enough her admirer emerged into the street, thirty yards away, bent low to the ground like a tracker or someone trying to keep out of the line of fire. This was the moment of telling. Cass had demonstrated her awareness of the tail and her ability to escape it. The implications would surely not be lost on her follower; either he would give up and walk away, or he would escalate his pursuit. She had no interest in punishing curiosity, but if the man meant ill, he would receive it in full measure. His fate was in his own hands.

And it was a man, she could see, though only in partial profile from her vantage. Thin, wiry, balding. His remaining hair was cropped short, his cheeks were heavily stubbled. Unfortunately his reaction didn't give her the clarity she'd hoped for. He straightened up and started looking quickly about him, obviously wondering where she'd gone. He took a few steps one direction, and then stopped, uncertain. Then he turned her way, looking up the street but not seeming to notice her. And she recognized him.

The Weir from the gate of Morningside. The one whose

life she'd twice saved. It glanced back over its shoulder, the
other direction. No, not *it*, she reminded herself. *Him.* He was
confused now, frustrated. Maybe even a little frightened.
Whatever he'd intended to do when he caught up with her,
it was clear he didn't have a plan for having lost her trail.
She wondered that he could have followed her for so long
without her noticing; clearly he must have been doing so
since she left the others. But then she hadn't been making
herself hard to follow necessarily. She'd ducked him with
such a simple trick. Even if he did mean her harm, seeing
him there, hugging himself in the midst of his uncertainty,
any doubts she'd been harboring about being able to deal
with him vanished.

She stood and stepped out into the road, called to him.

"Over here."

He practically jumped at her voice, hunched in on
himself as if preparing for an impact. They stood there
staring at each other for a few seconds, neither willing
to move. He was poised, tensed, ready to spring away, or
maybe towards her. She wanted to see which he'd choose
before she decided how to proceed.

Finally, when it became obvious that each was waiting
for the other to make the first move, Cass took the initiative.
She held her hands up to show they were empty, took a
slow step forward. The Weir coiled further, but the angle
and direction was enough to reveal intent. He was about to
bolt. Cass stopped.

"Easy," she said, not knowing whether or not the creature
could understand her words. It hesitated. *He* hesitated. Why
was it so hard to think of them as people? "I'm not going to
hurt you," she said. "Not unless you start something first."

The Weir's eyes narrowed as if he was trying to puzzle
out what she'd said. He responded with a quiet burst of
vocalized static; not quite the same as the typical sound of
a Weir, but in the same family. This was warmer somehow,
had some measure of emotional content. Cass couldn't
understand what he meant to communicate of course, but

she was certain he *was* trying to communicate.

"I don't guess you're going to tell me why you're following me, huh?" Cass said. It was hard not to think of the man as a creature, as something more akin to a dog or a wolf than a man. But there was more than just animal intelligence behind the eyes. The Weir squawked again, louder this time, and afterward he closed his eyes, clenched his fists. Cass recognized the emotion. Frustration.

"You can understand me, can't you?"

The Weir opened its eyes and cocked its head slightly. Cass glanced up at the sky, accessed her internal connection to check how long until sunset. Forty-two minutes. How long had it taken with Swoop? She didn't know how much time she'd need to find a place to hole up for the night. The fact that Swoop hadn't reacted to her with instant hostility when he was still a Weir had strengthened her suspicions that she might be able to move among them, but she wasn't ready to test that hypothesis quite yet. But her curiosity was nearly overpowering. What was this Weir before her now? Not Weir, not Awakened, but something caught in-between. The image of the woman she'd killed was still strong in her mind, the guilt lingering. The similarities were too great to be ignored or to be an accident. She had to know. And if she'd been able to Awaken Swoop from his fully-Weir state with Finn's help, maybe this creature was a good opportunity for her to try again on her own.

"I think I can help you," she said. "If you'll let me."

The Weir kept his place. Cass began walking towards him, slowly, hands held open and out to the side. And even though the man-creature didn't relax, he didn't run away either. She stopped about ten feet from him; enough distance for her reaction time, just in case. From there, she tried to reach out through the digital to him, to find his connection and attach to it. She could sense it now, or at least picture it in her mind's eye. For a brief moment, she thought she'd found it, but when she stretched out to it, it was like sticking her hand into mist or shadow. Form without substance, nothing to grasp or follow to its source. The Weir made another sound, this one with a vaguely questioning tone.

She had hoped it wouldn't be necessary to try to touch the Weir. She had no way of knowing how it would react. But after a minute or two of standing there, she couldn't think of any other way to proceed. And though she wasn't necessarily afraid of what might come with nightfall, she didn't really want to be standing out in the open when it arrived either. Cass held out her hand.

"Will you come with me?" she said.

The Weir looked down at her outstretched hand, and then back up at her.

"We'll find somewhere safer," she said. "Follow me."

Immediately the words left her mouth, a change came over the Weir. It relaxed, moved towards her. Almost submissive. Cass turned halfway and took a few hesitant steps. The Weir followed obediently. He continued to watch her intently, but for whatever reason his posture didn't suggest any fear or planned flight. Cass walked on, increasing her pace. The Weir matched it.

On her first trip around the loop, Cass had passed one building that seemed more intact than any of its neighbors. There was no way to know if it was a particularly good place to spend the night, but it seemed like a good option for some quick cover. She led the Weir back around her previous route, located the building. The front door had a barred gate over it, but the lock was broken off. They entered into a narrow foyer that led to a corridor with rooms on either side.

"Wait here," Cass said, and the Weir stopped by the door without complaint. It was uncanny how compliant he'd become. His eyes were just shy of wild, but he did exactly as he was told. As Cass explored the corridor and its adjoining rooms, the thought rolled around in her mind. Did exactly as he was *told*. Responds to commands, not questions. Was he still under some kind of control or influence? Did the

Weir-state make him susceptible to external demand? She checked the rear exit, the nearby staircase, and then after confirming that the back rooms were clear, Cass returned to the foyer and decided to put the idea to the test.

"Come here," she said. The Weir promptly walked to her. "Sit down," she said. He did, right at her feet. She knelt in front of him, looked into his watchful eyes. A war raged in them. She'd been wrong before about him not being afraid. He *was* afraid, very much so. And helpless. A wave of pity rolled over Cass as she realized her commands were indeed overriding whatever liberty the Weir-man had enjoyed before she'd spoken. He *was* trapped in some kind of in-between state, partially awake, aware of his circumstance and powerless to change it.

"Take my hand," she said. The Weir reached out and held her hand. "I'm going to help you," she said, though she didn't know if that would mean anything to him. "I'm going to get you out."

And with that, she closed her eyes and tried again to find his connection. Cass spent a minute or so calming herself, breathing deeply, clearing her mind. It'd been easier before when she'd let the connection come to her. She waited. Five minutes became ten, threatened to stretch into twenty, and still she could find nothing. She'd thought after her experience with Swoop, after having observed how Finn structured the signal, that she'd be able to replicate the process. And though holding the man's hand had made her sense of him stronger, the result was the same; there was nothing firm for her to cling to. It had been a strong memory of Swoop that had helped her find him, a perfectly clear image of him in her mind. This poor fellow holding her hand now was a stranger. Worse, he was a complete puzzle, his very existence an unanswered question. She didn't know exactly what she should be looking for.

Then Cass realized that wasn't entirely true. She didn't know this man at all, but she'd seen the datastream that held all the Weir together. The thought occurred to her that maybe instead of starting at the individual, she could pull back and find the collective first, then work her way to him. She switched her focus.

The effect wasn't immediate, nor was it easy, but Cass did find it. In her mind's eye, the churning datastream reformed, present but indistinct, as if viewed through a fog. Without Finn's help, her footing was less secure and she felt the strain of maintaining her connection to the signal. But her previous experience helped her keep calm. She could do this. Slow and steady.

Gradually Cass shifted her attention to the man's hand in her own. And though she wasn't using her eyes, the sensation was much like glancing down at a child, close at hand, while keeping an angry crowd in her peripheral vision. Her attention went to the man, but her awareness stayed with the datastream, passively watching for any sudden changes that might signal danger or require a reaction.

She could almost see him now, standing out from the raging stream. Not trapped in its flow, fighting the current like Swoop had been. This man's personality was distinct from the flow, yet still tethered by thick tendrils and surrounded by wisps of something other. And compared to Swoop, he seemed... thin. Not in shape, but in substance, like there was somehow less of him.

And there, behind him, was something else entirely.

It was distant in her mind, itself wrapped in a mist, but once she noticed it, she couldn't draw herself away from it. A convergence. In a manner that had no parallel to the real world, the thing seemed to both radiate and absorb the broad signal of the Weir, and others beside. A swirling nexus, half-whirlpool, half-star, both source and terminal point of the datastream. Cass's mind bent at the image, trying to comprehend the impossible angles and movement.

And yet it had structure. Structure so impenetrably complex she had no hope of understanding its architecture. Even so, she was compelled to bypass the man for the moment, and to stretch herself towards it, to try to find meaning in its impossibility. It grew larger in her mind, began to solidify. Cass continued to reach towards it. As she did so, she gradually became aware of a vague sensation of falling, or of being carried along by the current. The nexus was drawing her to it, and now that she'd allowed herself to be caught up in it, she feared she might not be able to escape it. And yet she didn't fight. Not yet. Just a little closer.

Though she couldn't see any others, her gut told her there were others out there, connected to it; a vast network. This was merely a single node, one of many. And there in the midst sat something bright, brighter than all else, yet pale with a sickly light. Even without knowing what it was or what purpose it served, Cass felt an immediate revulsion. It was a bulbous teardrop, shimmering at the center of the nexus, and she couldn't force herself to imagine it as anything other than the bloated body of an immense spider. There was something else too behind the instinctive reaction; a vague familiarity, like the sight of a strange animal triggering the memory of another's bite. There was danger here, Cass knew.

She turned her focus back to the man whose hand she still held, fought her way back towards him, struggled against the current that threatened to carry her into that alien mass. And as she strove to free herself, she heard in her mind sporadic warning cries of the Weir, as if they'd awoken to her presence. They'd noticed the intrusion. The glowing thing at the center of the nexus twitched and pulsed. Cass wrestled herself free, felt the convergence receding. But still the spider-thing shifted and remained clear in her mind. And to her horror, it began to unfold itself; not eight legs but eighty, or eight hundred. Tendrils stretched and spread and probed. It was alerted to her presence, if not her location, and was searching, bending itself towards her. Without consciously processing, Cass knew this was the same intelligence that had pursued her when she'd freed Swoop. This was the thing that had risen from the deep to seize her.

This was Asher.

She fled then, pausing only long enough to snatch the man free before she severed her connection. The physical world snapped shut around her. The man cried out in pain or in shock and fell forward, cradling his head in his arms. Cass too felt pressure in her skull; the onset of the strange headache that had accompanied her two previous attempts. She hoped she wasn't going to relapse into whatever state she'd experienced when she'd freed Swoop. She was counting on that reaction having been the result of the trap that had been attached to him, and not simply an escalation of the symptoms she'd suffered after her first attempt. Her ears were ringing slightly, and the experience of her second escape from Asher lingered with terrible clarity. The cries of the Weir still echoed in her mind. After a few seconds the pain reached a threshold and stabilized. Not pleasant by any means, but bearable.

The man was bent double in front of her, but he wasn't moaning or showing any other obvious signs of distress. Cass touched his shoulder lightly. He didn't respond immediately. His breathing was heavier than it'd been before she'd brought him out. Finally, he raised his head and his eyes to hers.

"What..." he said, and then stopped, apparently surprised at the sound of an actual word coming from his own mouth.

"It's OK," Cass said. "You're OK now. You're not connected to the Weir anymore." He shook his head and sat up, trying to comprehend her words and their implications. "It's a lot to process, I know."

He'd been staring right into her eyes since he looked up, but now became self-conscious, or maybe troubled by them. He looked away across the foyer at nothing in particular, mouth open.

"What's your name?" Cass asked.

Seconds passed before he responded. "Orrin," he eventually said, slowly. "... I think."

"Orrin, I'm Cass."

"What'd you do to me?" he asked quietly, still unwilling to look at her. The tone was more curious than accusatory, but there was an edge to his voice that was unsettling.

"I set you free," she said.

"You're the girl from that city," he said, flicking his eyes to her and then down to the ground in front of him. "Right? Aren't you?"

"Yes."

"And before that, you stopped a man from shooting me," he said.

"After the city," Cass corrected. "That came after."

He shook his head, though she couldn't tell if he was disagreeing or was trying to clear his thoughts.

"You followed me from there, Orrin. We saw you last night and tried to find you. You ran away. Then today, you followed me here. Why?"

"I don't know," he said sharply, agitated. But he quickly softened. "You were... you seemed different. From the others. I wanted to see why."

Between the headache and the strangeness of the interaction with Orrin, Cass had lost some awareness of her surroundings. It came back to her as if she'd realized she'd just caught herself right before nodding off. The foyer was darker; quite a bit darker than when they'd first entered. And those echoes of the Weir in her mind, she discovered, weren't just in her mind at all. They were real; the Weir were out.

Something about her change must have drawn his attention. He looked up at her, then back at the door behind him.

"Is that them?" he asked. "Are they coming here?"

"They're out," Cass answered, "but I think we'll be OK in here."

Orrin scrambled up to his knees and backed up against the wall.

"Is that them?" he asked. "Are they coming here?"

He said it in the exact same tone, with the exact same

cadence, like a recording stuck on a loop. His reaction hit Cass with a fresh note of dread. She'd been so intent on rescuing this man she hadn't fully considered the potential outcomes; it'd never even occurred to her that he might not be completely stable. Everyone that Wren had Awakened had reacted differently, of course. Some, like Kit and Luck, had been relieved, and grateful, and had adjusted well. Others, like Mez, had kept to themselves and never really seemed to recover fully from the experience. But none of them had come back in the sort of shape that Orrin was in. It was too late now, though; he was Awake and it was becoming increasingly clear that he was coming apart.

"You don't need to worry, Orrin," she said. "I've done this plenty of times. We'll be all right."

His eyes stayed fixed on the door.

"No," he said, shaking his head. "They're coming. They're coming here!"

"They're not," Cass said, trying to soothe him. "They don't know we're here, Orrin..."

And as she said it she felt it was a lie. Now that she listened carefully, it *did* seem like the cries were growing in both frequency and volume. They were calling to each other, certainly, but not in the sporadic, almost casual way that was normal to their hunt. They were coordinating. Worse. Converging.

Her experience with the datastream and the node. Maybe they really had noticed her, not just in that plane, but here too, in the real world.

"They're coming," Orrin repeated, shaking his head.

"Yeah," Cass said. "Yeah, I think you're right."

She rose to her feet, scanned her options. He turned and looked at her then, eyes wide. The rear exit wasn't necessarily a better choice than the front door. She knew better than to go up the stairs. Rear door might be locked or rusted shut. Out the front then, the way they'd come in.

"Come on, we'll find somewhere else. We can lose 'em," she said, heading towards the entrance. But he shook his head again as she passed, stayed huddled against the wall. Cass stopped, turned back towards him. "Orrin, I need you to stay calm, OK? I need you to trust me. I can keep you safe, if you just do what I say."

"You!" he shouted. "You *brought* them!"

"I'm leaving," Cass said, trying to keep emotion out of her voice. "I'm going to find somewhere safe. You can take chances on your own, if you want to. They might not even notice you if you don't do anything stupid. Or you can come with me, and I'll do what I can to protect you. Either way, I'm leaving now."

She turned back around and headed out the door. As soon as she exited, she saw the first of them. Fifty yards down the street, looking right at her. Too far for the jittergun. Not far enough to get much of a head start. The Weir made the decision for her. It rushed her, mouth wide in a howl.

Cass hunched down, tucked her chin, brought her hands up to eye level. Waited. The creature closed the distance in short seconds, leapt. And Cass sidestepped, delivered a perfect hook, buried her fist in the side of its head as it went by. It sprawled in midair, landed in an awkward heap, face down on the concrete. Motionless, once it stopped skidding.

There was a gasp behind her, and Cass turned to find Orrin standing in the entrance, eyes wide and wild.

"You... you..." he stammered. "You can't fight them!"

Cass looked over very deliberately at the Weir she'd just felled with a single blow, and then back at Orrin, cocked her head.

"Wasn't much of a fight," she said. Other cries picked up, no doubt responding to the Weir's previous howl. Orrin swiveled his head back and forth frantically, like a man trapped in a prison spotlight.

"Come on," Cass said. His head snapped back around, his eyes locked on hers. From his wild look, she knew he was lost.

"You're crazy, is what!" he said. "You're crazy!"

And he took off running in whatever direction his feet

happened to be pointing him.

"Orrin, no!" Cass called, but she stopped short of trying to grab him before he got out of reach. "Don't run off!"

If he heard her, he didn't make any sign of it. And though Cass felt she ought to chase him down, she noticed she wasn't actually doing so. She stood and watched as he fled back the way they'd come. Right back into the arms and claws of the very thing she'd just rescued him from. Orrin disappeared around a corner.

Maybe he'd be all right. Maybe the Weir wouldn't notice him, or they'd ignore him. But Cass had learned long ago you couldn't save people from themselves. If she went chasing after him in his current state, he might very well think she was trying to kill him herself. And even if his head finally cleared enough for him to realize what he'd done, it was likely his panic would make him unpredictable and impossible to control, the way a drowning man clings to a would-be rescuer and dooms them both.

She'd done what she could for him, and risked all she'd been prepared to risk. Guilt tugged at her as she turned around, but it didn't prevent her from heading off in the other direction. A lesson she'd have to think more deeply about later. Right now, getting clear needed all her attention.

Cass set off at a jog, head up, eyes constantly scanning for threats. Orrin had been partially right; she couldn't fight them *all*. Evasion was her primary goal. But if they came at her one or two at a time, she wasn't particularly worried about running a path right through them. She cut through an alley, and then back down a wide avenue, zigzagging her way more or less northward.

The biggest question was whether the Weir were merely closing in on her last known position, or if they were actually tracking her. The thought that they might have identified her individual signature was by far the worse possibility. If they'd caught her digital scent, it might be hours before she could completely shake pursuit. It might even take until dawn.

There was no way to know until it played out. And there was nothing she could do about it now anyway. She pressed on, ever watchful. After ten minutes of winding her way through the broken urban terrain, she had her answer. The Weir's cries hadn't converged in any one location and they weren't getting any more distant either.

They were tracking her.

Cass's heart fell with the knowledge. The situation wasn't quite as dire as when she'd bailed Gamble and her team out and gotten cut off, but it wasn't far removed. But if they were tracking her, they were reacting, and if they were reacting, they were a step behind. She'd have to stay ahead of them, evade contact as much as possible, strike only as a last resort. It was going to be a long night; an hours-long game of cat-and-mouse, with the highest possible stakes. And the cats had the numbers. At least this mouse had claws of its own.

Maybe it was because her conscious mind was so preoccupied with the now, or maybe it was just a gift from her well-honed survival instinct. Whatever it was, a thought slid sideways into her mind, like someone had slipped her a secret note. The Weir knew when one of theirs was killed or incapacitated. She'd seen it during her ambush run; it had nearly cost her her life when she'd stunned Swoop. And that thought triggered a distant memory that invited her to recall her old life, to go further back than she'd allowed herself to go in a long, long time. From her days with RushRuin. Back to when she'd given away her name. A tactic she'd occasionally employed with Ran and Dagon, when a target's security or a rival crew had them outnumbered on force or outgunned on paper.

The main downside was that it usually required at least two to work. Usually. Cass decided to put it to the test. She switched tactics. Evasion was still part of the equation but now only *part*. The other part was locating an isolated target. She didn't know what trail she was leaving that the Weir could follow; so she was going to leave a bigger one.

She slowed her pace, started using her ears as much as, if not more than, her eyes. The shattered cityscape wreaked havoc on sound waves, made it difficult to ever be certain of distance and direction. But after two or three minutes, she'd managed to pick out the direction that offered her what she figured was her best opportunity. Cass slipped into a lane between two buildings, barely wide enough for her to squeeze through sideways. If her guess was right, it'd lead her out to the lowest concentration of Weir. If not, well... she'd just wedged herself into a choke point that didn't even afford her enough room to throw a solid punch.

As she was approaching the midpoint, a croak came from behind her. She glanced back over her shoulder, but didn't stop moving. The end of the lane was clear, and it was impossible to know if something had just passed her by, or if the sound had merely been channeled by the buildings she was passing between. Cass picked up her pace, told herself it was the right move and not just because she was starting to get claustrophobic. When she was six feet from the exit, a shape flashed by. She inhaled reflexively. A heartbeat, two, three...

A twisted face manifested, blue-eyed, howling rage and warning. The Weir launched into the narrow space, lunged for her with arm and claws extended. Cass intercepted the Weir's forearm with her own, crushed it into the wall and pinned it. A quick cross-step, and she drove her shoulder into the chest of the creature, checking its forward movement and enabling her to grab its trapped wrist with her other hand. She rolled back, snapping her elbow up from underneath. The Weir's head whipped back with the impact, and Cass stomped a low-angle kick into its knee. The creature collapsed down, toppled forward towards her. She wrenched the captured arm back and around, dropped her hip onto the back of the Weir's head and let gravity do the rest. The creature folded up at unnatural angles with sharp cracks. After that, it didn't make any more sound.

Not quite how she'd planned, but she got the result.

From all around her, alerted howls went up as the Weir's companions sensed its demise. Cass vaulted up from the broken Weir, clambered over it and escaped the alley. She didn't take time to evaluate her options for paths; she just took off towards the nearest route that offered cover. If she'd judged correctly, the Weir would rush to encircle the location of their fallen broodmate, which would buy her some time and distance. Knowing where they'd be headed improved her chances of avoiding them.

As she cut her way back and forth through the crisscrossed lanes and alleys, Cass had another realization. Even with all she'd been through, after all she'd discovered about herself in the past twenty-four hours, she was still operating in her old mindset, using her default tools and skill set. When the danger had come, she'd fallen back on old ways without even considering if there might be new options available to her. After she and Wren had left RushRuin and gone on the run, her son had taught her how to mask her passive signal to escape intrusive traceruns and prevent Asher from tracking their movements. Maybe, she thought, with what she'd come to understand about the connection that the Weir shared, she could adapt the same concept. If she could just find the space to try it.

It was dangerous to stay on the move while splitting her focus, but she had to risk it. So while she navigated the urban wreckage, Cass recalled her experiences with Swoop and Orrin, formed a clear picture in her mind of that churning datastream. More, she concentrated on the way it had made her feel. The last moments of her rescue of Orrin rose sharply to the surface, when she'd turned and fled. When the Weir had first noticed her intrusion. There was something there, something for her to notice. She tried to roll the image around in her mind's eye, tried to shift the perspective to get a clearer view.

There *was* something there. Something she'd seen on Orrin. Wispy tendrils clinging to him. Though she hadn't noticed it before, she felt certain now that having interacted with the Weir's datastream, having spent so much time in its proximity, she'd somehow drawn traces of it out with her. Or, perhaps, had left some trace of herself tangled in. And the horrifying thought emerged that she may have inadvertently begun a process of reintegrating with the Weir. Had she given Asher what he needed to find her again? To reclaim her?

Something rose up in her then, something born of raw emotion and instinct, equal parts anger, revulsion, and desperate need to get away. And in that moment, in that swell, Cass felt power go out from her. The surge was like nothing she'd felt before; a sensation halfway between physical and imagined, a bubble of raw energy bursting and dissipating into the air around her. She went momentarily weak, her legs hollow, her hands and face clammy. Still she pressed on, pushed herself through the faintness. Time and distance were her only allies now, and she needed as much of each as she could get. It wasn't until three or four minutes had elapsed that she realized the cries of the pursuing Weir had faded behind her. She slowed to a jog, but it took another ten minutes before she let herself believe she'd done it. Whatever *it* had been exactly. Between intentionally drawing their attention to a specific location and disrupting her own signal, she'd managed to escape.

It was fully night by the time Cass found a place that looked sturdy and disused enough to shelter in. Some kind of warehouse or storage facility, wide and subdivided into many chambers. She spent the night tucked into one of the smaller cubical rooms on the top floor, hidden behind two stacks of metal pallets. Tired as she was, she refused to let herself sleep for the time being. Though she'd shaken the Weir off her trail for a while, she wasn't positive that her escape was permanent, and she had to stay awake and alert for sounds of danger. She'd sleep in the morning, once the sun was up and the Weir had returned to their holes for the day. The night was long, and it took an incredible effort to stave off sleep for the duration, but she managed. She even stuck it out for almost an hour after sunrise before she finally gave in and let herself get some much-needed, and much-deserved, rest.

When she woke shortly after noon, Cass had a small meal and some water and let her mind wander through all the broken thoughts and emotions that whirled in her head. Thoughts of Wren, and of the team, and of Orrin. Orrin. She was conflicted about him. There was no way she could have known about his fragile mental state before she brought him out. Even so, she wondered if there was something else she should have done; if she should have left him as she'd found him, or if she should have let Sky shoot him when they'd seen him the first time at the gate of Morningside. She'd almost convinced herself that interacting with him at all had been a mistake. But then she pictured the node, and knew that whatever the outcome for Orrin, she'd learned something significant from him. Small comfort for Orrin, if he'd met a nasty end, but she couldn't count it as a total catastrophe.

Cass had launched herself into the unknown based solely on the disquiet she felt in her spirit, not for any grand plan or purpose. She'd simply felt in her heart that there was something for her, for her alone, to be found out here. But as she sat in the decaying warehouse, contemplating her next steps, she couldn't escape the image of the node. The more she tried to ignore it, the more prevalent it became in her mind. And something else was bothering her. Something she'd been avoiding. For all her plans and high-minded ideas of living on her own terms, she knew deep down she was still running. Reacting. Even now she was letting Asher define her possibilities. And when she finally allowed herself to accept that realization as true, it filled her with indignation. She wasn't free. In fact, for all that had changed, for all her transformation, and for Wren's, she was still in the exact same situation that Three had found her in. Harried. Under pursuit.

She'd lied to herself long enough. No more hiding. No

more letting someone else dictate her path.

There was no way for her to know what the nodes were, or what function they served. But she guessed that the convergences she envisioned in the digital had corresponding representation in the physical. Whatever they did, they were important to the Weir, maybe critical, and that made them important to Asher. Maybe it was foolish. Maybe it was the last thing she'd ever do. But she decided then and there what her goal was: she would find whatever it was that created that nexus of data, and she would use it, or destroy it, to rob Asher of some portion of his power.

Cass had let herself come to believe that she'd never be able to confront Asher herself; that he had managed to set himself up in a plane of existence that she could never reach. Wouldn't he be surprised to find her knocking on his door? Asher had always been obsessed with power and with control. Cass could only imagine the height and depth of his godly delusions, now that he'd transcended the physical world and become a mind without a body. She smiled to herself at the image. And she couldn't wait to see how he'd react when she walked up and punched him right in the mouth.

TWENTY-EIGHT

"It's time," Foe said, jolting Wren awake. He'd fallen asleep over his meager breakfast, after successfully enduring another night outside.

Wren dragged himself out of the chair, followed Foe; his steps barely registered through the fog of fatigue. Mindlessly he slipped off his shoes and socks and even his pants. They always got heavy in the water, and more than once the water dripping out of them had given him away. It wasn't until his feet hit the cold water that he came fully back to himself. And it was a good thing too. Foe didn't even wait for him to get completely off the ladder before the lights went out. Wren felt a sting in his left shoulder blade an instant later.

He stilled himself, took two more hits from Foe's clicker as he slid to his right and advanced down the wall towards the back of the room. The pain was still as brilliant as it'd ever been, but it'd lost its power to frighten Wren. He didn't enjoy it, of course. But knowing it was inevitable, he'd come to accept it. That made it easier to focus on the things that actually mattered, like controlling his breathing, and moving smoothly through the water.

Everything about the Waiting Room encouraged deliberate, fluid movement. No sudden starts or stops. He hadn't exactly made a conscious effort to memorize the location of all the posts, but he'd spent so many hours

moving among them that he'd developed an intuitive sense
of where he was in relation to them, and also where he was
in the room in general. Before he came into contact with
a post or a wall, he managed to... well, to *feel* it somehow,
without actually touching it. He could sense a shadow of
pressure. Maybe it was the way the water sloshed against
everything that gave him a sense of his surroundings.

And just as he was beginning to feel pretty good about
having gone almost a full minute without a shock, he drew
his foot up a little too high out of the water. It made a gentle
slapping sound. Wren tensed up, anticipating the click. But
it didn't come. Either that meant Foe hadn't heard it, or–

Before he knew what was happening, Wren felt a sharp
tug in the bend of his left knee, and an instant later a
light impact on his chest, near his right shoulder. The two
together torqued him around, threw him off balance, sent
him backwards into the water.

He sat up, coughing and sputtering. The lights came up.
Foe was standing over him.

"That wasn't necessary," Wren said when he got his
breathing under control.

"Apparently it was," Foe answered. Wren got to his feet,
shook as much of the water out of his shirt as he could.
"Maybe now you will be awake enough to show some
effort."

Wren didn't respond. Just waited for the lights to go out
again. Foe bowed forward slightly, and dipped his hand in
the water. Then, without warning, he whipped his hand up.
Wren reacted reflexively, brought his arm up to shield but
too late; water slapped his face and eyes. The stings came
before he'd recovered. He opened one eye to total darkness.

He lashed out, firing at where the old man had been a
moment before, barely able to restrain himself from letting
out a frustrated cry. He wasn't sure where the old man
had gotten to, but he fired anyway, even though he knew
it would earn him a reprisal. Sure enough, a brand of fire
seared his neck. There was no way to know if he'd hit Foe;

the old man never reacted or told him. But considering Wren hadn't fired anywhere near the direction Foe's last shot had come from, it was probably safe to assume he hadn't hit anything.

The lights came up again, and Foe was halfway across the room. How did he move so fast without making any noise?

"Boy!" Foe said. "Intensity is good. Anger is not. Emotion is to be drawn upon, not *relied* upon. A little water in the face is nothing worthy of upset."

Wren nodded. Everything a lesson. Always a lesson. Foe was right. It was such a stupid trick. Something unexpectedly petty, and it had thrown him off. He was tempted to credit the minor outburst to how tired he was, but he rejected his own excuse. Asher wouldn't give him any room just because he was tired, or cold and shivering. Foe was giving him practice at mastering himself.

"Again," Foe said, and once again all was darkness. Wren lowered himself into a crouch, slid silently forward through the chilled water towards where he'd last seen Foe. He pressed into a pole, listened to the water sloshing gently. The old man was hiding his movement in those waves somehow, small as they were. But how? It was mindboggling, as if Foe had figured out a way to defy reality, to hack the physical world and bend its rules.

Wren closed his eyes, strained to listen for a hole in the water where the old man must be. Whether it was the fatigue or the undulating motion of the water, or some combination of the two, Wren felt his balance escaping him. He reached up and put a hand on the flat top of the post, using the solid surface to steady his sense of balance. And as he crouched there in the water, it finally struck him. He almost laughed, it was so simple.

Quietly as he was able, Wren slipped his clicker into a pocket on his chest and edged his way up the nearest pole. He put both hands on top of it and then slowly, carefully, he lifted his right foot out of the water. There was another pole

about a foot over; Wren stretched until he found it with
his foot, then followed it up and placed his foot on top. He
leaned forward over his hands, levered himself up, eased his
way completely out of the water. It was harder than he'd
thought it would be, and his muscles strained and trembled
with the effort. But he managed to keep his balance. A few
moments later, he stretched his left foot back and found
a third post to rest it on. The two poles his feet were on
were separated by maybe thirty inches. He rocked back in a
crouch and stood up on them. He stood there for a moment,
feeling the posts with his feet. They were hard and slightly
rough, but now his training with the petals came into play;
he had a sense of himself in space that didn't require his
eyes.

Wren knew in all likelihood he was going to fall from
his perch in some painfully clumsy fashion. But he'd take it
slowly. He took his clicker back out of his shirt pocket and
rocked to his right, got his balance, lifted his left foot. His
thigh muscles burned with the strain as he lowered himself
down, but he was able to stretch his left leg forward enough
to find the pole he'd had his hands on just moments before.
In his mind, he pictured what he could remember of the
posts' arrangement.

Left foot secure, he shifted forward to it, and then stepped
out, probing the darkness with his right. Wren found
another post, slipped his foot around on it to find the center
point, shifted his weight. Moving this way was brutal on
his muscles; not just his legs, but his whole body, it seemed.
Back, stomach, he'd never realized just how many muscles
it took to keep his balance. He was getting a complete lesson
on it now, though.

More importantly, Foe hadn't shot him yet. Wren found
his way to a pair of posts that were only a foot or so apart,
and he paused there, standing upright with a foot on each,
and listened intently. Still he could hear nothing but the
motion of the water. And even that seemed to be subsiding.

Wren determined to hold his position until he heard

Foe, or Foe shot him again. Three minutes, five, ten. It was always hard to judge time in absolute darkness, but Wren had no doubt this was the longest he'd ever gone without taking a hit from the old man.

And then, Wren thought he heard the slightest shift in the water, off to his left; a bare ripple. Maybe he'd imagined it, and it certainly wasn't enough for him to locate the source, but he turned and pointed his clicker in the direction anyway.

A moment later, the lights came up, dazzling. Wren squinted against the glare. Foe was standing about ten feet away and, much to Wren's surprise, Wren was pointing his clicker only about two inches too far to the right.

Foe just looked at him standing on top of the posts, and based on the stern expression on his face, Wren braced himself for a correction.

"What are you doing up there, boy?"

Wren crouched down and then hopped off the posts back into the water.

"It seemed like a good idea at the time," Wren answered.

"Because?"

"Because then I didn't have to worry about splashing when I walked," Wren said.

"Did Haiku tell you to do that?" Foe asked.

Wren shook his head. "No, sir."

Foe smiled. "Then perhaps you are ready to move on," he said.

Wren blinked at the statement. Move on? Had he just figured out what he was supposed to from the Waiting Room?

"We're done with the Waiting Room?"

"For today," Foe said. "Do not be anxious, boy. This room still has much to teach you. But you have done well. You have demonstrated a skill that is one of the most difficult to teach."

"Walking on poles in the dark?" Wren asked.

Foe rumbled with something between a cough and a

chuckle. "No, boy. Thinking sideways. Come along."

Wren had never heard the term before, and wasn't quite sure what Foe meant by it. They got out of the Waiting Room, dried off, and headed back upstairs. Foe allowed Wren to change into a dry shirt, and then took him into the room they used for their training in the digital. Wren couldn't help but feel disappointed. After his apparent success in the Waiting Room, he'd hoped that maybe he'd get to move on to some new level of training. Instead, it was back to the basics.

Wren took a seat on the floor, as he always did. A splotch of yellow in his periphery caught his attention. He glanced over. A set of shelves was attached to the wall and held all manner of equipment that Wren didn't recognize. On the bottom shelf, Haiku's ball was mostly hidden amongst some chunky devices.

Foe eased himself to the ground and sat crosslegged directly in front of Wren. He dipped his head forward in an easy nod. Signaling for Wren to begin.

Wren started as usual, by initiating a request for mutual connection, precisely the way Foe had shown him. They continued through the same basic processes of establishing the connection or refusing it, of redirecting it, shutting it down. Thankfully Wren got through all the steps without making any errors. He still hadn't been able to figure out why Foe was so insistent on doing things his particular way. The old man had shown him a different technique but the end result was always the same, regardless of whether Wren did it the way Foe taught him, or the way he'd always done it before.

"Good," Foe said. "Now. Tell me about your experience in the Waiting Room. What led you to use the posts in that manner?"

Wren shrugged. "It just kind of happened."

"No," Foe said. "It did not. Explain your thought process."

Wren thought back to the situation, tried to step outside the moment and work his way through it objectively.

"You had splashed the water in my face," he said, "and then when you turned the lights back on, you were farther away than I'd expected. It made me wonder how you could move so fast without splashing. I crouched down and had my hand on top of the post. I guess when I felt it, I realized it was big enough for me to stand on."

"And why did you not see this before?"

Wren wanted to give the quick answer, to say he didn't know, but he knew Foe preferred him to sit and consider, to spend time pondering, even if the answer was still going to be that he didn't know. He sat for a moment and asked himself the question again. Why *hadn't* he seen it before? What had it been about touching the top of the post in that particular moment that had changed his perspective on it? How had he thought of them before then?

He thought back to his first experience in the room, how he'd caught his foot on one and tripped. From then on, he'd looked at the poles as things to be avoided. Obstacles.

"I'd been looking at them wrong," Wren said.

"How?"

"When we first started, I thought I was supposed to be moving around them. And I didn't think about them again until just today."

"Could you walk through them?" Foe asked.

A bizarre question; Wren wasn't sure if Foe was actually expecting him to answer, but the old man waited, so Wren said, "No?"

"Then why did you say you were wrong about them?"

It took a moment for Wren to understand what Foe was saying.

"I guess I wasn't *wrong*," he answered. "I just hadn't recognized both ways to look at them."

Foe held up his finger, marking the distinction.

"The flexible mind," Foe said, "perceives what is possible, not what is expected. Even when what is expected comes from one's own preconceptions. A skill that can be developed, but one that I have found most difficult to teach."

"Thinking sideways?"

Foe nodded. "You have been frustrated with your training thus far. This portion in particular. Tell me why."

"I g..." Wren started, and then stopped himself. No *I think* or *I guess*; he was still trying to learn to stop qualifying his answers. If he didn't, Foe would remind him. "It's because I had different ways to do the same things, and it was hard to remember all your rules."

"Rules?" Foe said. "Were you able to achieve the same results through different means?"

"Yes," Wren said. Hadn't he just said that?

"If they were rules, how could you succeed without following them?"

Wren blinked back at the old man. Whenever Foe started peppering him with questions this way, Wren had learned it was more than just philosophical babble. It was his way of drawing understanding out. Another lesson within the lesson.

"They are not *rules*, boy," Foe continued. "If all I have taught you is *rules*, then I have failed you indeed. It is natural for people to desire them because it saves them from the hard work of properly judging their own actions. And they desire rulers because it saves them the hard work of ruling themselves. Mere rules are beneath us. Consider your oath. Are they rules?"

"No."

"Laws?"

"No."

"Then how can they govern your behavior?"

"Because..." Wren said. "Because they're... ideas of what's right?"

"Principles," Foe said. "We operate on principles, firm enough to provide guidance and structure, yet flexible enough to survive contact with reality. They can be applied to many situations, even those which we lack the capacity to imagine until they occur. Rules are rigid. And the real world is always a special case.

"Given that information and your success in the Waiting Room, perhaps now you have sufficient experience to understand why I have been so insistent on a particular methodology?"

Wren tried not to get too excited about Foe's use of the word *success*, even though it was the first time he'd heard the old man say it. Mentally he quickly rehearsed the steps that Foe had ingrained in him, looking for what it was he'd missed all along about them. But even with all the discussion of principles and flexibility, he couldn't quite see what the old man was getting at. It was all still just basic connectivity, broken down into... And then it opened to his mind, how Foe had segmented the process. What Wren had always considered one single act, he now saw in distinct phases. The same tools, from a different perspective.

"They're building blocks," Wren said. Foe dipped his head.

"When we first began, everything you did, you did by instinct. By feeling. By way of natural talent," Foe said. "You achieved results without understanding the mechanics of *how*. If you rely too heavily on feeling alone, it is difficult for the mind to perceive how else a technique may be employed. But now, boy... now we may begin."

A moment later a connection request came in. Wren accepted it. Foe sat up straighter, laid his hands palms-up on his knees, took a deep breath and exhaled. Wren did the same, as he'd been taught, tried to relax his shoulders and control his breathing.

"Now," Foe said, and he smiled. "Follow me."

Wren didn't understand what Foe meant but, as usual, it only took a few seconds for him to get practical experience; Foe's connection *slid*. It wasn't that he'd killed the signal or reflected it. It was still strong, but it felt like it was slipping away. Wren knew he was going to lose it and just before he did, it stabilized. Nothing he had done. Foe had backed off, given him a chance to catch up. But as soon as Wren had re-secured the connection, the same thing happened. He didn't know what to do; he'd never experienced anything like it before.

No, that wasn't true. He had, in Morningside. When he'd tried to connect to Underdown's machine remotely, and he'd needed Finn to help him. Wren tried to recall that moment, to draw up the image of what it was Finn had done... Too late; he lost his focus and the connection.

"Again," Foe said. They repeated the process; request, accept, follow. Wren felt the familiar frustration try to bubble up. He knew Foe could easily tell him or even show him what he was supposed to do. But now Wren was able to understand the sense of frustration, to acknowledge it and to accept it. Embrace it, even. He understood now, really understood.

If Foe had just told him about walking on top of the posts in the Waiting Room, he would have missed so much of what mattered in that lesson. Haiku's words came back to him, about not confusing the method of learning for the skill. Discovering the solution on his own was far more powerful than having it shown to him. He'd truly learned the lesson, at the deepest level.

And even when Foe's connection escaped him again, and Foe restarted, Wren was able to let himself settle into the moment, to let the frustration propel him towards the solution rather than thrash against the situation. Foe kept him at it for hours, and what Wren had previously considered the easiest, if most tedious, part of his training took on a new, far more severe character. Previous sessions had been shorter and much less intense. Though he'd always been physically weary when he'd undertaken them, he hadn't had to deal with mental exhaustion on top of it.

That was rapidly changing. The amount of sustained focus and mental effort it required to chase Foe's signal made Wren's mind feel like it was twisting in strange ways and drained him faster than he'd thought possible. By the end of the time, Wren had only managed to capture the signal a handful of times, and only briefly. And he hadn't been successful at all in the last hour.

"Good," Foe said. "Enough for today."

Wren was pretty sure enough had been a couple of hours before, but he was grateful for the reprieve. Foe led him back to the parlor where they took a small meal together with Haiku. Between the lack of sleep and the brain-melting training he'd just been through, Wren could barely follow a conversation, let alone participate in one. Just before Foe took him to his next lesson, though, he did manage to remember one thing.

"On the shelves," he said to Haiku. "Hidden on the bottom one." Haiku smiled at him.

"Tomorrow," he said, "we will make it a little more challenging."

Wren nodded, hardly comprehending the words. He followed Foe out and up the stairs. When they reached the top of the second flight and Foe turned on the landing, Wren's heart fell. This meant the game with the petals. He was so tired, reality had lag. There was no way he was going to be able to handle the petals today. It took every ounce of his will just to stand on the mat and not break down into tears. And then it began.

To Wren's surprise, after the first few minutes he found that rather than overwhelming him, the gentle fall of the petals began to soothe his frazzled mind. Though the exercise required focus, it was of a different kind; passive, expansive. It almost felt like it carried him outside himself.

"Missed one," Foe said. He walked in his usual slow circle around Wren, occasionally changing directions, rarely stopping. Somehow he seemed to know exactly when stopping would be most disruptive, when Wren was counting on him to continue his movement a particular direction, or was anticipating a change.

Wren reached out for a red petal and Foe, standing off to his side, moved as if to grab Wren's wrist. Wren didn't even think. One hand flashed out on its own and deflected Foe's attack, while the other secured the petal. Wren tucked the petal in his pocket, mildly pleased with himself.

"Still wasting too much energy, boy," Foe said.

Wren snorted a chuckle. He didn't have any energy left to waste or to use otherwise. Faster than Wren had ever seen him move, Foe whipped his fist straight out towards Wren's face, too fast to dodge, almost too fast to see. Wren barely had time to tense up and squeeze his eyes shut before the impact... except there was no impact, only a breeze from the strike. Wren opened his eyes to see Foe's knuckles a half-inch from his nose. Foe didn't take his arm back or lower it. Just let it hang there. Wren glanced from the fist up to the old man's eyes. The look on his face was one of his subtle hints that a clue had just been given.

"Missed one," he said. And then he lowered his arm. "Why did you tense?"

Even though Foe had asked a question, Wren knew he was still supposed to be catching red petals. He continued as best he could.

"Because I thought you were going to hit me," he answered.

"Mm," Foe said. He started walking his slow circle again. Wren had learned to read that reaction. The question, his answer, Foe's odd all-purpose *mm*. Taken all together, that meant he was wandering around close to a discovery. This use of energy was the issue Foe had commented on the most over the past week. Wren replayed his own words; *because I thought you were going to hit me*. He *thought* Foe was going to hit him. And the first time Foe had mentioned it, hadn't he feinted as though he was going to shove Wren? That was it. He felt it snap into place, felt the mild burst of relief of a difficult problem solved.

"I *thought* you were going to hit me," Wren repeated. "But you weren't. And if I had known you weren't going to hit me, I wouldn't have flinched. I'm wasting energy reacting to attacks that won't actually hurt me."

Foe didn't make any comment, didn't even acknowledge that Wren had spoken. He just continued around in his circle. Wren waited for confirmation. The longer he waited, the less confident he felt. Doubt crept in.

"Is that right?" he asked.

"Missed one," Foe said.

"Foe, is that right? Is that what you meant about wasting energy?"

"What do you think?"

Wren caught a red petal, tucked it into his pocket.

"I thought it was."

"But you do not now?"

"I'm not sure."

"Why not?"

"Because you're not acting like it's the right answer."

"Mm."

Wren shook his head, made a grab for a red petal that was passing his knee. How many lessons was he supposed to be learning? He was having trouble keeping all the threads separate in his mind. But no, he was sure of it. The pieces fit together too cleanly. Maybe there was some other hidden aspect to it, but Wren felt certain he at least had gotten part of the answer.

"Yes," he said. "I'm right."

"Then why did you ask me?"

"Just to be sure."

Foe held up a finger, the way he did whenever he wanted to draw attention to something Wren had just said.

"In the Waiting Room," he said, "how many times have you successfully struck me with your clicker?"

Wren didn't have to think about that long at all.

"None."

"How do you know?"

Wren started to say because Foe had never reacted to being hit, but he caught himself. Hadn't he managed to control his reaction to being stung? Surely if he could do it, the old man was far more capable of the same. He didn't quite know where Foe was leading him yet, but he felt the connection between the two lines of thinking. And then he had another thought.

"Actually I've done it a bunch of times," Wren said. "So many times I lost count."

Foe made his little rumbling chuckle.

"Good," he said. "Very good. Though if you cannot count beyond six, I have more work ahead than I supposed."

"I've hit you six times?" Wren asked, surprised. He couldn't help but wonder when and how he'd managed to score any hits at all.

"Not according to you," Foe said with a smile. "But how can I prove otherwise? Missed one."

He feinted as if he were going to shove Wren, but Wren saw it now, saw Foe's posture and his foot position, knew there would be no force behind it. Wren ignored the motion and caught another petal.

"What is your foundation?" Foe asked.

"Truth," Wren responded without even thinking about it.

"Why?"

"Because with clarity, I see that which is."

Foe nodded. And then he lunged at Wren. Instinctively Wren swept his arms up, twisted, deflected the attack and redirected its energy. Wren kept his place in the circle, and even managed to catch another petal after Foe moved away.

"Did I succeed?" Foe asked.

"No."

"Are you certain?"

"Yes."

"How do you know?"

"Because you didn't knock me out of the circle."

"And why do you believe that was my aim?" Foe asked, and as he did he held out his hand, open, palm up. On it were a few crumpled red petals. At first Wren thought the old man had managed to catch several at once, but then he realized the more likely case. He jammed his hand in his pocket. The petals he'd captured were all gone.

"You took all my petals," Wren said.

"Yes."

"You distracted me with the shove, so you could get them," Wren said.

"Well, no," Foe said. "I wanted to shove you out of the circle, but you prevented it." And then he smiled. "Appearing to get what you want can be almost as powerful as getting what you want."

Foe switched off the machine and watched as the last flurry of petals drifted to the ground. Once they had settled, he continued.

"Deception, like violence, is a tool. Your enemy will use it, if you allow him to. When properly applied, it can be of great use. When your enemy succeeds, deny him a sign of his success and you sow doubt. When you fail, behave as if you have succeeded and you sow panic."

Wren nodded. Foe had just taught him several lessons all at once, in one continuous stream, something he'd never done before. And yet Wren understood each, how they were different and yet related. The principles that underscored each.

"Truth is your foundation. Perceiving that which *is*, is critical to your success," Foe said.

"I understand," Wren said. Foe dipped his head, and then whipped his hand out again. It struck Wren on the cheekbone, a sharp rap of knuckle against bone. The blow wasn't severe; Foe had obviously held back. Still, Wren was completely startled by the fact that Foe had actually struck him.

"Mm," Foe said.

"You've never actually *hit* me before," Wren said, touching the place on his cheek. And as he said it, he realized he'd just told him why he'd allowed it to happen. Because Foe had never struck him, he had assumed like all the others that blow too would stop short. He'd seen what was expected, rather than what was possible. "I get it," he said. "I understand."

"Mm," Foe said again. And he switched the machine back on.

Maybe it was because of all Wren had absorbed that day, or maybe it was because of the success he'd had in the Waiting Room. Whatever the case, he felt a shift in his perspective. His training wasn't fun, or easy, or painless. But the suffering took on a new dimension. It was for a purpose. Haiku had tried to explain it to him before, but Wren hadn't been able to understand. He'd lacked the experience to truly comprehend what Haiku had meant. But now he saw. The training was efficient, and effective, and it was building him into something he never could have been otherwise. The adversity became to him then not a thing to be resisted or escaped, but one to be embraced. Foe had said his teaching would be as fire to the flesh, and that image now had its full significance revealed to Wren's mind and, more importantly, heart. It was a fire, yes, but not one that consumed and destroyed. It was a refining fire, the fire of the forge. Shaping him into an instrument of purpose.

Though he didn't recognize it until much later, that realization was the turning point in Wren's instruction. Even after that day drew to an eventual close and bled into the next, the new outlook didn't wear off. Rather than seeing his time in a particular chamber all as one event to be endured, each individual repetition became an opportunity to practice a specific skill. He no longer sought Foe's approval or Haiku's commendations to gauge his success. His heart told him when he had executed what he had intended, and when he had not.

He even began to make a conscious effort to prevent his thoughts from lingering on the past, on how things had been or how he wished they would be. He took control of his interior life, and whenever he caught himself feeling apprehensive about what lay ahead for him, either tomorrow's pain or his eventual confrontation with Asher, he recalled himself to the moment, focused his mind on whatever was immediately before him, whether rest or work, comfort or pain. Sleep came more readily, less plagued by anxiety of how little time he had until he had to wake again. When he was exhausted and hurt and at the end of all his strength, Wren allowed his world to shrink down to that one minute, that one breath, and committed himself to finding his way to the end of that moment, and that moment alone.

The more he succeeded, the more Foe and Haiku increased the intensity of his training. Even on his days of rest, when Foe took him up to the top of the tower and had him arrange flowers, the complexity of the arrangements increased exponentially, Foe's critique of his ability heightened. Though he couldn't be sure, on a few occasions Wren suspected they'd even pushed him as much as two or maybe even three days without allowing him to sleep.

"You will come to the end of your strength, boy," Foe told him. "And beyond it there lies only the will. Many claim to possess the will to prevail; few demonstrate the resolve necessary to prepare to do so."

Much as Wren had experienced on his initial journey with Haiku, his mind proved that it could drive the body far beyond its perceived limits. And as he devoted himself to the process, Foe and Haiku poured themselves into him. Through it all, as much as he learned about the world of House Eight and how to operate within it, he learned even more about himself.

Wren's lean childhood had built a foundation; though one for which he could not be truly thankful, he nevertheless grew to appreciate it. Cold, hunger, fear, pain, exhaustion – these were not new horrors to him, but old ghosts returned to haunt him. At least three of them visited him each day. Often all five. In his previous life, these sufferings had been a thing to escape if possible, or to endure if not. But under Foe's teaching, they became merely information; recognized by his mind, acknowledged, evaluated for relevance. The cold. Was he becoming hypothermic, or was he merely uncomfortable? The pain in his shoulder. Muscular? Was there any significant injury? Would it limit mobility? If so, to what degree? Hunger expanded into many categories. Hunger for protein distinguished itself from hunger for carbohydrates. Beyond that, though Wren couldn't necessarily identify the exact nutrients his body was demanding, he developed enough sensitivity to his body's needs that cravings no longer took his tastebuds into account. Food became fuel.

But the greatest change was a secret growth; a change so gradual the full measure of it escaped Wren's notice or regard. Yet true growth it was. A patient cunning. An awareness. Haiku expanded his game beyond the small yellow ball. Each morning he would show Wren a set of items, sometimes two, sometimes as many as five. And when Wren was routinely able to identify each, Haiku took to showing him the items at the end of the day, to see if Wren could recall having seen any of them during his training, and if so, where he'd seen them. To Wren's amazement, he discovered that sometimes, somehow, he could. And each day it became easier.

Wren had ceased to try to measure time but over the course of days, or more likely weeks, Foe gradually opened his world back up to him a grid at a time, enabling Wren to expand his reach. And with that slow reintroduction to the density of connection in the world, Wren found he had developed an entirely new perspective on all that was available to him. What before had been a single mass of electromagnetic noise he now saw as an intricately woven network of signals; as if he were seeing not only the painting, but also seeing the brush strokes and fibers of material that comprised it.

Nights that he was forced to sleep outside became increasingly frequent, and familiarity with the dead city eventually drained those dark hours of their capacity to fill him with dread. He never quite gained a sense of peace out amongst the Weir, but his confidence grew sufficiently to enable him to manage his anxiousness.

Whenever Wren began to feel like he had gained some level of mastery, Foe would throw in a new twist, would challenge him in some unexpected way. The old man combined training sessions, forcing Wren to face off against him in the Waiting Room while simultaneously trying to capture his signal, or to escape his attempt to capture Wren's while Wren caught petals.

Sometimes in the midst of a training session through the digital, Foe would insist on Wren doing extensive calisthenics; pushups or handstands or squats and any other number of unusual exercises that kept him shaky, out of breath, and dizzy with effort.

It was during one such session that Foe opened Wren's eyes to just how great the challenge ahead of him was, and just how dangerous. Everything had been going as expected up to that point, which should have served as a warning to Wren in and of itself. He'd become quite adept at capturing Foe's signal and maintaining it no matter what Foe did to escape him. Or so he'd come to believe.

Foe shifted his signal around, attempted to withdraw it or to actively resist Wren's signal. But Wren had developed a sensitivity to the processes, an almost physical sensation of pressure and balance that warned him when a change was coming. An instant before it occurred, Wren correctly anticipated the transition; Foe's signal gained strength, threatened to flood Wren's processes and overwhelm them, but Wren was ready. He applied the correct counter, boosted his own output to match and stabilize. But this time, Foe's signal continued to grow, to press back against him. Wren ran through different protocols in a matter of seconds, attempting to bleed off some of the strength of Foe's attack, or to redirect. When none of that worked, he tried to kill the connection. Even that was impossible; any process Wren executed to sever the connection was intercepted by one of Foe's, counteracted. It felt almost as though Foe had seized Wren by the wrist and lifted him off the ground. No matter how Wren kicked or swung or struggled, he couldn't find any footing from which to launch an attack. And the pressure from Foe's signal continued to grow.

Wren was out of ideas, had reached the end of what his training had taught him. He could feel himself starting to come apart. Foe was penetrating all his defenses. He was reaching directly into Wren's mind. Wren knew the old man wasn't going to harm him, but natural instinct and honed determination refused to let him accept defeat. Hoping to catch his instructor off guard, Wren dug deep and broadcast. The eruption of energy slammed into Foe's signal, halted its advance. And though Wren thought for certain that his mind would tear in two with the exertion, he boosted his own signal even further, to a greater intensity than he'd even known was possible.

Foe's signal was turned back. Repelled.

And in the next instant, it gave way, and Wren felt himself falling forward, racing into the void where Foe had just been. Before he could stop himself, he slipped into some new plane, dense with connections, and processes that raced like lightning flashes. Floating. He'd seen something like this before, when he'd faced his brother through Underdown's machine. He had pierced through the digital interface and slipped deeper. He was seeing thought. Consciousness. Foe's mind. And Wren realized he no longer knew how to withdraw from it. He felt his sense of self slipping away. The sensation was like being out of breath and deep under water. He could perceive the way of escape, shimmering in the distance, but though nothing restrained him, Wren knew he was too far away to reach it before he lost himself completely.

And then, a shock of force, like someone had grabbed him from behind and snatched him violently backwards. The connection snapped shut. Wren was himself once more, seated crosslegged in front of his teacher. His whole body ached from the strain.

"Careful, boy," Foe said. "The mind is fathomless. If you overextend, you may well lose yourself forever."

"You let me in on purpose," Wren said. "I overcommitted."

Foe nodded.

"What would have happened if you hadn't pulled me back out?" Wren asked.

"What is the body without the mind?" Foe said. Wren sat quietly for a moment, absorbing the implication.

"I could have died?"

"Meeting power with power is a dangerous tactic," Foe said.

"I didn't know what else to do," Wren replied. "You haven't shown me how to deal with... whatever you did."

"Have I not?" Foe asked, and though his expression didn't change, there came a glint in his eye. An invitation to reconsider. But even though Wren thought about it for a full minute, he couldn't recall anything Foe had taught him that would have applied to the situation he'd just experienced. He was just about to open his mouth to say so when it came back to him in a flash. The first time he'd broadcasted, when Foe had been evaluating him.

"You demonstrated it," Wren said finally. "But you didn't teach me how you did it."

"Mm," Foe said.

An invitation to consider further. Wren tried to recall the circumstances. He'd broadcast, and as he'd done so, he'd felt tremendous pain. The more he'd boosted his signal, the worse it had become.

"A feedback loop," Wren said. "You fed my own signal back to me."

"Show me," Foe said. And he launched the attack again. It caught Wren by surprise, and out of reflex he tried to resist the signal by matching its intensity. He knew it wasn't the right solution, but he just needed a little time and space. And almost without consciously trying, his mind assembled the right protocol: a combination of Foe's basic building blocks, initiating a connection and redirecting Foe's signal back into itself. Immediately the pressure dissipated. Wren could still sense Foe's signal, still attach to it, but now it wasn't something to war against. The connection dropped.

"Good," Foe said. "Your enemy may come against you

with such force. If such an attack comes, it is best not to be in its path. But should you find it unavoidable, such a technique may spare you."

"Could it kill him?" Wren asked.

"Kill him?" Foe repeated. He paused and sat in thought for a moment. "I suppose theoretically it would be possible. If your enemy is blind to the nature of the technique and also foolish enough to persist in his attack. It would take a tremendous amount of output, though. On a scale that in all my long years I have yet to witness."

Foe continued to look at Wren for a moment, and then took a deep breath and exhaled.

"That is enough for today," he said. He got to his feet. Wren followed him out and they made their way to the parlor, where Haiku was preparing a meal. The sun was already down, but the night was still young. Wren was allowed to rest for a full twenty minutes before they sat down to eat together. During that time, he reflected on what Foe had told him about the feedback loop. Asher was no fool, certainly, but Wren didn't believe he needed to be. There was a chance that Wren might be able to disguise the feedback loop as some kind of direct challenge, mask it so it appeared that the signal was Wren's, rather than Asher's own. Foe had said it would take a tremendous amount of output. Well Wren had faced Asher, and he knew what he was capable of. Asher was, in fact, probably even stronger now than he'd been when they'd last fought each other. If only there were a way that Wren could be sure.

"I was thinking," Wren said, when they were all seated around the table. "About the feedback loop. Before I have to face Asher, is there a way I could test it on him?"

Foe stopped just before putting a bite in his mouth. "No!" he said, and his word was so forceful that Wren flinched. "No, boy. Testing is a fine way to introduce your techniques to your enemy without harming him. More often than not, you will teach him what to look for and how to defeat it. Whatever you do, commit yourself fully to it, so that you only have to do it once." He put the bite of food in his mouth, chewed it quickly, and then added, "When you decide to kill the king, kill the king. Don't slap him first."

"Well, I don't know if the loop is going to work. How do you think I should... defeat Asher?"

"In the most effective manner possible," Foe said. Wren made a face at the non-answer. Foe responded to it. "Boy, surely by now you understand all of this training has been precisely because we don't know what you will face when next you meet your adversary?"

"I do," Wren said. "I would just feel better if I had some idea of a plan before I had to do it."

"A plan is a fine thing to have," Foe said. "As long as it is flexible enough to be applied to the real situation. Too often a plan is nothing more than a preconception that prevents clear vision. It fixes the mind on what is desired, not on what is. Whatever the distance between what you *want* to happen and what is *actually* happening, that is enemy territory. How much territory would you like to cede to your enemy?"

"None at all," Wren said.

"Then be careful how you plan."

They ate in silence for a few moments, before Haiku spoke.

"When Asher controls the Weir," Haiku said. "Is he... *in* them?"

"I'm not sure," Wren said. "But I don't think so. I think he... It's more like he directs them, I guess. Like he tells them what to do."

"Hmm," Haiku said.

"Why?" Wren asked. "What were you thinking?"

"It is not, perhaps, an elegant solution," Haiku said. "But I wondered if you could draw him into a physical being. Trap him there."

"I wouldn't know how," Wren said.

"Mm," Foe said. But the tone was different than usual; not his signal that Wren had overlooked something. Rather, as if he was considering. "In your accounting, you said your brother used a Weir as a spokesman. Painter, I believe you called him?"

Wren was shocked to hear the name leave Foe's mouth. As far as he could remember, he'd only mentioned it in passing, back when he'd first recounted the fate of Morningside, before Foe had even agreed to train him. Was there anything the old man couldn't recall?

"Is that accurate?" Foe asked, prompting Wren.

"Yes," Wren said. "Painter."

"A Weir using language would require much more than casual control."

"Painter isn't a Weir," Wren admitted. "He's Awakened." Foe sat quietly, looking at him for a moment. "He was my friend," Wren added, mostly to himself.

"Mm," Foe said. "Perhaps that is even better. If Asher uses him in such a manner, his presence must be strong indeed."

"So, you think if I can find Painter, and get Asher to... possess him, or whatever?"

"You will have to prevent him from severing the connection," Foe said. "Once it is established."

"And then...?" Wren knew where this was going now, but he hoped he was overlooking something.

"*Then*, boy," Foe said. "You kill him."

And so here it was, then. Everything Wren had tried to ignore, everything he had tried to leave unconsidered, was laid before him. The inevitable outcome.

But he remembered Foe's words, about taking life feeling like a violation of his nature. He was right to react this way. And he remembered Three's words from long ago. When he'd first trained Wren with a knife. The image broke clear in his mind's eye.

I don't like it when people get hurt, Wren had said.

Hey. Hey, look at me, Three had answered.

That's good. That's really. Good. OK?

Wren could still hear his voice. But the words meant so

much more to him now than they ever had before. And Wren realized then that his training in House Eight's ways hadn't started with Foe, or even with Haiku. It had started long before, all that time ago, with Three. *Life, my charge,* Wren thought. As it had been Three's. Tears came to his eyes, welled up from within him, but not from grief. From gratitude. And from an overwhelming sense of belonging. Three was gone, nothing was going to change that, ever. But Wren shared Three's life now, shared experiences, understood on a far deeper level than he'd imagined possible who Three had been, and why. And though he missed Three with all his heart, he couldn't help but feel something of the man had transferred to him. Maybe the best parts of who he'd been.

"Do you have any weapons?" Haiku asked.

"A few," Foe said. "We will have to find what suits."

"I have one," Wren said. "I have the one I need."

At Foe's prompting, Wren returned to his room, and withdrew it from his pack. Three's pistol. It had always seemed a dangerous thing to him before, a wild thing not to be trusted or carelessly handled. Now, he carried it reverently, a sacred instrument, an ancient weapon of legacy.

Wren laid the gun on the table, and the shells beside it. For a moment, no one said anything. Then, Haiku broke the silence.

"Well," he said. "Three never did much like to have to shoot anything more than once."

"Have you used it before, boy?" Foe asked.

Wren shook his head.

"Then perhaps we should find something more suitable–" Foe said.

"No," Wren said, interrupting. "No, Foe. This is the right one."

Foe looked to Haiku, who nodded in return.

"Come with me, Wren," Haiku said. "Bring the weapon."

TWENTY-NINE

Cass had become a ghost, haunting a necropolis. For weeks she wandered the sprawling boneyard east of the Strand, endlessly cycling between the roles of hunter and hunted. The day after she'd left Orrin behind, she'd thought she had escaped the Weir completely. That night, however, had proved her wrong. They hadn't tracked her as aggressively as before, not as though they knew exactly where she was, or were following a clear trail. But there was no doubt they were still searching for her. For several days, she'd tried different tactics, sometimes ambushing, sometimes avoiding. She even traveled from sunup to sundown to gain as much distance as she could, and though that did seem to buy her a few hours, inevitably the Weir would increase in number before dawn. No matter what she did, she couldn't seem to get clear.

And it was obvious that it had been no coincidence. These weren't the few roving Weir that commonly wandered the night. The numbers were too great, too consistent. They were searching for her. Asher was searching for her.

On the one hand, it was exactly what she had been hoping for. Asher had no reason to believe Wren was anywhere besides with her. As long as he was spending his effort on locating her, Wren was safe in Greenstone. Safer now, maybe, than he'd ever been, assuming Gamble and her team had made it there. And she was certain they had.

On the other hand, she had underestimated just how difficult it was going to be to find the physical location of the node. And there was an added complication that revealed itself after the first few days of wandering. Every time she entered that unseen world, each time she attached to the Weir's datastream to find the nearest node, she was leaving something of herself behind. She could feel it. Filaments of signal clinging like tendrils, or webs of smoke. It was how they were tracking her. How they knew where to move next. Cass had figured out how to disconnect them, but they seemed more resilient each time, more numerous. As a result, she tried to minimize how often she connected, and she was careful only to access the digital in the early part of the day, hoping that whatever trail she was creating would grow cold and confused over the hours before nightfall.

But after the first week, she realized that there was more going on. Even when she didn't connect at all, those digital threads crept up on her. Whatever process she had begun wasn't one she could stop. And it was accelerating. They were trying to reintegrate her. Her fear was that she was once again racing against time; that Asher was actively seeking to reclaim her before she could reach her goal. It drove her, made her angry at each new delay, threatened to make her impatient.

Cass had been here before, though. It wasn't exactly the same, of course, but nor was it entirely different from what she'd faced with her addiction to quint – when her body had burned itself out, and yet demanded more of the poison that was consuming it. An ever-growing, ever-accelerating demand that she'd known she couldn't sustain. Here, now, though, she could at least actively combat it. She would do so for as long as she had strength; and probably well beyond.

Ranging through the wastes revealed just how widespread Asher's ruin had become. Though Cass mostly tried to avoid settlements if she came across them, every once in a while, when her supplies were running low, she had no choice but to enter. She'd scavenged from three separate outposts, none of which had any people left at all. Whether they'd fled or been carried off, Cass didn't know. The signs were similar either way. People were gone, and they'd gone in a hurry.

At least she had discovered no ·more monuments of the dead. She guessed that had been a special desecration reserved for Morningside. Asher's godly wrath poured out on the city that had defied him. A city whose greatest sin was to elevate Wren to a seat of power. She'd taken what she needed, and moved on as quickly as she could, back out into the wastelands.

Out there in the open on her own there was no one else to worry about, no one to distract her from herself, no noise to cover over the storm that raged inside her. She hadn't even realized just how much chaos there was in her heart and mind until she was forced to spend so much time alone. As she wandered the broken world, Cass began to make discoveries about herself.

The first started with an obvious observation: she missed her youngest son. She missed him deeply, with a dull ache that lived like ice in the center of her heart. But as much as she thought about him and wondered about him, she noticed her feelings had taken on a different dimension. She missed him, but she didn't long for him the way she once had. She didn't feel that blood-deep *need* for him. The need to have him close by, to have him in her view. Under her control.

She wrestled with the implication. From the day of his birth, Wren had become her primary concern, to the expense of all else. Everything she'd done, she had done for him. To protect him, to care for him, to do what she believed was best for *him*. She had never before recognized how much of herself she had poured into her role as his mother. How much of her identity she had placed there. Now, with the separation, forced to live life on her own terms and hers alone, she discovered just how much she had needed him to be that little boy. How much she had required him to need her, how jealous she had been whenever he'd started to pull away.

The decision to send him to Greenstone while she stayed behind had seemed like an impulse decision, one made in the heat of the moment, when running back into the fire to pull out whoever she could felt like the only real choice she'd had. Later, it had begun to seem like a mistake.

Now Cass wondered if there had been more to it. If something in her subconscious had recognized her need to let go, lest she lose herself completely. She felt vaguely guilty, then, as if what she'd thought of as perhaps the most noble gesture of her life had in fact been selfish. Or perhaps she felt guilty that she didn't feel more guilty. As much as she missed her son, if she was honest with herself, she was actually enjoying the distance. Having been robbed of the power to do anything for him, by her own hand no less, she felt free for... perhaps for the first time ever.

She would never reveal the thought to Wren of course, would never speak of it to anyone, even if she had the opportunity. Which she wasn't counting on. The thing that had torn at her most was that Wren had gone so long thinking she was dead. But surely Gamble had communicated the news to him, and though he might have been upset at her absence, at least he knew she was alive. Or, had been when Gamble had last seen her. It would give him hope. And Cass decided then, at the very end, if it came, when it came, that she would risk a message to Gamble. She would send final word of her death, a final goodbye, so that Wren wouldn't go through life wondering.

She cried a little when she thought of that moment, when she thought of her son facing another death. Her death, again. But he had proved himself resilient beyond all her imagining, and he was amongst family now. jCharles and Mol, Able, Mouse, Gamble, all of them... they'd look after him as their own. Cass realized just how blessed she'd been to have found such people. How undeserved those relationships were, and how rich. The thought led her inevitably to Three. The first one in her life to look at her not as something to be taken from, but as someone worth giving to.

And she wept for him again. For the gift he'd given her, and for how he'd been rewarded. The weight bore down on her then, a weight she had never been able to let herself accept or acknowledge. A weight that had been hanging over her ever since she'd met the man Chapel. A truth she had been running from.

All of this could have been avoided. All of it.

If she'd been stronger, somehow. Like Chapel. Chapel had freed himself from the chains of the Weir. Maybe if she had fought harder, if she had been faster, or smarter, and had broken her own bonds, she could have ended Asher's life then and there. A simple swipe of the hand and she could have wiped him from the world. Asher would be gone. And Three would still be alive.

And beyond that, she'd given birth to Asher. Raised Asher. How many ways had she gone wrong to unleash such a man on the world?

That was the darkest time for her, then, confronting that reality. The guilt haunted her for three days and nights, hung on her and pulled at her, whispered to her that she should allow herself to succumb to the process of reintegration. That she deserved it. That it was justice.

And in a way, it was wrestling with those dark thoughts that opened her eyes to what she'd really been seeking out here in the open. The node was her goal, yes, her target. But it was her own judgment she was after. A chance to face the consequences of all her failures. She'd managed to escape them until now. But now, she was looking for that place where she could come face to face with them, and accept her doom. It was what she deserved.

She almost believed it.

Almost.

But in the midst of that turmoil, her thoughts broke open. Memories stirred that she had long suppressed.

Memories of Asher as a boy, a young boy. Of how she had loved him, and how she had fought for him. How she had done as much to protect him as she had for Wren. And how he had ultimately rejected her. How he had resisted her pleas, had struggled against her. She had poured herself out for him, and in response he had denied her.

She let go then, let go of a deep-seated grief she hadn't even known she was harboring. A grief for the little boy she had lost long ago. And more significantly, she let go of the idea that the consequences of his actions were *her* fault. It was another aspect of her desire for control, and now that it had been revealed to her, it was almost embarrassing to consider, as though she alone were powerful enough to shape the course the world took. As though her actions, her successes or her mistakes, were all that mattered in the determination of the future's outcome. Even if she could change one thing about the past, that was no guarantee that anything that followed would match her vision of what might have been.

Asher, and Asher alone, was responsible for his actions.

Three's death wasn't her fault. It was a choice he had made. And not a coward's choice, not an easy escape from the suffering of the world; he had given his life to hold true to himself.

After that days-long process of coming face-to-face with herself and confronting her own demons, Cass emerged transformed. Whatever she had thought she'd been looking for out there on her own, she knew now she'd found what she'd needed. What she had truly needed.

And her objective transformed as well. She wasn't out here searching for death. She was fighting for life, both for her own and for those she loved. She didn't fear death, if that's what she was facing, but neither did she accept it or embrace it. It took patience and courage to be willing to suffer. She had both. The image of that lone star, shining in all its brilliance even amidst the empty blackness of the night sky came back to her then, and gave her strength.

In that new strength, Cass devised a different approach. Rather than trying her usual direct method, she embraced the slow advance; she began to circle the node. To stalk it. If Asher were analyzing her pattern of movement, she knew it might be possible that he would discover her intent. But she also knew her son. He most likely wouldn't give her the credit of having a plan, and would instead assume he was driving her in a panicked spiral. It occurred to her that such an assumption would work to her advantage; the more Asher thought he was in control of the situation, the more likely he was to let it linger, to toy with her.

It took several days but the new pattern paid off, and enabled her to spend even less time connected to the Weir's stream. The search had led her west; a few times she even lapsed over into the fringe of the Strand. Gradually the distance closed, her loops shrank.

And then one morning, she found it.

Or, rather, she found where it was buried. She stood on a dust-coated street a mile or two from the border of the Strand. Based on everything she could discern, she was standing right on top of whatever it was that was creating the node. But it was underneath her. Way, way, underneath her.

For an hour she searched for some tunnel or access to no avail. And then, just as she was sitting down to take a break, she saw an unassuming cinder-block shelter with a heavy steel door. It was barely seven feet tall and almost a perfect square, four feet to a side, with a slanted roof. A chainlink fence surrounded it, topped with razor wire. Behind it, a slender pole stretched up thirty feet into the air. There may have been a light on top of it, though it was impossible to see in the daytime.

It was the razor wire that caught Cass's attention. The little building was too small to hold anything particularly valuable. And the fence itself only protected a patch of ground that was maybe ten by ten feet. She approached the gate of the fence and found that it was unlocked.

The steel door of the shelter too wasn't secured. She pulled it open, and the hinges squealed as they awoke to their long-forgotten purpose. The only thing the building contained was a damp, cool darkness. No, there was more. Stairs. Concrete stairs leading down into the emptiness.

Cass stood at the door for a few minutes, sipping water and taking some food. She wasn't particularly hungry, but she wasn't quite ready to see where those stairs led, either. The last time she had seen a place like that had been a storm water system. The memories it stirred weren't pleasant.

Still. She was a different woman than she'd been back then. A new creation. Darkness held no power over her now. It was just the fear of the unknown that was resisting her now, and the easiest way to slay that beast was to gain its knowledge. She capped her water and started her descent.

The walls of the stairwell were smooth concrete, as were the stairs themselves. A sturdy railing separated one half-flight of stairs from its counterpart further below. Cass leaned over the rail and looked down into that depthless blackness. It was like staring down into a chimney, or a fathomless tomb. Concrete as far down as she could see, stairs winding around and around on themselves. As much as she dreaded the walk down, she despised the thought of the walk back up.

Even though she had no problem seeing in the total darkness, Cass took it slow, careful of her steps, minimizing her noise level. She counted flights as she descended, but lost track somewhere in the sixties. It was around that time that she became aware of a faint hum, one that at first she couldn't be sure she was actually hearing. Trying to determine its source was what caused her to lose her count of the stairs, but she made a best guess and continued on. Sometime later as she approached the bottom, she was in the low one hundreds, give or take a few. The count might not have been perfectly accurate, but it was close enough to make the point. Cass was deep, deep underground. A thousand feet or more, by her estimate. Though marginally warmer than the temperature above ground, it was still surprisingly cool and here the air was very dry. The hum had grown quite distinct; a resonant drone, mildly soothing. And Cass knew she was reaching the end because she could see a doorframe outlined in a moonlight blue. Her first instinct was to freeze, fearing that she was seeing the light from a Weir. But after a few moments she realized something else was shining mutedly below her.

Cass followed the final set of stairs, and stepped up to the sliding door. It beeped and clicked, and opened to a small chamber. There was another door at the other end, and when she went to it, it behaved exactly as the first. When it opened, however, Cass stepped out and then stopped short.

Whatever she'd been expecting, this wasn't it.

The chamber opened out to a cavernous room, with a ceiling that stretched easily twenty-five feet above her. It was hung with an enormous steel grid laden with huge stacks of pipes. No, not pipes. Bundles of cables. The room was filled with rows of machines, laid out in uniform aisles. Stacks and stacks, for dozens of yards in both directions. Each one hummed softly, but taken all together in that huge room they joined in a droning chorus that filled the emptiness. And each had a tiny light of familiar hue, undoubtedly reporting its status. Cass walked among them as if in a dream, awed by the immensity of the system, and by its perfect order. This was surely a relic of the old world, something left by the people lost to time. And yet, though its creators were dust and ash, this technology remained. More than remained. Persisted. It continued on in its purpose. And Cass knew that purpose.

This was the mind of the Weir. Or, at least, a single node of it. She wondered how many of them there were, how far their reach extended. As she explored them, her vision of the node through the digital came back to her. The Weir's datastream had been connected to it, it was true. But hadn't there been more? Now that she thought of it, she remembered the swirl. Yes, the Weir, but other signals as well, individual strands rather than the complicated churning mass of the Weir's collective stream. Not just the mind of the Weir, then. Was the node also responsible for her own connection? For the connection of everyone else out there who relied on it?

And how was it still functioning so well after all this time? There was hardly any dust to be seen, the air was cool and dry. The environment was well-controlled to protect the machines. But it seemed unlikely that it could have been designed so well as to remain in such pristine condition for who knew how many decades.

Cass moved further into the facility and made yet another astonishing discovery. In the midst of the aisles of smaller machines was an open space, a miniature courtyard of sorts. And in the center of that space sat a single, massive machine. Ten feet tall at least, and twice as wide. The most striking thing about it, though, was that Cass had seen it before. It had been smaller, more compact, less intricate in its inputs, but the same nonetheless. She had seen it in Morningside, in the governor's compound.

Underdown's machine.

This, she knew then, was what she sought. The center of Asher's power. Or, at the very least, a critical component to his control over the Weir. For a time she evaluated it, walked around it, studied it. Wondered how it functioned and what exactly it did. She told herself she was looking for the best way to cripple it, but all that time she found herself having to resist an urge to connect to it. She'd seen it from afar so many times, but only had glimpses since her first discovery. Now, here was a chance to see it in its full glory, unhindered by distance. Before she knew what she was doing Cass started to stretch out to it.

It was then that she realized her great danger. The urge she was feeling was not her own. She was being compelled towards it, as if her physical proximity had hastened the process she had been fighting against for so long. And it was as she wrestled herself back under control that she learned the answer to the mystery of why the machines were so well-maintained.

From somewhere deep in the facility, a cry echoed, sharp and distorted, white noise translated by an organic voice.

Cass stood, paralyzed by the shock, even as the cry was answered by other voices, too many to count or process. The Weir. The Weir were in the building.

And in her mind, a connection forced its way to her in a lightning flash, a burst of signal lasting less than the blink of an eye. The afterimage was unmistakable. Asher. He had glimpsed her, he had found her, his eyes were on her.

She broke into a run then, twisting her way through the aisles back towards the stairs, but too late. Far too late. The Weir were swarming toward her now, their electric howls saturating the room and overwhelming her senses. Every turn she took led her to a Weir.

Cass whipped the jittergun from its holster, cut her way through the onslaught as it crashed into her, filtered by the rows of machines. If it hadn't been for the aisles forming so many narrow corridors, the numbers would have engulfed her in seconds. But the Weir were constantly forced to redirect, and the separation kept the attacks coming in bursts of only two or three at a time. Cass's speed and reaction time, coupled with her unconquerable ferocity, were too much for so few to contain. With gun, fist, and claw, she rent all who stood in her path.

But in the confusion and chaos, Cass was driven off course, forced back, and she found herself circling against her will towards the great machine. Though she slew them as they came, the Weir used their superior numbers to direct her. They were corralling her. Asher's will. To drive her to the machine. There, to do what? Sacrifice her at its foot, at the altar of Asher? Or to complete the process of reintegrating her, of casting her once more into bondage?

There was no escape for her, she knew that now. But she wouldn't give Asher the privilege of taking her life, whether by slavery or by death. She'd wanted to punch him in the mouth. This was her opportunity.

She fought her way back towards the machine, and found that as long as she made progress in that direction, the attacks were fewer, less vicious. A few of the creatures still dared to test her. One lashed out just as she came out from an aisle. They were so slow compared to her, she saw it all before it developed into a danger. She stepped outside the attack and brushed the creature's arm by, then stepped in and embraced it, trapping its outstretched arm over her shoulder where it could do no harm. With a swift twist, she lifted the creature off its feet and crushed its skull into the concrete. Another tried to pounce from behind, but she turned in time and slapped its head sideways, guiding it into a rack of machines.

Though she hadn't intended to, something happened when she touched the creature, and she felt power go out from her. The Weir shrieked for half a heartbeat and then abruptly went silent and collapsed to the ground as if it had just been switched off. After that, though they continued to keep pace with her and hem her in, no other Weir approached her.

The machine was just ahead of her, and she slowed her advance to it. When she reached it, she put her back against it, and kept the jittergun moving in a lazy arc, ready to cut down any foolish enough to move towards her. For the moment, none of them did. They were hanging back, either having accomplished their purpose of encircling her, or afraid to come any closer.

It was then that Cass became aware of the ripple in her thoughts. A dark pressure that stretched into her mind, threatened to force control of herself to the side. It brought pain that she felt somehow other than physically; a mental agony as if her mind was literally bending. She pushed back against it with all her will, and as she strove against it, she knew its source.

Asher. Asher was trying to force his way into her mind again.

Cass felt peace descend on her then. She'd only begun to understand the power that had long been latent within her. There was no way she could withstand a determined attack from someone as skilled and powerful as Asher. She reached to her belt, to the grenade that Finn had given her. Just in case.

In those final seconds, she did what she had decided long before to do. She pimmed Gamble, speaking quickly to minimize the connection time.

"They got me, G. But I took a bunch with me. Tell Wren I love him."

And before she got a response, she activated the grenade. Five seconds, from the time she released it from her hand.

But just before she did, the pressure in her mind released immediately, and she felt a sudden void where it had been. A moment later, the line of Weir broke. Some lunged forward, but most scattered into chaos.

Cass cut loose with the jittergun, dropped to a knee. Weir fell before her, and to either side. But for that instant, she saw a clear path back towards the stairwell. She left the grenade at the base of the machine and surged forward. Five seconds.

Even if she could get clear of the concussion blast, she had no idea what that pulse would do to her. She smashed through a Weir who had either tried to stop her, or just been unlucky enough to cross her path.

Three seconds.

Two.

One.

"Cass?" came Gamble's voice.

And then hell broke through and threw her into darkness.

THIRTY

Wren held the pistol just as Haiku had showed him the night before. It was early afternoon now, and they stood together a little distance from the tower. The pistol was heavy, and large for his hands, but so well-balanced that it almost felt like it was helping him. Haiku had set an empty water canister on top of a three-foot tall block of concrete, about fifteen yards away. Wren focused on the front sight, lined it up with the rear, and placed it in the center of the slightly-blurry canister. It felt strange to keep his attention on the gunsight instead of on what he was shooting at, but Haiku assured him that was the only way to do it. Once he was on target, Wren took his finger from the side of the gun and slipped it inside the trigger guard. Touched the trigger.

He took a breath, held it. Steady. Keep the sights lined up. As long as those sights were lined up, Haiku said, the round would go where it was pointing.

Wren put pressure on the trigger, tugged. The trigger clicked back, the hammer fell.

Click.

"Too quick," Haiku said, from off to his left side and slightly behind him. "You want steady pressure on the trigger. Don't jerk it. Did you see what happened with the sights that time?"

"They went down and left."

"Down and left," Haiku repeated. "So you'll shoot low

452

and left. Try it again."

Wren repeated the process, more mindful of the pressure he was putting on the trigger. Slow and steady. He drew the trigger back fraction by fraction. Any second it was going to release. Any second. He reached the point where he knew the trigger "break", pulled through that last bit.

Click.

The sights dipped again.

"Same thing," Wren said.

Haiku nodded. "You're anticipating too much."

Haiku stepped up next to him, adjusted Wren's grip slightly.

"You have two jobs," he said. "The first, and most important, is to keep those sights lined up on the thing you want to destroy. The second, is to put smooth pressure on that trigger. You're not firing the gun. That's not your job. You do your two jobs, and the gun will fire itself. That's its job. OK?"

"OK," Wren said. Haiku stepped back to his previous place.

"Again."

Wren tried again. Same process. On target. Finger on trigger. Smooth pressure. Eyes on the front sight. Smooth pressure. Front sight.

Click.

The sound of the click actually startled Wren that time, he'd been so focused on the front sight, he hadn't noticed how close the gun was to going off. And, he was happy to notice, the sights had barely moved.

"Well?" Haiku said.

"I think I see now," Wren answered.

He tried it a few more times. Sight, on target, finger to trigger, pressure. *Click.*

He kept at it so long his arms got tired of being extended. Haiku watched him practicing, made occasional comments and minor corrections, but once Wren had seen how it was supposed to work, he was able to make a lot of his own corrections. A benefit of his training, carrying over to a new skill. It was mildly thrilling to see how quickly he could learn something new.

"One second," Haiku said. "I need to check something." He came over again and took the pistol from Wren. He gently guided Wren back a few steps and then stepped up to the firing line, between Wren and the target. Wren rubbed his eyes, massaged his arms while he waited. He heard the clicking of Haiku manipulating the weapon, checking the cylinder to make sure it was clear, dry firing, checking the cylinder again.

"Here," Haiku said, bringing Wren back to the line. "Show me one more time."

Wren took the pistol, careful to avoid pointing it anywhere except the ground, just as Haiku had taught him. He waited for Haiku to step back to the side and behind him, and then went through the process.

Gun up, sights aligned on target. Finger to trigger. Steady pressure.

The pistol belched hellfire and leapt in Wren's hand so violently he almost dropped it. His ears rang with the echoing thunder that rolled across the open plain and back again. Wren's mouth dropped open. There was no sign of the water canister. It had been completely obliterated.

Wren looked at Haiku, who was standing there with his fingers to his ears and a grin on his face.

"You didn't tell me it was loaded!" Wren said.

"You should've checked it yourself," Haiku said, taking his fingers away. "And I needed to see how you handled it."

"I only had three shells for it," Wren said.

Haiku looked over to where the canister had been, where the concrete was smoking faintly.

"Don't think you'll need more than one," he said. He picked up another canister from the ground by his feet and motioned to Wren. "Show me it's clear."

Wren flicked open the cylinder, took out the spent shell, showed the three empty chambers to Haiku. Haiku nodded.

"Keep it that way. Be right back."

He walked back down to the concrete block and placed the cylinder there. When he returned he held out his hand for the pistol again. Wren reluctantly handed it to him. His nerves were still rattled by the unexpected blast.

"If you can hit something that small at that distance, you'll be able to hit something bigger and closer no problem," Haiku said. He had angled himself to the side as he spoke, but he had the cylinder open again. "If your target's farther away than that, don't bother trying to hit it."

He snapped the cylinder shut again, handed the weapon back to Wren, and then stepped off to the side and put his fingers to his ears. He gave Wren a little nod.

Wren got back into his proper stance, and then paused. He flicked the cylinder open, saw the back of one shell in the chamber. Closed it again. He glanced at Haiku, who was smiling again. Wren took a breath, brought the gun up and on target. Sights, finger on trigger, gentle pressure.

As he got closer to the trigger break, he braced himself for the roar, gripped the gun more tightly. Closer. Closer. The trigger released.

Click. The hammer striking a dead shell. A dud?

Wren opened the cylinder, withdrew the round. It wasn't a dud. It was the one he'd already fired. He looked up to Haiku, an unspoken question.

"How'd you do with those sights?"

"Low and left," Wren said.

Haiku nodded. "Anticipating the gun going off. Don't worry about that. What are your jobs?"

"Sights and trigger," Wren answered.

Haiku held his hand out again. Wren gave the pistol to him, the process repeated yet again. This time, though, Haiku didn't let him check the cylinder.

Click. Click. Click.

Over and over, for the next twenty minutes, Wren practiced sighting in and pulling the trigger, cycling through all three chambers, never knowing if the gun was going to go off. Eventually it didn't matter. He felt himself relaxing, maintaining his grip and a good sight picture on target. Then, at one point, after one *click* and the trigger broke for the second time, the gun again leapt and thundered in his hand. The water canister evaporated. Wren didn't even flinch.

"I think you've got it," Haiku said.

"I hope so," Wren said. "I'm all out of practice."

Haiku shook his head. "Practice continuously," he said. He held out Wren's last shell to him. "But save that until you need it."

Wren nodded as he took the last remaining round and slipped it into his pocket. He removed the empty from the pistol, and got the other back from Haiku. Three had always carried the empties around.

So would Wren.

When she woke, Cass found herself lying face down on the concrete, about twenty feet or so from the stairwell. For a moment, based on how she felt, she thought she had fallen from a great height. Her entire body hurt, and when she tried to lift her head, the whole world sloshed. Everything around her was dark and still, but there was a strange buzzing in her ears. She lay there for a minute or two, unsure if she was capable of moving and unwilling to test it. The buzzing grew louder, took on strange shapes in her mind. Eventually they resolved themselves to words.

"Cass..." a woman's mutilated voice was saying. "... there?"

Static overwhelmed all other sounds for several seconds, and then the voice came again, process, distorted, full of audio glitches and artifacts. "... signal is still there... see you... respond..."

Cass had heard that voice somewhere before. Somewhere long ago. Was it her own voice?

No.

Gamble.

The recognition snapped Cass back to herself. She opened her mouth, stretched her jaw. Slowly drew her arms towards herself, placed her palms flat against the floor. Pushed up on shaky arms. To her relief, and mild surprise, she was able to support her weight, and even pull her legs in enough to get her knees under her.

"Gamble," Cass pimmed. "I can hear you. I might make it after all. Not sure yet."

She felt the message got out, felt it stutter and glitch. Something was very wrong with her. She managed to sit back on to her knees without losing her balance. All around her was chaos. Between the concussion wave and the electromagnetic pulse, the neat aisles of machines were in shambles, both physically and in that unseen, digital realm. She'd made it a lot farther away in that five seconds than she'd thought. And thankfully, the stacks of machines seemed to have absorbed most of the energy from the blast, concussion and pulse. She hadn't quite cleared the blast radius, but she'd almost made it.

The room seemed to be a lot hotter than before. And here and there she could make out the broken forms of Weir. Most were still. Some were twitching spasmodically. Two were still on their feet, but of them, one was staring blankly ahead, and the other was turning slow circles to its right.

"Cass... coming in str..." Gamble's broken voice said, but it was a little cleaner now than it had been before. "... location when..."

Cass realized then the problem wasn't with her. It was with her connection. Possibly with every connection for who knew how many miles. The signal was degraded. And then the Weir that had been turning in slow circles stopped. Switched direction. Facing her. It opened its mouth. Started towards her in an ungainly lope.

Whatever was wrong with the connection wasn't permanent. It was being repaired. The other Weir turned its head to look at her. Cass's jittergun was a few feet away. She crawled to it, scooped it up off the floor. The Weir that was moving towards her was having trouble staying on course. She dropped it before it ever posed a serious threat. But the other was still tracking her with its head.

Cass looked over at the stairs. She'd come down them knowing full well she was going to have to climb them to get back out. The idea of trying to run up them was almost enough to keep her from getting off the floor. But whatever she'd done had hurt Asher. Better. It had scared him. He had fled her mind when he realized what she was up to, fled the machine. She wasn't ready to give up yet. Not by a long shot. Cass called up her last reserves of strength and got herself up and moving towards the stairwell. She cycled through the small chamber, and when she got into the stairs proper, she turned around and gave the controls on the door a half-second burst from the jittergun. Maybe that'd slow them down a little bit.

Then, with arms and legs of lead and a heart full of fire, Cass climbed.

To Wren's surprise, Foe had given him the rest of the day off from training. Wren had gone to his room and washed the grime off himself, excited about the prospect of getting long hours of sleep. Instead, he was still awake in his room. He'd turned off the overhead light, which cast his room in near total darkness. The bathroom light was on, though the door was drawn all the way shut. Just barely enough light for him to make out his coat hanging on the back of the door to his room. Wren stood against the opposite wall, practicing drawing Three's pistol from its holster. Not for speed. Just for familiarity. Hand to grip, smooth draw from hip to firing position, front sight on target. Finger to trigger. Steady pressure. *Click.*

He returned the pistol to its holster, which he'd fixed to his belt. The weapon was heavy and felt like it might make his pants come down on the side, even though his belt was as tight as he could get it. Again; smooth draw, on target, finger to trigger. *Click.*

Wren had tried to sleep. He certainly needed it. But every time he'd started to drift off, he'd had terrible nightmares. Nightmares of unspeakable and bizarre things, things his mind couldn't even properly reconstruct now, leaving him with broken fragments of images and a haunting fear. Practicing his draw and shot all as one movement was focusing, the repetition calming. He'd done it so many times now that even in the low light he was developing a feel for how the weapon should feel when it was on target, and whether or not he'd executed a proper trigger break.

For all he was facing, it was Painter that was causing his turmoil. There were too many emotions surrounding the circumstances for Wren to identify exactly how he felt. Maybe he was feeling *everything*, or all the bad feelings anyway, all at once. Fear, anger, grief. And maybe even a sense of vengeance. He had saved Painter, after all. He'd done everything he knew to do to help him. And Painter had repaid him in the cruelest way possible.

Wren didn't want to kill anyone. He could barely imagine what it would be like, to have someone on the other side of that pistol when he was pulling the trigger. It was one of the reasons he was practicing borderline obsessively. When it came time, he just wanted his body to do it.

But the thing that scared him most was that with Painter... well, with Painter, he *could* imagine it. And though he tried to ignore it, he found that the longer he waited, the more difficult it was to resist the urge to reach out and find Painter. He would have to do it eventually. And though his inclination was to wait until he could ask Foe for permission, he felt like maybe he was beyond that now. After all, Foe had fully restored his own connection. Maybe this was one of his final tests. Maybe Foe was waiting for him to see the opportunity and to take it. Then again, maybe he was just trying to justify it to himself.

In the end, he decided to compromise.

Wren sat down on his bed, laid Three's pistol beside him. Laid his hands in his lap, took a deep settling breath and let

himself relax. And then he stretched out. Eastward, towards
Morningside. The last time he had done so, he'd been in
Greenstone, on the roof of the Samurai McGann. How young
he'd been then, he thought. Just a kid. And for a moment, a
sad thought crept in. He was still just a kid, technically.

The great digital fog was still out there, still roving just
as it had been before. But now Wren feared it less. It wasn't
a single mass of darkness to him anymore. It was a deeply
complex pattern of signals, crisscrossing one another. But
there were gaps, holes that he could see now. Paths through.

Wren extended himself through it, even as he knew he
was playing a dangerous game. Once he had penetrated the
perimeter he realized that the signals weren't stable; they
constantly fluctuated around him, dropped and reformed.
He didn't know what would happen if his signal interrupted
one of the filaments, but he assumed it wouldn't be anything
good. To be safe, he initiated a protocol Foe had taught him
to minimize his signal's profile. For a fleeting moment, he
thought of how easy it would be to look for Mama. Just
to see if there was any way that she might still be alive.
Any way to confirm the hope that his heart still clung to.
But no, he turned himself away from that line of thinking.
In part, because he knew it might jeopardize her safety, if
she did happen to still be out there. But in even greater
part, because he knew that was not his purpose. Painter
was integral to his objective, to his plan. Risking anything
at all just to soothe his emotions would be inexcusable. And
whether she was alive or dead, the knowledge of either
would wreck his focus. He had grown comfortable living
in that in-between state. Now was not the time to upset it.

He didn't have to search for Painter, not really. He knew
all of Painter's credentials, assuming they hadn't been
modified by his new state. So Wren followed the simple
steps of a basic connection, almost like sending a pim,
except rather than allowing it to attach, he observed where
it went, followed it to its destination and then killed it before
it could finish. All of this took only a few milliseconds, but it

gave Wren a clear sense of Painter's location. Not his exact position, Wren hadn't attached long enough to do that, though it would not have been hard for him now. But a reasonable estimate. He was a long way from where Wren had expected him to be. Further north and west. Not too far from the border of the Strand, in fact.

Asher was keeping him busy.

Wren withdrew his signal, and then settled back on his bed after the brief foray. A few seconds at most, but it was enough to scratch the itch. His restlessness subsided. He'd taken a step towards carrying out the plan. Maybe that would be enough to convince his racing mind that he had done something useful, and it would let him sleep now. He couldn't quite bring himself to sleep with the pistol next to him; it seemed foolish after all of Haiku's safety warnings, even though it was unloaded. He dragged his pack over next to the head of his bed, and laid the pistol inside, on top. Close enough to reach out and touch if he really needed to.

He rolled over on his back, hands behind his head. Took a few deep breaths. Closed his eyes.

He had reached out and touched the storm across the Strand. And a few seconds after he'd closed his eyes, he got a response.

By the time Cass got to the top of the stairs, she literally couldn't go any further. She dropped to her knees, and then fell forward to her hands, and then rolled to her side. She lay on the concrete under the afternoon sun like a dead woman in all ways except her heaving for breath. By her estimate, it'd taken her just under fifteen minutes to run those steps. The last five, she'd been almost blind with tunnel vision. For a time, she genuinely wondered if she would ever be able to use her legs again.

"Gamble," she pimmed, as soon as she had recovered enough to do so. "I'm up. I'm alive."

The message went out after a brief hitch. A moment later, Gamble responded.

"Cass! What's your status?" There was still fuzz and static, and some distance as if Gamble had said something from inside a well, but it came through clear. Whatever she'd done to connectivity, it was being restored, and quickly. She wondered what would be coming up those stairs behind her. And how soon.

"Alive," Cass said. "For the moment."

"What happened?"

"I found something, Gamble. Something big. I need you to pass a message to Wren."

Her response didn't come back as quickly as Cass expected.

"Gamble?" she pimmed.

"Yeah, yeah I read you, Cass. It's just... uh, Cass, Wren's not here."

"It's fine, just tell him when you see him."

"No," Gamble said. "He isn't here, Cass. In Greenstone. He left the town."

Cass knew she hadn't heard that right. She sat up, ignoring the raging protest of her muscles.

"What do you mean he left? Did you see jCharles? At the Samurai McGann?"

"Yes, I'm with him now," Gamble said. And then Gamble broke the news to her, quickly. About Wren, and a man named Haiku. Three's brother. How Finn had tried to find him and couldn't. It was all too much to take in, too much to process.

"Maybe you should try," Gamble said. "Maybe you can reach him."

"No," Cass said. "No I definitely can't now. Asher's seen me. He's after me. I don't know how much longer I can stay ahead of him. But I don't think he knows Wren's not with me. Not yet."

The line was quiet again for several seconds before Gamble's reply came in.

"Lead them here," she said.

Cass shook her head, even though there was no one there to see it. "No, Gamble..."

"Bring them here, Cass," Gamble said, and her voice had that authoritarian edge to it. "We're expecting it."

Again, what had once been a single process revealed itself in its smallest components to Wren. Before his training, the first step to receiving a pim had been a notification of its sender and, unless set to autoaccept like he did with Mama's, a permission request to accept the connection and message. But now, even before receiving the indication of who the pim was from, Wren felt the formation of the signal, trapped it before it could develop, held it, and analyzed it. And all of this he did with deliberate control, with understanding. No longer by *feeling* alone.

Wren unwrapped the datastream, identified it as a pim, and identified its source.

Painter.

There was danger in that simple process; an active connection was far more obvious, and much more vulnerable to tracking to its location. It was obvious there was no coincidence here. Somehow Painter knew Wren had found him. Was this Asher's way of uncovering Wren's location? It seemed the likely answer. Maybe the only answer.

The safest thing to do was to redirect the signal, to cast it off into some faraway place to die. But if Wren's ultimate goal was to confront Painter anyway, why would he give up such an opportunity? Accepting the message would only expose him for a tiny window, and he was watchful. He decided to risk it.

He accepted the message, allowed the connection, though he diffused it. If Asher were watching for him, he'd get an idea of the region that Wren was in, but not his exact position; similar to what he knew about Painter's location. Equal footing, at best.

Painter's voice came through. "Hey, Wren."

Two words, from a familiar voice. It was like Wren had found a recording from months before, when he and Painter had been friends. *Hey, Wren*. Same voice. Same cadence. Same Painter. The wave of emotion that broke over him was disorienting. Maybe it had been a mistake. Maybe he should just ignore it, pretend it didn't happen.

But no. He'd started everything in motion, whether he'd meant to or not.

When you decide to kill the king, Foe had said, *kill the king*.

"Hi, Painter," Wren replied. Two seconds. Three. Five.

"Didn't expect to be talking to you again," came Painter's response.

"No," Wren said.

"I'm glad you're alive."

Wren didn't know how to respond to that, so he didn't. The dead air hung between them for several seconds. What else was there to say? The anger started to boil up in Wren.

"I was wondering why you were looking for me," Painter finally said.

"How did you know I was?"

"I felt it. And I recognized you." Wren didn't say anything, but Painter seemed to know what he was thinking. "I'm different now."

Curiosity layered atop the seething anger that Wren was trying so hard to suppress. Together, the combination was more than he could stand.

"Why, Painter?" Wren asked. "What happened to you? We did so much for you. And we would have done more, anything, if you'd only said something."

The words came out fast, heated. Wren expected a response in kind. Instead, Painter's answer was soft, chastised.

"I know," he said. "I lived in your world, Wren. I tried. I really did. But apart from you and your mom, and Mr Sun... I was garbage there, Wren. Less than. And Asher gave me purpose."

"Purpose?" Wren said. "Destroying a city was your purpose?"

"He gave me my sister back."

Wren heard it now in Painter's voice. The sorrow, the remorse. But he heard, too, Painter's true sense of purpose. He'd done what he thought he had to, to get his sister back. To protect her. To keep his promise to her. And something cracked in Wren then. Not enough to take away his anger, not enough to forgive Painter. But just enough to give him perspective on how someone could make such a choice. Wren couldn't accept it, couldn't justify all that Painter had done, but he saw a sliver of something hidden within; how it was born of love, however misguided and twisted.

"You can stop," Wren said. "Why don't you stop now? Refuse Asher? Turn against him?"

"It's too late for me, Wren. I made my choice. Whatever happens to me now, I deserve."

"You don't have to serve him, Painter. You're not his slave."

"No, I'm not," Painter answered. "I'm his voice. That's how it is now. But..." He trailed off, as if he was afraid to continue. When he did, Wren understood his hesitance. "Wren, not for me, I would never ask you for anything for me. But when all of this is over, if you can... would you please free my sister?"

Painter sounded so fragile, so broken. Wren's heart defied his own anger and was moved.

"I'll try, Painter," he said, and he meant it. "If there's anything I can do for her, I'll do it. I promise."

"Thank you." The connection rippled, and a few seconds later, Painter pimmed. "I should go. Asher's coming."

"Wait," Wren said. "Painter. What is Asher doing? What does he want?"

"I can't keep it out for long–"

"Painter, please."

"It's your mother. He's tracking her now."

Wren's heart leapt with joy and dread.

"She's alive?"

There was a long pause, even though the connection was still active.

"For now," Painter responded finally, "but I don't think she will be for long. I'm sorry, Wren, Asher's coming. If he finds you, he'll come for you next, I'm sorry."

And with those words, Painter severed the connection. Wren could have prevented it, could have held on and forced Painter to tell him more, but the risk was too great. He may have already risked too much.

Was it a trap? Had Painter told him that Mama was alive to try to get him to reach out to her? To trick him into giving them what they needed to track her?

It was only as he was thinking these things that Wren realized his mistake. Possibly a catastrophic one. He'd responded with surprise. *She's alive?* Painter hadn't known Wren wasn't with his mother. That explained the pause. He had been warning Wren that Asher knew where she was, that Asher was tracking *her*, assuming that it meant Asher was after both of them. The message was meant to explain how the Weir were finding them. Now Painter knew they weren't together. And whatever Painter knew, Wren had to assume Asher knew as well.

He sat on his bed for maybe an hour, sweating, on the verge of panic, wondering if he had doomed everything in that one, simple mistake. He would have to tell Foe, there was no doubt. And something else was certain.

He would have to leave.

Cass had wrestled herself up to her feet, forced herself to move again. She still had a few hours of daylight left, and she needed every last drop of it to get distance. None of the Weir had exited the stairwell while she was in front of it. She'd never even heard any on the stairs. But she wasn't waiting around to see if they might show up.

Her mind was racing, and as much as she wanted to focus on her current predicament, she couldn't control the swirling thoughts. Where was Wren? Who was this man Haiku, and what did he want with her son? Why had jCharles and Mol let him go?

Back in Greenstone, Wick was busy trying to find her and work up a route for her back to them. She'd agreed to it, even though in her heart she didn't believe she'd be able to make it that far. It was a long way back, and she'd have to make a run across the Strand.

While she was still getting her pace settled, a pim came in; since she was expecting Gamble she didn't even notice the source.

"Mama?"

The voice drove Cass to her knees, stole her own words from her. Her son. Her baby boy.

"Mama, are you OK? Are you there?"

She found her voice.

"Wren! Wren, baby, I'm here! Where are you, are you OK?"

"I'm fine, Mama. Where are you? Are you hurt?"

"I'm OK, baby! I'm OK right now. Where are you?"

"Mama, you have to run," he said, insistent. His voice had changed somehow. It was stronger, more confident. "Asher knows where you are. He's tracking you."

"I know, Wren. I know. Wren, where are you?"

"I can't talk now," he said. "I have to go. But I'll pim you when I can."

And just as suddenly as he had appeared, he vanished. Cass tried to pim him back, but her message died in the ether. Died completely; he hadn't refused her message. It was as if he didn't exist at all.

Cass forced herself up, got back on the move. Her boy was alive, and apparently safe. For a time she had to work to convince herself that she hadn't hallucinated it. But whether it was a dream or not, it renewed her hope. She would make it back to Greenstone. She *would*.

Wren came out to the parlor to find Foe sitting at the table, looking at him expectantly. As if he was waiting for Wren to tell him something.

"I talked to Painter," Wren said. "And my Mama."

"I know," Foe said. "I saw you."

Wren wondered if he should apologize, if he should beg Foe for his forgiveness, for violating his promise not to contact anyone. But then, Wren wasn't truly sorry. He'd gained information he'd needed, and maybe even set his plan in motion, even though that hadn't been his original goal.

"Then you know I have to leave," he said.

"Mm," Foe said.

"I'm sorry, Foe," Wren said. "But I'm out of time."

"By what reckoning?"

"Asher's found my mom," Wren answered. "If I don't do something now, he'll get her back."

"And what does that have to do with you?"

"She's my mom, Foe."

"When you came to me, you swore to lay down your past. To count your old life as lost. Are you so eager to take it back up again?"

"But... I can save her."

"Can you?" Foe asked. "What good will it be for you to go unprepared? For you to stand in harm's way, incapable of withstanding it? All that you have worked for will be lost."

"You've taught me well, Foe. I'm ready."

He didn't respond then, and somehow that was even more terrible than any of his questions had been.

"I understand my purpose," Wren continued. "Life, my charge. Service, my strength. To give of myself, that others may live. I understand that now."

Still, Foe made no answer.

"Will you let me go?" Wren asked.

"You are not a slave, boy," Foe said. "You are not my property. I have not held you here against your will, nor shall I do so now."

"So you think I'm ready?"

"That is yours alone to know."

Wren nodded, disappointed not to receive Foe's

encouragement, but grateful that the old man hadn't spoken against him either.

"If you are determined to go, I ask only one more thing of you."

"I am."

"Then come with me," Foe said, rising from his seat. He called to Haiku, who appeared almost immediately, and held a quiet conference. Haiku dipped his head and disappeared again without acknowledging Wren.

"I need to get moving soon," Wren said. "I don't have much time."

"So you mentioned." Foe turned and left the room, not waiting to see if Wren would follow. "This will not take long," he added just as he exited.

Wren caught up to Foe on the stairs, and followed the old man to a room he'd never seen before. It, like so many others in the tower, was small, and sparsely furnished. A narrow workbench, a stool, a chair, an oddly-shaped table that looked like it was meant for people to lie on.

"Sit in the chair," Foe said, while he went to the bench and gathered tools. Wren hadn't seen the tools before, but one looked like a small paintbrush, with just a few stiff bristles. Foe's back was to Wren and blocked the view of what he was doing. After a few moments, he said, "Remove your shirt."

"What are we doing?" Wren asked.

Foe turned, holding two instruments, both of which looked like brushes. The one in Foe's left hand was definitely a brush. In his right hand Wren saw now that what he'd thought was a brush with bristles was actually a wooden handle with a narrow grouping of needles.

"I don't like needles," Wren said.

"It is the tradition of this House," Foe said, "that when one has reached a sufficient level of training, before being sent out on a test, one receives a mark. It is both a distinction and a commemoration. I will not force you."

Wren sat in the chair, looking at those needles. Then he took off his shirt.

The process was simple, if a bit painful. Wren tried not to watch while Foe did his expert work. Foe worked quickly but when he was finished, the symbol he left behind was so elegantly executed, it almost looked like it had been painted on with a few simple strokes. Foe cleaned it, coated it with some kind of salve. Wren didn't recognize the mark.

"What does it mean?" Wren asked as he slipped his shirt back on, tried to ignore the soreness of the fresh tattoo.

"It means you are being sent out," Foe answered. He left his tools soaking in a solution, and opened the door, motioning for Wren to exit. "And," he added, "it means you are a son of this House."

Wren had expected to be taken back to his room, so he could gather his belongings. Instead, Foe led him downstairs to the exit. The door was already open, and outside they found Haiku waiting, with all of Wren's belongings already packed. When they were all outside, Foe turned to Wren and addressed him.

"Failure will likely mean death," Foe said, bluntly stating what Wren had not wanted to consider. "But death is never the final word in the life of a righteous woman or man."

Wren nodded. "People live on, as long as we remember them."

"Remember them?" Foe said, scoffing. "I am not talking about platitudes. If someone's death does not provoke you to meaningful action, then why bother to remember? Would you not rather forget?"

Wren didn't respond, and felt somewhat foolish for having said anything at all. He'd just repeated what so many people had told him so many times before.

"I mean," Foe continued, "that a life well-spent is not ended in death, but rather planted. You thought Three was a man. You were mistaken. He was a seed." Foe let the words hang there for a moment. "Honor him with your actions, son."

"Thank you, Foe," Wren said, and the words felt less than inadequate. Almost empty. "Thank you for everything."

Foe dipped his head in his slow nod.

Haiku stepped forward with Wren's pack.

"Food, water, a few supplies," he said. "Your weapon is in the top. Ammunition..."

"... is in my pocket," Wren finished. Haiku nodded, and placed his hand on Wren's shoulder.

"Good luck, Wren," he said. "Remember your oath. Hold to your code. Trust your training."

"Thanks, Haiku. I will." Wren lingered for a moment, wishing there was something more he could do or say.

"I'll come back if I can," he said.

"Mm," Foe responded.

Wren slung his pack on, adjusted the straps. The end had come so suddenly, he hadn't really had time to prepare. He knew he had to go, but leaving felt surreal. He gave the two men a little wave, and then turned and started out. It wasn't until he was fifty yards away or so that he realized what Foe had called him.

Not "boy".

Son.

He stopped then, turned to look back, but both Foe and Haiku were gone. He remained for a few long seconds, taking in that final image. The tower looming in the afternoon sun. Much like when he'd first seen it. Then it had filled him with fear. Now, it looked like home. He took a settling breath. Turned around.

And with that, Wren set off into the open, and into the arms of his mortal enemy.

THIRTY-ONE

"They're coming," Gamble said.

"What?" jCharles asked. "But we're not ready. We're not even close to ready."

"I don't think that's going to matter to them at all."

"How long?"

"Wick?" Gamble said.

Wick was sitting with Mr 850 at the table in jCharles's apartment, drawing up plans together on a hastily sketched layout of Greenstone.

"Yeah, huh?" Wick said.

"ETA on Cass?"

He didn't look up from his work. "Three days, give or take. Depends on how much static she gets between here and there. And how much she stops."

Gamble looked back at jCharles.

"Gonna be a long three days," jCharles said.

Gamble gave a curt nod. "Better get to it then."

"*Get* to it?" jCharles said with a chuckle. "I've *been* at it. Seems like I've been living there."

"Well," Gamble said. "It'll all be over in three days, one way or the other."

"Gonna be a long three days," jCharles said again. "I'll go talk to Hollander."

"All right, check," Gamble said. "I'll make the rounds. Might have to scrap some plans. Better to have a few

472

completed ones than a bunch half-done."

"That's your call, G," jCharles said.

She nodded again, and headed for the door. jCharles checked in on Mol, but she'd fallen asleep on the bed in the back room with Gracie in the crib next to her. He stood for a moment, looking at them both, soaking in the peace that emanated from that scene. Treasured it. He needed it. After blowing them each a silent kiss, he backed out and closed the door quietly, and then made his way out of the Samurai McGann to go see Hollander.

As he walked, he thought about the past few weeks; about how Kyth and Bonefolder had become strange allies, about how things had gone ever since Gamble and her team had showed up.

Hollander's folks had stopped them at the gate for obvious reasons. They came in ready for war. It had taken jCharles almost two hours to convince Hollander that they were The Good Guys, even though he hadn't ever met them before and most certainly hadn't called them in. By the end of it, it hadn't seemed like Hollander believed any of it, but he agreed to let them all stay in Greenstone as long as jCharles assumed all consequences if anything should go wrong.

And that had been the easy conversation. Shortly after, he'd had to break the news about Wren leaving with Haiku. Even after jCharles had explained all he could about the circumstances, Gamble and her team had been none too happy to hear that he'd let Wren go off with a stranger. Much less so when he told them he had no idea where the man had taken him, or when he'd come back.

There had been some discussion of them going out and trying to track him down, but in the end, in great part due to Mol's patient and gentle intervention, the two of them managed to convince the team to stay in Greenstone. They resisted at first but after the first day or so, they got involved in the preparations for the city. Once that had happened, things had smoothed out dramatically. They'd all come to get along pretty well, though the roughest one of them, the Awakened one – Swoop was it? – kept calling him "Knucklehead" like it was his name.

And those people were absolute beasts. If they slept at all, it wasn't much, and after a couple of days, they had divided up tasks and were splitting time between manual labor and training volunteers. jCharles hadn't called them in, but now that they were here, he didn't know what he would have done without them.

Materials weren't coming in as fast as he'd hoped. Volunteers were just that, volunteers, and not necessarily the most skilled of the bunch. jCharles had dug into his own coffers pretty deeply to hire some pros, but as good as they were at their work, half of them didn't believe what jCharles had told them, so they weren't exactly *motivated*.

Looking at where they were in preparations, and in numbers of personnel, jCharles gave them about a twenty-five percent chance of survival. Which, was actually pretty good. Which was, of course, depressing. Even if they had six more months, it was still going to be a roll of the dice.

He found Hollander sitting in his office, as expected. Hollander's head was down as he pored over some reports on a tablet on his desk; his way of keeping something like a work/life balance. jCharles knocked on the door frame.

"Yeah?" Hollander said without looking up.

"Got a sec?"

Hollander glanced up, waved him in, and went back to scanning the feed.

"What's up?" Hollander asked.

"Bad things," jCharles said. Hollander continued to read for a span, and then set the tablet to the side, ran a hand over his face and sat back in his chair. He raised his eyebrows expectantly. He looked exhausted.

"We've got three days," jCharles said. "Give or take."

"You sound pretty sure about that," Hollander replied.

"I am."

"How's that?"

"Because I've got a friend headed this way."

"And he's seen 'em?"

"No," jCharles said. "They're chasing her."

Hollander's eyes narrowed. "How many we talkin'?"

"Not sure. Guess we better assume *all* of 'em."

"You know... I've given you a lot of slack lately, jCharles."

"You have."

"And I still don't like you having those two blue-eyes around."

"I don't care, Hollander. They're doing a lot more for this town than you are right now."

Hollander raised his hand partially up off the desk; a warning.

"You got a lot of eyes around town," he said, "But you don't know everything, bud."

"Well, you know the plan," jCharles replied.

"I know *your* plan," Hollander replied. "But like I told you before. Anything comes over that wall, first thing it's going to see is me." He let it hang for a moment, and then added. "Whether you're there or not."

"We're after the same thing here, Holl."

"We'll see."

jCharles still hadn't been able to figure out whether Hollander didn't trust him, or just didn't understand the scale of what they were facing. But he knew the officer had a good heart. He hoped it'd be enough to see him through.

"Will you at least get the people moving Downtown? When the time comes?"

Hollander nodded. "As long as you handle the logistics of having all those folks gathered in one spot, we'll send out the alert. Don't count on us forcing anybody to do anything they don't want to, though."

"Pretty sure you won't have to," jCharles said. He gave Hollander a nod, and headed back to find out what Kyth and 4jack were up to. And as he left, he felt like he had to adjust their odds of survival down to a twenty percent chance.

•••

The sun was up, good and strong, and after a long night of running through the Strand, Cass was trying to decide whether she should take an hour of rest, or just push on. Would that hour of rest give the strength to make up the ground she'd lose? The Weir had been following her relentlessly, and the farther she got out into the Strand, the more effective they seemed to be growing. After she'd destroyed the node, they'd been scattered and broken, apparently unable to coordinate as well as they had before. For a time, the tendrils from the Weir's datastream seemed to have a harder time finding her, too. It was beginning again, now. She could feel it. But it was slower now, easier to shake off.

"Mama?" the pim came in, making it sound like Wren was in Cass's head. "Are you there?"

"Yeah, baby, I'm here."

"Sorry I didn't pim again yesterday. I was afraid to at night."

"It's OK. Where are you?"

"I'm coming to help you," he said. Her baby. He sounded like he really meant it. More. Like he could really do it.

"No, Wren," she said. "You stay where you are."

"I'm already on my way. Can you come to me?"

"No, I'm headed to Greenstone. Gamble and the team's there."

There was a pause, and when he replied, she could hear the surprise and joy in his voice.

"They're alive?"

"Yeah, baby, they're all alive."

"Well... all except Swoop, you mean."

It hit her like a thunderbolt. He didn't know. Of course he didn't know. There was *so much* he didn't know. She had so many things to tell him, and so little energy to do it.

"Swoop too, baby. There's a lot to explain."

"He didn't die?"

"He's Awakened, Wren."

Another pause. This one longer than the first.

"He woke himself?"

"No. I woke him. And another man too. A lot's changed, baby."

She thought he'd be stunned by it, but he responded quickly.

"Everything's changed, Mama."

Her turn to pause. She didn't recognize the tone in his voice at all, and she wasn't sure she liked it.

"Wick drew a route up for me," she said a few moments later. "I'll send it to you."

"No, don't," Wren said. "Asher might intercept it."

In the explosion of emotion she'd felt when Wren had contacted her, Cass had completely forgotten that Asher might be monitoring for their signals. Not that it mattered in her case, but was she endangering Wren by talking with him now?

"What about pimming?" she asked.

"It's OK," Wren said. "I'm taking care of it. But we should be careful. I'll see you in Greenstone, OK?"

He sounded so confident.

"OK, baby," she said. "I love you."

"I love you too."

The connection closed, and Cass couldn't quite make out what her heart was doing. Hearing her son's voice had flooded her with chaotic feelings. The first time they'd spoken, she'd teetered right on the edge of lapsing into a desperate need to find him, to be with him. Now, though, after hearing how different he sounded she wasn't sure that he needed her as much. If at all. And instead of the fear she expected, there was an unexpected peace. She couldn't wait to see him, of course, to pick him up and hold him close. But it was a desire, not a need. And as she pushed herself on, farther into the Strand, closer to Greenstone with each step, she knew what Wren had said was true.

Everything had changed.

And she was at peace.

•••

Wren squelched the connection with his mama. Not just disconnected. Closed it and compressed it, just as Foe had taught him. It was still possible for Asher to find him, but not without Wren knowing about it. And to anyone else, he wouldn't exist. Well, to anyone except a nearby Weir, maybe. He still hadn't had a chance to test that yet.

Running the open after he'd left Foe's tower had been an incredible experience. Exhilarating. He'd traveled a lot, and it had always been oppressive and full of constant anxiety; a slow-burning fear that worked on the mind and soul, even if all around seemed safe and secure.

Now, the depth and power of Foe's training had begun to reveal itself to him. And the farther out he went, the more evident it became that Haiku's "game" had been more than just a game. Much more. Where before the world of the open had been a grey wash of ruin, now it was vivid and alive with a subtle life of its own. How very much he had missed before. He'd taken to walking that fuzzy border between the Strand and the dead cityscape, and now it seemed like everywhere he looked he saw quiet whispers of stories untold. He'd spent the first night hiding out on the third floor of a five-story structure. But as the sun was slipping below the horizon on the second day, he noticed signs that suggested people had traveled through not all that long ago. And when he followed the trail, it led him to a wayhouse, cleverly concealed. A welcome surprise, not only to sleep in absolute security for a night, but also to have discovered his own ability to perceive the world around him so clearly.

The same skill enabled him to skirt a pair of scrapers that were either pushing their luck traveling so close to the Strand, or had wandered into unfamiliar territory. He saw signs of them before he heard them, and when he heard them, he went quiet, remembering how he'd moved in the Waiting Room. The habits he'd formed in the tower were showing their worth. Now he understood the value of constant practice. And he understood how every moment was an opportunity to practice.

There was another skill that Wren continued to develop all along his journey.

Draw from the holster, sights on target. Finger to trigger; smooth pressure.

Click.

Over and over he rehearsed, with careful attention to each step. As he walked, he picked out different targets, various bits of scrap or marks on the walls of the buildings he passed. At times he would even stop, close his eyes, and draw, just to see if he could get on target by feeling alone. He didn't quite master that technique, but he could get pretty close. And while he worked, Wren tried not to worry about being fast. He just wanted to be smooth. Oddly enough, as he got smoother, the speed came too.

Unfortunately, the speed of his draw didn't improve the speed of his travel. He too was running a route laid out for him by Wick, one that was intended to get him to Greenstone, coming in from the opposite side of the Strand. And though Wren had thought it was a good enough plan when he'd first received it, with each hour that passed, it seemed less like the right path to take. He was supposed to branch off westward, but kept delaying transition. Eventually, he made the decision, and committed to it.

If he stuck to Wick's path, he might make it in time, might be able to stand with Mama, and jCharles, and Gamble and the team. But he wasn't going to Greenstone. He knew what would happen if Asher reached it. He wouldn't let that happen.

Wren turned eastward, back out into the Strand, cutting the corner. Asher and his Weir might make it to Greenstone.

But they'd have to pass Wren to do it.

When Cass reached the gate around noon, coated in dust and exhausted, jCharles and Gamble were both there to meet her. Gamble gave her a rough embrace and then, in typical fashion, got straight to business.

"How far ahead of them are you?"

Cass shook her head. "They were on my heels until daybreak. Two, three hours after dusk at most."

"Team's waiting at the McGann," Gamble said. "We'll get you up to speed."

When Gamble had said *the team*, Cass had assumed she meant Gamble's people. But as soon as she walked in the front door of the Samurai McGann, she realized how wrong she'd been. All of Gamble's team was there, of course, but the entire saloon was full of people, the vast majority of whom she'd never seen before. Greenmen, rough looking citizens, a red-eyed girl who looked like trouble.

The welcome from the team was brief, but sincere. There were murmurs throughout the crowd from those that didn't know her, but no one actually gave her any trouble. It took Cass a few moments to realize that contact with Swoop and Kit must have acclimated people somewhat to the idea of the Awakened. Not that they liked it. But they seemed to accept it. At least for the moment.

As Cass scanned the crowd, to her utter shock and surprise, she glimpsed a familiar face towards the back.

Lil.

Lil smiled and gave a gentle wave, but didn't try to push her way forward. Cass understood. The urgency was too great. There might come a time for reunions, but if so, they would have to earn it.

Gamble gave her the briefing, explained the plan from something between high and low level. At the end of it, Cass wasn't quite sure if she'd gotten too much detail or not enough. Fortunately, the basics were simple, if a little crazy. An early stand. A tactical withdrawal. Ambushes along the way. Hope for the best.

"You're letting them into the city?" Cass asked.

"Not for free," Swoop said.

Cass shook her head. It was a good plan. Maybe the best plan, all things considered. But it wasn't going to be enough. She knew it in her gut. She'd seen it at Morningside. The most terrifying aspect of Asher's Weir was the speed with which they could react as a single entity. On an individual level, she could outpace any one of them. But when the entire force could split itself into two forces in an instant, or scatter and then reform at another point... There was just no way to defend against it.

Unless.

"Wick," Cass said. "I need you to find something for me."

Haiku stood on the catwalk, looking out over the wide, flat plain below and at the broken bones of the sprawl beyond. Foe stood by his side, keeping silent watch. Since Wren had left, the tower had returned to its usual quiet, but with it had come a strange emptiness. For so long, days and nights had been filled with constant activity and purpose; now they were a yawning void. Even so, there was no rest in them. Haiku couldn't stop analyzing all he'd taught Wren, and all he hadn't.

"I wish he had stayed," Haiku said. "Just a little longer."

Foe didn't respond. Haiku hadn't really expected him to.

"Do you think he'll be able to resist Asher?" Haiku asked.

"It is what he is trained to do," Foe said. He fell silent after he said it, and Haiku thought that was all the old man would say on the matter. But a few moments later, he added, "He truly believes he is ready to face his brother, and thus, so do I. But there is one doubt that lingers. Something for which I fear I failed to prepare him."

"To win?"

Foe shook his head.

"To bear what it will cost him to do so."

"I don't know," Wick said. He was kitted out, ready to go to war, back in prime shape. "That's pretty far out, Cass. You think you can get there in time?"

"I can," Cass stated. "I can do it. Do you have any grenades or explosives?"

The little guy named 4jack barked a laugh, and then

apologized. "Sorry," he said, "but yeah. Yeah, we've got some explosives."

"Most of them are already in place," his shy friend Mr 850 said. "What do you need?"

"Anything that'll go boom," she said. But Mr 850 shook his head.

"How much boom?" he asked. "Do you want fire? No fire? Wide area blast, concentrated? Are you wanting to collapse a structure, or penetrate thick plating? There are a lot of parameters–"

"I don't know," Cass said. She turned to Swoop. "Maybe like what you did at Ninestory. Something like what you did with the door?"

Swoop nodded and looked at Mr 850.

"Hexcord," he said. "Three... no let's say four strips."

"Green or grey?" Mr 850 asked.

"Green if you got it."

Mr 850 nodded and bustled off.

"How do I rig it?" Cass asked.

"You don't," Swoop said. "You cover me while I rig it."

Cass shook her head. "No, Swoop, you stay here. Your team needs you. These people need you."

"I appreciate that, Cass, but nah. You're not goin' out by yourself."

"We have this conversation a lot."

"Think you woulda learned by now."

Cass looked to Gamble for support, but Gamble shook her head.

"You know he doesn't listen to me anyway."

Kit muscled her way through the small knot.

"I'll come too," she said.

"No you won't," Cass and Swoop said at the same time.

"I'm not going to make much difference here," Kit said. "Out there, with you two? I bet the Weir won't even notice us."

"Kit," Cass said. "I'm just going to come out and say it. I'm not coming back. When Asher figures out what I'm up to, he's going to throw everything he can afford at me. And he can afford a lot."

"Hey," Kit said. "I already died once, Cass. Same as you."

"No need to do it a second time," Cass said.

"You a shooter?" Swoop asked, looking at Kit.

"Done a fair bit," she answered.

"Good enough for me," he said. "Two guns up while I'm riggin'."

Mr 850 pushed his way back through the saloon, gripping a small satchel in his hand.

"I could only find two greens, but I had three greys," he said. "They're all in there."

"Thanks, brother," Swoop said. He took the satchel, tossed the strap over his head, looked at Cass. "We still standin' here?"

Cass looked at Swoop, then at Kit, then back to Swoop. They were coming, and there was nothing she could do to stop them.

"Nope," she said. Someone Cass didn't know handed Kit a rifle. Kit took it, checked it over like a pro. Once she was satisfied that she knew the controls, she leaned over and gave Wick a kiss right on the mouth. When she pulled away, he looked simultaneously startled, confused, and a little goofy.

"Let's do it," Kit said.

Cass turned and led the way out the front door of the Samurai McGann. As she stepped into the street, a pim came in.

"Mama," Wren said. "They're coming."

"I know, baby," she answered. "How close are you to Greenstone?"

"Not far."

"OK. Hurry, baby. I'm not going to be here, we're going to try to–"

"No, Mama, don't tell me. If I don't know, he can't find it out." Cass didn't like the sound of that at all, but before she could say anything, Wren added, "Good luck."

"OK, baby. You too. We'll see each other soon." She said it without thinking, without meaning to lie. But once she'd said it, she couldn't bring herself to change it.

"I hope so," Wren replied. "But if not, it's OK."

And a moment later, he vanished.

Painter moved along at the very front of the force. Asher had always sent him well ahead before, to deliver his messages. Now, Painter was with the army itself, driving hard. The sun was still above the horizon, and when Painter glanced back he could see how much trouble it was causing in the way his Weir companions loped along behind him, stumbling at times, veering off course. And he could feel it in the strain of Asher's control. Though Asher hadn't forced his way into Painter's mind, there was a lingering presence there, a sensitivity that seemed to grow with each day. Painter couldn't help but wonder if one day he would cease to be himself entirely; if one day Asher would be all there was.

Asher was exerting himself to a degree that Painter had never experienced before. That told him everything he needed to know about what lay ahead. This was the big one. The thing Asher had been preparing for all this time. He had summoned everyone. Every single Weir he could reach and influence. Even Painter didn't know how many that was.

Roh and Snow were with him, up front. Asher's voice and Asher's hands. And many more besides. Roh's grotesque behemoths followed closely behind, terrible to behold. There were more out there, too. Painter had felt them, somehow. Once he'd met Roh's, once he'd gotten the sense of their signature, he recognized it elsewhere in the datastream.

Snow made a quiet *whuff*, part question, part warning. Painter glanced over at her, saw her looking intently ahead. When he looked back, he didn't see anything at first. After they'd covered another thirty yards though, he was able to make out what she'd seen. He'd missed it before because it was coated in the grey dust of the Strand and was so small.

A lone figure.

A boy.

Wren.

jCharles stood on the northern wall, a pair of jitterguns in holsters high on his belly. It'd been a long time since he'd worn those. He tried not to think about how much he'd missed their comforting weight. Hollander stood to his right, geared up, eyes fixed northward. He held his rifle shouldered, but cradled barrel down; he'd be able to snap it up when it was time, but now wasn't the time. 4jack was on jCharles's left, shirtless, and casually manipulating his knives, one in each hand. jCharles would have called it a nervous habit, but 4jack never got nervous. Especially not when he was supposed to be.

The sun still hadn't quite sunk below the horizon yet. The crowd was gathered a couple of hundred yards away, and it wasn't coming any closer. Not yet, anyway.

"You wanna send out that alert?" jCharles said. "Better to get people moving now than when it gets to be a real emergency."

Hollander shook his head. "I know you're worked up, bud. But I don't think you appreciate just how strong this place is. I've got my folks in good order. We can handle this."

To Hollander's credit, jCharles was a little surprised at the size of the force out there. It was big, sure, but not like he'd imagined. Maybe he really had let his imagination run away with him. For some reason he'd expected them to come more from the east, though he didn't know why.

As he was thinking that, a sudden cry arose, the sound of many Weir shrieking in the distance. A moment later, the crowd broke into a run towards the wall.

"Here we go," Hollander said, but he didn't raise his rifle.

There was something strange about the advance of the Weir. Something in the way they moved that seemed off. Haphazard.

"My God," 4jack said, seeing it before anyone else.

"What?" Hollander said.

And then he saw it too. All of them did. This wasn't a wave of Weir rushing the wall.

It was people.

"What do we do, Holl?" jCharles asked. They'd closed to a hundred yards. Ninety. Seventy. "Holl?"

"People or not," Holl finally said. "They're not comin' over this wall." He raised his rifle.

It was hard to tear his eyes away from the people as they covered that final distance, but jCharles managed to look up, out in the distance. There were Weir out there. He could make them out. But they were hanging back, waiting to see what happened to the people first.

He looked back down. They were close enough now to make out faces, expressions. The terrified look, the desperation. And jCharles understood. Slaves, of a sort. Captives, at least. Forced to fight for their lives. Facing certain death if they refused, and death merely likely if they attacked. Taking the wall was their only, desperate hope for life.

Hollander fired the first shot. After that, as the sun sank below the horizon and darkness seeped into the sky, jCharles had to shut off his brain and let his body do what his mind couldn't.

Cass and her two companions had covered more distance than even she had thought possible in such short time, fueled by thoughts of what might be happening in the town they'd left behind. Dusk had settled and was edging towards night when they approached the waypoint Wick had laid down for them. Cass saw the spire first, thirty feet high. A single, red light glowed dully on top.

They hadn't seen a single Weir yet. Hadn't even heard one.

"Here we go," Cass said.

"Stay tight," Swoop answered as he pulled ahead of her. "Let me lead."

Cass waved Kit forward.

"Hand on Swoop's shoulder," Cass directed, "cover left. I'm rear guard."

"Got it," Kit answered, and she fell right in step. Cass didn't know much about what Kit had done in her days before she was Awakened, but it was obvious she'd done more than just a little shooting.

The structure wasn't the same as the one Cass had seen before, but the feeling was similar. She knew the node was here, down below them, even though she was afraid to reach out to it to verify. The reintegration was working on her again. And she didn't dare draw Asher's eye now, for fear of giving them all away.

There was no fence around the building, this one rounded and thin. It looked almost like a smokestack. Swoop eased the door open and, as expected, found a set of stairs leading down into darkness.

"Slow and steady," Swoop said.

"Maybe just steady," Cass said back.

Together, the three of them began their descent.

Painter couldn't believe it. What was Wren doing here? What was he doing at all? The boy was just standing there, like he'd been waiting for them. Just as he'd been the last time Painter had seen him; a little dirtier maybe, but still small, fragile. Whatever was left of Painter's heart twisted and sank. He'd known this would happen some day. But not today. Not like this.

Painter felt a pulse go through him, a feeling he'd learned to interpret as Asher extending himself. And the Weir surged forward, racing past him, charging towards Wren as a merciless wave. Painter closed his eyes.

And then he felt something, another wave of force, this time not from Asher. From Wren.

He opened his eyes and terror seized his heart.

Where Wren had been just moments before, there stood now a towering being of divine wrath and judgment;

ten feet tall, forged of lightning, wreathed in flame. And even as Asher drove Painter forward, he resisted, his fear temporarily overriding Asher's influence.

Painter had seen this before. It was only Wren. It was only little Wren, doing his trick. Doing what the woman Lil had taught him to do. It filled Painter with terror for some reason, but he knew it could do him no harm.

The wave of Weir slowed and for a moment looked like they might balk, but again Painter felt Asher extend himself, and the Weir resumed their surge. Painter had assumed that whenever Asher found Wren, there would be some sort of dialogue, some exchange before the end. Or at least that Asher would toy with his kid brother. Now, it just looked like Asher was going to erase him.

And then the strangest thing happened.

As the Weir drew near to Wren, when they met the radiance of his shimmering image, they fell. Fell as if their minds had been instantly extinguished. They fell in piles, heaped up one upon the other until the crush could stop its advance. The Weir stopped, crowded into one another, trapped between the compulsion to drive forward and the terror of what lay before them.

And then Wren walked towards them, and as he approached, they parted, scrambling to get out of his way. Wherever one failed to escape his aura, it too fell and lay as dead.

Asher burst his way into Painter's mind.

"Oh look. Little brother's learned some new tricks," he said. "Fine. I'll do it myself."

Asher issued some wide area command, and Painter understood intuitively that he was being directed on to Greenstone. But as he stepped forward, Asher spoke to him.

"No, Painter, not you. You stay. You will bear witness, so that you may proclaim my final victory."

And then, with Painter as witness, Asher leapt upon his brother.

•••

The Weir had rushed in after most of the civilians had been cut down. The people hadn't fought particularly well, or even bravely. Theirs was pure desperation, and it had made them easy targets. At first, jCharles had thought it a foolish tactic, to throw bodies at the wall. But as the Greenmen around him started calling for extra magazines, he soon realized what effect it had really had. The Weir were advancing much more quickly, coming much closer to actually reaching the gates, and as more and more Greenmen were forced to reload their weapons, the volume of fire dropped off. Each time it did, the Weir made leaps towards the gate.

"Holl! Send out that alert!" jCharles yelled.

"Yeah," Hollander called back. "Yeah, I think you're right."

jCharles hadn't really had time to look back behind him, but he'd heard some screams and some scuffles. Some folks had gotten the idea early enough on their own. Soon after Hollander sent out the alert, though, it got a whole lot noisier. The streets filled with citizens, all rushing towards the one place the vast majority of them had avoided at all costs. Downtown.

As expected, the plans for a well-ordered evacuation were immediately blown, and though the chaos in the streets wasn't as bad as that just outside the wall, jCharles knew many lives were going to be lost before the night was through. Why hadn't Hollander just listened to him?

And then, the call came in. The eastern gate was under attack. By a much larger force.

The Weir that jCharles had been fighting, the one that was dangerously close to breaking through to the gate, had merely been a diversionary force. And jCharles knew then that all his worst nightmares of this night were coming true.

Cass was relieved to reach the bottom floor without any sight or sound of another Weir. Kit was breathing a little harder than anyone else, but otherwise they all seemed to be in good enough shape to finish the job. Though Cass hadn't counted the stairs, she was pretty sure that they weren't as far down here as she'd been in the other node access. Like the other, however, the stairs terminated at a single door and when they opened it, the small chamber they entered was, to all appearances, identical.

Cass closed the door behind them, and then pulled Swoop and Kit closer. They spoke in whispers.

"I don't know if the layout's going to be the same beyond that door," Cass said, "but we're looking for a single, big machine, about ten feet tall. Swoop, you remember the one back in the governor's compound?"

"Pretty much," he said.

"It's like that one, but much larger."

"Check."

"How much time are you going to need to rig it?"

"How bad you wanna hurt it?"

"I want it dead."

"Hexcord's prepped. Just got to slap it on and activate. Forty-five seconds, if you can keep 'em off me."

"We'll do it," Cass said, looking to Kit. Kit was grim-faced, resolute.

"We have to," she said. "So we will."

Swoop adjusted the satchel so it was hanging around front, but still out of the way of his weapon.

"When we go in," he said, "if it looks familiar, you take point. If not, leave it to me."

"OK, check," Cass said.

Swoop nodded, and he and Cass executed the same door-opening routine she'd learned from Gamble. The room was clear, at least as much of it as they could see, and they rolled smoothly in. To Cass's relief, the layout seemed to be identical; racks of machines forming aisles, same pristine environment. She nodded to Swoop, and moved up front. He kept close behind as she began to lead them towards the location of the target machine.

It was remarkably quiet, except for the pleasant drone of

the machines and the cooling fans. The only real difference she noticed between this node and the first she'd found was that the blue status lights on the machines seemed to be brighter in a few locations. She didn't remember that variation before. It was as she came around a corner that she discovered the source.

A cluster of Weir was waiting for them.

Cass didn't wait, she just unleashed with the jittergun and cut down four before they reacted. But it was only a few seconds before she realized just how much trouble they were in. Cries sounded from all around the room, and Weir poured towards them from three directions.

"Back!" Swoop shouted, "Back!" and he unloaded with his heavy weapon, mowing down their enemy and momentarily checking their advance. Cass and Kit withdrew behind him, Cass with a hand on his harness, pulling him along behind her to guide him. Kit backpedaled and fired clean, controlled shots, *pop pop pop*, one after the other.

But the Weir kept coming, kept forcing them back. Back.

And Cass recognized what was happening, too late. The Weir drove them back by sheer force of numbers to a wall, and ringed them in. The machine. The Weir had waited in ambush, and then steered them away from the machine.

They were cut off. Surrounded.

Wren sensed it coming, that initial impact of Asher's signal, and without thinking he shifted his mind, redirected the attack, robbed it of its energy. The next seconds, or minutes, or hours, were a white hot blur of reaction, reflex, and training, as Wren's mind and body fused into one entity and strove against Asher. All the cold, all the exhaustion, all the fear and adrenaline and pain, every ounce of what Foe had put Wren through paled in comparison to the experience he now endured. Asher had grown tenfold, a hundredfold since Wren had faced him last. His signal had grown in complexity, and the processes came from multiple directions.

But Wren remembered the petals, how overwhelming they seemed when he had tried to focus on each one individually. And his mind gained a new perspective, saw everything, but only noticed the processes that could truly harm him. Still he strove to grasp Asher's signal, to attach to it, to find his opening.

And then, a lightning flash. Wren saw it. The opening. And as soon as he saw it, he executed the plan, just as he had countless times under Foe's watchful eye. After all of the struggle just to hold on, the strike was surprisingly easy. Wren attached, and clung to Asher's signal, locking him down in Painter's mind.

He felt it then, the moment when Asher realized his danger, the moment of panic. Asher flailed and thrashed against Wren, but for all his power, he couldn't break free. He had never experienced anything like it, this simple capture protocol. He didn't know how to escape and though surely he had the power, he was too frantic to find a counter.

And here, now, was the moment, the one Wren had been visualizing, had been training for. The instant he thought it, his body was in motion as if of its own volition.

Draw from holster, raise from hip.

Sights on target.

Finger on trigger.

Painter stood frozen, eyes wide. Asher seemed to scream within him, pure rage, but Painter was paralyzed by fear.

No, not by fear.

Wren saw it in his eyes now. Painter wasn't panicking. He was *holding* himself still; resisting, in fact, Asher's commands to move or attack or anything.

"Do it," Painter said, his voice strained. "Do it, Wren."

Smooth pressure.

Painter stood bravely, facing his death.

Justice.

But this wasn't justice. Wren knew it in his heart. Asher had proven himself time and again, had shown his will; he would destroy until he himself was destroyed. But Painter,

Painter had been deceived, enslaved. Killing him may have been revenge, or it may have been mercy. Either way, in the end, he would be another life that Asher had claimed. But a life that Asher would claim by Wren's hand.

No, he wouldn't.

Wren released the pressure from the trigger, took his finger out of the trigger guard.

"Wren," Painter said. "Wren, hurry! I can't hold him much longer!"

Wren didn't lower the gun, just kept it centered right on Painter's chest. He would have gotten him, easy. He would have done it.

Painter cried out and fell to his knees, clutching his head in both hands.

And Asher slipped free of Wren's hold, and turned all his wrath upon his brother.

By the time Hollander and jCharles made it to the eastern gate, they knew it was going to be lost. Too few Greenmen remained, too few of Bonefolder's hired guns, too few of everyone that jCharles needed, and too many of the enemy. 4jack came up close behind with the team of Greenmen they'd brought from the northern gate.

A thundering blow rattled the gate, followed by a guttural howl unlike any sound jCharles had ever heard.

"That plan of yours," Hollander said. "Better get to it."

"Get everyone off the gate," jCharles said, "and get your men Downtown."

"We'll cover our–" Hollander started, but jCharles cut him off.

"Just go!"

Hollander stared at him for a hard moment, but then issued the order for the Greenmen to withdraw. Most of them did, though a few stayed on the wall despite his repeated orders. 4jack slapped jCharles's shoulder.

"I'm gonna get in place."

"Yeah," jCharles said. "See you in a few."

4jack nodded and took off, and jCharles didn't stick around. He ran to the nearest stairwell, made it down to the ground level.

Gamble was waiting for him, along with Sky and Finn.

"We set?" she said.

"Almost," he answered. He swapped out the magazines on both jitterguns. "Hoping to get those last few off the wall–"

The gates shuddered again. A moment later, Sky's rifle hummed once, and then twice more in succession. jCharles didn't see anything through the gate yet, but when he looked up, he saw Weir on the wall. They'd topped it somehow. There were still Greenmen up there.

"We're going," Gamble said.

"There are still–"

"They're dead," Gamble said abruptly. "Finn, hit it."

The gates shuddered a third time, and the squeal of flexing metal rent the air. It held, but the Weir were swarming the top of the wall now, and jCharles saw the last of the Greenmen fall. Seconds later, a clap of thunder struck so loudly the ground shook and a shockwave passed through him. The gate was smoke and fire, and whatever had been on the other side of it had evaporated. Most of the Weir on top of the wall had been thrown off, one way or the other, or were laying stunned atop it.

"Mouse," Gamble said, "Gate's down. Moving in ten!"

"Check," came Mouse's reply. Finn had dialed jCharles into the team's channel, and he was getting a front row seat to how they operated.

"Finn, Sky," Gamble said, and then she motioned with her hand. The three moved out into the street in a wedge and started dumping rounds through the smoking husk of the gate.

"Four... three... two..." Gamble counted down, "one, Alpha's moving!"

"Alpha moving, check!" Mouse said through the channel. Gamble and her two teammates started falling back, just as the first of the Weir came stumbling through. Sky picked two off. jCharles fell into position with them, jitters at the ready but holding fire. As expected, the Weir saw them first, and immediately charged.

"Go!" Gamble said, and they all took off on their route.

It was the worst twenty seconds of jCharles's life. He didn't dare look behind him, but he was certain that at any second claws were going to drag him down. The howls of the Weir were devastating, echoing off the buildings and narrow streets of Greenstone. jCharles was the last to make it through the designated alleyway, and the instant he crossed, two loud pops sounded just behind him, followed by a strange metallic whine. He didn't stop, though, until he reached the cover point. He leapt over a three-foot concrete barrier and ducked down. Only then did he risk peeking up and over.

A fibrasteel mesh now covered the end of the alley they'd come through, like a web up to about ten feet. A horde of Weir stacked up against it, those in front forced into it by those in the rear. A few moments later, jCharles saw thin metal cylinders tumbling down from the rooftops, reflecting the gaudy lights of shop signs as they fell. They disappeared into the churning crowd of Weir, and a second later, a series of white flashes lit up the alley, like lightning on the ground. jCharles didn't have time to see what the effect was. Gamble and her crew were already up and running.

"Zulu's done!" Gamble said through comms, "Zulu's done! Alpha moving to Two Peaks!"

"Alpha to Two Peaks, check!" Mouse answered.

As they ran, jCharles heard gunfire and explosions from all sides, between their location and the gate. His cell was just one of many, fanning out, trying to split the mass of Weir up into as many separate lines as possible. The first few chokepoints were the easiest. As they made their retreat back towards Downtown, though, everything was going to get increasingly complicated. They'd done their best to barricade certain roads and paths, to funnel the Weir through the target zones.

Gamble led them through a crossalley at a sharp angle. As fast as they'd been moving, a dozen Weir or so had already managed to get ahead of them. Fortunately, they'd come out on the Weir's flank and together the four made short work of their enemy and moved on.

Two Peaks was actually just a street that had two round-topped buildings, one on each side. When they reached it, they fell into position, covering the two feeder streets that led in from the eastern gate.

"Alpha's in position at Two Peaks!"

"Alpha at Two Peaks, check!" Mouse answered. "Bravo moving to Water, Bravo to Water!"

"Bravo moving to Water, check!" Gamble replied. Ten seconds later, a group of Weir pushed in just down the street from Two Peaks.

"Finn, hit it!" Gamble said.

"Check!" he answered, and a series of pops ran amongst the Weir, sending them sprawling. They poured another volley of fire into the latest group of pursuing Weir. Moments later, their fire was joined by withering fire from a nearby rooftop. The rooftop with a prominent water tank. "Water." That was Mouse, Able, and Wick up there, covering their teammates.

Together the two teams leapfrogged their way back towards Downtown, delaying, delaying, delaying the inevitable tide that threatened to overtake them the instant they made a mistake.

jCharles was the first one to do so.

Cass refused to accept that this was how it ended. Even as she and Kit and Swoop fired round after round into the advancing mass, her mind was in some other place, watching it all unfold. And she refused it. She thought of her son, and her friends, and of what must have been happening back at Greenstone. This was the critical moment, the crucial target that could tip the balance, and it was resting on her.

A cold fury rose in her heart then, a raw anger, and

power rose up in her to match, in a way she'd not before experienced. And as she looked around at all those Weir, waiting to pounce, Cass realized she could fight with more than just her claws and her gun.

From somewhere deep inside, a righteous wrath swelled up, and Cass reached out into the digital, down into that datastream she'd be fighting so hard to resist, down into the collective consciousness of the Weir. And she embraced the flood of information, the flashes of wild emotion and fractured images that screamed towards her, drawing them to herself.

"Go!" she shouted, and she leapt forward upon the Weir. As they collapsed upon her, she unleashed herself, and met them fury for fury. And though there was but one of her, she was as many among them, cutting them down with gun and claw. And though she couldn't be certain, it seemed that many fell before she even struck them.

"Dry!" Finn shouted, and he lowered his rifle to swap in a fresh magazine. jCharles spun and went to a knee, let loose with both jitters into the crowd of pursuers that were ever gaining ground. Two seconds later, Finn shouted "I'm up!" and returned to firing. "Move, Twitch, move!"

jCharles gained his feet, and took off again, but he watched over his shoulder as the Weir bounded after him. When he turned back to face forward, he'd overrun his turn by two yards. He swiveled back, saw Finn looking back at him from the alley, eyes wide, and starting back towards him. But an overeager volunteer made the decision for him by firing off another fibrasteel web that sealed off the alleyway. Finn flinched away and was lucky not to get hit.

jCharles was not so lucky.

"Run!" Finn shouted, and he jammed the barrel of his weapon through the metal mesh and fired into the Weir. "Run, man!"

jCharles let off another long burst from both pistols as he backpedaled. There was no choice now, no plan except to make it to Downtown. Behind him, he could hear the report of gunfire from above; Mouse and Able and Wick no doubt trying to cover him as best they could. It wouldn't be enough, though.

He ran then, ran faster than he'd ever run in his life, hoping that he wouldn't miss a step, stumble, or slip. It was just four hundred more yards to Downtown.

Three hundred.

His lungs felt like they were going to burst.

Two hundred.

The cries of the Weir were so close now he knew if he even glanced over his shoulder, that would be the end. Just ahead came the cutthrough. Through there, his friends were waiting for him. And just as he entered the alley, he felt a sting and a tearing across his shoulder blade, filled with fire. He twisted away from it in reflex, stumbled, felt himself careening forward. There was another Weir blocking his way, rushing at him. They'd cut him off.

He fought to get his balance, to bring his weapons up, but before he could, the Weir in front was upon him.

Except, it wasn't.

It stepped up on the alley wall, ran two steps along it and leapt, claws flashing, as jCharles finally succumbed to gravity and spilled headlong to the ground, out into the open.

He flipped around on his back, brought his jitterguns up. But no Weir followed after. Hands seized him, started dragging him backwards and to his feet.

"Come on, come on!" he heard a voice say. A voice he knew. Mr 850. His friend was dragging him towards safety. And as he was regaining his footing, he caught a glimpse of his savior, emerging from the alleyway. Not a Weir. 4jack, knives in hands, spattered from war.

Together he and Mr 850 ran towards the massive concrete bunker where everyone had gathered. Or, everyone who had survived. The last stand.

•••

How Cass recognized Swoop amidst the awful melee, she didn't know, but when she saw him, she came back to herself, heard him calling her name.

"Cass! Cass! We gotta move!"

He and Kit both were cut up and bloody, firing their way back towards the door. And then, finally, Cass understood. Somehow, some way, they had found their way to the machine. Cass dropped low to avoid a Weir's attempt to grab her, punched up into its solar plexus with her jittergun, squeezed off a burst, and then leapt over it as it collapsed backwards. Swoop and Kit, made it through the first door into the chamber. Cass grabbed a Weir that tried to block her off and drove it backwards into the chamber, and killed it as they fell to the floor. Swoop slammed the door shut behind her, put two more rounds into the Weir on the floor when she got up, and together all three started up the stairs.

They'd made it almost three flights when the whole building filled with thunder and shook.

Wren's defenses practically disintegrated. Whether he was too spent from the battle, or Asher had finally figured out how to break through, Wren knew he had failed.

Pressure grew in his mind, a feeling that his own thoughts were bulging and warping, as if the thoughts of another were shoving his aside. As a last defense, Wren tried the feedback loop, just to buy himself some time, but Asher was too strong and pushed through it before he could finish getting it in place.

Asher was trying to force his way in to Wren's mind. Wren could feel his brother's presence stretching into his own consciousness. Everything that he'd fought for, everything he'd trained for, was coming apart now, and even as the rage and anger built within him, Wren knew it would not be enough. Asher was simply too powerful. Wren couldn't resist him...

And in that moment, Foe's other teaching came to mind. The warning he'd given Wren. About how fathomless the mind was. And Wren knew what to do.

He reversed. Opened himself completely and fully to Asher's invasion, felt Asher's consciousness sweep into his own, flooding him, elated, full of vengeance. Asher's laugh echoed through Wren's mind.

"Oh, Spinner," he said, a voice in Wren's head now. "Beautiful, stupid Spinner."

Wren remembered what Foe had said, about a name emerging from suffering. But in those last few moments, he didn't find any new name. Wren was what Mama had called him, and that was who he wanted to be, until the very end.

"My name is Wren," he said. "Baptized in blood, forged in fire. Son of the dawn."

"What are you babbling about?" Asher said. And Wren answered.

He attached to Asher's signal, locked on, fed both back into his own.

Immediate, breathtaking agony seared Wren's every synapse, every nerve. But he took a further step, and broadcast, multiplying the power of his output, feeding it back into itself, combined with Asher's own power. Wren's body convulsed with the pain, but still he pushed on.

And to turn his mind from the torment, he reached back to his oath.

Truth, my foundation.

Discipline, my shield.

Life, my charge.

Honor, my way.

Service, my strength.

Only then did Asher seem to realize his danger. And, just as Wren knew he would, his only solution was power. He raged against Wren then, trying to escape, and in doing so only added even more disruptive energy into the feedback loop.

Discipline, my shield.

Wren mastered himself completely in that moment,

turned mind and body to a single purpose, without regard to cost. Asher screamed.

Service, my strength.

This was it. The final moments. Wren understood now what Three must have felt. A fulfillment of purpose. Sadness at not being able to see how life would change afterwards. Gratitude for the life he'd been allowed, however short. Wren focused on all those who had done so much to protect him. All who had given, that he might live. And here, now, he laid down his life that others could go on. Peace descended on him.

And in Asher's last fit of explosive rage, Wren felt the cascading failure, and darkness took him.

There at the bunker, jCharles ran to join with the rest of his ragtag army. Greenmen fought side by side with Bonefolder's thugs, citizens with improvised weapons stood amongst Lil and her well-armed warriors. Lil was singing her warsong, urging her companions to stand strong. And next to Lil, firing a pistol he hadn't seen for at least a decade, was his wife, Mol. Emptying round after round into a monstrosity that was charging its way toward her.

It happened in slow motion. Mol fired the last round from her pistol as the behemoth reached out for her.

jCharles was too far away to do anything.

The abomination bulldozed into Mol and she fell backwards, the creature collapsing down on top of her. jCharles's heart stopped cold.

And then the creature kept going, flipping up and over her, landing like an earthquake on its head behind her. And there, on the ground, little Mol, his wife, lay with her legs extended, having thrown the creature with expert technique.

She rolled with the motion, and twisted, got to her feet and somehow, before jCharles could close the distance, she already had a fresh magazine in her gun and was firing again.

jCharles barely had time to feel relief at seeing his wife unharmed. He came up next to her, and together they fought side by side, moving together, helping those they could, as they worked their way towards the main structure.

Everywhere it was chaos. Whatever cohesion the Weir had shown at the beginning of the assault had disintegrated. Now they came from all sides, from every direction, attacking whoever was nearest. Each posed a deadly threat, but the sudden lack of coordination between them was impossible to overlook.

And as they made their way through the tangle of friend and foe, a second change came over the Weir. The first had been subtle; this was like a lightning strike. All at once, it seemed as though the Weir were breaking down. Putting up less of a fight, reacting sluggishly, looking confused, even turning on one another. It was still another hour before the collection of warriors and civilians could gain clear control of Downtown, and another two before anyone considered anything safe.

But somehow, miraculously, as dawn broke over Greenstone, the people discovered that they had weathered the storm. Somehow, after the crushing wave of Weir had crashed and receded, Greenstone was still standing.

There was no spontaneous celebration, no great collective cheer of victory. The survivors were far too exhausted, too shellshocked, and the losses too great for anyone to see much joy in it. But those loved ones that found one another still alive huddled close and held each other and wept together and laughed together. After the battle was over, and Gamble and Hollander both gave the all clear, jCharles and Mol went back to get Grace; Mol had left her with an older woman, secured safely inside the massive concrete structure that had incredibly never been breached. Apparently their daughter had slept through the whole thing.

Mol of course had *promised* jCharles that she and Grace would stay in the bunker until it was all over, though to hear her retell it, she insisted she'd never said anything about herself. The damage to the city was substantial, between the ravaging Weir and all the explosives they'd used to stem the tide, but as the people searched through the city, jCharles was amazed at how many citizens they'd been able to save. The Greenmen had born the heaviest blow. Hollander didn't have much to say, and jCharles didn't expect anything from him, given the circumstances. But each knew what it had cost the other to see their way through to the end, and whatever their relationship had been in the past deepened into a rare friendship. jCharles doubted there was anyone in Greenstone who hadn't lost a loved one or a neighbor or a friend. But for his part, as selfish as he felt even thinking it, jCharles counted himself most blessed.

jCharles, Mol, and Grace picked their way back through the city towards their home. When they got there, jCharles wasn't sure whether to laugh or cry so he did some of each. The street was cluttered with debris and there were some scorch marks on the building across from the Samurai McGann, but otherwise the place was intact. It didn't even look like anyone had tried to open the door.

Mol was the one who pointed out the worst of the damage.

"Oh, Twitch," she said. "They got him."

She pointed up at the drawing of the ronin, still red-eyed, still holding his sword aloft, defiant, victorious. There was a hole where a stray round had struck, right in the whisky bottle hanging from his belt. It was so absurd, jCharles burst out laughing.

"Couple of inches either way, and that could've been real nasty," jCharles said. "Think our ol' friend's got a new lease on life. How about you?"

"Oh, you know, Twitch. Greenstone's always been a place for second chances," Mol said. And she went up on her tiptoes and kissed him on the cheek.

•••

It was the sound of quiet sobbing that first brought Wren to his senses. A gradual awakening that found him first hearing, then feeling the ground beneath him. He opened his eyes to a dark sky above, dotted with stars. But though his eyes were open, and he could perceive his surroundings, he felt as though he'd gone blind. Deaf, though he could hear crying. Utterly isolated and alone, though there beside him sat another.

Wren had felt this before, though not so intensely.

He looked over at the person who lay doubled over nearby. Recognized him. Painter.

"Painter," Wren said. And Painter started at the sound of Wren's voice. He sat up, wild-eyed.

"Wren? Wren... you're alive?"

"So it would seem," Wren answered.

A choking sob erupted from Painter's mouth, and for a time he couldn't speak for his weeping. Wren waited patiently, too stunned, too spent to offer any consolation. When Painter finally recovered himself enough, he spoke.

"Why?" he asked. "Why didn't you just kill me?"

"Because," Wren said, "if I had taken your life, I couldn't have given it back."

Painter fell into silence again, staring blankly at Wren. He shook his head once, and then again. Finally, Wren pushed himself up to his knees, struggled up to his feet. He felt hollow, as if his insides had been burned out. Painter remained on the ground, looking up at him.

"Painter, I need you now," Wren said. "I need you to help me get back to Greenstone."

"I can't," Painter said weakly. "I can't go there."

"Please, Painter. I can't find my way. I need your help."

"You don't need me, Wren. I saw you. I saw what you can do. There's nothing that can hurt you now."

"I do need you, Painter," Wren said.

"Why?"

"Because you're the only one here," Wren answered. "And I'm disconnected."

•••

It was mid-morning before Cass got back to Greenstone with Swoop and Kit. They were all suffering multiple wounds, and whatever Swoop had done with his charge on the machine had had a much more substantial effect on the signal in the area. It'd been degraded pretty severely until just a couple of miles outside of Greenstone, and that was the first time they were able to establish firm contact with Gamble and the team. The initial reports were all fairly good, all things considered, but when Cass got to the city itself, she couldn't believe the news could be good at all. She searched all through the city, through the rubble, amongst the wounded and the dead. It wasn't until almost noon that she found what she was looking for.

He was standing outside the eastern gate, a little distant from the town, with two others. Cass recognized his silhouette as soon as she saw it and she wasn't sure if her feet even touched the ground as she flew to him.

"It's all right, Mama," he said, as she held him tight. "It's all right now. We did it."

EPILOGUE

Painter and Wren had found Snow as they walked to Greenstone. She'd just been sitting there when they found her, like she'd been waiting for them to catch up.

"Wren?" Painter asked. "Do you think...?" And then he trailed off.

"Not anymore, Painter," Wren said. "I'm sorry."

Painter nodded.

"But," Wren continued, "maybe my mom can help."

jCharles headed back to the Samurai McGann after a long talk with Hollander. Gamble and her team had been talking about next steps, and with the loss of so many Greenmen and all the work that needed to be done, it seemed like a natural fit. It hadn't taken much to sort it out for Gamble to move into an officer's role, and for the rest of the crew to step in as instructors and senior Greenmen. When word went out, the number of volunteers for the Greenmen jumped to such levels, Hollander had to turn folks away. Why jCharles had even been involved in any of it was kind of a mystery. People had started treating him like his opinion mattered when it came to Official Town Business. He'd helped get the materials together to patch up the east gate until it could be properly repaired, and he'd handled some logistics of getting people temporary housing while the town got put back together. And every time he helped somebody out, it seemed like two more people showed up. It'd been happening ever since the battle, gradually at first, but steadily growing. It was all starting to feel uncomfortably political.

When he came in to his saloon, he was surprised to find Kyth sitting at the bar, nursing a short glass of something amber. Something off the top shelf, he guessed. It was still early, not even midmorning yet. Nimble hadn't even taken the chairs down off the tables. jCharles went over and plopped down on the stool next to Kyth. 4jack and Mr 850 had both rolled out already, returning to their normal lives, relationships refreshed and some stories to tell that no one would believe. He figured Kyth would be following suit shortly.

"Rough start to the day?" he asked, looking pointedly at the drink.

"Not at all," she said with a smile. "Had a good, long talk with Mol."

"Uh oh."

"All good things, honey," Kyth said, and she took a sip, rolled it around in her mouth. "Think we both understand each other a little better now."

"You know she told me to call you?" jCharles asked.

"She did not mention that, no. But it makes sense. She always was the one with the good ideas."

jCharles sat quietly with her for a bit, waiting to see if she had anything to add. Apparently she didn't, so he switched topics. "Headed out soon?"

"Nah," Kyth said. "Think I'm gonna stick around for a while actually. Place has character."

"How long's a while?"

"Oh, you know," she answered with a wink. "A while."

"Kyth."

"Fine... I got a job offer, OK? I want to see if it pans out."

"You did not," jCharles said. "Kyth, tell me you did not agree to work for the Bonefolder."

Kyth shrugged, flashed her smile.

"Oh don't worry so much, Twitch. She's about ready to retire. And she likes my ideas."

"Ideas?"

"It'll be good for you too," Kyth said. And then she got serious, serious in a way jCharles couldn't remember ever having seen her. "I mean it, Twitch. I owe you."

"Kyth—" he said, shaking his head, but she wouldn't let him finish.

"No. I still owe you. I'll owe you to the day I die and beyond. Bonefolder's been a thorn in your side a long time, I know. Least I can do is pluck it out."

jCharles didn't know what to say in response. Kyth didn't give him much time anyway.

"And maybe get rich in the process," she said, and she drained her drink, got up off her seat, and kissed him on the cheek. "See you around, neighbor."

"Yeah," jCharles said. Kyth turned and walked towards the front door. "Hey, thanks for not destroying my *whole* town," he called after her. She waved over her shoulder without turning back, and then disappeared through the door onto the street. jCharles shook his head. His life had become exceedingly strange indeed.

They'd made the decision on their own, though Wren had been the one to prompt it. Cass had been reluctant at first to leave Greenstone. They had friends there, friends so good they might as well have been family, but Wren had made some good points. They'd both changed so much, so quickly, he said, that he wanted to get away, just the two of them, and work things out together, the way they used to do. And he had someone he wanted her to meet. Someone he thought could help her.

The goodbyes had been easier this time around, since everyone fully expected to see each other again sometime soon. All of them except when she'd gone to see Mouse, and he'd pulled her aside, and laid his heart bare to her.

"Mouse," she said, blinking back the tears that his gentle words had brought. "Mouse, I do love you. I do. And it might be cruel to say it, but if I made a list of qualities I wanted in a... relationship, like that, well. I think it'd pretty much just describe you. But my heart isn't in a place where I can love you the way you deserve. Not right now." She reached up and touched his face. "You deserve better than I can give."

"Maybe you could let me be the judge of that," he said. Cass smiled, took her hand away. Shook her head.

"I can't ask you to wait for me," she said. "Don't wait for me." He smiled sadly when she said it.

"I don't reckon I have much say in that, Miss Cass," Mouse said. "Been telling my heart not to love you for a long time. Hasn't listened yet."

She didn't know what to say to him then, so she'd just hugged him, and thanked him for all he'd ever done, and then they'd said their goodbyes. They left in the morning, Wren leading the way northward, and eventually eastward. He wouldn't explain much about where they were headed, but Cass didn't need many clues. She knew enough about the high level that she didn't need the details.

They took travel at an easy pace, and Cass was amazed at her son; how perceptive he'd become, how clever, how confident. Over their five days of travel, they talked through all of the experiences they'd been through while they'd been separated. Cass didn't understand all of it, for either of them. But Wren was able to talk her through a lot of techniques and share insights she didn't even know he possessed. With Asher gone, she didn't seem to have to worry about any reintegration with the Weir, but Wren said the man they were going to see would be able to tell them for sure.

Asher was still in him, somehow. His consciousness. His personality. Trapped in some portion of Wren's mind. But Wren was already learning to control that portion of his brother, or rather, of himself now. Asher still had some power, Wren suffered frequent tormenting nightmares. But even just over the course of the few days they traveled together, these too he began to tame. Even so, his hope was that the man they were going to see could help him too.

They reached their destination just before sunset, but instead of completing the journey, Wren had asked if they could spend one more night out in the open. They lay together there on the roof of a long-abandoned building, side by side, his head on her arm, with the Weir roaming the ground below. But neither of them were concerned. Neither of them had cause to fear the night. Not anymore. The stars above shone brilliant against the sky, a spray of diamonds on a velvet sky. They stayed up late into the night, talking about whatever came to mind. Enjoying each other's company. Enjoying, for the first time maybe ever, true peace.

Cass smiled to herself.

"He promised me this," she said. "Did you know that? Did I ever tell you?"

"Tell me what, Mama?"

"The night you went into the Vault, and you fell. When Jackson took you. Three carried me up to the maglev line. And when we got to the top, the sky was full of stars. Just like this. And I said I wished you could see them, and he said you would, one day. He promised."

"Three was pretty great at keeping promises."

"He was," Cass said. They sat together in silence for a time.

"What happens now?" Cass asked.

Wren thought about it, seemed to be weighing his answer carefully. Then he said, "I think I'd just like to be a kid for a little while. If that's OK."

"Of course, baby," Cass said, as the tears welled. "Of course that's OK."

"Just for a little while," he said, and then added. "I still have a lot of work to do."

"We all do, sweetheart. But there's time. Time enough to make things right. To make things new."

"Kind of like a new day," he said.

She drew him close to her.

"Just like."

ACKNOWLEDGMENTS

As always, this book could not have appeared in your hands in its current form without the help and support of a great many people. I won't give you the *entire* lineage, but here's a pretty good subset of excellent folks that helped me throughout the writing process. My most sincere thanks to:

... Jesus, for your limitless grace and great faithfulness.

... my wife and children, for your constant love and encouragement, for your patient understanding, and for being my most favoritest thing in the whole wide world.

... Marc Gascoigne, Phil Jourdan, Mike Underwood, Caroline Lambe, and everyone else at Angry Robot for all their long-suffering patience, general excellence, and the coolest orbital platform in the known galaxy.

... Lee Harris, for suddenly deciding to take a chance on me.

... Dan S, Z, Legion, and Luke T for being seriously cool fans.

... and all the folks out there who stuck with me to the end of the trilogy.

HEY, YOU!

- ***Want more*** of the best in SF, F, and WTF!?
- ***Want the latest*** news from your favorite Agitated Androids?
- ***Want to be spared***, alone of all your kind, when the robotic armies spill over the world to conquer all weak, fleshy humans?

Well, sign yourself up for the Angry Robot Legion then!

You'll get sneak peaks at upcoming books, special previews, and exclusive giveaways for free Angry Robot books.

Go here, sign up, survive the imminent destruction of all mankind:

angryrobotbooks.com/legion